BOOK 1 OF THE SHATTERED MIRROR SAGA

TWISTED SOULS

SKYE CRAWFORD

Dead Fox Publishing
deadfoxpub.com

Editing: Lauren Woods, Kelley York
Cover Design: Sleepy Fox Studio – sleepyfoxstudio.net
Interior Formatting: Sleepy Fox Studio – sleepyfoxstudio.net

Digital 978-1-960322-19-7
Paperback 978-1-960322-20-3
Hardcover 978-1-960322-21-0

CONTENTS

Sidhe Lineage Tree iv

Glossary vii

Prologue 1

Chapter 1 3

Chapter 2 14

Chapter 3 25

Chapter 4 38

Chapter 5 51

Chapter 6 64

Chapter 7 77

Chapter 8 87

Chapter 9 96

Chapter 10 107

Chapter 11 118

Chapter 12 130

Chapter 13 142

Chapter 14 154

Chapter 15 165

Chapter 16 178

Chapter 17 192

Chapter 18 211

Chapter 19 227

Chapter 20 241

Chapter 21 256

Epilogue 266

Acknowledgments 270

About 271

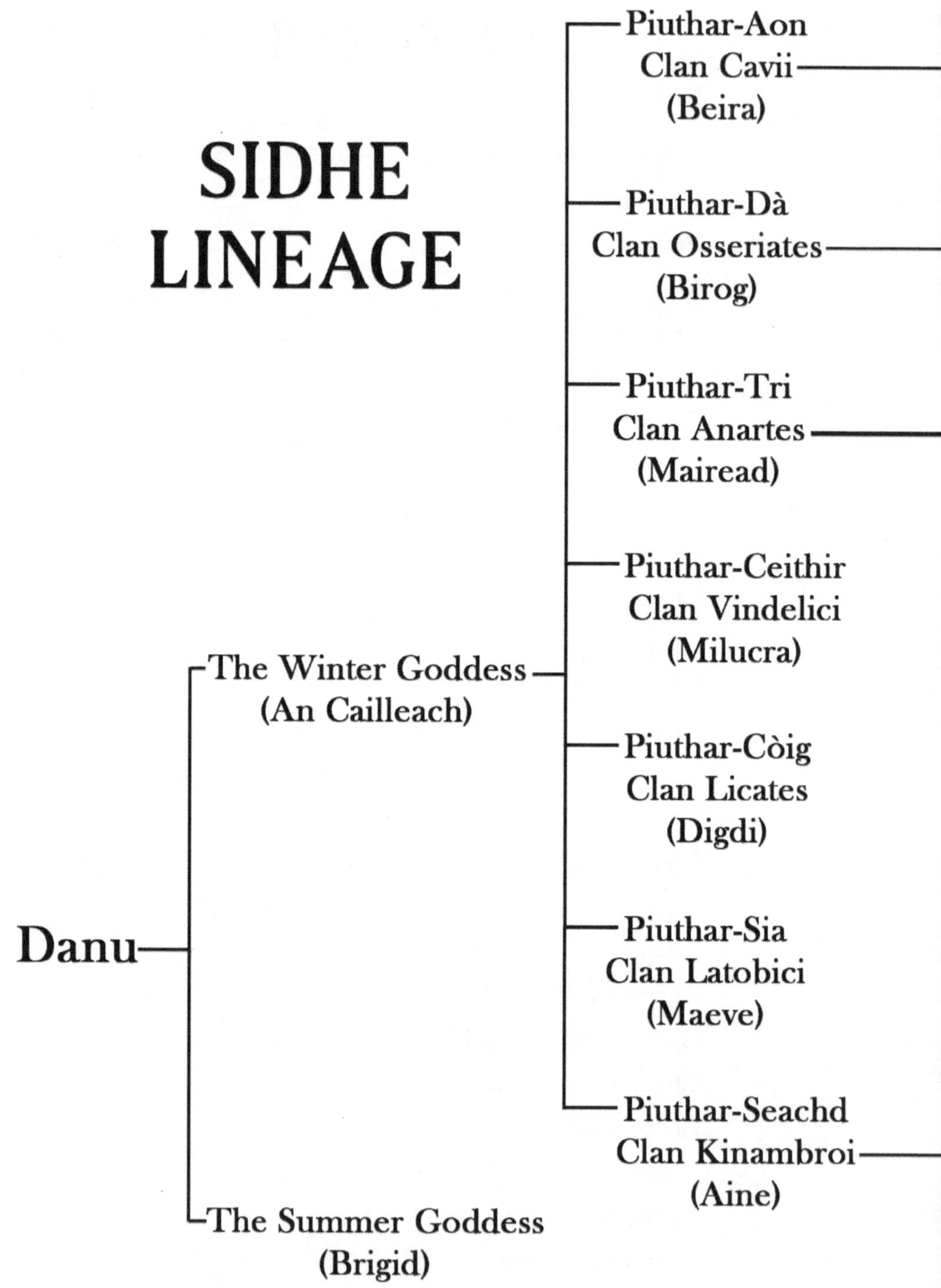
SIDHE LINEAGE
Danu
The Winter Goddess
(An Cailleach)
The Summer Goddess
(Brigid)
Piuthar-Aon
Clan Cavii
(Beira)
Piuthar-Dà
Clan Osseriates
(Birog)
Piuthar-Tri
Clan Anartes
(Mairead)
Piuthar-Ceithir
Clan Vindelici
(Milucra)
Piuthar-Còig
Clan Licates
(Digdi)
Piuthar-Sia
Clan Latobici
(Maeve)
Piuthar-Seachd
Clan Kinambroi
(Aine)

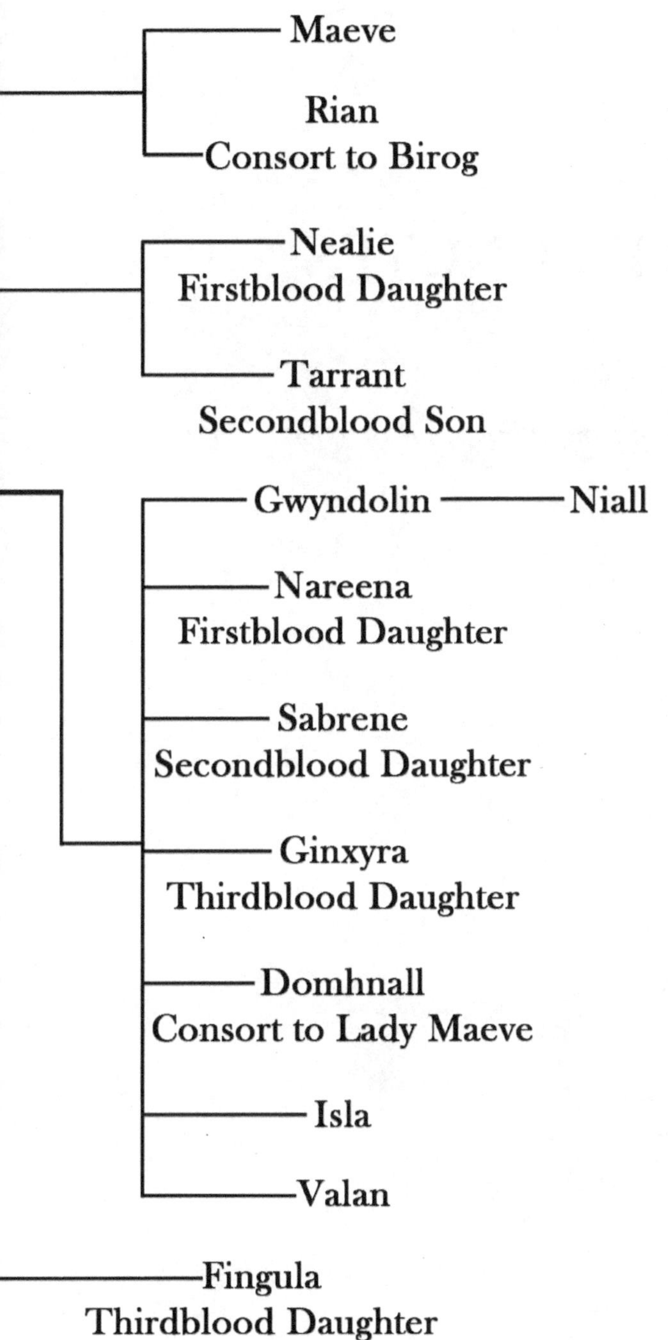
Maeve
Rian
Consort to Birog
Nealie
Firstblood Daughter
Tarrant
Secondblood Son
Gwyndolin
Niall
Nareena
Firstblood Daughter
Sabrene
Secondblood Daughter
Ginxyra
Thirdblood Daughter
Domhnall
Consort to Lady Maeve
Isla
Valan
Fingula
Thirdblood Daughter

CONTENT NOTES

For a list of potentially triggering subjects, please refer to page 269.

GLOSSARY

aon - one

dà - two

tri - three

ceithir - four

còig five

sia - six

seachd - seven

ochd - eight

naoi - nine

deich - ten

aon deug - eleven

dà dheug - twelve

buime - nurse, nanny, nursemaid

cella - the inner chamber of a temple

nóiméad - minute

orlach - one thumb length

troighid - one foot of distance

uairean, uair – hour

To my parents, who gave me the chance I needed to become my most genuine self without judgement.

PROLOGUE

It crawled up the walls.

Shadowed claws intermingled with rotting flesh flexed and pulled its tiny, battered body ever upwards out of the pit. This was a thing composed of nothing, of having never known life, but still it moved with a will of its own, governed by laws of reality deemed impossible by mortals. For the first time, it learned how to think, to eat and absorb the surrounding darkness that clung and condensed its body into a more solid form. It filled in the spaces that, up until now, were ruled only by death and decay. This thing held no sense of the passage of time, since what care was it to that which lives forever? It simply moved unceasingly, digging fingers into stone; it was with the fully formed hands of a small child that it finally reached the top.

CHAPTER 1

The current Piuthar-Tri, Lady Mairead of Clan Anartes, was in deep conversation with Cernunnos when her daughter interrupted. It was already bad enough she had to draw back clan members to Fo Erkunia after losing three outposts near the surface, for the Piuthar-Aon to constantly try to pluck away the strongest remaining members of her clan for those fake Latobici—but now she must be reminded of another failure.

Before her last consort had died, Mairead had not only given birth to Domhnall—who turned out to be a promising wizard—but hoped to repeat such a success when she later gave birth to twins. Alas, it became increasingly clear Isla lacked wits and Valan nigh physically disabled. If only she could combine the two together and get a half-decent sidhe.

"That is quite the accusation," Mairead said, the tone of her voice pleasant, smooth, and not angry in the slightest. The perfect diplomat. Her appearance was typical of most of the Higher Court of Unseelie: dark skin which lacked the warm brown undertones of mortals, elaborately braided white hair that fell to her ankles when standing. Under the glow of will-o'-the-wisps, Mairead's hair took on a green sheen that gave the impression of something metallic. Her eyes, edged at the corners with faint crow's feet, were a bright green that gave off a matching glow on the rare occasion she let herself display emotion. At first glance, most found her a lovely, mature beauty, failing to notice that her fingers were a little too long and tipped with black nails shaped like the talons of a bird. The elaborate robes she wore hid most of her hands under layers of silken red, black and, between the two, a gray leathery material adorned with images of screaming faces.

Standing beside her as she sat on her throne, Cernunnos eyed the two of them, his silence revealing that he knew better than to insert himself into their conversation just yet. Her hall may have no longer been as elaborately gilded nor as full of powerful allies anymore, but not all power lay in what was obvious.

Isla smoothed down the front of her robes, clearly nervous, but the words tumbled out of her anyway.

"He's been found sneaking one of the guards to bed—and to the baths—every night for a month now. A *male* guard. He thinks himself a female and lays with men, Mother. He needs to be reeducated."

Beside Mairead, Cernunnos made a noise dangerously close to a snort. It was an odd sound that echoed around the chamber. Aside from the deep green carpet runner which led from Mairead's black throne to a set of double doors made from shades of green glass, it was difficult to make out much more of the hall's detail, as if the surrounding dark had a visible weight to it that refused to be easily seen through. The only light came from small will-o'-the-wisps that floated about on an invisible air current. A soft glow slowly pulsating from the small orbs revealed marbled walls at varying distances, making the geometry of the room constantly fluctuate from those brief glimpses.

"Is there something you'd like to add to this conversation, Cernunnos?" the Piuthar-Tri sighed.

"Oh, pardon; I'm imagining the spectacle of a future veiled one following around her brother for a month," Cernunnos replied.

"Indeed."

"I wasn't the one who followed him around!" Isla said. "I merely hired someone to do so for me."

"Completely believable!"

Mairead turned just enough to glare at the male fey for his outburst before focusing back on her daughter. "And you decided to come here alone, without this other person to help support your claims? Do you think me gullible, child?"

"O-of course not, Piuthar!"

"Stupid, perhaps?"

"No, not at all. If anything, I wish to learn from your genius," Isla replied. "I want to make you proud!"

The praise did give Mairead pause, having her reevaluate this daughter. Isla was simple but earnest, and eager to further the Unseelie version of *An Cleas,* according to her spies. She was quite skilled at inflicting pain on others, truly showing promise in turning cruelty into an art.

The problem with Isla was that there wasn't much else; she would never make a leader— just as well with so many older sisters—but she could make a decent tool. This young sidhe woman just needed to be cultivated carefully.

"There may come a day, especially if you continue to excel in your devotion to An Cailleach, that I will be proud of you," Mairead allowed. "But bringing me mere words and not a single bit of proof will not do, child."

Isla dropped to her knees. "I'm so sorry, Piuthar! I will try to do better!"

How did this girl come from me? Mairead wondered. *I am indeed being punished for my past failures.* It was the slightest of movements, but she did sense Cernunnos shift his weight, which for him was the equivalent of jumping up and down in glee.

"Yes, Cernunnos?" Mairead asked.

"If I may offer a suggestion—"

"Would it stop you from talking if I said 'no'?"

"It is only the simplest, most humble of suggestions," Cernunnos replied, his words not quite matching his tone of voice, just neutral enough that she couldn't accuse him of sarcasm.

"I'm certain that it is."

"To find out the truth, ought we to hear the boy's side of the story? Perhaps even from this *special* guard of his."

"I think you are enjoying this too much."

Cernunnos pressed a hand over his heart as if wounded. "After all, isn't the boy decrepit? How would he be able to fraternize for an entire month before collapsing into a pile of sticks? I must know his secret—it must make you curious, too. If there is the slightest bit of truth—"

"Oh, very well!" Mairead snapped. She hated that he was right; she *was* curious—though it had more to do with how Valan had managed to convince a warrior supposedly loyal to her to watch over her weakling son instead. If anything Isla said could be believed. "Let's continue this little drama. It is not as if I have *better* things to do."

Valan sat in his favorite place—his room. Technically a noble, albeit the youngest male, his room was sparse but still a space he didn't have to share with anyone. It wasn't even located in a nicer place within Clan Anartes' stronghold; the walls themselves comprised different stone materials, with one part looking especially roughly made. Another wall consisted entirely of shelves stuffed with books, papers, and musical instruments. The odd bleached bone here and there. A large closet and chest containing various clothes. In one corner, as if given a place of honor, stood a frame with the complete skeleton of a goblin; the bones still glowed faintly from the will-o'-the-wisp used on it the night before. Sometimes at parties, he wouldn't just play music but make the skeleton dance and twirl in the ever-shifting glow of faerie. The macabre sight was very much appreciated by the other young sidhe.

Perhaps someday he'd be capable of animating more than one skeleton—two, no, even three!—but right now the challenge was to play a song on uilleann pipes that didn't sound like he intended to put people to sleep. He felt ridiculous enough as it was sitting with such a large—large to him, anyway—musical instrument, but it did provide an excuse to sit down and rest, to better hide any exhaustion. He could not afford to be seen as weak.

Valan was still in the middle of a particularly difficult reel when he heard a loud knock on his bedroom door. He glanced over at Balfore, who had been leaning against the wall next to the door, and gave a small nod.

In response, Balfore gave a long, pointed yawn, indicating that the noble could answer his own door.

“Please,” Valan insisted. As a hint, he gestured at himself with the bagpipes still strapped across his body; by the time he moved the instrument aside and stood up…

“Fine, but only because you pay me—and if it stops you from playing that thing,” Balfore grumbled. Apparently, he wasn’t impressed by how uilleann pipes were meant to entertain people at parties, either. Perhaps they were considered lovely to any other race; however, the hearing of sidhe was different, not just in being able to detect sound from an increased distance but also in the amount of octaves registered. To a human, most of the music produced by the fey sounded like half of the song was missing.

Whoever was on the other side of the door didn’t wait for permission to enter. Just as Balfore moved, the door swung open. He was agile enough to avoid getting his toes clipped, but seeing Isla standing there was still a bit of a surprise. Balfore hastily bowed and Valan tried to do much the same over the side of his musical instrument. It also helped hide the look of irritation that crossed his face; Valan made a point of being around his twin as little as possible. Family gatherings being what they were, attending them wasn’t made easier by Isla’s clear animosity toward him. She, the blessed daughter, had no issue with demanding things of him while he had little choice but to obey. Among the Unseelie, males must never fail in paying respect to women. As far as Valan knew, things had always been this way, that he as a member of the weaker and more emotional gender needed to follow the orders of the women of his race. He had been assured, sometimes violently, that it was for his own good.

Isla looked around the room, especially toward the bed, as if she expected to see something there—*does she know her motives are so obvious?* Valan for not the first time wondered—but there was nothing unusual to see. Perhaps his bedding wasn’t completely smooth in one spot, but likely because he was sitting near it.

“The Piuthar-Tri wishes to speak to you—and *him*, now,” Isla proclaimed, brazenly pointing a finger at Balfore in disgust, as if to say, *that thing.*

The two male elves exchanged looks, but Valan responded. "It is an honor. We shall come at once."

Balfore, due to his rank, wasn't allowed to say anything, even to a not-quite-veiled one, without being granted permission first. He remained bowed. The level of deference she received, while appropriate, somehow managed to irritate her further. "Then hurry up!"

Mairead never really bothered to spend time with her spawn while they were young, since they were of little use to her at that age. Since her last husband's death, she wasn't interested in seeking another consort either, simply preferring to order whomever caught her eye to her bed. There had even been a brief dalliance with *that one* while she was still with Torran, which she would just as soon forget about. A fairly easy task, since Isla looked nothing like him. Valan—much to Mairead's annoyance—was starting to look like and take on some of *his* mannerisms.

When Valan entered and bowed before his mother, strands of his long, soft, ghostlike white hair escaped the folds of his cloak to fall across a thin shoulder. It framed his delicate, pretty face as if planned; there was no way to outright accuse him of that, as it appeared too natural looking. Still, the sweeping hair was too perfect, something she'd expect *him* to do. In that moment, Mairead understood why Isla hated her twin and so terribly wanted to break him.

Would his hair remain as soft when stained with blood? How easily could she destroy those fragile limbs? What would his screams sound like? That these thoughts had arisen unbidden in her mind soured her mood further. How Valan had managed to survive to his current age was a mystery to her. Perhaps Isla was even more incompetent than she had originally considered.

Behind her two kneeling children was the commoner Isla mentioned earlier, also on his knees and bowing even lower. Mairead spared her guard a cursory glance before focusing back on her children. The twins side by side made it all the more apparent how they were not identical. Isla did not have skin quite so dark or hair as pure white as Valan's, but she was taller with a curvaceous figure mortal men often found too tempting to ignore—at their own peril, as she was more succubus than dark sidhe. The roots and tips of her knee-length hair were a faint green, reminding Mairead of another daughter who had recently died.

"You may look at me," Mairead said. Isla and Valan did as she commanded, while the male commoner remained kneeling, though he didn't keep his face lowered quite so much as before. This pleased her. Everyone was acting very well-behaved. Cernunnos, still standing somewhat near her throne, was even remarkably silent.

Now *that* made her suspicious. She made a point of turning to face him, even allowing herself to smile. Despite his split warrior's kilt emphasizing his white-furred legs ending in cloven hooves, all the glint of his gem-encrusted torc, and the dramatic gold-tipped stag antlers on his head, Mairead assumed it greatly bothered Cernunnos that he was just barely more eye-catching than Valan, who only had to let down his hair.

Cernunnos, the Great White Stag; some mortals spent their entire lifetimes hoping to catch a mere glimpse of the elusive fey. Mairead expected to see Cernunnos scowl or show some other petty expression, but the male's face remained carefully blank. Whatever he felt, he did not want it to be known, which was revealing in its own way.

Cernunnos, of course, noticed her looking and smiled, raising an eyebrow. "How old are they, my dear Piuthar?"

"Too old to be what you think they are," Mairead replied, answering his unspoken question first. "Almost twenty, thereabouts."

"My, how the time flies. Things blur together after a while. So easily we forget! A pity what happened to Torran: going mad and dying before meeting these two. Such similarities he would see! I wonder what he would think."

"You almost sound sentimental. And old. It is unbecoming."

"Now I am truly wounded."

Lady Mairead waved a hand like she wished to shoo away a particularly annoying fly. Her two children did not understand much of the exchange, going by their expressions. Isla looked rapt, as if trying to absorb every word before it escaped out of her head; she really needed to learn how to control her emotions better. Valan just looked bored, his expression a bit too well-practiced. Mairead easily discerned it was nothing but a mask. These two were born minutes apart from each other, so why were they so different? It couldn't mean—no, she dared not even think it.

"Isla has made quite the accusation against you, boy," Mairead said. "What is it that you think you did wrong?"

"I would not dare to presume to know the thoughts of a female." Valan pushed his errant strands of hair behind a delicately slender, pointed ear. The movement drew attention to the contrast between the soft white hair against pitch-black skin. His face remained neutral, but he wasn't quite skilled enough to completely hide his nervousness. A faint trembling claimed his hands before he could steady them. He understood the trap Mairead had put him in.

"But you dare to refuse to answer your Piuthar," Mairead said.

Valan knelt again, bowing lower than his guard had earlier. "If I have offended you, it was done unknowingly." A perfect response.

Seeing him bowing down like that, Isla could barely contain herself, looking ready to kick him out of both glee and frustration. Mairead took in the emotions that flitted across her daughter's face, especially the frustration there over Valan having managed to talk his way out of trouble. If Isla couldn't provide proof of his misdeeds, then he couldn't be blamed for not knowing what these faults were. Lashing out at him now would be a sign of her own weakness.

"Oh, get up! Truly, you males are a pathetic lot," Mairead said. "I'm talking about my warrior, boy. How *I* am the one to assign him his duties—and I do not recall ever giving him the order to watch over you. Do you think yourself so grand as to usurp me?"

"I would never dare." While Valan did stand, his shoulders remained hunched, his head hung low. "I hire him as a bodyguard only when he is off duty."

Isla still appeared to struggle with the desire not to kick him. "That's a lie! You two are always together! In the baths! Your room! You even share meals!"

Valan gave her a look of wide-eyed puzzlement. "I don't know what you are talking about. The Slavemaster knows if Balfore has kept to his work schedule—you can ask him to see his records. You can trace the payments I made outside of that schedule. I apologize for presuming, but perhaps you mistook several of my friends for the same person? We males tend to look alike at a distance."

Another well-crafted response. Mairead wondered how often he must have practiced it. Still, a fool of a girl Isla turned out to be; it wouldn't do to let a male get away with proving her foolishness in front of a Piuthar. He had to know his place.

Cernunnos slowly clapped. "My dear lovely Isla! My, your diligence in keeping a sibling in line is truly remarkable—quite praiseworthy! He is completely cowed by your mere presence."

Mairead side-eyed him. *Is Cernunnos trying to help the boy?*

"Under such constant oversight, it is truly no wonder that there is a betting pool over who is to take over Valan's tutelage once he leaves for Crann Bethadh."

"I've never heard of this 'betting pool'," Mairead said. "And I do not fully believe Crann Bethadh is the best fit for him. He could be just as useful seeking training within the royal harem."

"And give up the chance to finally knock Rian Cavii down a peg or two?"

"Domhnall Anartes is already well on his way to surpassing Rian in magical prowess."

Cernunnos lightly tapped a cloven foot against the black-and-gold marble floor in over-dramatic thought. "It's true that this Valan boy doesn't seem as magically talented as Domhnall, nor his father, but we both know there is more than one way to twist the knife."

She understood his meaning immediately. Rian Cavii was another of those males known to be very vain about appearances, going so far as to carve out a body made of stone to inhabit in pursuit of perfection. It was insulting for him to have lived for so long without anyone managing to kill him.

Sidhe were nigh-immortal beings, but they could still be destroyed through the use of specific weapons or methods, which the Unseelie were fond of employing against their rivals. Outside of outright murder, one favorite method was to make the eternal lives of their enemies as miserable an experience as possible. So why not trot out an even prettier male in front Rian Cavii, keep him distracted and annoyed until Domhnall killed him? Then Clan Anartes, who provided two wizards proven greater than the old man and with the Anartes's reputation for magical prestige, would become once again unchallenged by any other clan.

"Was Rian part of this…bet?" Mairead asked.

"Even better: he is *not*."

Lady Mairead regarded this son of hers. Head still bowed, but she did not doubt he listened to every word—after all, his future was being discussed. Still, how did he manage to have his hair frame his face and figure so well? If this was a skill, it was not one easily learned—or even more horrible, a natural talent. Valan would do well by learning how to properly please the veiled ones, which could then be used as a bargaining tool with other Piuthar. There'd be no more talk of him possibly sleeping with men, either. Certainly, there were plenty of rumors of males turning to each other if no woman chose them, but it was never something done *openly*. She firmly believed that only a deviant male would readily prefer other men. Males served no other purpose but to please and obey women.

Nothing prevented Valan from attending Crann Bethadh and learning the finer arts of pleasing women, either. If he failed at one, there was always the other—if he didn't die first. Isla remained too obsessed with him. Mairead knew at some point one of the twins would kill the other; if the surviving sibling turned out to be inferior, she'd have to remove that one as well. She doubted that trading the twins off to separate clans would do much to cool this rivalry. Neither was this a time for Clan Anartes to lose two children at once. Better to handle the rivalry now while things were still under her control.

"Isla, is a guard and a mercenary the same thing?" Mairead asked.

"Of course not, Piuthar." Isla smiled after she spoke. Next to her, Valan remained still as a statue. The twins knew which one their mother sided with.

"To even try to pay off a guard to look after someone else—the sheer level of stupidity! A warrior of a clan is not some easily bought, goat-legged trash," Mairead said. She *felt* Cernunnos bristle over that description. "It offends me that a mere male thought this to be acceptable.

Valan, you are to report to Sabrene immediately for reeducation. Tell her exactly what you have done wrong."

"Yes, Piuthar-Tri."

"Piuthar," Isla began in a voice that was perhaps a little too eager, "may I be the one to teach him? I've been practicing, and the other veiled ones say I've been doing well. I know how to break him to best serve you."

Mairead considered this. The eagerness displayed, while admirable, also revealed the likelihood of her having to deal with a very *dead* boy. He could still be made useful. Isla was too untrained and lacked control over her emotions. Yet… "You may, but Sabrene will supervise you—you are not allowed to kill. And this will be it, Isla; you will no longer obsess over this male afterward—it is embarrassing behavior for a future veiled one. Do you understand me?"

"Yes, Piuthar." Isla didn't sound quite so eager.

"Good, now you will leave," Mairead commanded. "And you: Balfore, was it? You are to return to the slave pens, but this time, you will stay in a cage. You should have known better; a warrior of my clan is loyal only to me."

A shift in the walls followed her statement, one of shadow itself contorting and twisting along both sides of the Clan Anartes throne. Dark elf warriors stepped through the shifts in reality. Four guards quickly surrounded Balfore and dragged him away from Mairead's sight. Isla was next to leave, practically skipping off, followed by a much slower-moving Valan. The image of Cernunnos wavered and then blinked out of existence, almost as if he had never really been there at all.

CHAPTER 2

The Anartes complex was a massive tower comprising two parts. From the outside, located in a dark cavern below the layer of earth upon which mortals tread, hung a gigantic stalactite that was mere *troighids* away from joining with the floor to form a solid pillar. The partially exposed mycelium of a gigantic mushroom filled in the remaining gap. The mushroom's stalk, which glowed a faint blue, branched out and wrapped around the almost-pillar as if it were a vine, dotted here and there with caps of a darker blue. The entire construction was technically hollow, with the highest, biggest mushroom caps serving as rooms for the more important members of Clan Anartes. The rest of the clan made do with windowless apartments formed of stone.

The inside of the complex did not match the outside. In some places of the world, the border between the material and ethereal was thin, which most fey used to cross into the Otherworld. This thin veil between states of existence made it easy for the sidhe to manipulate time and space near such locations. Thus, the far larger interiors featured plenty of balconies and walkways to allow easier flight to certain locations. It also possessed a grand spiral staircase which connected each floor to the next; however, it was rarely used since "falling accidents" were far too easy to stage.

Valan decided a falling accident would be a kinder experience than what awaited him, so he took the stairs in search of Sabrene. Instead of going up to the eldest daughter's private quarters, he headed toward the breeding pens. This direction also gave him a secondary purpose. While his frail frame often made him seem like an easy target for assassination and walking up so many stairs practically left him comatose from exhaustion, Valan had discovered a solution. Through favors given here and there, he'd been able to enchant a few items that helped him function more like a sidhe his age should. A display of physical normalcy might help convince others he wasn't quite the easy target after all.

Valan never spent any time with his second-eldest living sister, fairly certain she wasn't even aware of his existence, but he did know enough about her rumored habits. Outside of her regular duties, Sabrene spent her time designing new chimera. Her best creations were turned to stone and used as decorations throughout the tower, enchanted to turn to flesh to attack intruders. Her most popular chimera was a mix of a haunted chest, a jellyfish, and a giant bat. Anartes' youth would play a game called *mhealladh*, which took place in a room lined with identical containers such as large jars or chests. Most of the containers were traps filled with poisonous gas or spikes, but at least one possessed a magical item provided by the clan's Archwizard. And, of course, another was the chimera.

This haunted container blended in with the others, but when opened, a giant mouth would suddenly burst forth with translucent, stinging tentacles. It could also sprout more tentacles underneath it to scuttle after its target on land or in the water; even worse, it could grow wings and fly. More than once, Valan had witnessed it eat an unlucky cousin.

The area reserved for Sabrene's experiments was located right next to the torture chambers. There was a time when his older sister had used sidhe limbs in her creations until the Piuthar put a stop to it; such a terrible thing to waste so many Anartes males over something so trivial. If Sabrene wanted to use a male, she'd have to buy a slave from a seller in the city herself.

It reminded Valan that as soon as his punishment was over, he needed to set the wheels in motion to buy back Balfore before he ended up as an experiment. Despite what Lady Mairead claimed, Valan *did* see the warrior as loyal. It wouldn't do to have rumors spread that anyone loyal to him ended up with a fate worse than death. He wouldn't be able to directly buy Balfore himself, but he did know who could do so for him—something he had planned for a while but hoped to never actually follow through with.

He just needed to survive being tortured. Torture wasn't something new to Valan; he could handle it as long as he kept in mind that the pain would eventually be over. The memories of Isla digging her nails into his neck or pulling on his hair, all the weird noises she made… The very thought still made his skin crawl. He tried to see the positive side: Isla wouldn't dare defy their mother by torturing him again. This would be the last time. It had to be. It wouldn't be long now before he was sent to Crann Bethadh. Afterward…afterward was a problem for another day. *I've survived up 'til now, and I* will *continue to do so.*

Sabrene's laboratory comprised a round room with two parallel oval tables in the middle. Small, haphazard towers of jars and formaldehyde-smelling boxes leaned precariously against the walls, framing two partially open doors through which he saw rows of cages. The high ceiling was hidden from view by all the preserved body parts hanging from chains. Between the two tables, a ghoul stood frozen under the effects of a spell. Sabrene herself bent over one of the tables, which neatly displayed the dissected and broken remains of a tiny fairy, its carefully sawed-off limbs arranged nearby. The other table had the remains of a giant beetle, cut up just as cleanly, having been skinned for its natural armor.

If Valan were to guess, Sabrene wanted to improve the ghoul by giving it extra armor magically infused with crushed pieces of fairy, which would make it harder to kill. A useful experiment, but not her usual inspiring horror. The bodies were of creatures easily found in great numbers near the Otherworld, so repeating this process wouldn't be difficult. Advance shock troops for Clan Anartes that Valan knew other families were undoubtedly looking to take advantage of.

"You wouldn't happen to be willing to take on another apprentice?" Valan asked. He already knew the answer, but it never hurt to start off a conversation with implied praise. Despite Isla having run off to find their elder sister first, his twin had apparently chosen to look elsewhere. Enough time, he hoped, to spin things more in his favor.

Sabrene didn't bother to stop sawing off the limb she was working on. "I already have four, male. The only way you are getting near me is if I decide to hang you with the rest."

Valan *had* noticed earlier that several of the body parts hanging from the ceiling were male.

"I apologize. I've always been an admirer of your work." Valan bowed. "The Piuthar-Tri has sent me to you for reeducation."

"Another demand, is it?" Sabrene muttered. She finally set aside her saw, turning to face him. A look crossed her features, one he had seen often enough, before her expression became controlled emotionlessness: *Oh, it's the pretty one.* "So, what did you do?"

"I paid a guard."

"To…?"

"Guard."

Sabrene didn't bother hiding her next expression. Pure irritation darkened her face. "That's it? My efforts are to be wasted on *this*? It's bad enough that… Just go ask Kirwyn to whip you a few times."

"Gladly, but the Piuthar wishes for Isla to do the actual whipping. You are wanted to supervise so things don't get out of hand."

"And where is she?"

"I don't know. She was supposed to be looking for you." Valan shrugged. "I guess we'll have to wait."

"Wait," Sabrene repeated flatly. "*I* am to wait on *her*."

Valan moved closer to the ghoul, making a show of studying it. Several beetle plates were already sewn onto the abdomen and over the heart, with other places marked for more covering. He knew the string she'd used consisted of finely crushed fey bone, spider's web, and matter pulled across a veil from the Otherworld. Over time, the string became absorbed by the body, the parts fusing together. A method often used to fix up the undead as they started to fall apart.

Several magical runes were also carved into the armor, the handwriting reminding him of the clan's Archwizard. "The stitching here differs from what was used on the goliath in the family dining room."

"The goliath is made up of heavier parts. The flesh needs to be folded back and then double chain-stitched, otherwise it'd collapse under its own weight."

"And this is catch stitch here?" Valan looked at her with wide, earnest eyes. Eagerness tugged at the corner of his mouth…and just as quickly, he looked away, suddenly shy. "I'm sorry for asking. You must be very busy. I don't want to waste your time."

"It's already being wasted," Sabrene replied. Her voice had lost its harsh edge from earlier. "And yes, that's catch stitch. It works best on lighter material that is expected to shift on top of muscle. Was there… anything else you wanted to know?"

Valan turned his overly-earnest eyes toward her again. "I've always been fascinated by your skill in combining creatures made of gelatinous material. I didn't even know such a thing was possible until I saw your creations. A chaos slime, floating giant's eye, and a squid? Genius!"

"And the vocal cords of a surface cat," Sabrene had to add. "I really should let that one run rampant more often. Its cries can't be appreciated if it is always a statue."

This time, Valan walked over to the table where she worked, coincidentally now closer to her. He moved a slender, delicate hand over one of the knives Sabrene had placed nearby, not quite touching but as if he badly wanted to. Several of her tools were still clean. "These scalpels here… Do you plan on creating something else soon?"

"Well…" Sabrene leaned closer to him, then flicked Valan in the middle of his forehead. Hard. "That's not for you to know."

"Ow."

Alright, he had to admit at least to himself. *I've been a bit too dramatic and heavy-handed, but I'm on a time limit here.*

"Nice try." Sabrene made a shooing gesture for him to get away from her table. "I can't decide if it was brave or stupid of you to try to appeal to me—*that* certainly hasn't happened in a while. You do know what I like to do to the males who displease me?"

"Yes, and I'd go with 'brave'."

Which, apparently, wasn't the response she expected. Fear, more like. Fear was the normal, healthy response. She studied him as if he were a bug that had just started to wiggle unusually. Silently judging the value of his limbs and skin. "I might change my mind when I'm not so busy."

"Yes, Sabrene." Valan kept the disgust out of his voice, making it a point for her to hear the sound of her name coming from his mouth. Just look at how easily he obeyed. Valan didn't really want to end up as a consort within his own family; this was more about trying to get her to *like* him enough so that she wouldn't let his twin sister go overboard in "reeducating" him. As soon as this was over with, he planned to stay as far away from Sabrene as possible.

He decided to pretend to not see the slight twitch to her lips as she picked up the saw again with the intention of ignoring him. Saying her name like that really affected her. He doubted she ever had males willingly show interest in her. Who would want to risk being stitched up as part of her latest monster? But Sabrene was now the second-eldest daughter after Gwyndolin had died during the fall of one of the Clan Anartes outposts, which meant her influence over household politics was now worth a lot more. Aside from Nareena, she had the best chance of becoming the next Piuthar-Tri. Valan might be the first male to play nice, but he doubted he'd be the last.

To give her more space, Valan pretended to study all the jars and boxes, commenting here and there on some of the rarer specimens contained within. Conversation between the two of them remained light. Sabrene was in the middle of explaining to him the differences between a pooka and a changeling—important information, such as which produced the best excretions to disintegrate a body—by the time Isla finally appeared. His twin brought with her a large fold-up carrier full of tools meant for torture. Apparently she wasn't just wandering lost and confused over where her oldest sister could be, but struggling to decide what to use on him.

Isla stopped several steps into the room once she noticed Valan was already there. "You! But—"

Valan bowed, hiding his grin. *Did she really get lost?* As if she honestly expected to have a chance to talk to their sister before he could after all her running around.

"Oh, Isla, there you are." Sabrene didn't look too pleased to have her lecture interrupted. "Well, let's make this quick. We'll have to finish our discussion on different slimes another time, Valan."

"I look forward to it."

"Q-quick?!" Isla all but screeched. "The Piuthar said I could do what I wanted with him! It will not be quick!"

"*I* am the one to determine what is and isn't done, and I, you stupid, lazy little girl, have more compelling matters to attend to," Sabrene said. "You've wasted enough time just getting here. Do not dare to disagree with me again: ten lashes. That's it. And if you are going to whine about it, I have no issue with fixing *your* bad behavior. Know *your* place."

"B-but I—"

Sabrene *looked* at her and Isla fell silent. Even his twin finally realized how bad of an idea it was to argue with a higher-ranking female. Valan struggled not to smile; it wasn't often he got to watch Isla being admonished so blatantly. This might not become one of the most horrifying days of his existence after all.

"Now, follow," Sabrene commanded. She led the way through one of the side doors and down a hallway lined with cages. Most of the cages were covered by thick sheets of spider webbing, making it difficult to see inside, but not all. Valan certainly heard the creatures moving in the cages: the occasional clawed foot scratching at the floor, the hissing, and soft weeping from some of the more humanoid captures. The three nobles passed a commoner male dangling a piece of meat over the top of one cage, just out of reach of something that shook the cage's bars and growled hungrily. Valan tried not to stare too long at the fish gills attached to either side of his neck.

The hallway ended in a massive reinforced door, which marked one of the many entrances to the torture cells. Sabrene whispered a word and the door opened on its own, revealing another circular chamber, the walls flanked by small alcoves with chains attached to the stone. The floor sloped downwards into a spiral that led to even deeper depths. As Valan looked down the hole in the middle, he spied two clan guards patrolling along a path that went so deep into the earth that he couldn't see the bottom even with his superior dark elven vision.

Rumors were rampant about the kinds of guests entertained in the more secure areas. Most of the interrogation spaces were empty, but Valen did recognize one of his nephews, Niall, asking someone else questions. The low hum of an activated glyph, one made to protect against eavesdroppers, prevented him from hearing the discussion. Each alcove was reinforced with such runes. Depending on the questioner's desire, any sound produced would be amplified or obscured. Sometimes the screams of one prisoner were used to help convince the others to start talking. Other times, the torturer simply found the sounds pleasant.

"I want this one!" Isla eagerly rushed past her twin to stand closer to their sister, pointing at one of the nearest alcoves.

Why that one? Valan wondered. At a glance, all the cells appeared identical. Each were stocked with the same amount of chains, a stool, a small table for tools, and hooks attached to the wall above the table which held a few of the more basic torture instruments. As far as he could tell, the runes inscribed on the floor didn't look any different; Isla wasn't skilled enough to alter those, anyway. Still, he didn't like it. Something was going on that he knew nothing about in a place where he held no power.

"Fine," Sabrene said, "and we may as well make this educational. Valan, strip in front of the wall, there. Isla, I want to see how skilled you are at using a scourge. You will *not* embarrass me once you enter An Loch."

This was always the worst part for Valan. Taking off his clothes meant removing all the magical protections and enhancements he used to feel normal. Removing his bracers made him slower and clumsier. Without his wide belt, his strength drained away, his bones turning brittle. His legs especially caused him the most trouble. While they looked normal, the simple act of walking convinced him that his muscles were somehow attached to his bones the wrong way, making every movement painful.

The removal of the silver earring studs and hoops meant the back of his throat started to itch, forcing him to hold back a cough—an old injury inflicted by Isla when they were younger, from the first time she had tried to strangle him. Only after summoning acid onto her face had she stopped. The *buime*[1] in charge of them healed Isla, assuring her she

1 **buime:** Nurse, nanny, or nursemaid.

wouldn't develop any scarring, but placed a curse on Valan so that his throat could never fully heal as a reminder to never attack a female.

"Ugh, I'll never get used to how disgusting he really is," Isla said behind him once he'd fully undressed. "He's pathetic. So weak."

Valan ignored her. It wasn't like these were things he hadn't heard from her before. He looked up at the heavy lead manacles dangling from chains, each one inscribed with small symbols that prevented the wearer from using magic. Locking one around his own wrist was easy enough—and preferred, since sometimes he'd end up with a broken arm afterward if put on too tightly by someone else—but securing the other one always required help of the usually unfriendly natured.

Sabrene grabbed his wrist as he was about to shackle himself. Valan didn't dare try to pull away since it wouldn't take much energy on her part to crush his wrist. Any show of resistance at this point meant Bad Things for him.

"I've never seen anything like it," Sabrene said. She twisted his arm to better expose the crease between his ulna and radius, digging her fingers into the space there before moving on to force his fingers apart. A feverish look entered her eyes as she stared at his fragile, slender bones there. "No— I have. These are like the little bones of a baby bat."

Valan couldn't bring himself to look at her. He fought to suppress the rising fear that she was going to break his fingers, one of the easiest places to damage that took the longest to recover from. Without his hands, he wouldn't be able to play musical instruments and would struggle with the most basic forms of self-care; his life would effectively be over since far too many sidhe would see it as an opportune time to kill him, and there was nothing he could do to stop her.

Just focus on the wall in front of you, he told himself. *It'll hurt but only for a time, and then I can go back to him. This is only temporary. I can drink a couple healing vials hidden in the heels of my boots and see his face again. It'll be over soon.*

Sabrene finally stopped playing with him and shackled both of his wrists, standing back to rejoin Isla. "Show me how you were taught to hold the whip."

"Like...this?"

"Very good. Now, you raise your arm back like so—no, not like that. You want to use the muscles in your upper arm and shoulders. It's less tiring and you can do more damage. Try it."

Just count the cracks in the walls. One, two…

"Not bad, but aim more for the upper back. If you let the barbs wrap around the front, you risk digging too deep and spilling the organs. Just imagine the travesty if he were mortal. Having your prisoner die too soon helps no one."

…seven, eight. It doesn't matter what happens to this body.

"And avoid the back of his head, girl. Do I have to hit you with it for you to understand? Now try again."

What number was I on? It was… I better start over again. This isn't me. I'm somewhere else.

"Again."

This is temporary.

"And again."

And one day…

"Once you start seeing the spine and back of the ribs, you need to adjust the angle of your swing. Otherwise the hooks will catch on the bone and possibly damage the lungs—even now the point is to punish. They can't be punished if they die too quickly."

"I understand, Sabrene."

…and it may take years. Decades…

"Oh! You've learned quickly. That was perfect."

…but I'll make them pay.

"Again."

He lost track again. The number of times the barbed hooks ripped away his flesh all just became *pain*. No, he was supposed to focus on the wall. Surely…it was ten by now. Who lost count first? If he could just… concentrate on the wall in front of him…

"There, that's enough for now."

"But this isn't fair!" Isla pouted. "He is supposed to scream and cry and beg for me to stop. This isn't how it's supposed to go at all!"

Valan felt a trickle of blood slide down the corner of his mouth and drip off his chin. His bottom lip was a bloody mess from biting down so hard to keep from screaming. He struggled to keep his eyes open.

"Not everyone screams at first," Sabrene said. "With more experience, you'll come to understand that different prisoners have different breaking points. It's important to learn their habits, their desires, what it is they think they cannot survive without, and use that against them."

He could agree with that much, at least.

Sabrene walked up behind him and patted Valan on the top of his head like a well-behaved dog. "Don't worry, beautiful boy. I'll stitch you up." She leaned in close to whisper into his ear. "And I know how to improve you."

Valan's eyes widened. *I-Improve? What does she mean by that? She can't be talking about…*

He had seen the statues of what she made of other sidhe men. The things she turned them into. How could he have been so foolish? He should have done more research on her, not tried to get close and feign an interest in her. He'd assumed she wouldn't be *this* impulsive. He was stupid. So stupid. Too wrapped up in avoiding Isla trying to kill him. He should have—

Sabrene ran her nails down the exposed parts of his spine. The pain was so excruciating that he couldn't think of anything anymore.

CHAPTER 3

His eyelids felt heavy, gummy. Valan tried to scratch at the corner of his eyes with his hand but discovered he couldn't move his limbs. Neither could he turn his head, locked in some sort of brace and forced to get a good view of all the body parts hanging from the ceiling. He could look down at himself just enough to see that he was still naked, strapped to one of the oval tables in Sabrene's workspace. No sign of any of his clothing, either.

"Lady Sabrene, he's awake."

The male commoner from earlier, the one with the gills, moved to block his view of the contents on the other oval table. Valan caught a quick glimpse of a massive black body covered in fur, something with claws and a snout.

"Oh, dear, I must have watered down my sleep concoction too much," Sabrene said from elsewhere in the room. Valan was too groggy to tell exactly where. "I need more practice on delicate creatures. I have to be so very careful. Go tell Mabina to prepare that Seelie we captured, so I can practice more later."

"At once, Lady Sabrene." Her apprentice bowed and left, heading in the direction of the cages.

Valan hadn't even realized he was struggling to rise from the table until Sabrene pushed his shoulders back down. Her face appeared above his, upside down. "It's much easier to work on subjects under a stasis spell, but you've already undergone too much pain. It's incredibly disappointing when I spend hours building something only for it to pull itself apart from the shock. Try not to wiggle; it'll spoil my work."

"It has occurred to me," Valan began, his mind racing. Dredging up everything he'd ever heard about her and learned from his own interactions. "That as an admirer of your past creations, it'd be a shame for all of that to come to an end."

Sabrene dug her nails into his shoulders. "'An end', you say? Really? *You* certainly can't stop me."

"And I normally wouldn't want to—big admirer, after all. I heard that the Piuthar-Tri threatened you with punishment if you ever used a clan male in your experiments again."

"You're just the youngest male. She'll come to forgive me."

"Will she? Harming a noble without permission? Consider how she reacted when all I did was *hire a guard*. I'm about to be sent to Crann Bethadh. She has plans for me that are already set in motion, *and*," Valan made it a point to really emphasize *and*, "even if you killed me to cover up what you do here, how are you going to explain why so few reinforced ghouls have been built since you've focused on me? I suppose you could always blame Isla for my death, but you were specifically put in charge of her—you'll get blamed anyway."

Sabrene scowled at him. "You talk too much."

"I'm told it's an inherited trait."

Which clearly didn't make much sense to his sister, going by the puzzled expression on her face. Due to her age, Valan guessed she'd known Mairead and the late Torran a lot longer than he had and neither one were known to talk overmuch. Naturally, he was lying in order to save himself, which would be to the surprise of no one, least of all Sabrene, since all dark elves were fond of trickery, but he knew he raised some concerns she needed to consider. Was she really willing to risk her ability to create new marvelous creatures over some male?

"I'll make your improvements *subtle*," she grudgingly allowed. "That way, everyone will be happy. Now stop distracting me."

Valan had hoped for a better result, but before he could try to convince her further, Sabrene jammed a needle into the crook of his arm. He jolted from the stab, not able to brace himself for the pain and unable to get a single word out before his world turned dark.

The upper floors of the Anartes complex were the most decorated and guarded. Bejeweled strands of frost overlaid the sweeping banisters lining the paths that appeared to float on the chilled spikes, leading to the bedrooms of the female members of the family. Azurite statues of creatures guarded the corners, coming to life on Lady Mairead's whim. Arcane tapestries edged in silver and gleaming with faerie light decorated the walls. Males were not allowed there without express permission, and yet those paths were exactly where Cernunnos walked now. Even without anyone openly glaring at him, there was a sense of *something watching* that did not want him here.

Midway down an apparently empty walkway, Cernunnos abruptly stopped, stuck out the spear he held, and forced an invisible something to trip. That *something* landed with a light *thump!* and cursed at him, but he decided to ignore that part. He waggled a finger in admonishment at the unseen being sprawled on the floor.

"What you are about to do is very stupid," Cernunnos said. "You'll be caught and the wrath of this entire clan will fall upon both of you. Go back, brat. I'll take care of things here."

In response, Cernunnos got a dagger thrown at his head, which he batted aside easily enough with his spear.

"Get out of my way, old man." The air wavered and revealed a lean, muscular male figure wearing tattered, blackened leather armor. The hood of his equally ragged cloak hid the details of the upper half of his face, with his nose and mouth concealed by a fraying, poorly knitted blue scarf. A very tacky scarf, by Cernunnos' standards. He was bleeding in several places, having gotten into a few fights before reaching this point, by the look of things. The young man already had two more daggers out. The hard white glint in his gray eyes radiated immeasurable anger.

Cernunnos pointed his spear at him. "Brat, I'm trying to *save* you."

"Nobody asked you to."

Another attack, this time the brat moving even quicker with both knives. A green tint flashed along the edges of the blades, illuminated by the nearby faerie fire. *Poisoned*, Cernunnos noted as he parried both blades and gave the brat a shallow cut through the lightly armored left arm. He moved directly in front of the brat to keep him from easily running past him down the walkway…and was a little curious. Supposedly, this young man never had an instructor teach him to fight, and while he was not skilled enough to be a challenge for Cernunnos, he still possessed some talent. Especially for someone who wasn't even six decades old yet. It was a shame Cernunnos couldn't keep testing him, but this interruption had already gone on for too long.

He wasn't sure what movement of his gave it away, the shift of his wrist or the slight change in balance to his stance, but the brat noticed; he dodged Cernunnos's attempt to knock him out, backing away several steps and crouching low. His feet silently slid across the floor and then he leapt at Cernunnos. A very straight-forward attack Cernunnos had no trouble dealing with, though as he blocked, a weird, dark distortion appeared at the edges of his vision, and he could no longer focus on the person in front of him. His mind kept trying to reinterpret what he saw as not really being there. Just another empty shadow in his surroundings.

Now it was Cernunnos's turn to step away. He glanced down at a jagged gash across his abdomen, the edges of the wound peeling back, painfully shedding layers of skin from the poison coursing through him. By the time he looked up again, the younger man was gone.

Was my bed always this soft? Valan wondered sluggishly. *And intricately patterned?* He noticed the details now that he got one eye open. One eye, not two. Hesitantly, he reached up to touch the blind side of his face and felt a bandage that spanned his forehead down to part of his neck. He suddenly felt overwhelmed. *What did she do to me? Why can't I—*

"Awake at…Bel's *ochd uairean*," somebody in the room said, marking down the time.

Valan jerked upright, a weight attached to his back lurching and throwing him off-balance. He reached out and grabbed the bedpost to keep himself sitting.

"Subject appears disoriented." Sitting in a plush, high-backed chair next to a vanity sat a dark elf female scribbling notes in a book. Her garb was plain, stains of unknown substances here and there reminding him of what Sabrene's gilled apprentice wore. Valan surmised this bedroom belonged to his sister.

"How long have I been unconscious?" Valan asked.

"Subject is capable of simple sentences," the female apprentice said as she wrote more into her book.

"Answer my question!" Valan shouted. He moved to the edge of the bed, forcing himself to stand. His legs began to buckle, but he ignored the weakness. *I* will *stand. Even if I must hold on to the bedpost to remain steady, but my body* will *obey me.* Sabrene had her fun with her little experiments, but it did not change that he was still a clan noble. Some *commoner* did not get to treat him like he was nothing.

The apprentice pursed her lips, clearly wanting to say something sarcastic, but ultimately decided to keep the thought to herself. She bowed her head, if slightly, before answering his question. "You've been unconscious for nine days."

Valan lost his grip on the bedpost and vomited on the floor. Once he started, he couldn't get himself to stop dry heaving uncontrollably. The *things* attached to his back kept twitching in response. He must have misheard her. It couldn't have been nine days. That was too long. Far too long to remain unawares in Sabrene's bed and everything that implied. A cold sweat coated his body, and he realized he was covered in yellowing bruises he didn't remember acquiring.

No—nothing had happened. He didn't remember anything, so there was no point in assuming the worst. It didn't matter.

What did matter was that nine days was the longest they'd been separated. *All this time, he's been alone out there. They didn't find him…did they? If they found him, if anyone harmed Sorn while I've been stuck in here, I'll…*

Valan couldn't let himself continue thinking like that. Of course his family hadn't found Sorn; they'd both be dead already if that was the case. He wiped spittle off his chin and got back on his feet. Enough weakness. He just needed to solve one problem at a time. First, he needed to know how much damage had been done to his body.

The mirror above the vanity stretched nearly to the ceiling, with elaborate blackened silver and gold skull filigree covering half of it. Plenty of space remained for him to see the *things* attached to his back: wings.

The black, leathery wings of a giant bat. The clawed tips of the wings curled a solid ten *ordlach* over the top of his head. Horrible. As if he really needed something that emphasized his ongoing issue with appearing frail. How was he expected to fit through narrow pathways with these things? What about this counted as "being subtle"?! He couldn't wear a cloak over this. All of his clothing from now on would need to be custom made. His long hair was going to *constantly* get in the way every time they flapped. Flapped. He *flapped* now.

"I'm never going to be able to live this down," Valan said. He needed to get these things cut off as soon as possible. As long as he had them, he couldn't be seen in public and hope to retain a shred of dignity. Worse, he still didn't know the extent of the damage done to his face.

Valan pulled off the bandage to reveal the mess underneath. His left eye was simply *gone*. Some sort of shiny black rubbery mass filled the socket where there once resided the elegant red of a normal Unseelie eye. He could still blink, but it felt *wrong*. An orb a lot less solid than it should be. At some point during his recovery, the substance had leaked out of his eye socket and burned swirling, mottled patterns along the left side of his face and neck.

Acid burns. She had ruined him. One of very few upsides of his physicality had been an attractive face, the symmetry inherent of dark elf nobility. Even if, say, Sabrene was so attracted to him that she never wanted to share, it was counterproductive to ruin his appearance. Physical flaws in sidhe nobility, especially damage like this, would be enough to strip him of his title. Up until this moment, Valan hadn't considered himself a particularly vain person, but seeing what he looked like now filled him with despair.

"Why…?"

He didn't expect an answer, but the female apprentice provided one anyway. "Lady Sabrene was inspired by your interest in slime, so she took part of an acid ooze and infused it with magic from across the veil to serve as an improved form of eyesight."

"Improved." Valan was beginning to hate that word. It sounded foul when he said it out loud.

"As you fly around, the processing power of your existing eyes wouldn't be able to keep up with the movement, thus, you were given synesthesia. The new eye registers sound bouncing off of objects at great distances." She flipped several pages in her book. "Past experiments with synesthesia have determined that it is not recommended to try to use both synesthesia and normal vision at the same time. Side effects include migraines, bleeding from the eyes and nose, vertigo, and inability to breathe. To relieve these conditions, it is recommended to remove the parts of the brain that process information for the eyes and replace them with an appropriate creature already adapted to synesthesia. Installing vocal cords and eardrums that better send and receive sound is also suggested." She glared at him as if the incomplete experiment was all his fault. "This was not applied to you out of fear of going 'too far'."

"My apologies," he snapped back.

Unbelievable. Complete insanity. This was them showing restraint. If they had it their way, he'd be hanging from the ceiling and eating insects. As soon as the opportunity presented itself, Valan was going to kill Sabrene and every apprentice who'd helped her.

He then had another sinking thought: he was no longer technically a full-blooded sidhe. His title, such as it was, could be stripped from him for being so heavily scarred, but animal parts from a lesser race meant he wouldn't be able to continue calling himself a sidhe at all. He would join Balfore in the slave pens to become fine breeding stock for the other giant bats.

He needed to leave. Now. While he still could.

A pair of obsidian scissors inset with emeralds rested in a neat row with matching hair care tools on the vanity top. Valan grabbed them, spun around, and stabbed the apprentice through the left eye. She gasped in shock, dropping her book as she jerked away from him. Even with the element of surprise, he was annoyed that he almost missed hitting her from losing his grip on the scissors. He didn't have enough strength in his hand to drive the blades deep enough into her brain to overwhelm her senses and render her unconscious.

As a sidhe, she permanently died only when hit with a "mortal" blow from a tool made of iron. Being reduced to a pile of ash or goo would technically work, but those methods took time. Usually when a sidhe wanted to kill another of their kind, a more efficient method was to slow them down with poison, remove their limbs, then take bets on whether the targeted sidhe could regenerate faster than fire or acid could damage them. Granted, using poison followed by acid or fire was becoming less popular in favor of simply tricking the enemy into teleporting into an active volcano.

The sidhe woman reached under her cloak, pulled out several poison-tipped darts, and threw them at Valan, quicker than he could ever hope to move but not as quick as he could think. An invisible barrier made of thickened air sprung up between them, the darts striking the surface and causing a rippling effect that surrounded Valan before the tiny projectiles dropped to the ground. Valan stuck out his tongue at her, revealing a row of gold piercings down the center, with the biggest stud shaped like a skull.

Valan held out his hand and summoned a gust of wind that sent the female sidhe flying across the room. Her head snapped backwards against a stone wall, the wind driving the scissors deeper into her skull, finally knocking her out. Other objects scattered and tumbled about the room from the gale force, including a statue that wobbled and tipped over. When the statue crashed to the ground, the head of it snapped off the body…and blood spurted out of the neck stump.

Interesting… Statues don't normally bleed.

Valan let go of his control over the air.

Until now, he hadn't bothered to take in many of the details of the room. All the statues in the bedroom were sidhe men in various poses. The broken one was a handsome nude figure with a curiously blank expression on his face; where his genitals should have been was a mass of tentacles. Another statue was missing his lower jaw, instead equipped with a long, protruding prehensile tongue. The statue closest to the bed was constructed from two males missing the lower halves of their bodies. The torsos were sewn together and posed so the bottom half "walked" on his hands.

The display of Sabrene's depravity left Valan stunned, then angry. How close had he been to becoming another part of her collection? He *really* needed to kill her. Her and every apprentice who had helped turn him into the monstrosity he was now.

"One down, three more to go," Valan muttered under his breath. He approached the apprentice's body and held out his hand. His bruises started to glow a saturated shade of green. On the ground, her body withered, decaying faster than it should have naturally as he siphoned her energy. His task complete, the bruises faded.

Secretly studying necromancy, specifically sacrificial magic, was turning out to be useful after all, though the ability worked only if he had personally harmed the person beforehand. Sacrificed them to himself, more like, same as mortals did to appease whichever fey they decided to call their deity. Valan was just skipping a step. This method was the least popular to use against other fey, especially by a male since it involved siphoning and converting the target's soul into energy, which was then absorbed. That way, even if an enemy's body did manage to regenerate, it would be only a shell with no mind inside.

From his studies, Valan had learned there was a disagreement between authors if the converted energy qualified as a soul—which was, after all, a human word—and if the practice should be used only on lesser races. As far as Valan was concerned, that type of magic kept enemies from healing and attacking him again, so whatever special term was used to describe the energy wasn't all that important. He was just turning someone who'd otherwise harm him into something useful.

With any luck, he'd also be able to get rid of Sabrene before he was caught. He summoned globes of acid to burn away the skulls of the statues, followed by more necromancy in hopes of killing them fully. Nobody deserved to be stuck living forever like that, so why not offer them a little mercy before the end? Then he left the bedroom, but not before conjuring a bolt of fire to hit Sabrene's bed and destroying that, too. The sound of crackling flames behind him brought a smile to his face.

Now, if I were a lunatic bent on turning others into little horror projects, where would I be? he mused, walking across the floating platform that connected to a set of stairs leading down. Far down. He'd never been this high up in the tower before. It was a lot of steps, even for a healthy fey. Without his belt and bracers, Valan did not have the capability of walking down all those stairs. Maybe he should just fall down. Falling sounded nice. Even he could climb over the low railing and just jump. No more dealing with the deranged machinations of the females of his species.

He wondered where he'd end up once he died. The fall wouldn't kill him, but whoever found his body certainly would, especially if given over to the Piuthar-Tri. Or to any of the Piuthars, who took their task of providing counsel to An Cailleach very seriously, who everyone else was supposed to worship. Previously, he'd merely paid lip-service to An Cailleach, if only to increase the chances of his survival. But over the years, it was made very clear to him that the Winter Queen didn't care too much for males. With his luck, instead of dying from hitting the ground, the veiled ones would just wait until he healed enough to endure torture for the rest of his existence. Sorn might still be here, too, and Valan would have been leaving the other man by himself in this world. If his love wasn't already dead, that is. Which was most likely the case if nine days had passed.

Valan sighed, and then coughed; the smoke from the fire was beginning to bother him. With the mess he'd made in Sabrene's room, it was now too late for a great many things he'd rather have happened... and didn't he have these wings now? Why, this was the perfect chance to try to fly. If he couldn't figure out how before he hit the bottom, well, then it must have been fate.

The smile on his face grew wider, a little more manic. Was this how Torran had felt toward the end of his life?

He climbed over the banister, tried an experimental flap with his wings, and then stepped off the edge. The ground rushed up to meet him, closer and closer. He had to time things just right...and several *troighid* from hitting the stone floor, he stretched his wings as far out as he could and then closed them with such force that he managed to lift himself back up into the air. He meant to attempt an easy landing with minimal damage, but the abrupt movement tangled his long hair around his left wing. Suddenly, he started to fall again, this time at an angle that sent him smashing into the ground. He heard a loud *snap!* of the bones in his left wing breaking and a spreading numbness emanated from his left shoulder as he lost the ability to move the attached arm. Multiple sharp pains in the left side of his chest let him know he'd broken several ribs as well.

"What was that?!"

"Who—?"

Valan snarled and called forth a wave of darkness that centered on him, blinding both himself and everyone else nearby. Long years spent living under the earth made the Unseelie adept at seeing in the dark, but it wasn't an omniscient ability. Sidhe eyes still required at least some light to register surrounding shapes.

Valan struggled to his feet, clutching his dislocated arm to his chest. He closed his normal eye and tried to *look* through the one affected by synesthesia. At first, he couldn't make sense of what he was seeing; dark ripples vaguely outlined objects before fading into nothing. Noise. Noise hitting the objects in his surroundings as the other fey in the area moved to get out of the range of the darkness spell.

He couldn't afford to be caught here. Not yet. He had to keep moving. He hurried toward Sabrene's laboratory, sidestepping anyone who came too close as they ran by but did not see him. The broken wing hung limply from his back, practically dragging on the floor.

Once he reached the main entrance to the lab, Valan took one last cautionary look around. His synesthesia picked up a narrow, rippling wave flying in his direction that he guessed must be an incoming projectile. Someone had figured out that they just needed to aim at the center of the darkness to find him. He entered the lab and closed the door behind him, nearly smashing his own fingers in his haste. His time was running out. He needed a place to hide. Multiple footsteps rushed toward the door, but he managed to manipulate the veil radiation around him in enough time. The room's shape warped, distorting in size, with the ceiling curving down toward him to form a much smaller room. Valan jumped up, clinging to a chain hanging from the ceiling, using a corpse as a platform to stand on as the lab snapped back to its original size. Body parts surrounded him. Dead eyes of creatures staring, waiting.

It's as if they know I'm going to be dead right next to them.

He hurriedly scanned the bodies, making sure he didn't recognize anything familiar. Nothing looked like it could have been a part of Sorn. There was that, at least. Something small to be happy about. Valan struggled to stifle the sudden, near hysterical urge to laugh at his own dark thoughts. Far below, two sidhe guards ran into the laboratory, their hurried steps drawing the attention of one of Sabrene's apprentices as they came out of one of the cage-lined hallways.

"Hey, did you see a winged creature go through here?!" one of the guards asked.

"What? No, and who said you could come here?" the apprentice replied.

"This is important! Something set a veiled one's room on fire, and now we might have an intruder running around. Did you hear anything? See anything odd at all?"

"No. And if it was an intruder, the wards would have activated, you idiot. Whatever you're looking for isn't here."

The three sidhe traded several insults before finally separating. Valan saw the echoes of their departure within the synesthesia: two left through the main door while the third stepped into one of the side hallways. He waited to make sure he didn't perceive any other movement, then distorted the space within the room a second time to step down onto the laboratory floor. As a younger noble sidhe, the area Valan effected was limited to the space immediately around him, and such magic worked only near places easily connected to The Otherworld.

The two oval tables were still where Valan last saw them, if recently cleaned and emptied of body parts. A few instruments were set aside on a tray. The stacks of jars and boxes looked much the same as before. Instead of heading straight for the side hallway the apprentice had used, he went toward the other one. This hallway of cages was not the same one he'd taken to reach the torture chambers earlier; he simply wanted to check inside it first to avoid any nasty surprises.

Valan tried to open the side hallway door as quietly as possible, but he wasn't exactly known for his stealth. The creaking door announced his presence, causing the two people cleaning one of the large cages on either side of the hallway to look up from their work. One of the two sidhe had very recognizable gills. Nearby, an ogre was kept on a short chain attached to the cage's side; too short of a leash to hurt the two assistants as they cleaned.

It looked like it really, really wanted to hurt them, though.

That's an excellent idea, Valan thought, agreeing with the creature's sentiment.

Valan snapped his fingers, releasing a pulse of magic that carried the sound waves to the lock that was chained around the ogre's neck. The lock abruptly disappeared from *here* to be sent to *there* in The Otherworld. In theory, the bigger the noise, the bigger the object he could move, but it really wasn't something he could practice often since it would alert everyone nearby to what he was doing.

He wasn't too concerned if a sidhe traveling on the Otherworld side of the veil might stumble across a random lock and report it to a Piuthar, since demi-fey loved to collect what others thought of as junk. To those races, owning items from the mortal world was seen as a sign of bravery. Their very bodies relied on the magical radiation caused by The Otherworld, so they couldn't travel too far away from a veil without risking death. Little things like socks were usually the kind of objects fairies stole, so it was far more likely he'd just made a lesser fey very happy.

Without the lock to hold the chain in place, the two assistants watched in horror as the last thing which had kept them safe from the ogre fell away, a hesitation that cost them when the creature lurched to its full height and slammed down with its fists onto their heads. Valan closed the door on the sounds of the ogre ripping their bodies apart to eat.

CHAPTER 4

THE OTHER HALLWAY door opened and a female apprentice appeared. The last one. "What was that?"

Valan remained silent, stayed still, and maintained the illusion that his side of the lab looked perfectly ordinary and he wasn't there. The illusionary wall and door worked, but it couldn't prevent the assistant from reaching for the fake door handle and finding her hand passed through it, trying to find the source of the noise she had heard earlier. The illusion wavered and faded away at her interference. From her point of view, suddenly Valan stood a mere few feet away from her.

"Want to hear something amusing?" Valan asked, taking advantage of her surprise. He put his *will* behind that question, the veil radiation turning his intent into something more real, and felt her mind bend under the weight of his.

Being a noble implied more than just holding a title, since it meant he could trace his lineage to An Cailleach, and then to Danu, who held the most influence over the Otherworld. Against another noble from an older generation, Valan would be in big trouble, but it did mean he held more power over the veil than a commoner. Being labeled a peasant meant that not only were they too physically flawed, but also that their lineage was riddled with too many non-sidhe to hold much affinity with the magic of the Otherworld. The female assistant in front of Valan never stood much of a chance in fighting off his commands; so compelling did she seem to find him that she couldn't help but giggle a little.

"If I had been asked beforehand if I was interested in synesthesia, I might have agreed to let you all cut me up," he said. "I'd have *thanked* you for it."

He forced that compulsion onto her to find that it *was* funny So funny, in fact, shrieks of laughter burst forth and she fell to the floor, clutching her sides from the sheer hilariousness of it. He made her believe she was going to die. He was going to die. And all of it over something that could have easily been avoided. *Thanked*, he said! Hilarious!

One of the table's surgical knives in-hand, Valan slit her throat, silencing any further hysterics. Her laughter ended in a wet gurgle, a quickly decaying rattle of rotting lungs as necromantic energies left what remained. He felt his ribs heal and fought down his own urge to laugh, though it wasn't caused by his own spell. He rolled the top of his tongue against his teeth, idly counting the piercings as a way to recall how much time had passed since he'd first used magic to alter the world. Again Valan used his will to try to bend the walls around him, but his surroundings remained as inanimate as they appeared. As he feared, he had used too much of the magic trapped on this side of the veil, and a veiled one had just cut off his access. Whoever it was might not know exactly how or who had used up so much magic at once, but it was important to not let that energy get so low that the lesser fey on this side struggled.

He was now down to his own much weaker innate abilities involving darkness, air, and ice. His wounded arm and wing would make any physical attempt to defend himself incredibly difficult, and he still didn't know where Sabrene was. No sign of Sorn, either. Since his elder sister was a veiled one, she'd likely be in the family temple of An Cailleach, but that wasn't anywhere near here. Valan would need to move around without darkness or spatial manipulation to help him. Even if he managed to reach the temple, undoubtedly other veiled ones were also with her to offer prayers for whatever their latest twisted desires happened to be. Probably new ways to make males miserable.

Going to the temple was suicide. No plan he could devise gave him a chance to succeed. He had to acknowledge that this was as far as he could go. Valan briefly closed his eyes, exhausted, a dull ache spreading through his chest. If this was all his life amounted to, he might as well regain a little control of how things were going to end.

He dropped the bloodied knife and picked up the handsaw. If he was going to die, it would not be with *those things* still attached to him. His one unbroken wing was easy enough to fold over his shoulder and stretch to the front of him. Granted, he only had one working arm to saw off the wing. Removing the new limb wasn't going to be easy or clean, but maybe if he rested it on a tabletop and applied enough pressure, he could cut through the bone without getting overwhelmed by the pain. Well, it was worth a try, and if he was still conscious afterward, he'd go see how useful a bit of fire worked against a room full of veiled ones.

He moved closer to one of the oval tables and made his wing lie flat across it, took a breath so deep it aggravated his throat, and dragged the saw across the bone that connected it to his back. Valan hissed in pain, his arm trembled, and then he tightened his grip on the saw to prepare to move the toothed edge against his flesh again.

"Valan?"

No, it's too late.

"Do you think you can hold this steady for me?" Valan asked, voice dull and distant. "It's going to take me forever to cut it off myself."

Running footsteps. He dragged the saw against the bone again. Halfway through. Two more of that and it'd be gone. Ignore the blood. The second wing would be easier to remove.

Don't look at me.

Stronger hands than his wrapped around his fingers and gently pried the saw away. He knew the feel of those hands.

"I'm not going to let you hurt yourself."

Valan shook his head, looking up as Sorn knelt down in front of him to see each other's faces. "You don't understand. *These* are not *me*. I will not die as somebody's pet! And where have you been this entire time? Enjoying yourself?! Just when I needed you the most a-and you...w-were..."

The stricken expression on Sorn's face made him stumble over his words. His love's dyed dark blue hair was an unbrushed mess. Light gray eyes bloodshot. Face thinner than he remembered. Valan hadn't been the only one going through his own personal nightmare. "… I'm sorry. I'm sorry. I know none of this is your fault. It's mine," Valan admitted. "Turns out I'm not nearly as smart as I think I am."

"No, I'm in the wrong. I shouldn't have left. I thought I'd see to freeing Balfore and ran into a complication," Sorn said. "We can't trust Morfran anymore." Sorn brushed Valan's white hair out of his face, saw the damage there, and winced.

"That bad, huh?" Valan commented and then pulled away from his lover's touch.

"Don't you dare," Sorn said, wrapping an arm around his waist to keep them close. He pointedly brought their foreheads together, forcing Valan to meet his eyes. Letting him see the anger there. His hatred of everything that *wasn't* Valan. The world should sink into the closest black hole for daring to harm him. "*I know you.* All of you. I love you. You remain without flaw to me. Now, let's murder that older sister of yours."

"I love you, too."

Too much. Valan had to forcibly restrain himself from undoing Sorn's leather armor right then and there. Now really wasn't a good time to get distracted. Sorn just smirked under his blue scarf, fully aware of exactly what kind of effect he had on Valan.

"And I would like to kill her, too," he continued, "but I don't know where she is."

"I do. She's in one of the lower cells," Sorn said.

Valan smiled slightly. "My hero."

"Keep thinking that while I see to this," Sorn replied. He gently moved Valan's dislocated arm. "Ready?"

"Yes," Valan said. Sorn didn't give him a moment to change his mind, first twisting his arm and pushing it back into the shoulder socket. Valan struggled against any outward displays of emotion, then very carefully tried to move the fingers of that arm; he could. He nodded. "Let's go."

It had not failed to occur to Valan that despite the noise created by his sound traveling spell, or during the time the two of them spent wrapped up in each other's concerns, not a single guard had shown up. They should have been found, captured, if not flat out killed by now. He didn't like it. Something else was going on that he didn't know about.

A trap of some sort, surely, but what would be the point? As skilled as he knew Sorn to be at more covert matters, and Valan liked to think he wasn't completely useless himself, there were far more in Clan Anartes who were stronger. An elaborate trap wasn't needed.

"Why would my sister be down there?" Valan asked once they entered the side hallway leading to the cells. "How...long has she been down there?"

"Seven days ago, someone reported to the Piuthar that they heard you screaming in her room. One of your eyes was outside her door," Sorn said. "She refused to let anyone check the interior." He scowled. "My efforts to get into her room all failed. She had changed the wards to prevent even Mairead from getting past them. They've been torturing her for trying to permanently alter the clan tower without permission ever since. I couldn't...come back until four days ago."

He knew Sorn was telling him only the bare bones, but Valan was too concerned by the first part of what he'd said. *Seven days*. The apprentice had told him nine. He might have been screaming, if that *someone* hadn't been lying, for two days, and he had no memory of it. It didn't surprise him to learn that the Piuthar-Tri was more upset about the wards than what happened to him; he was just a lowly male.

Valan was glad Sorn didn't turn to look at him while speaking, since he was struggling to control his emotions. He distracted himself by studying his love's back. The cloak barely remained hanging off of Sorn's shoulders, slashed by some sort of blade, and his leather armor was ripped in places. Through the tears in the leather, he spied partially healed cuts. Someone had tried to stab him multiple times in the back, with Sorn just fast enough to avoid a fatal blow to land if his opponent used iron. A clear tension gripped Sorn's back muscles that traveled down his arms to end in tightly clenched fists. The exposed parts of his skin were a shade of gray that could have blended in with stone.

As if feeling Valan's gaze, Sorn glanced back at him.

"Never again," he swore.

"Never again," Valan agreed. He didn't want them to be apart ever again. He stepped closer and lightly rested his hand on the middle of Sorn's back, as if to say, *I see you, too*. His love relaxed slightly against the touch, his expression softening before he faced away. After a moment, Sorn motioned to the door. Valan understood, the two of them having done similar things before, and moved to the opposite side of the door as Sorn silently pushed it open.

Valan hummed a low tune, vaguely insect-like, and the soundless image of a *ceithir troighid* cockroach appeared, darting through the doorway and into the torture chamber. The insect's many legs scuttled across the ground before he made it disappear down the central hole in the middle of the floor. Nothing jumped out to attack the illusion or otherwise reacted to it, but that didn't necessarily mean other sidhe were not around. Many dark elves employed methods to obscure themselves from view, such as special clothing to reduce the heat their bodies gave off, creating their own illusions and shadows, or even magical compulsion to claim the element of surprise. To counteract that, other fey had to be even better at subterfuge. As such, the insect illusion was meant to serve as a distraction for Sorn to more easily enter the other room unnoticed.

Through Valan's normal vision, Sorn was practically invisible. Gone from his side of the doorway. Something dark that blended in with all the other darker shadows. When Valan switched to his synesthesia eye, he perceived the faint ripples of sound that had been caused by his humming earlier hitting objects and giving them shape. One shape happened to be Sorn-sized, crouched down with two daggers out, ready. Interesting. He tried to keep from smirking over how he could now find Sorn whenever he wanted to. He resisted the temptation to jump in front of Sorn and shout "Boo!" … That would be a great way to get himself stabbed.

Nothing else in the room looked even vaguely humanoid shaped. Odd. Where were the guards? If a veiled one was being held below in one of the reinforced cells, it was safe to assume more warriors would be on patrol. Valan politely waited for Sorn to deem things safe enough to return to the door, stepping out of the shadows to be seen in normal sight. Sorn was frowning, eyebrows furrowed.

"What are the chances you managed to kill everyone else in a fit of rage?" Valan asked.

"Low. After I killed three, I haven't seen anyone come by to replace them—and that should have happened days ago."

How conveniently abandoned.

"Well, since everything has been wrapped up with a nice gift bow just for us, let's go see our present," Valan said. He began to walk down the sloping path to the lower cells, but Sorn darted in front of him. The rogue removed the tattered remnants of his cloak and tied it around Valan's waist instead.

"You're distracting me too much," Sorn explained.

Valan smiled. And yet up to this point, the blue-haired man had no trouble seeing him wander around in the nude. Good to know that despite what had happened to half his face, Sorn still desired him. "That would be a very bad thing to do."

Sorn shot him a heated look and made a point of walking in front again, leading them down to the correct cell. Along the way, Valan noted the bodies of the three dead guards Sorn had mentioned, along with the faint smell of rot.

"Why did you remain down here?" Valan asked.

Sorn's shoulders twitched, but he otherwise refused to answer the question. How very moody. It soon became abundantly clear what he had been up to anyway. Littered across the ground, embedded into the stone here and there, were the half-melted or shattered remains of what had to be *tri* dozen—no, there was far more than that.

"That looks like your entire knife collection."

"Almost," Sorn admitted, and then added as if it explained everything, "...you know I hate puzzles."

Which...didn't explain much of anything yet. Once Sorn got *moody,* however, it was nigh impossible to drag the truth out of him. Valan sighed and stepped closer, hoping he could figure out what exactly Sorn had been trying to do. Unlike the torture cells near the top of the curving path, these lower rooms possessed barred doors lined with lead on the interior side. Lead contained multiple uses in arcana, the most notable being blocking spells. Iron would have worked even better, especially so close to a veil, but then a sidhe would have to trust slaves with carrying a material capable of killing their masters. It'd be too foolish. At least since lead wasn't lethal to sidhe, it could be used to line prison cells. Nobody could use magic inside a lead "box" and nobody on the outside could easily use magic to get in. Perfect for trapping any fey without killing them.

He examined the spots in the walls and floors that looked like Sorn had been aiming at the most with his daggers, noting they were roughly located over various magical glyphs. Magical symbols were not something someone of Sorn's skill-set could easily read—much less see clearly. He probably had sensed them, guessed they were something to do with keeping the cell door sealed, and thought he either had to activate them in a specific order or try to drain them by triggering them constantly. A desperate action that could have backfired horribly. Any single one of these could kill someone if the rune repulsed whatever damage it received back onto whatever tried to break it. Thus, all the broken and melted knives. Incredibly reckless. Dangerous. A person would try to do this only if they didn't value their life. On top of that, the runes were also likely rigged to an alarm system that alerted when someone tried to break them.

"Sorn…"

"I thought you were dead. Worse," Sorn grudgingly explained. "I had to try to kill her myself."

"I understand," Valan replied, his voice low. He did understand, recalling how he'd felt before walking off that platform earlier.

This shared weakness of theirs was something they needed to address soon, before anyone tried to use it against them. If they both went into suicidal spirals at the mere chance the other was gone, they would be in trouble. Until recently, they'd been safe since no one knew Sorn existed, but it was only a matter of time before their luck ran out. A mistake made here and there. Someone curious about why the thin, borderline sickly Valan always wanted twice the amount of food delivered to his room. Why, when Balfore was on duty, someone else wearing an identical guard uniform with the faceplate always closed stayed next to Valan.

Balfore hadn't known about Sorn; he was a "friend" who agreed to hang around a noble for a few hours to earn extra coin, one of many Valan hired and alternated between. He didn't feel bad about using the other sidhe as an early warning in case someone else became too curious.

Valan had hoped that being so blatant about having a guard around would make other sidhe see it as a too-obvious trap and wouldn't act on it.

And they hadn't, not until his twin sister couldn't help herself.

With these wards tripped, somebody definitely knew about Sorn now, or at the very least knew an unknown person was wandering around causing problems. But perhaps since no one had bothered to check the cells in this all but abandoned part of the Anartes tower, Valan could assume it was a *friendly* somebody.

Yet nobody ever did anything for someone else for free. There was going to be a price to pay for this "kindness" eventually...and he was letting himself get distracted by worry. Valan returned his focus to the runes on the floor and walls.

The runes and wards comprised layers, the oldest likely created when the stones were first placed. Over time other markings, done by different hands and varying levels of skill, were added to cover any weaknesses left behind by someone else's latest addition. A rune right in front of the cell door looked like it was meant to trigger a bolt of lightning if anyone without the proper key tried to open it; another symbol inscribed over it didn't just summon lightning, but also triggered a mechanism that released a cloud of acid to kill the cell's occupant. The last layer protected the destruction of the rune against dispelling magic, triggering a set of floor spikes if the magic powering the rune suddenly disappeared. There was likely another layer he failed to notice, and this was only one main set of runes among many. Nasty and thorough, designed by generations of sidhe wizards.

Valan scowled. Even if his faith in his intelligence had not been so completely shaken by recent events, he knew there was no chance of somehow outsmarting wizards of this level of skill and power. So, what to do? Intentionally open the door without the key and hope to dodge lightning while Sabrene was killed with poison gas? Or set off a chain reaction from the other rune clusters, which activated untold other Nasty Ways To Die? He glanced over at Sorn.

"What?" Sorn asked.

"You're not dead."

"I threw the knives from very far away."

"And don't think I didn't notice the remains of the fifth anniversary dagger I bought you." Valan had saved up a lot of money to get that custom-made without raising any suspicion.

"It was overdone, the balance was bad, and it had a shitty inscription," Sorn retorted, then shifted his weight as if uncomfortable. "Before you ask: yes, I still have the first and the tenth."

Alright, so, that knife had been all of those things, Valan acknowledged to himself, but it wasn't meant to be used, just to serve as a physical reminder of surviving together after so much of their lives needed to be hidden away. Valan couldn't exactly ask the local metal inscriber to include anything that could be confused with *feelings*. He had to settle for a short poem about two snakes eating each other to death. At the time, Valan thought it was funny, but Sorn apparently not so much and he'd never forgiven him for it, either. Knowing his moodiness, it was probably one of the first knives he'd thrown at the glyphs.

"I'm going to replace it as soon as I can—and it'll have *flowers* on it," Valan teased. "It'll be *so pretty*."

Sorn shot him a Don't You Dare look. "No, it won't. And I'll be the one to design the damned fifth anniversary knife."

They smiled at each other.

Right. The runes. The wards. Focus. Valan turned away from Sorn. *Play with him later.*

He couldn't outsmart generations of wizards nor overpower the runes with magical prowess, which left him doing something so stupid, so simple, that it could actually work. So, what would Isla do? Isla would… walk up, self-assured in her right to be anywhere she wanted within the tower, and use the key. Just use the key.

"Did you find any keys on the guards?" Valan asked. "And I will need my family sigil back."

"I found keys, but none of them are labeled. I was going to try using them before I heard you use that loud spell." Sorn pulled out an amulet bearing the Anartes sigil that he kept tucked under his armor and scarf, handing it over to Valan along with a ring of identical keys. Only nobility were allowed to wear the Anartes symbol, and not just because of rank. The amulet gave the wearer free access past various checkpoints, such as the front gate, the family dining room, and other areas where commoners were not allowed. There are also secondary enchantments, like poison resistance and increased skill with hiding in the dark, but these were all things Sorn benefitted from more than he did. With his health limitations, Valan couldn't risk traveling outside the Anartes stronghold too often.

He also hadn't wanted to point it out earlier, but not all the magical wards Sorn had been using as targets earlier had their traps limited by distance; the magic recognizing the house symbol likely negated the worst effects from harming him once triggered.

Valan put on the amulet and studied the keys, running his fingers over each on the off-chance he could pick up any differences between them by touch if not by sight. He detected nothing unusual, but the trick couldn't be too complicated for a standard guard to use and yet still remain evasive enough that only a member of Clan Anartes would be taught. Since the keys weren't special, perhaps the trick lay in the ring they were on.

This device had keys equal to the number of grooves. Valan slid them between each notch, then twisted along the indentations. Eventually, the shape of a many-pointed star took form with each key at a point and the previously hidden bent sections revealing tiny runes.

Valan glanced around and noticed a symbol, located in the middle of the door, that appeared less faded by age than the rest—and just so happened to match a point on the keyring. The symbols were probably changed regularly to prevent spies from taking advantage of the information.

But this all felt too simple. Anyone could accidentally bend the ring at a joint and see the symbols. This had to be a trap. A spy might have been pleased they'd reached this far and thought they've solved the puzzle, but Clan Anartes was a house of wizards. There had to be more to it.

Holding the center of the star, Valan bent the points inward like he was trying to make a bowl, then twisted the curved sections in the opposite direction, ending with a shape closer to a layered snowflake. All that extra bending shifted the symbols to match completely different keys.

There, done.

Valan pushed the matching key into the lock but purposely didn't twist it. The keyring warmed in his hand, reacting to the symbol on the door, and then the door itself opened. Magic reacting to magic. He was glad Sorn must have noticed the lock itself looked odd and hadn't tried to lock-pick his way past it; that would have led to a very dead blue-haired rogue.

Valan waited near the doorway since the lead-lined walls would make it difficult for him to defend himself. Sorn darted into the room first.

Sabrene was chained spread-eagle to a large, upright stone cross. Torture tools were strewn about, including a cold, unlit brazier with different sized branding rods and pokers still in the basin. Superficial cuts covered her body, several nails had been pulled from her fingertips, and partially healed burns scabbed the bottoms of her feet. Whoever did the torturing had been gentle with her so far. The injuries could be easily covered up or quickly regrown.

She lifted her head, revealing a swollen, bruised face that reminded Valan of his own past experiences of being backhanded several times, her eyes widening at the sight of him in the doorway. A look of hope flickered across her features. Did she think he was here to save her?

"Val—"

The name remained half-spoken on her tongue. Sorn stabbed her in the crotch, twisted the blade viciously, and then dragged it up through her stomach cavity. She screamed as her guts spilled out onto the floor.

Valan thought back to when she had grabbed his hand, made her little comments, and patted his head like a dog after helping his twin torture him. Of what she had done to his body—her so-called *improvements*—only for him to wake up in her bed, having been there for days. The bruises he had no memory of acquiring.

He hummed a tune to himself to harmonize with her wails and used the left-behind flint to relight the brazier. He was going to start by burning off her hands, then the rest of her limbs, until only ash remained.

Sorn leaned back against the wall, arms crossed and with a dark glitter in his eyes, as he watched Valan reduce her to nothing.

It took hours.

"Well," Valan said once he was done. "What would you like to do next, my love?"

"We're going to go home, fuck each other's brains out, sleep, and then fuck again."

"Fantastic."

And if they happened to still be alive afterward, he'd have a slave deliver them steaks.

CHAPTER 5

VALAN SET HIS favorite chair on fire, watched it burn for a moment, and then hastily summoned shards of ice to put out the flames before the damage became irreparable. He then kicked the chair for good measure and winced from hurting his toes, which just made him angrier.

The chair was a plush, overstuffed wooden monstrosity better suited for some grand hall in a human castle, not shoved in the corner of their tiny, hidden room behind the staged room that only held belongings appropriate for the youngest male noble. When Sorn had first "acquired" the chair after seeing it being auctioned off at Fo Erkunia's Bazaar, smuggling it in pieces before reassembling it again, the chair was covered in ugly, fat baby faces with fluffy wings. How a throne had ended up within Fo Erkunia was the result of an Unseelie playing a prank on a human: a king thought it wise to summon a sidhe to help defeat his enemies before they could take his throne, wanting them killed. The sidhe decided to reinterpret the king's words and took the fancy chair so that no one could have it. Can't steal a throne that'd already stolen by somebody else. Sorn had overheard the sidhe thief bragging about his cleverness and figured he might as well steal the useless thing, too.

Over time, Sorn had carved up the faces to look more like rudimentary skulls and the wings into spiderwebs. Even with the "improvements", there was no hiding that the chair was made for a much bigger, wider person—although Valan enjoyed the extra space to lounge in while reading, sometimes even falling asleep in it. Sorn would know better than to tell Valan what he looked like when that happened.

Just like Sorn would know better than to try to insert himself into the middle of Valan's tantrum. He lay in their bed on the opposite side of the room, his eyes mere slits, hungover from drinking too much mead the night before. The place was a mess, with open books and scrolls scattered everywhere, along with cut-up shirts tossed—and looking stomped on—on the floor. Normally, the walls were covered with the knives Sorn collected, giving the room an oddly incomplete look while at the same time as being disorganized.

Valan wore only pants—due to his massive wings—but apparently the chair did something especially upsetting. They had depleted their stock of healing potions and salves once they had made it back to their room a couple of days ago. Their wounds would heal naturally, but it'd put them at too much of a disadvantage the next time an enemy attacked and they hadn't fully recovered. None of this was enough to prevent Valan from preparing to kick the chair again despite the nasty bruise forming on his toes, though seeing the growing worried expression on Sorn's face made him hesitate.

"If this is about last night," Sorn began, then winced at the sound of his own voice. "We'll be more careful in certain positions." He shrugged. *No big deal.*

Which was the absolute worst thing Sorn could ever say. Valan glared at him. "I can't even sit in my chair anymore!"

"You can sit on me."

Valan responded by giving a long and thorough explanation of just where Sorn should shove that idea repeatedly.

The blue-haired man didn't respond immediately, pretending to seriously think about Valan's suggestion. "Only if you watch."

Valan laughed, then immediately scowled. He wanted to be angry, and Sorn was ruining things. The winged sidhe walked over and pulled the blanket off of the other male, tossing it to the floor. Sorn didn't try to stop him, completely comfortable in his own nudity, merely raising an eyebrow as if to say, *Well?*

Accepting the challenge, Valan climbed on top of the bed, his knees on either side of Sorn's waist, and then they kissed. Sorn attempted to pull him down the rest of the way, but Valan resisted, shook his head, and then started to kiss down the center of Sorn's chest. His fingers brushed across a brand marring the skin, forever marking Sorn as a slave of Clan Anartes. He moved lower, running that pierced tongue of his just below Sorn's navel, his warm breath heating the trail of saliva he left there. He looked up at Sorn. "Are you certain you want to *just* be my chair?"

Then the winged sidhe got up, snatched away one of the four pillows stolen during their last rest—why did Sorn need to hog all the pillows anyway?—and used it as a cushion while he resumed going over all his opened books and unrolled scrolls on the floor. Sorn stifled a groan and sat upright, now thoroughly awake and annoyed.

"I've killed people for less," he grumbled.

Valan ignored the other's obvious suffering—Sorn deserved it—and focused on fixing his latest problems. The most brutal solution was to cut away the scarred tissue, then hope that when he healed, his face would go back to the way it was before. Unfortunately, the damage had been done to him with acid, which could break down sidhe flesh completely. Valan's face had already scarred, which now meant his skin would remember the injuries. Removing the damage caused by the acid would have been easier if only he hadn't fully healed first.

He could try more mundane methods, like using cosmetics to cover the color and smooth over the scar tissue. There were also spells he could cast to make his eye look normal. It wouldn't be enough to hide the damage from intense scrutiny, but he figured he could always style his hair over that side of his face and maybe add jewels to distract someone from noticing that one side wasn't quite like the other. Gems infused with faerie fire were everywhere; using a few wouldn't even look out of place. Not exactly a style he would normally choose, but it wouldn't be the first time he pretended to not be himself. Still, he needed to be careful not to look like he was trying too hard to hide his appearance; that in itself could cause others to get a little curious.

The most obvious problem was the wings. Too big to hide under a cloak, and the spells that would mask their appearance were beyond his skill to cast. At any rate, he could not leave this hidden room until he had a solution. To even get back to his chambers unnoticed after killing his sister, Sorn had to dress up as a guard with Valan wrapped in a body disposal sheet and carried over his shoulder—not exactly something they could do forever. Even though their unknown *friendly helper* had made it easier than it should have been to take care of Sabrene, she was still a veiled one. There were going to be questions since a "flying creature" had been spotted going into her lab, and his eye had been found outside of her bedroom. All clues pointed to Valan, and being caught killing a female of Sabrene's rank was a death sentence...after a very long, extensive amount of torture, first.

As far as Valan knew, he was still considered missing, and nobody had connected the winged thing to him. All of that would end once he went out in public. Lady Mairead should have summoned him to explain himself by now—that was, if she thought he was actually still alive, or if she wasn't already getting answers from someone else. He just didn't know, not while trapped in this room, so he had to assume the worst. Better to plan for it and be pleasantly surprised later.

He idly turned the pages of the tome in front of him, skimming over a spell that discussed the finer points and uses of locating magical objects, but he wasn't fully paying attention. Valan listened to Sorn get dressed in the mended cloak and leather armor left for him next to a set of chairs and small table. The Anartes crest and that tattered scarf were also nearby for him to wear; Valan had left the scarf unfixed on purpose, knowing Sorn preferred it that way.

A carafe of water with matching goblets waited on the table, along with a big bag Sorn would recognize, one they usually kept hidden in a hole under the stone floor. He heard Sorn sit down and drink straight from the carafe, pause, and then drink some more. Afterward, he pointedly set the ceramic container down with enough force for him to hear. Sorn's way of making it clear that if Valan wanted to talk to him, Valan needed to be the one to speak first.

"What we should do next, I'm leaving up to you," Valan said, turning his attention to a scroll with brittle edges, a spell meant to lead someone to a place they had already visited once before. Very handy if he ended up traveling somewhere unfamiliar and needed to recall the quickest way back to a previous location. He was still figuring out what all the rune combinations meant, what with it being a multilayered assortment of symbols that he really shouldn't be studying without any guidance, but he felt it was a necessary bit of magic to learn. So many things were becoming necessary.

"As things are now," he continued, "I can't leave this room. The wings are too recognizable. I'll be blamed for Sabrene's death, and then I'll be dead, if I'm lucky." Valan kept the simplest choice to himself—just cut off the wings and burn down the stumps—but Sorn had already vetoed the idea of self-mutilation. He was very careful to keep his voice empty of emotion.

"So, here are the choices: we could run, using the money we've saved to start over somewhere else, even head for the surface. Or we could steal someone else's Fáinne Athrú. There should be plenty in Fo Erkunia with a ring like this; it's just a matter of finding who has one and taking it. And I've counted: we've managed to set aside enough money that you could hire someone to make the ring, if you wanted." Almost every choice meant Sorn would have to do things alone, separating the two of them, after they had *just* promised not to do so again. "...All I can do is swear not to leave this room until you come back, whatever you decide."

Valan felt a hand dig into his hair, tilting his head to look upward. He hadn't even sensed Sorn move. The very furious gray eyes of his love stared down at him.

"You only pretended to sleep again," Sorn accused.

Not the response Valan expected. The anger certainly, but not that statement.

"Well...yes," he admitted. He thought he'd hidden the fact that when they went to sleep, Valan...hadn't. Thinking over all the things to be done, any potential countermeasures, anything that kept him from closing his eyes and waking up in Sabrene's bed again. She was dead, but it would take him some time to move beyond what had happened.

"Rest," Sorn demanded, releasing his hold on Valan's hair. "And if I find out you've left this room before I get back, I'll kill you myself. Got it?"

"Yes."

Considering the potential eventualities if things went poorly, dying by Sorn's hands sounded almost pleasant. Valan gestured at part of a wall, a section free of weapon mounts, and the wall slowly melted, actually being composed of mud and grit. On the other side was the staged bedroom. His large clothing chest partially blocked the exit, but Sorn didn't have any issue jumping over it after grabbing the bag of gold.

Valan waited until Sorn pulled the hood of his cloak over his head, easily disappearing from normal sight, before using magic to reform the mud wall. He smoothed back his hair and looked around. He had a map of local trade routes somewhere here, didn't he? It'd been drawn up several years ago but should still be at least somewhat useful.

Then he needed to review the limits of scrying. Valan wavered on his feet, his thoughts scattering. He needed to…maybe take up Sorn's idea of advice and at least try to rest. He crawled onto Sorn's half of the bed, laying on his side as he soaked up the residual heat that still lingered there. His wings annoyingly hung halfway off the bed's edge. This side at least had all the pillows. He stared at the nearest wall, the wall hooks empty of daggers, and still couldn't close his eyes.

The exterior of the elegant, if still massive, tower that made up Clan Anartes was surrounded by barren, hard-packed rock. By all appearances, the landscape was empty and unguarded, with nothing alive nearby except where tree roots extended from the cavern's ceiling down to the floor to form their own kind of forest. The massive wall of roots served as a natural barrier between the tower and the wealthy district of Fo Erkunia. Only a fool would cross that barren stretch of land around the Anartes stronghold without permission.

Sorn often traveled across this seeming emptiness, hidden as always under his cloak; even though he wore the Anartes crest, he still avoided the areas around the tower that felt heaviest, wary of the places so thick with condensed magical protections that it made it hard to breathe, along with all the things that wandered about unseen. The forest he navigated carefully as well, avoiding the main road that was used by veiled ones as they traveled with their guards, with even more guards stationed on patrol. Mushrooms grew on the floor and within the alcoves caused by the tree roots, providing homes for equally dangerous creatures that also needed to be avoided. Sorn knew it was easier to get around those mushrooms than have to potentially explain to a veiled one why he had possession of a noble's amulet.

While still within the forest, Sorn removed the bag of gold he kept hidden under his cloak. He'd had his suspicions when he first picked up the bag in their room and heard a crackle of paper, now confirmed once he opened it. The bag didn't contain just gold. Three scrolls made up of multiple sheets of paper lay on top of the pile. The first batch of paper was a long list of gear Valan thought they needed if they wanted any chance of surviving by themselves, including suggestions of looking into which mercantile groups might soon travel to elven border towns closer to the surface. Off to the side of one paper, Valan wrote, *How to travel with my books?*, *Horse?*, *Object Shrinking?*, and *Would a throne fit onto a carriage?* before scratching it all out to the point of ripping into the paper. One question had been left alone: *Who forgot to make sure the emergency stash isn't rotten? EXPIRED SIX YEARS AGO.*

Sorn scowled with all the righteous indignity of somebody who was trying not to feel guilty. Weren't travel rations supposed to last forever? That wasn't his fault. Best to move on to the next batch of rolled up papers. The second batch detailed, with a very bad drawing, what a Fáinne Athrú should look like. By the artwork, it was just about anything, except for a specific set of runes carved into the band.

These rings are attuned to their owners, Valan had written, *so you'll need to kill the wearer.*

Not a problem. Valan had included a list of names he suspected might be using such a ring and how they each had a sudden change to their appearance that couldn't be explained by simple cosmetics or temporary illusions, as well as a list of all minor nobles, along with their clan locations. Rumors picked up from his years of playing music at parties, perfect for situations like this that could be made useful for narrowing down potential targets. He noticed Valan didn't mention anyone from the major clan, the ones with better protections. Worried about him, was he? A minor clan wouldn't make much of a fuss over one of their own dying, anyway.

The third scroll held the least amount of info. A list of stores that might sell a Fáinne Athrú along with a note of how much the ring was usually worth. *You know which stores are more likely to sell it than me*, Valan had added. The winged sidhe visited the city as little as possible, knowing full well that there were too many adversaries interested in gaining prestige by removing a noble—even just a male one—from a major clan. And rumored to have health issues as well? The poisons practically made themselves. Even if Valan stayed within the richer districts, more than likely a female would demand he spend time with her and he wouldn't be able to tell her no, especially not publicly, because she'd outrank him. One last paper, which had few words, with the ink blotched in places from being rolled up before it could completely dry:

I love you. I don't care what you decide to do, just come back.

After memorizing what parts he wanted to remember, Sorn ripped up all the notes, then chewed on the pieces. He dug into the bag for a small waterskin that had sunk to the bottom from the coins shifting around earlier, needing the extra help to swallow more paper than he was used to. The ink tasted like brown sugar. Not the usual flavor; Valan must have been experimenting.

He already knew what he wanted to do.

The expensive shops, theaters, and restaurants of the shopping district of Fo Erkunia looked to be made from fantastical structures in a mix of natural stone and giant mushrooms so crowded together that it gave the impression of each building being organically grown out of the one next to it. The pristine, winding paths saw a lot of traffic at Bel's *dà uair*, with dark elves taking a mid-cycle break from what made up their lives. Slaves hurried after their masters, arms laden with heavy packages, with the occasional whipping if one moved too slowly, but it was by all accounts a peaceful day. The beatings given weren't even all that particularly noteworthy.

Cernunnos sat with his feet propped up on a tabletop next to a bistro, the air thick with the smell of fried cheeses and wine. He wasn't sitting alone. Next to him, a rather dour-faced sidhe pretended to take a drink out of his glass of wine. He looked like he had been carved out of black marble streaked with white veins that matched his hair, his every move possessing a rigidness as if he truly were made from stone. Cernunnos didn't even bother to touch his own glass. Both drinks were likely poisoned three times over already. Standing on either side of the stone-faced elf at a respectable distance were several armed warriors from Clan Cavii.

"I do not see why this is so important as to interrupt our other plans," the statuesque sidhe said, his voice lacking emotion. The absence of emotional expression wasn't so odd in and of itself when dealing with dark elves, but the pure *empty* quality of it made him unnerving.

"Oh, I know you are just brimming with curiosity! You're here, after all."

"And planning to make you pay for every hour."

Cernunnos waved a hand as if that was of no consequence, then perked up further when he spied a familiar figure walking on the road opposite the bistro. "Hey brat! Slave boy, whatever you are! Come over here!"

The figure across the street continued walking as if he hadn't heard Cernunnos.

"I like him already," the stony sidhe commented.

"Hey! Idiot slave wearing the ugly blue scarf!" Cernunnos yelled again. "Get over here!"

That made the brat stop walking. It also caught the attention of several nearby sidhe. Slaves had little protection in this district, their only hope of remaining unscathed was to stay close to their masters, who *might* get angry if another dark elf tried to kill their property. When a slave traveled alone, it was usually at the behest of a powerful clan and with the crest displayed somewhere on their person. Cernunnos could see the brat did not have that advantage. Normally, moving through this district was not an issue, since his appearance was unassuming and other sidhe were typically absorbed in shopping or socializing. Being singled out so loudly put an end to that disinterest.

The scarfed elf grudgingly crossed the street and knelt down in front of Cernunnos, keeping his face turned to the floor as any slave would. However, he did nothing to hide the scorn in his voice. "If this is about me poisoning you, go get your own antidote."

"Are you ever *not* angry?" Cernunnos asked. "Feral brat, this is called *having a conversation.*"

The stone-faced man leaned forward, peering over the table at the top of the slave's hooded head. *Something* happened, forcing the brat to clutch the side of his skull and glare at the man. "Quit it!"

"Well, Rian?" Cernunnos asked.

Rian leaned back in his chair, shifting uncomfortably in his seat. "Interesting choice of defense. Three months? No breaks? … Almost a waste of stamina potions."

"Details, Rian."

"No, and he might be *his*. Not all the possible mothers could have been killed off, but I really don't care enough to delve deeper—and you shouldn't either. He doesn't even remember how he ended up in a cage."

"Can I go now?" Sorn all but growled.

"Almost," Rian said.

Cernunnos pulled a silver ring out of a hidden pocket in his kilt and tossed it. It slid across the table and spun off the edge, landing in front of Sorn. "This is the last time I'm going to help you, brat, so *listen carefully*. If you keep following your master, you'll end up dead—so I'm going to give you a way out. Just you. I can drop you off at a major human city on the surface so you can start over. You don't belong here."

"He seems resourceful enough to survive on his own," Rian allowed.

"See? A ringing endorsement. He's practically gleeful. I can tell. Just give your master the ring he wants so much and meet us back here before *dà dheug*—and then you'll be a free man."

"You can go now."

Sorn was already gone, the silver ring along with him.

"So…" Cernunnos said. He raised his glass and toasted the empty air. "Do you think that's a *yes* or a *no*?"

"I think you are making a mistake," said Rian.

Cernunnos eyed his glass closely, as if trying to count the number of poisons within it. "I'm betting on a *maybe*."

"Let me offer you some advice: stay away from *that one*. He's survived this long on his own. He can continue to do so."

"Definitely *maybe*."

"If he's anything like his father, he'll be fine."

"That could become a problem."

"It will," Rian replied. He turned that empty gaze on Cernunnos. "This world is already suffering from having one of him around. It doesn't need two. If necessary, I can take him on as an apprentice. Reshape him. You need only ask."

Cernunnos didn't seem to hear the other man. "Eleven poisons!"

The problem with books, Valan groused, *is that I never have enough of them.*

He had given up on trying to rest, deciding to go over a *Beginner's Tome of Disenchantment*. Much to his frustration, half of the book referenced material within other tomes he had no access to. He *should* have access to these other books, either from Anartes's own library or after reaching puberty and becoming a student of Crann Bethadh, but the Piuthar-Tri thought Isla needed more time to "mature" before seeking higher education. It'd be completely unfair to Isla to send off the male twin to learn before her, after all. Valan had to settle for whatever Sorn could steal or convince somebody else to part with—in other words, none of the truly powerful, knowledgeable stuff.

If not for one small description about gem enchantment versus their monetary value, this tome would have been completely worthless. Even as he sat on the floor reviewing it, he wondered if this beginner's book would serve better as a stepping stool.

Still in the middle of this contemplation, a dull, droning noise started to build inside his head. Somebody had just tripped the wards he'd placed on his bedroom door. It was too soon for Sorn to have returned; in any case, he'd been granted the ability to safely move past the wards.

Valan didn't move, listening for any noise in his staged bedroom, but there was nothing. Either the mud wall was thick enough to muffle the sound of movement or whoever had entered was being very careful. His mind raced over who the intruder could be, automatically latching onto the worst possible scenario: the Piuthar hadn't summoned him yet because she'd rather send assassins to get rid of him quietly.

Valan reached over to a pile of scrolls on the floor next to him, carefully picking up the topmost one. He'd been saving this spell to memorize later, but if the intruder made it into the hidden room, he had no need to memorize it anyway. In such a confined space, this spell could easily obliterate everything within it, including him, but he wasn't willing to risk making noise by searching for something less dangerous.

He waited.

Nothing.

Silence.

And then, screaming. The clash of weaponry. Something dragged itself across the ground, followed by whimpering and the crunch of bones.

More silence.

A smile formed on Valan's face. He stood, walked over to the mud wall, and *willed* the creation of a hole large enough to see through. Usually, his clothing chest blocked the way into the staged bedroom, but now it rested in the middle of the room surrounded by blood and a few discarded dark elf body parts. It had occurred to Valan, the last time he played *mhealladh,* that he shouldn't settle for some minor magical trinket when he could have a pet monster instead.

"Good girl!" Valan congratulated his pet on its latest meal.

The large chest rattled in response. A long, translucent tentacle slithered out of a corner of the chest's lid and wrapped around a sidhe's severed leg before popping the limb into its hidden mouth. Valan resisted the temptation to get closer to pat it on top of its head and instead let the chimera settle. Calling the chimera his "pet" was perhaps too strong a word. It was more of a beneficial relationship; the more he fed it with assassins and the like, the less likely it would get an urge to attack *him.*

Well, now he had a clue as to what was going on outside. "Assassin" was also too strong a word to describe whomever had entered his room. Aside from the gore, the fey left behind packs half-stuffed with the belongings he kept on the shelves. Just thieves. Dark elves who thought to take advantage of his disappearance and steal the belongings of a noble. They probably thought that if he was dead, or at least still missing, any magical protections he had in place would either be weakened, if not deactivated entirely…and then they made the mistake of opening his presumed clothing chest.

It was going to be a chore to clean everything up, but that could wait. Valan reformed the mud wall to let the monster enjoy the crumbs it left behind in peace.

CHAPTER 6

Once Sorn returned, the first thing he noticed was the bedroom door ajar. He further eased it open noiselessly, his gray eyes quickly taking in the condition of the room itself in search of whoever had been through here. Seeing the chest in the middle of the room, the blood, and then the untouched bare wall that led to their real chambers eased the worst of his fears, so he silently entered the room the rest of the way and closed the door behind him. Loitering in the hallway, invisible or not, was the least safe option.

As he moved toward the wall, Sorn picked up the faint sounds of snoring. He couldn't keep himself from grinning into his scarf. Valan was the most graceless elf he'd ever met.

"Valan, love, wake up." Sorn lightly tapped the wall with his knuckles. He made a point of saying that word *love* so the other sidhe knew it was really him and not someone pretending. In general, dark elves were very familiar with lust in all its forms, but *love* was anathema. Not something ever spoken of, if even known about at all. Neither Valan nor Sorn would have ever known about that word if it hadn't been for a book of Seelie poetry introducing the subject. They had made fun of the contents at first—*Twirling through trees? Singing about flowers? Crying about being in darkness? Really? Disgusting. Pathetic. How did the Unseelie not completely wipe out these whiny light elves by now?*—but to their growing horror, not *all* of it seemed ridiculous. It provided a name to how they felt about each other; up until then, Valan had admittedly thought their bond was just some sort of abnormal lust curse.

"Sorn? Oh! Um." Then came the sound of books sliding across the floor as Valan inevitably tripped over them in his haste to get up. Sorn practically felt the other's embarrassment through the wall.

"... Valan?"

The wall melted, revealing a very sleepy looking sidhe with his soft, messy hair sticking up everywhere. Valan smiled. "You are back early!" Both of his eyebrows rose and he blinked owlishly. "Or...late? I don't actually know what time it is."

How can looking at someone make me so happy? Maybe it is *a curse*, Sorn thought. He reached into the underside of his many-pocketed cloak and held out his hand, now holding several rings. Some were still streaked with blood. "Here."

"You are amazing."

Sorn tilted his head to the side as if to say, *I know.* The elf took the rings from him with one hand and used the other to pull down Sorn's scarf. Valan lightly kissed him, but Sorn wasn't about to let things end quite so innocently, pressing their lips harder together and slipping his tongue into Valan's mouth to stroke and pull at the skull piercing there.

"Sit on the throne," Valan said a little breathlessly once they pulled away. "I want to finish what we started earlier."

"Later," Sorn replied, his eyes narrowing. He was about to bring up one of Valan's least favorite subjects. "It's about Cernunnos."

"Can this wait?" Valan muttered into the other sidhe's chest.

"No," Sorn said regretfully. He then explained what had happened earlier between him and Cernunnos, carefully repeating to the best of his ability what the older sidhe told him. By the time he was done, Valan had pulled away and was glaring at the books on the floor.

"Before we deal with that, I need to determine if any of these rings have the right enchantment," Valan said. "Once I'm done, we can go."

At Bel's *dà dheug*, a dark carriage pulled by two skeletal horses stopped in front of an empty bistro. Emblazoned on each side of the carriage was the Anartes Sigil. The skeleton of a goblin crawled out from underneath and opened the door for the carriage's occupant.

Valan stepped out, noting that quite a few other dark elves were still about at this hour, despite most of the shops having closed. Noise and faerie lights indicated that a party was well underway at the district's bathhouse nearby—he'd have to look into that later. He couldn't afford to fall behind his peers' social machinations in order to avoid a dagger in his back.

Several tables lined the outside of the bistro, and all but one had been cleaned in preparation for the next day. Somebody had doodled across the tabletop using wine, the sticky residue forming crudely drawn, seemingly random images. The "art" portrayed a round figure with a stick chasing after a horde of other stick figures, something that could be mistaken for a kobold, random squiggly lines, all encircled by a roughly round shape that curved and wavered. It didn't look like the artist had tried to make the circle even, but quite the opposite, in fact…

I've never been to Lake Bel, Valan thought to himself. He'd seen enough of the city's maps to recognize the shape of the lake, though had never bothered to visit the center of the city itself. That section was the domain of Clan Licates, the home of the Piuthar-Còig, and not exactly a place a member of Anartes could wander into without drawing attention. He'd have to leave the carriage behind and walk the rest of the way. He'd chosen it due to not needing a slave to drive it around—a slave who could later be asked questions about where Valan had gone—but it would stand out too much in the middle of the city where the lake was located.

However, the city center was not a place that anyone alone, especially if well-dressed, could wander around without being noticed. His other option was to take a series of tunnels that connected all seven of the Piuthar-controlled clans to the city bazaar, tunnels normally used by slaves and merchants carting supplies between clans. It wasn't exactly a discreet place for a noble to walk, either. At best, he had to hope that no one else would be using the tunnels at such a late hour. That route posed its own difficulties: below the merchant tunnels lay the labyrinthian sewers. A host of slimes and sidhe who were deemed too degenerate to belong to any clan often lived down there and sometimes visited the above sections during a break in patrols. The chance of not being seen by anyone was extremely low.

Valan gritted his teeth. *Why couldn't Cernunnos have picked an easier spot to meet?*

He still needed to figure out exactly where he was supposed to go. The lake was far too large to aimlessly wander around and hope to run into the older elf within a reasonable amount of time. He eyed the table again, looking for additional clues. The odd droplets of wine had dried here and there, with the largest marking where boats normally docked on Lake Bel's edge to take visitors to the *other side* of the lake. The detail seemed obvious enough. At this point, he had to hope he guessed right and this wasn't just him seeing too much into things.

"Oh! Valan?"

He looked up from the table to see two dark elves break away from the crowd outside the bathhouse and start toward him. They waved at him. Valan recognized the two immediately and walked over to meet them halfway. He plastered a smile on his face and bowed, his unusually elaborate and long cloak brushing the ground. The dark material of the cloak matched that of similar types, but the extra decorative folds gave it more of a bat-like appearance.

Nealie Osseriates, oldest daughter of the Piuthar-Dà, of the second-most powerful family of Fo Erkunia, returned his smile. She wore very little, showing off her pristine ebony skin and slight curves. Her white hair was longer than even his, plaited in multitudes of tiny braids held in place with black-gold clasps shaped like snakes. A step behind her, if still technically with her, was what appeared to be a male from Clan Latobici; not as elaborately decorated, white hair the shortest out of those present, but this fey was the most dangerous as far as Valan was concerned. As much as Nealie looked to be at ease with her physical charms, the Latobici appeared the opposite. Technically, the Latobici's clothing fit around a narrow frame, but this sidhe looked deeply uncomfortable to be standing there as the shortest out of the three, with metallic gold eyes in stark contrast to an otherwise very plain appearance.

When Clan Anartes had become weakened by the loss of several outposts, Clan Latobici had tried to take advantage by expanding their control of the Fo Erkunia sections Clan Anartes held power over, only to be pushed back again. That loss had to sting. Awkwardness between him and any Latobici was a given due to clan rivalries, but especially so when it came to other shared history he'd rather they both forget about.

Valan made a point of letting his gaze linger in appreciation over Nealie just a little bit longer. He pretended not to see the annoyed expression on the Latobici's face. "Stunningly beautiful, as always."

"If we'd known you were still alive, I would have invited you." Nealie pursed her lips. "I suppose I still could. It's not over yet."

"You look...different," the Latobici stated. From the tone, Valan couldn't tell if the fey thought this to be a good or bad thing.

"Well, me being dead is certainly news to me. I've been preparing for the evaluation in my room," he said. Valan pushed his hair away from the left side of his face for them to get a better look. Against his already dark skin, an even darker tattoo of swirling shapes centered over his solid black left eye. It looked like it was all done by the same artistic hand. Intentional. Tattooed eyes weren't exactly unheard of, just considered too costly and painful for most to consider worth the aesthetic. Especially when it needed to be done repeatedly since the dye faded when a sidhe healed. What noble would want to mar their natural beauty, anyway?

The Latobici frowned. "I was told your sister stole your eye before killing you."

Aren't you well-informed about other people's clans, Valan thought. "And yet here I am, still alive with two eyes. I just...got bored, alright? Reading all those books about fungi made me feel like stabbing out my eyes with needles, so I just decided, why not? Let's see which is actually worse. At the very least, it'll freak out the instructors. Does it really look that bad? I guess I could see about reversing it."

"Whatever." Nealie pressed herself against him, her fingers already playing with his belt buckle. He didn't try to stop her. She glanced back at the shorter dark elf, the smug look on her face plain for all to see, intentionally testing the Latobici. "I can find out for myself how *dead* he really is, can't I, Gwyn?"

Left unspoken was why the higher-ranking woman thought to seek a reaction from the lower-ranking sidhe.

"I didn't hear any rumors about anything else being removed, at the very least," the Latobici said. "You can always stick a sack over his head."

"Come, male. You will entertain me this evening."

Valan made himself look regretful. "I can't. Someone else has already laid claim to my time tonight."

Nealie stared at him in disbelief; she was not used to being told no, especially by a male. She stepped back and then slapped Valan across the face. Hard. The strength behind the blow rocked him sideways. He just barely managed to stay upright.

"You dare deny me?!" Nealie shouted.

"Who?" Gwyn asked.

"All I can tell you is that it's a Cavii," Valan said. He kept his gaze toward the ground. Nealie raised her hand as if to slap him again, but hesitated. Taking in his appearance once more. The elaborate cloak, the additional rings on his fingers, the unusual fancy tattoo; like he really was trying to appeal to someone of significant rank. Someone more powerful than her who might take offense at her damaging him.

"Get out of my sight," Nealie practically spat.

Valan bowed low and then did exactly as he was told, returning to his carriage. Through the Anartes amulet he wore, he directed the carriage to return to Clan Anartes. From there, he had a long walk down some tunnels to look forward to. In the dark confines of the carriage, he felt someone rest a hand over his. He closed his eyes, savoring that touch, and then focused on watching the landscape outside the carriage window. "I'll be alright. I'm just admiring my ability of avoiding one problem by creating an even bigger issue for myself later."

His original plan, and part of the reason why he'd chosen a carriage with the Anartes Sigil so prominently displayed, was to start up some rumors that he wasn't dead after all. To be seen without wings and with both of his eyes. What he didn't consider was that even though his "tattoo" marked him as eccentric to other nobles, he hadn't made it look unappealing enough to completely prevent others from becoming interested in him—and he blamed his own vanity for that. He should have chosen more grotesque imagery to hide the scars, thus avoiding this problem entirely. Now he had to pull a Cavii lover out of thin air before someone found out he had lied.

As the carriage neared the forest, it began to slow as two dark shapes darted out, followed by the carriage speeding up again as if nothing had happened on its way back to the Anartes tower.

"And so the prince descends from his tower!" Cernunnos announced, loud enough for all to hear at the westernmost edge of Lake Bel in the middle of the night.

The lake itself was suspended high above the city. A large chunk of the cavernous roof wasn't made of rock but of pale blue water in which the shadows of swimming fish could be seen. The transparency of the water made it difficult to determine its depths since the other side reflected the image of the moon as it was seen on the surface world. Water dripped down to splash on the ground every so often, before suddenly reversing course and returning back up to the lake at various intervals. Valan knew the dripping water was intentional, serving as a way to help further break down the passage of time by *nóiméad* and *uair*. Hanging upside down at the lake's edge was a small wooden boat that a creative sidhe could use to sail through to the other side. Cernunnos stood directly under the boat.

"Really, Father? You had to give me a ring to summon sunlight?" Valan muttered, walking toward the older sidhe. He glanced to either side of him uneasily while rubbing one of his eyes, and then coughed, covering his mouth and nose. Sorn tilted his head to the side as if he heard something else, then stood directly behind Valan, though facing in the opposite direction; back to back, as if expecting to be surrounded at any moment.

Cernunnos didn't seem to react at all to his son's wariness. "What? Think of it as a birthday present. You can practice with it."

"Birthdays are for lesser, short-lived races."

"Ah, so you *have* been reading those books I've been giving you." Cernunnos grinned in the face of Valan's obvious discomfort. "Enjoy learning about the surface?"

"No."

"So you don't want any more books?"

"... No." Valan scowled over his own hesitation to that question. "And you can take back your uilleann pipes. I like my violin more. I'd appreciate it if you stopped trying to mess with Sorn, too." He paused, thinking of something else. "And the constant spying, *please* stop with the scrying into my life."

"Worried about what I'd find out?"

"I'm more concerned about who might be looking over your shoulder and noticing me."

"The time you have left to hide is coming to an end, kid." Cernunnos tugged on a lock of his own unusually soft white hair for emphasis. His red eyes darkened for a moment. "There's no getting away from your looking like me any longer. At this point, I'm getting concerned that you are *trying* to look like me. I suspect in about five hundred years, you too will grow horns!"

Valan looked particularly aghast at that idea. Him? Grow horns? Sorn already complained about how long it took for Valan to brush his hair free of tangles—and it tangled constantly, and never stayed in a braid, and always got into his face, and there was that time it had wrapped around his wing... Adding horns to that mess would be far too much to deal with on top of everything else. Was already too much to deal with, but more importantly to Valan, *giant horns weren't attractive.*

"Is there a reason you wanted to meet out here?" Valan asked, folding his arms in front of him. Sweat trickled down his temple and he hoped his hair hid it from view.

"I'm going to leave soon," Cernunnos said.

"Okay. Bye."

"Can't even pretend to miss your father, eh?" Cernunnos smirked, but his eyes had narrowed, carefully studying his son's reaction. "I'm going on an adventure! Why don't you come with me? It'll be fun. You can leave this city behind. You can even bring along that feral one with you."

"No," Valan replied, his voice flat. "Why don't you take any of your other children instead? Find another one who looks like you so you can parade them around in front of all your friends. I'm sure they'd be very amused by the similarities."

"Brat, at this point, *you* probably have kids running around."

Valan remained silent. He struggled to keep his anger from showing on his face. As far as he was concerned, this man did not deserve to know how he really felt. What other things he had planned. Why he wanted to stay in Fo Erkunia. It was clear to him that the only reason Cernunnos had shown any interest in him at all these past few years had more to do with the rumors of them looking alike, and so the older sidhe just couldn't resist meddling. Possibly already using the similarities to his own benefit. It's the only explanation that made sense to Valan. Cernunnos surely had other children; Valan just happened to be the one who resembled him the most. There certainly hadn't been any familial interest back when Valan was younger, back when he might have needed this man's help the most.

"Just…quit bothering us. Go back to your surface friends. Prance around the forest with your followers."

"I can't help you anymore after this."

So, Valan thought, *I did fail that test of yours.* His father's interest in sending him all those books about the surface, stories of warriors and "goodly" races doing heroic deeds, what the surface dwellers saw the sidhe as; if Cernunnos had also arranged for Sorn and Valan to face Sabrene alone, then just maybe his father wanted to see what they'd both do once given a choice, how "goodly" they'd be. He turned away and started back the way he he'd come.

"You've been here too long," Cernunnos said, as if his son really had spoken aloud.

"And you not long enough," Valan replied. He stopped walking and glanced back, about to say something, but then shook his head and went on his way again.

"And I *will* be checking your grades in Crann Bethadh!" Cernunnos shouted cheerfully.

"Stop scrying!" Valan shouted back.

Cernunnos chuckled, letting his son leave his sight without further needling.

"That has got to be the most ungrateful little twit I've ever met," a shadow to the left of Cernunnos said.

"Is that what you understood?" Cernunnos asked. What he gained from their exchange was something entirely different.

By the time they reached the tunnel entrance leading back to Clan Anartes, Valan stumbled, his legs giving out underneath him. If not for Sorn grabbing him around the waist, he would have fallen to the ground. Both his legs started to spasm and he had to bite down on the sleeve covering his forearm to keep himself from making any noise. This was far more walking than what he could normally handle. When talking to Cernunnos, the only thing that'd kept him upright was leaning against Sorn's back. That had little to do with "checking for enemies" and more about not falling over in front of his own father.

"Nobody is around," Sorn said into his ear. "We can take a break here."

Valan dug his heels into the ground, trying to stretch out and apply enough pressure to his leg muscles to keep them from cramping. Eventually the tremors stopped, though left him drenched in sweat from the effort. Controlling his breathing became the next issue; this was not the place to have coughing fits.

Others walk around all the time. It's not a big deal, Valan thought through clenched teeth. *Of course I can do the same.*

He just needed to get through this tunnel. Once he got closer to the tower, he could always summon the family carriage again. It wasn't something he liked to be caught using, especially since it wasn't exactly subtle. It also gave the impression that he needed such obvious magic just to move around, but at this point, he had little choice in the matter. *Just get through the tunnel. Worry about the rest later.*

He took a step, the muscles in his legs still too tight, his joints aching, cautioning him that if he wasn't careful, too much movement would just start another fit. He ignored the warning, tried to take another step—and that's when Sorn picked him up, arms hooking under his knees and lower back to carry him.

"Put me down!" Valan snapped. He grabbed onto Sorn's shoulders to keep himself steady. "I know how to walk!"

"This is for me, not you," Sorn said.

Which didn't exactly mollify Valan, but further insistence on his part would be even more humiliating. Besides, he was fairly certain that if he continued to make a fuss, Sorn would have no problem just dropping him to make a point, and then he'd have to deal with the possibility of broken bones.

"Fine," Valan said as if he still had control over the situation. "But only until the end of the tunnel."

Sorn just kissed him lightly on his forehead.

Isla was used to eating alone, but she thought things would change with her twin finally dead. She even kept his eye in a jar next to her bed to soothe her before resting each night. She had assumed that once he was gone, the other sidhe who sought to talk to him would then turn to speak to her, for clearly she was the most superior of the two. She even entertained the idea of buying that guard friend of his as a slave to serve her, though by the time she had gotten around to it, someone else had already paid for him first.

So, why am I not happy?

She stared down at her plate, frowning at a dish of clams lathered in a spicy sauce. Her favorite food. Usually, she ate her midday meal in the family-only dining hall, not the one available to guests and minor nobility, but these days, not many visited the family-exclusive one. Today, she thought she should try mingling with the lower ranks. Valan was dead, Sabrene was dead, and the Piuthar-Tri was speaking to no one except a few older members of their clan. Apparently, a family gathering would take place soon, and even Isla noticed how the male relatives were especially scarce.

She brightened. Maybe she'd even be announced as a higher rank now! She was certain she could make her mother proud.

Lynet Anartes, an adopted member of the family, sat down across from Isla. She recognized the female as someone who Valan had sometimes played music with. Instead of being thrilled that things were finally going her way, Isla found herself struggling with dueling emotions: pleased she would finally get her much-deserved attention, yet irritated that somebody lesser dared to sit near her without asking permission first.

Lynet smiled, resting her elbows on the tabletop. "That was very cheeky of you, Isla! I didn't know you had it in you."

"What are you talking about?" Isla all but snapped.

Lynet's smile quickly disappeared, taken aback by the other's venom. "Your…trick to convince everyone Valan was dead…?"

"He *is* dead."

Isla had watched her sister remove him from the torture cell so she could experiment on him. She'd wanted to see what Sabrene did to him but was soon kicked out of the laboratory. It was mere chance, and not at all her lurking around near Sabrene's bedroom completely innocently, that led her to finding Valan's eye. If her twin wasn't dead, then he was enjoying life as a part-time statue, which was as good as dead. Sabrene's keeping a private collection of her favorites was an open secret among the female members of their family. If her older sister hadn't died, Isla had planned to visit Valan after a few decades to see what little was left of him, but that was no longer possible.

It crossed Isla's mind that maybe the weird flying creature that had broken out of Sabrene's room might actually be her twin, but going on a rampage through the laboratory and torture cells was not something the Valan she knew was capable of. He'd been just another pathetic excuse for a male who spent all his time either at parties or hanging out in his room, more concerned over his appearance than actually being useful to the Piuthar.

"Really?" Lynet asked, and then quickly moved on as if not expecting an answer. "Anyway, I thought to invite you to a party we're all throwing before final evaluation."

Isla didn't respond immediately, savoring that word: invited. She was *invited* to things now. Every time she had attempted to get close to anyone, they'd quickly become spooked. She would either never hear from them again, or they stayed as far away from her as possible. She never understood why; there was nothing wrong with being seen in her company. Born blessed, destined to become a respected veiled one of the An Cailleach and acquire all the power that entailed, so what was there not to like? If it was about looks, there was certainly nothing lacking about her in that regard, either.

"When and where?" Isla asked.

Lynet smiled again, the expression a touch more genuine, and told her.

CHAPTER 7

A ROW OF floating mirrors arranged in a semi-circle held images of the six most powerful women in Fo Erkunia. Lady Mairead, studying those visages arrayed before her as she sat on her throne, brought the number up to seven. Legend told that the very first An Cailleach gave birth to seven daughters who, upon reaching maturity, participated in a rare display of cooperation, deciding to work together instead of allowing the Unseelie Court to devolve into a civil war over who was the best heir. Ever since the first Queen of Winter died, the sisters would decide every thousand years who among them should become the next An Cailleach, with the others serving as councilors. The Piuthar chosen would then give up her clan rights before moving to Oidhche Gheamhraidh in the Otherworld permanently. To boost all of their power further, it was agreed to make worship to An Cailleach mandatory.

The Piuthar-Tri patiently listened to two of the women, Lady Birog Osseriates and Lady Milucra Vindelici, argue over new farming lands for the third time. Normally Mairead would have intervened, helped to find an acceptable solution, but this was the result of Lady Beira Cavii's mess after deciding to play puppet-master to Clan Latobici.

Eventually, an agreement was reached. A cavern to the east of the capitol city was given to Lady Milucra, though reaching such a simple decision had taken far, far longer than it should have, leading to a few of the others present reaching the limits of what they were willing to abide by. Only then did Lady Mairead decide to speak.

"I would like to discuss a growing issue I am concerned with," Mairead began, but before she could speak further, another of the women sneered, cutting her off.

"Must we argue again over you wanting the return of your precious eldest boy?" asked Lady Aine Kinambroi.

Despite untold years of experience with controlling their emotions, a few of the other Piuthars' faces held expressions of exasperation; Mairead had been arguing for Domhnall Anartes to not become a part of Clan Latobici for years now. And even though the new Piuthar-Sia showed little interest in having Domhnall as her consort in favor of cycling through the royal harem, she still refused to divorce and let him return to his original clan.

"Oh, that," Mairead replied dismissively. "That has been settled to my satisfaction. They can keep the boy. I am referring to the growing size of human forces near the surface who use iron. We cannot continue to allow so many of our kind to be discovered by that race—it weakens us. Their *An Cleas* instruction is now more important than ever. It is only a matter of time before they start to rally behind a leader not in the favor of An Cailleach."

That news rattled the other women. All the arguing Mairead had subjected them to suddenly evaporated into nothing. Most of them should have also known by now about Clan Anartes's recent troubles with the sudden death of its second heir, and yet here she was, still with the full support of An Cailleach and treating the loss of her eldest son as nothing. So what could possibly make up for this damage in an already weakened clan? Why had the Winter Queen not deserted her? Most of the women present should have already been acting on their plans to destroy Anartes entirely, just waiting for that final fall from grace so their own clans could scavenge what they wanted from the remains without risk. The next clan to be gutted after the Latobici.

Some might suspect this was all merely bluster on Mairead's part, a last desperate attempt to hide weakness to focus on something more important, but were they really willing to openly go against Clan Anartes just to prove her bluff? Despite current losses, that clan was still the most powerful when it came to manipulating magic. Would their Winter

Goddess choose their side if it came to war? Dare they change the subject away from *An Cleas* influence to try to find out more about Clan Anartes's current state?

"And really, Lady Beira, if you wanted one of my males for a consort so badly, you need only ask," Lady Mairead said. Her eyes narrowed. "I am pleased with the continued cooperation of both our clans."

"I don't recall making such a decision," Lady Beira Cavii replied. A flicker of emotion crossed her face, too quick to determine what the expression actually was, but Mairead knew what the others might possibly read from it. That just maybe the Piuthar-Aon was lying, that the "alliance" between Clans Anartes and Cavii was deeper than what the other Piuthars knew about. Dare they cross not just one, but two of the most powerful clans? And then there was Clan Osseriates giving up some of its renowned neutrality to ally more with Cavii by having one of their own take Rian Cavii as a consort. Three of the most powerful clans apparently enjoyed being allied in full support of the Cailleach.

"Ah, of course." Mairead nodded slightly. "The rumors must be wrong. Perhaps it is better to reserve my concern for our next meeting. This discussion has grown overly long, yes?"

A murmur of agreement circled around the women, now more interested in accessing their own spy networks. One by one, the mirrors reflected nothing but Mairead's throne room until only Beira Cavii's mirror remained active.

"A rumor perhaps *you* have started?" Beira asked.

"Isn't this your rumor?" Mairead appeared perplexed. "If this is false, I could send messages to all the other ruling clans of my error."

"Do go ahead," Beira replied sarcastically. "I'm certain that would be very convincing."

"What bothers me is if neither of us started the talk of you having a new consort, who has the most to gain by making you upset with me?" Mairead mused aloud. "I can think of any number of clans who wouldn't mind weakening Cavii by having your clan attack mine."

And Beira cannot afford to appear weak either, Mairead thought. *It is only with a united front that the lesser clans dare not act. Not even Clan Osseriates, who despite their own "alliance" with you have been most unhappy with the results of being given Rian as a consort for one of their own.*

The two women looked at each other, expressionless, and yet understood each other perfectly. Beira Cavii dulled the magic of her viewing mirror first. Mairead did much the same, and outright dispelled all but one mirror from her throne room, that of Lady Birog Osseriates, which had appeared as faded as the others. The Piuthar-Dà reappeared in the mirror and she did not hide the fury from her face.

"See? It is as I warned: she has more to gain from this than I," Mairead said. "She found out about me promising you a consort and wishes to undermine you. Again."

"Our alliance holds *for now*, Lady Mairead," Birog practically snarled before her own mirror dulled again.

With barely a flick of her wrist, Mairead fully dispelled that mirror as well. She had long cultivated the image of being the Amicable One, the only Piuthar more than willing to listen to both sides before offering suggestions that were the most agreeable to all involved. Why, some of those other women even considered her soft, since she appeared not above taking into consideration the opinions of lesser fey. It was very easy to consider someone like her to be unthreatening, to overlook the slow but steady increase of Clan Anartes' power under her rule. How *close* she had come to rising above the limitations of the entire Unseelie Court with the creation of so many outposts near the surface, which until recently had withstood the threat humans posed.

Perhaps some of the other Piuthars truly understood the threat Mairead posed, but why make an enemy out of such a helpful, useful ally? And so she continued to spin her own duplicitous plots, long after so many other Piuthar had died sudden deaths and were quickly replaced by others. Only the Winter Goddess possibly knew the full extent of her schemes.

"All hail An Cailleach," Lady Mairead whispered into the emptiness of her throne room.

Time to make use of the more errant members of her household.

It had been a while since the last big family gathering. Valan remembered standing next to the *buime*, with Isla on the opposite side of the sidhe woman whose job it was to care for them; the buime had to physically stand in between them, otherwise they'd start a fight again. The chapel of An Cailleach had been crowded with other family members, with several lingering near Lady Mairead and the frozen altar dedicated to the Winter Queen. Valan never understood what they had talked about back then, but the sounds of battle beyond the safety of the chapel had made it clear that things were going very, very wrong.

He recalled being so excited about visiting such a distant Anartes fortification, not realizing at the time he'd been chosen only as a show of confidence because he was so expendable. A visit from nobility was meant to inspire the troops—there would even be a small parade!—but the joy of finally being able to go somewhere other than the Anartes tower had quickly given away to fear of a greedy, lesser race and their poisonous iron. Humans declaring the fey were evil had sought to destroy Anartes and take what his family had worked so hard for. To survive, they would have to return to the capital of Fo Erkunia.

Now, as he looked at three other sidhe children hiding behind a different buime while his remaining family gathered in the throne room of Clan Anartes, Valan wondered what they thought of all this. They all had their heads down, never looking up, so it was difficult to see any physical similarities between them. Valan decided to focus on the rest of the room. He did not want to be seen paying attention to any particular sidhe; that would just start up rumors.

No sign of Domhnall, Valan thought. All his cousins, such as the other Anartes wizards who normally spent most of their time at Crann Bethadh or An Geata, were here. A clear divide indicated where everyone stood in the throne room, with the males on one side and the females on the other. Which was just as well; several of his female cousins, while expressionless, gave off a hostile aura primarily directed toward the male side of the room. Isla looked especially angry to see him still around.

Those closest standing next to him were the Archwizard Ferehar, Slavemaster Hueil, and General Morrowe, even though the gap between them and the throne was quite obvious. No sign of Domhnall, and

Mairead had never chosen a new consort, which meant...Valan struggled to ignore the sinking feeling that threatened to overwhelm him. He was the only one left on his side.

Parallel to him on the opposite side of the throne stood his sisters Nareena, Ginxyra, and then Isla. Further down on their side were other high-ranking positions that only women were allowed to obtain.

The space between Valan's shoulders began to itch; if he suddenly disappeared, Lady Mairead would likely start choosing from his more distant blood relations to adopt—he had a lot of very powerful male cousins and nephews. Even if Mairead decided to elevate others to serve as her sons, he would still be seen as a threat due to having a closer blood relation.

Anartes males in general didn't have the best record in survivability.

The double doors of the throne room opened at last, and Lady Mairead strode through. Two steps behind her was a male Valan didn't recognize and couldn't get a good look at. All the nobles of Clan Anartes bowed or knelt, according to their station, as Mairead moved past toward her throne. As she sat down, the unknown male knelt next to her seat, closer to her than Valan.

Well, that's one worry out of the way.

"You may look at me," Lady Mairead announced. She studied them all: those who dared to meet her eyes the quickest, whose gaze lingered too long on the ground as if to hide. "I have decided to take a consort. For now, we will welcome Tarrant Osseriates to Clan Anartes." After a short, borderline dismissive pause to acknowledge Tarrant's worth, Lady Mairead then addressed each noble one by one, giving them orders of what she expected them to accomplish for the glory of their family.

"Niall, I elevate you to Secondblood. In two weeks hence, you are to be sent to Crann Bethadh. Domhnall Anartes will serve as your master." Mairead then turned to her new eldest boy. "Valan, in two weeks, you will stay in Oidhche Gheamhraidh. Viviane will serve as your Mistress. Now, as for you, Maccus..."

Valan stopped listening. *Mistress*, not master. Not a wizard to help teach him the magical arts. A female originally from Clan Licates before she became powerful enough to be independent, known in general for her fanaticism to *An Cleas* and the training of ideal males.

"… With that decided, I shall now address any of your concerns." Lady Mairead nodded first toward the female half of her nobility. "I give you permission to step forward and speak."

Ginxyra moved the quickest, walking a few extra steps toward the center aisle as if to make sure none could be considered before her. "Piuthar-Tri, with your permission, I would like to take over Sabrene's research."

"Your place is to serve at An Geata," Mairead said.

"I can do both," Ginxyra replied.

"Can you really?" the Piuthar asked. "I suppose I will allow you to try, but know this: any failure on your part to maintain our sacred spaces will lead to *you* being the next I offer in sacrifice to the Cailleach."

"I understand."

Other women stepped forward to share their own concerns until finally Isla could no longer contain herself and had to speak.

"Piuthar, shouldn't he be dead?" Isla pointed an accusing finger at Valan.

He had been gloomily stared down at the floor, looking up only when singled out by his twin. He didn't say anything, since technically Isla's question was meant for the Piuthar to answer.

"I am not aware of anything that would suggest such." Mairead turned to him. "Should you be dead, boy?"

"No, Piuthar-Tri," Valan replied.

"But, his eye, I…I mean, what about the winged creature we never found?" Isla asked.

Lady Mairead sighed. "He clearly has both of his eyes, Isla. That creature has already been found and securely caged, like all the other chimera. You need to learn not to believe every single rumor you come across."

Isla looked thoroughly confused. She returned to her normal place. "I'm sorry for listening to rumors, Piuthar."

"*Please* do better from now on, girl," Mairead said. She stared at Valan. He resisted the urge to squirm under the scrutiny. He was used to being ignored at most family meetings, as there had always been an older brother who she focused her attention on more. Nobody really cared what the useless, frivolous youngest male was up to; he never thought there would ever be a time when he suddenly became the oldest.

"You ruined your face," she finally commented.

"Yes, Piuthar-Tri," Valan replied. He decided now really wasn't the time to give a long-winded excuse about why he had such a tattoo.

"Though I suppose half of it is still recognizable."

"Yes, Piuthar."

Why point that out now? he asked himself, but then just as quickly came up with the answer. This was likely what Cernunnos had warned him about. Lady Mairead wanted to use him as leverage over his real father if another clan attacked Anartes. As a male, Cernunnos held very little power within the Unseelie Court, but he did maintain worshipers on the surface willing to do his bidding. A small army that, through Cernunnos, could be used for Mairead's own benefit under the threat of harming his son if he did not comply.

Indeed, the connection between father and son could not be denied. The so very open public meeting Valan had attended with Cernunnos present all but confirmed for anyone watching that their facial similarities proved their familial connection. But…

"I can't help you anymore after this."

Cernunnos would not help if a war started. Valan was on his own again. How long did he have before Mairead realized he wasn't quite the bargaining chip she expected him to be against his father? He wanted to curl up into a ball and sink into the floor. Well, that was how it'd always been, hadn't it? And it was not like he was entirely alone; he had Sorn. The only one he could trust. Some father figure popping up a few years ago only to just as quickly disappear didn't amount to much. Any kind of reliance on familial connections was a weakness. He should understand that by now. He didn't know why he'd allowed himself to entertain anything different. Maybe Isla was right about how pathetic he turned out to be.

"Are you still paying attention?" the Archwizard of the Anartes Clan asked. The old elf reached over the desk and hit Valan on the head with a stick as they sat across from each other in the Clan Anartes library. Valan flinched from the blow and nodded. A fresh set of bruises covered his throat, so he didn't want to talk if he didn't have to. "So what did I just say?" the Archwizard prodded.

"Unseelie are the nightmares," Valan forced himself to say, his voice hoarse.

"And?"

"A-and..."

The Archwizard sighed and smacked the boy on the head once more for good measure. "And that is to our benefit. With our world linked so closely with humans these days, sometimes their strongest dreams reach the Otherworld and grab the attention of the Cailleach, who combines them with the soul of a fallen sidhe to then be reincarnated through a Piuthar."

"But..." Valan trailed off again. He didn't understand. He didn't have claws or sharp teeth or look scary in any way, so surely the Cailleach had made a mistake in his case. Saying the Winter Goddess got something wrong seemed like a great way to be punished, so he didn't finish speaking. Nobody cared about his opinion on things anyway, only if he could repeat back what he was told.

The Archwizard almost hit him a third time, taking the boy's lack of a response as a lack of understanding. He tried to word things in a different way. "Enough mortals dreamed of you, or of someone like you, and felt so strongly—so terrified—that it inspired the Cailleach to give that dream a soul. A Piuthar and her consort then provide the flesh. Do you understand now?"

Valan nodded slowly. "Does that mean...everything is decided for me?"

"No, it is like what I told you about humans: how, where, and by whom are also decided for them along with the shape they are born into, but after that, a human is still capable of making their own decisions." The Archwizard eyed the boy. "To a certain degree. It's best if you listen and obey your betters."

The boy with a face as pretty as a girl's met the wizard's gaze furtively. "I don't understand why I'm scary."

"Most of us don't understand why we are the way we are—humans are not exactly the most intelligent of creatures. Their concept of nightmarish changes all the time. A thousand years ago, a dream similar to the one that inspired the creation of you could have led you to joining the Seelie Court instead," the Archwizard said.

"What you need to know is that we are strong because we represent that which terrifies humans the most—a fear that will no doubt aid you once it is your time to contribute to An Cleas." He frowned. "We used to be able to petition for a switch in clans from the ruling body of each Court if a member of the fey turned out to be more Seelie than Unseelie, but that is not possible anymore. We all must adapt."

When Valan refocused, Lady Mairead had long turned her attention to the other males of her clan, listening to their own questions and concerns. General Morrowe wanted to expand the barracks for new soldiers. One of his older cousins, a master at Crann Bethadh, accused another master of never putting the books back in the library. Eventually, after addressing all of their concerns, Mairead finally dismissed her nobility, with Valan just as empty of expression as the others.

CHAPTER 8

"'Play Dead' hasn't worked since you were eight," Sorn commented. The staged bedroom was now free of bloodstains and body parts. Sorn sat on the edge of the clothing chest chimera, once again placed in front of the rough wall that led to their real bedroom, with a key lock propped up on his knee as he used thin wires to practice opening the device. Several other locks of various sizes and complexity were scattered around him.

"I'm restarting this trend with the other children. I think it'll become really popular," Valan muttered into the blanket covering the bed of his staged bedroom. He lay face down with his limbs splayed, his feet hanging off the side of the bed. He raised his hands just enough to signal back, not looking up, as if to say, *Give me a moment.*

He wanted to run away. He wasn't sure how much more of Mairead's plans he could handle. Running away would be the easiest option. Just join a caravan heading for the surface and start over somewhere far away from Fo Erkunia. Spend as much time as he wanted with Sorn without having to be constantly concerned about somebody noticing. No more worrying about hiding his physical limitations. Things were supposed to somehow be *better* up there according to all those surfacer books, right? In time, perhaps, he could forget about having left *them* behind.

He listened to the soft clicks of Sorn using his wires to move the tumblers in his practice locks, the sound oddly comforting. Valan looked up just enough to see the half-sidhe's face, noticing that the blue scarf hung loosely around Sorn's neck to expose more of his not-quite-dark-enough skin. With the hood of his cloak down, his gently pointed ears were visible. By dark elf standards, the blue-haired man was not handsome, at best plain in appearance, and certainly did not possess the well-polished, carefully maintained looks of sidhe nobility. The type who wouldn't be caught dead in the finery Valan sometimes put up with.

Sorn noticed he had an audience and glanced over. "What?"

"I'm admiring the view." Valan smiled. Those rougher features came across as achingly handsome to him. Sorn had never needed to learn how to mask his emotions or pretend to feel something he actually didn't. The half-sidhe's default facial expression, with his slightly downturned mouth and harsh gray eyes, was the look of someone largely unimpressed with the world…until that gaze focused on Valan, becoming something softer.

"You should see me without any clothes on."

"You'd actually take off your scarf? Just for me?" Valan teased. Sorn gave his best *come hither* stare that left them both grinning at each other.

Valan resisted the urge to ask to fix that scarf. He was pretty sure the only thing keeping it from completely falling apart after so many years was the simple enchantment woven into the strings. A long time ago, back when his *buime* was still around, she took Valan and Isla shopping in the Bazaar for new slaves. She wanted to teach them what characteristics to look for when picking out a servant for different roles, though he suspected the real reason was just so he and his sister would have a new target to torment instead of each other.

"Over the next month, I want you to take care of your own slave," the buime *told them. "It'll be your job to train it, to make sure it eats and that it obeys you. Whoever's slave lives the longest will get to have their favorite dish for dinner for a whole week. Now, isn't that exciting?"*

Isla and Valan glared at each other. Challenge accepted. Isla immediately ran over to the cages with the special creatures: a dark-haired human, an albino kobold, a mermaid with a bright pink tail. Valan went the opposite way, ending up next to the cages that the buime *had told him were meant to be sold for use in the arena. Fodder used to rile up the more fearsome creatures in battles for sidhe to watch. He quickly moved past the troll likely to eat him for dinner and the dogwhatsit that looked boring in comparison, eventually arriving at a cage that caught his attention. A sidhe boy stared at him from the opposite side of the bars.*

The other boy had dull, matted gray hair, not the lustrous white of most sidhe. He wasn't pure-blooded, with ears not quite as pointed as they should be and skin not as dark. They looked around the same age, but a roughness to his features made it difficult to tell if this boy was older or younger than Valan.

"Hey." Valan walked up to the cage, picking at scabbed-over scratch marks on his shoulder as he excitedly looked the other boy over. This was the first half-sidhe he'd ever seen. "Do you know what lesser race you are? Human, maybe?" He frowned. This slave might be too difficult to care for. "Does that mean you can't see in the dark? Do you eat weird stuff?"

The gray-haired boy refused to say anything, moving as far back into his cage as the space allowed.

"But I want all three!" Isla cried loudly. "It's not fair."

"Only one, Isla, and no, it can't be your brother. He has to do something bad first." The buime *looked around, finally noticing that the other twin had wandered off. "Valan, get back here!"*

"I want this one."

After the buime *bought the two slaves the twins decided on, the slavemaster made a show of freshly scrubbing down the cages, applying the Anartes brand on the albino kobold and half-elf, and promised to deliver them to the Anartes tower as soon as possible. By the time they finished shopping and returned home, Valan did indeed find a large cage in his bedroom. The* buime *told him he wasn't allowed to open the cage, that another slave would clean up after it every morning, but the rest was up to him.*

The gray-haired boy lay on the bottom of the enclosure, unmoving, and Valan wondered if his new slave might already be dead. Valan knelt down, trying to get a good look at the slave's face, but the other boy just curled himself into a tighter ball so he couldn't see.

"Do you have a name?" Valan asked.

No response. Not even a twitch.

He scowled. Keeping a slave was a lot harder than he thought it'd be, but for now, he had better hurry back to the family dining hall. He was supposed to eat there with the rest of the nobility, and the buime *might have noticed that he'd wandered off again.*

"I'll come back with food," he whispered conspiratorially and quickly left.

He did return later, with a fresh set of bruises—the buime had *noticed he was missing earlier—and he placed a bowl of soup with a wooden spoon on the ground within reach of the cage. He didn't know what was actually in the soup—he'd just told the main cook in the kitchen that he wanted "slave food" and this was what he'd been given. The slave could easily reach through the cage's bars for the bowl if he wanted to, though apparently he still hadn't moved much from earlier. Valan frowned. What should do if he couldn't get the slave to eat? But this was just the first day; he really didn't have to worry about the slave starving to death until a few days had passed. He needed to turn in for the night, anyway.*

He fell asleep in his own bed easily enough, though was soon startled awake by a sudden noise in his room. Valan looked toward the cage and noticed that the bowl of soup had been knocked over. The slave was still curled up on his side, facing away, but it was very obvious who between the two of them had spilled the food. This kind of bad behavior, Valan had been taught, meant that a slave deserved to be punished. He was supposed to hit the boy hard enough so that food wouldn't be wasted again.

Valan got out of bed and picked up the practice sword leaning against a wall. He walked over to the cage and stared down at the other boy. It'd be really easy to strike through the bars. Stab him in the back a few times. Hurt him until he obeyed.

"It's because you're freezing, right?" Valan asked. He put the sword back and grabbed the blanket off his bed instead. It was his only blanket, but maybe the other boy was just cold. He looked sad, positioning himself like that. Granted, in giving up the blanket, Valan himself would end up chilly, but at least he had his bed and could always hug his pillow for warmth. The other boy had nothing. Valan pushed the blanket through the bars and went back to sleep.

In the morning, Valan got up and noticed the slave had wrapped the cloth around himself…and that presented a bit of a problem. Slaves weren't supposed to be given gifts, especially not for bad behavior. The buime *was going to be very angry with him. Valan reached through the bars of the cage and grabbed a corner of the blanket, pulling. The other boy refused to let it go.*

"Hey, you've got to give this back." Valan pulled on the blanket again. "You can have it again later."

The other boy clung tighter to the cloth. They both continued to pull on the blanket back and forth until finally the slave yanked it out of Valan's hands with enough force to knock him over. Valan struggled to stand back up, now sporting a newly sprained wrist. The gray-haired boy sat upright, startled at how a simple tug-of-war managed to hurt the other child. Under such scrutiny, Valan adjusted his clothes to hide his other bruises better, especially his badly swollen ankles from all the walking he'd done yesterday.

"Give me the blanket or we'll both be in trouble," Valan said quietly.

The slave reluctantly pushed the blanket through the bars, and just in time; another slave walked into the bedroom carrying cleaning supplies. Valan pretended not to see this other slave clean the mess in his room and the cage as he got ready for the day. If he did anything unusual, he knew the cleaning slave would report it to the buime. *He had to be in the family dining hall again this morning, but only for a short time since his older sisters wanted to do some sort of ritual. He wasn't told what kind because he wasn't important enough. Once the cleaning slave left, he gave back the blanket, watching the other boy immediately return to hiding underneath it.*

"I'll be back soon, okay? I'll bring food then," Valan said.

Valan was true to his word, returning to his room several hours later. He held a book with a plate of food resting on top. Instead of just asking for slave food, he brought along more of his own favorites, hoping the other boy liked the same things. He set the platter right outside the cage and then sat down as well. The buime *told him that teaching slaves was important but hadn't really given any examples of what exactly Valan was supposed to teach. He wondered what topics he knew that he could talk about, realizing that he could share how to read books. If the other boy couldn't—or wouldn't—talk, then chances were he didn't know how to read, either. Besides, books were fun for Valan; they taught him all kinds of things, and he could travel to all these other places without having to take a single step. It'd be great to have someone to learn with.*

So, he opened his book and began to read aloud a story about a group of dumb, kind-hearted adventurers who climbed a mountain to get their wishes granted by a tri-*headed monster. Instead of giving them what they wanted, the monster killed them off one by one. He really liked the part of the story when the wizard adventurer found a cursed set of dice. The wizard couldn't resist rolling the dice, hoping to gain good luck, but then lost all of his intelligence, and every time he talked, he'd sound like something called a duck. At some point in retelling the story, Valan became so engrossed that he forgot about the teaching part of all this, stopping midway throughout of embarrassment.*

Valan peeked over the top of his book. "S-sorry, I'm supposed to teach you. I'll just start over again. Um, this symbol here means—"

"What happens in the rest of the story?" demanded the boy under the blanket. Half the food on the plate had somehow disappeared without Valan noticing.

"You can talk!" Valan's eyes brightened. "This is great! I was getting worried, but—oh, uh, right…yeah, we can do the teaching thing later. So, what happens next is…"

Each day, he brought a different story, sometimes a new puzzle to play with, though the gray-haired boy didn't seem to like those as much, and eventually days turned into weeks. By the end of the third week, Valan found out Isla had accidentally killed her kobold slave, and when she had a bad day, it meant he was going to have an even worse one.

Valan was looking through the non-magical section of the Anartes library to find a book about thieves—the other boy seemed to like those kinds of stories the most. Finding the book he wanted, he turned around and headed out the door. At least, he tried to, but his sister stood in the doorway.

"You are not *better than me," Isla said. She held a pair of scissors in her hand.*

"O-okay," he automatically agreed. Valan slowly backed away, heading deeper into the library. He wasn't faster than her, but sometimes he could climb and hide between the stacks of books so she couldn't find him.

Today was not one of those days.

When the buime *found him, he was hiding in the corner of the library with most of his hair chopped off. Isla had not been careful with the scissors and his scalp was bleeding in several spots. The* buime *dragged him out, pulling him by the arm, and they walked down the scary hallway that led to the throne room. Isla was already there, standing in front of the Piuthar-Tri, her eyes puffy from crying.*

"Isla, did you do this?" Lady Mairead asked.

"No, he did that to himself," Isla said.

Valan just stared down at his feet.

"Did anyone see this happen?" Mairead directed her question toward the buime.

"No, Piuthar."

Mairead sighed. "Very well. Valan, you should be ashamed of yourself for cutting your hair short. I forbid you to do so again. The length of your hair is a reflection of the standing of your clan." She gestured to the left side of her and a guard stepped out of the darkness. "I want his face unrecognizable until his hair grows out, understood?"

The guard nodded and walked over to the boy, raising his fist.

By the time Valan made it back to his room, it was very late at night. Everything hurt. All he wanted to do was lie down and not move for a while. His eyes were so swollen that he didn't notice that the cage door was unlocked. He certainly didn't have the energy to stop the gray-haired boy from pushing him against the wall, unable to react to the upraised, sharpened end of a wooden spoon as it came slamming down toward his head…and then strike the wall next to him.

"W-who did that to you?" the half-elf asked.

"It doesn't matter," Valan said. He was just so tired of everything always hurting. "Why did you stop? Go ahead."

"What?" the other boy asked, taking a step back. Confused over the encouragement. "I can't kill you when you're leaking everywhere, okay? So you *stop."*

"Shut up!" Valan wiped his tears away. "I'm not leaking!"

"Yes, you are!"

"Am not!"

Valan limped over to his bed and pulled out something from underneath the frame he had been working on in secret. Over the past few weeks, he'd been trying to make a blanket using some yarn and needles he'd stolen from the buime *when she was distracted by Isla. He'd never tried to make something like this before, so the result ended up more like a mangled scarf. He even tried to make it super special, weaving what he knew of magic into it, willing this thing he made to help the other boy hide and stay warm. He didn't really know if it ended up with any sort of enchantment or not. Valan thrust the scarf onto the other boy's chest.*

"Here. It's not done, but maybe it can help you run away, so you don't get cold out there… So, bye. It was nice meeting you."

"… Sorn."

"Huh?"

"That's my name."

"Nice to have met you, Sorn."

Sorn fidgeted with the scarf. "And I don't eat weird stuff."

"Okay."

"And of course I can see. I'm not dumb."

"Oh," Valan sounded disappointed. He had enjoyed all the teaching lessons involving books; it hurt to find out the other boy might have been pretending not to know the entire time. "So you already know how to read?"

"... You're weird." Sorn kept glancing from the scarf to the door and then back to the other boy.

"Just go, okay? It's not like I want to stop you." Valan crawled into bed, hugging his pillow to himself. His face hurt from trying to talk so much. He wanted to sleep just a little bit, even though he knew when he woke up, the swelling would be worse. Tomorrow was going to be another bad day.

"T-that's right. You can't stop me. I can do whatever I want."

Valan didn't feel up to responding to the other boy anymore, his blackened eyes drifting closed. He woke up to the sound of the cleaning slave running out of his room, undoubtedly to report that Sorn had run away. His blanket slid down as he sat up, and Valan stared at it in confusion. He didn't remember taking it back last night. He then heard an unusual noise coming from underneath his bed.

He'd read stories about monsters that lived under beds and ate children. Valan very slowly peered over the edge, but saw nothing odd. Summoning up every ounce of bravery he possessed, he hung over the side and looked directly underneath.

Sorn stared back at him.

"Why didn't you run away?" Valan asked, bewildered.

"... I don't want to talk about it."

"Um, you don't have to hide there if you don't want to."

"Shut up. I know that." Sorn glowered. "I'm keeping watch. Go sleep some more."

Valan tried to smile, happy that he could still play games and read more books with this other boy. Today wasn't going to be so bad after all.

"Why didn't you choose for us to run away?" Valan asked, thinking back to when he had given Sorn three options over what they should do next.

"You wouldn't forgive me if we did that."

"Not at first, but I would have in time." He left unspoken just how much he needed this blue-haired man in his life. Of his desire to give absolutely everything to Sorn. Valan's greatest fear had more to do with how there might come a time when he would no longer be enough for the half-elf. That Sorn would grow tired of having to constantly stay in the shadows, that dealing with him would eventually become too exhausting, and that he would want someone more normal. *As long as you are with me, I can handle anything.*

Sorn set aside his lock, seeing the expression on Valan's face. "What's bothering you?"

"Everything that isn't you." Valan frowned, rubbing at his eyes as if to remove the remnants of self-pity he indulged in. "It's nothing. I'll... be fine."

He really couldn't let his emotions spiral further. There were plenty of other problems to solve, no need to invent new ones. Sorn was with him now and that was what mattered the most. Things weren't going to improve by doing nothing, so might as well try to do the stupidly dangerous plan that he came up with so that the other man could come with him to The Otherworld without detection.

Originally, he'd considered more mundane methods. He could somehow forge documents and register Sorn as another new student, use another Fáinne Athrú so Sorn looked fully sidhe, and then enter the fighter training courses since that gave him the highest chance of passing as a student. But students needed to be granted permission to visit different sections of the academy. They'd still spend their time largely separated from each other—and as talented as Sorn was at hiding, was it really something to put to the test every day, surrounded by the most skilled veiled ones and wizards of Fo Erkunia? It wouldn't work, especially as a long-term solution. Students were also not allowed to bring their own slaves and servants—the academy had its own staff, and part of the "learning experience" for students was to serve various masters in exchange for knowledge. Lastly, Sorn getting past all the school's protections from the outside was next to impossible.

But all wizards kept familiars, small fey-like beings that gravitated to and became bound to serve more powerful sidhe. It was something of a symbiotic relationship, since a weaker fey could siphon off some of the Otherworld radiation that sidhe exuded to help keep them alive even when away from a veil.

Unfortunately, the magic that made it possible to drastically change one's shape was beyond his ability to cast. Not something a Fáinne Athrú could cover. Which really only left him with one solution.

"Rat, snake, or spider?" Valan asked.

CHAPTER 9

Tarrant Osseriates did not want to be here. There were too many wizards. Everywhere he looked, robed figures navigated the irritatingly overly-complex layout of the Anartes tower. Nobody, it seemed, cared to use the spiral staircase designed specifically for connecting each floor in the easiest manner possible. Oh no, they all had to glide, fly, or *blink* everywhere. How were soldiers supposed to reliably protect this place? Who had decided it was a great idea to make the upper tower a series of ice-suspended floating platforms that need to be jumped to? It took him half the day to figure out where the main training facility even was; Tarrant needed to climb to the fourth floor, then use a series of side passageways to take him to the eighth, only to end up on the floor directly below the main entrance of the tower.

And what was with all the bizarre statues?

He uneasily passed by a stone monstrosity that somehow possessed six legs, a pair of massive crab-like pinchers, and was covered in needle-like fur in order to pick up one of many halberds left on display next to it. The soldier training cavern was serviceable enough, a big room with plenty of weapons to choose from, but it was clear to Tarrant that this clan wasn't too interested in trying to build the most individualistically skilled fighters.

Even now, half the cavern was taken up by a company of four platoons of soldiers practicing, alternating between using their shields and weapons in unison as someone they called General Morrowe yelled out specific commands. No unique warriors there. Neither was it free from wizards. One stood next to the general and summoned fire around any warrior deemed too slow to respond to shouted orders. On the other side of the cavern, by the roughly made walls, stood two more wizards using spells to break down more of the stone and widen the space even further. A group of goblin slaves hauled away the rubble.

The entrance Tarrant had used was not the only door, merely one of over a dozen that led to places unknown to him. He'd heard conflicting rumors that an entire village made up of the commoner families of Anartes soldiers also stayed in the tower, but to Tarrant, it was more likely just an extensive barracks like at his old clan. Still, that was a long row of identical doors. The only one that looked unique was center-most and heavily barred—one he'd seen earlier that led to the torture chamber section. Lady Mairead hadn't given him much of a tour when he'd first arrived. Apparently, she thought he only needed to know where her main chambers and the torture cells were located.

He hoped that by coming here, he could challenge and spar with someone to retain at least some normalcy from his former life as a twentieth-year student of Crann Bethadh. Perhaps even show everyone that while he was Mairead's new consort, he still had more going for him than just being the latest husband until she became bored. Tarrant could not escape the simple truth that while he was technically the highest-ranking male in this clan, he was also the most expendable. When his old Piuthar had handed him over, his time left to live had shortened dramatically.

All those years spent mastering the use of polearms, being selected to join the Wild Hunt twice in a row, and he'd ended up with a bunch of magic-loving freaks.

One of the identical doors opened, and Tarrant watched the Firstblood Son pass through. Valan approached the two wizards, spoke to one, and then they exchanged scrolls with each other before he headed toward another of the exits. It occurred to Tarrant that while the General looked too busy to spar, perhaps he could order the Firstblood Son to do so instead.

"Firstblood!" Tarrant called.

Valan very reluctantly turned to face his clan's consort. "… Yes?"

Tarrant sized up the other sidhe. This male was thinner than the average dark elf, but that wasn't unheard of. Some members of Clan Latobici were notoriously small-framed and made up for it with their sheer ferocity. More importantly, he wore leather armor and not a robe like other Anartes; it was more likely this elf was some sort of fighter and not yet another wizard. Valan didn't look like he was carrying any weapons, the closest thing being a heavy looking, coffin-shaped leather case awkwardly strapped to his back over a bulky cloak, but most sidhe kept their best weapons hidden. Besides, besting the Firstblood in front of the others present would help cement Tarrant's own standing as more than just Mairead's new plaything.

"You know how to fight, don't you? Spar with me," Tarrant demanded.

Valan looked at him, a single eyebrow raised. "Why don't you choose someone closer to your own skill level?"

Tarrant's eyes narrowed. *Does this bastard think he's better than me?* With his halberd, he gestured toward the wall racks holding an assortment of weapons. "Pick one."

The Firstblood reluctantly picked up a longsword and stood in a basic fighting stance in front of Tarrant, holding the weapon with both hands. Tarrant noticed an unusual amount of strain in the other's arms to hold the weapon steady, something he was more likely to see in a fighter holding a heavier weapon like a great axe or maul. Valan wasn't even paying that much attention to his opponent, looking off to the side as if bored. It was irritating.

Tarrant was going to start off easy as a warmup, testing the other elf's skills, but changed his mind. The sheer lack of respect set his teeth on edge. *Let's see how well this skinny bastard can handle my full strength.*

Tarrant shifted his halberd in his own two-handed grip and immediately thrust the spear point directly at Valan's face. Valan blocked—slowly, he noted—so Tarrant then used the resistance to swing his halberd the other way around, to the side, with enough force as if to cleave Valan in half.

At least, that was what should have happened. Tarrant noticed a dark blur at the edges of his vision before he could fully follow through with his counter swing, and he ended up trying to dodge out of the way of whatever his senses were warning him was there at the last minute. He stumbled to one knee; somehow Valan's sword had sliced through the armor protecting his upper thigh. The wound was not shallow; blood oozed down his leg and dripped on the floor.

How? He eyed the other sidhe suspiciously, even looked around, but didn't see anyone who could have been close enough to attack. Valan, by all appearances, hadn't moved much from the first blocked blow.

Valan dropped his sword to the ground, flexing his fingers to return feeling to them. His voice came out flat. "Oh, great and powerful warrior, you have bested me. I must now slink away in shame. Goodbye."

He turned away, heading toward one of the doors.

"Hold on. What—"

Laughter erupted from one side of the cavern. Tarrant glanced over and saw the General making the mocking noise. All the soldiers were looking at him, having seen what happened: Tarrant kneeling on the ground bleeding as Valan walked off.

"Did the consort just lose to the *worst* fighter here?" one soldier commented to another.

Tarrant's face flushed in shame. He, too, tossed his weapon to the ground in a fit of rage. Things weren't supposed to go this way. He shouldn't even be there. He needed to kill the Firstblood as soon as possible. It was his only recourse to regain any sense of pride. Making a point to ignore the General and soldiers, he followed after Valan, fully intent on a confrontation.

Sorn and Valan watched Tarrant walk right past them, hidden behind an illusionary wall the Firstblood had created. From the consort's perspective, the hallway would have appeared to only allow one way forward, though in reality, it split in two. Someone with more knowledge of the tower might not have fallen for such a simple trick, but Valan doubted an outsider like Tarrant would have been able to memorize the layout so quickly.

The Firstblood grabbed Sorn's arm to keep the other from following after Tarrant. Valan shook his head.

"I can solve this problem right now," Sorn said in a low voice, close to Valan's left ear.

Valan leaned against the rogue, also keeping his voice down. "And possibly create a bigger issue later. He is a newly arrived gift from Clan Osseriates. His death so soon can cause problems. There will be questions. Let Mairead be the one to eventually kill him, which shouldn't take too long, anyway."

Valan knew of only two of Mairead's past consorts: Condan and Torran. Both experienced wizards. Both driven to insanity and committed suicide. Then, there was her unhealthy interest in Domhnall, another wizard. Tarrant did not fit that emerging pattern. Which, now that he thought about it, could mean the current consort's novelty would help him live a little longer—though it still would not change the inevitable outcome.

"Let's go," Valan said. He stopped concentrating on his illusion and headed back to the training area, this time with the intention of going through the correct door to his real destination. He hoped Tarrant enjoyed exploring the sewers.

There were *tri* suspended gardens within the Anartes tower. The highest, and the one Valan had never been to, supposedly served as a chapel to An Cailleach, which grew plants—typically poisonous—that the Winter Queen was fond of, and was also home to a massive nest of giant bats. No one except a veiled one was allowed inside, not unless they were the next sacrificial offering. Located more centrally within the tower, the second garden was for growing various alchemical ingredients for use by Anartes wizards, though technically any of the nobility could visit. The last garden, located on the second floor and nearest to the commoner dining hall, was a carefully maintained roaming path full of the more unique vegetation brought back from travels abroad. Perfectly safe, as long as a visitor didn't get too close to the bladed fronds.

The Firstblood Son sat on a stone bench under a large mushroom in the third floating garden, with a bit of teal will-o'-the-wisp lighting the cap in a gentle glow. He had the *còig troighid*-long coffin case—which he used to carry his violin with enough interior space to hold quite a few other objects—open at his feet, though he held the violin in his hands. The case already had a number of coins, a few rings, and a scroll: the sort of items usually given as a gift to a playing musician. Aside from the section lined with felt to keep his instrument secure within the case, the sides were lined with lead.

The song he played on his string instrument, his thin fingers moving the bow in such a way that it caused a low, disturbing thrum, was perhaps something only a dark elf fully appreciated. It conjured images of dead things whispering in the dark, crawling unseen and following forever a step behind, promising power if one listened hard enough, tried to understand, before sinking into an oblivion of obscenities, only for the maddening cycle to repeat once again.

Other sidhe occasionally walked by, and sometimes the items in his case changed. The scroll was replaced by a folded paper, the gold gone and a sack with a bloodstained bottom left in its place, and more coins. Lynet Anartes walked by, whispered something directly into Valan's ear, causing him to give a brief half-smile, and she picked up two of the three rings to drop another bag next to the bloodied one. Valan continued playing for an *uair*, patiently waiting for the last exchange of favors.

Tarrant watched a *buime* carrying several books down the stone path to pause and listen to the song the Firstblood was playing. The sidhe woman dropped the books down on the stone bench and reached to pick something up from the case on the ground, then walked off as if nothing unusual had happened. Valan stopped playing soon after this, closing the case with his foot with more force than something made out of wood and leather should need, and used his will to change the color of the teal light above him to a shade of dark blue that matched the other grow-lights in the area.

From where Tarrant hid further along the path, his own cloak obscuring his features, it looked like the obvious exchange of goods left Valan with a bunch of junk.

Books on children's rhymes?

A diminutive skeleton crawled out from underneath the bench and picked up the books and case, following after Valan as he left the garden. Tarrant also followed, keeping enough distance between them so that he wouldn't be easily noticed. All he needed was a moment to catch the little bastard alone.

At that moment, another dark elf passed his hiding spot, wrinkling her nose from the smell. A slave must have over-fertilized the garden.

During a bend in the path, when Valan was fairly certain nobody could see him, he opened his music case and reached into the bag *without* blood on it. He quickly pulled out his old bracers, belt, and earrings and put them on. Something else was in the bag, but that would have to wait until later. Normally, he would have deemed it too risky to put on his additional equipment so openly, but with the way things were going, he might end up needing the extra help a lot sooner than he had originally planned.

He jumped off the edge of the suspended garden to land on a platform attached to the central staircase a few feet away and descended the steps. His animated skeleton managed to make the leap as well. Valan took the stairs down to the first floor, then through the nearest door of the torture cells. He didn't bother to look around him, barely noticing others occasionally bowing to him as he moved past; becoming Firstblood was not something he was entirely comfortable with yet. Already the title was drawing far more attention than he liked.

Two guards glanced at him along the spiral path of the cells, but otherwise left him alone. Valan headed all the way to the bottom, past even the protected cells, his journey ending abruptly at a blank wall. A thin layer of dust rested over everything, the only footprints being his own. Clearly, it was not a place visited by anyone recently. Sorn must have stayed further up the path to keep watch for anyone looking down here. Valan ordered the skeleton to drop the books and case, then he moved several feet away before issuing more orders.

Under his command, the skeleton opened the case and started to take out the items gifted to him during his public performance. The bloody bag was opened first, the skeleton removing the still alive, gagged head of a sidhe male. Bound as the mouth was, the only facial features that could move were the eyes as they darted back and forth in panic. Valan recognized the face of Morfran, the slaver who had tried to renege on their deal and attempted to stab Sorn. He had not forgotten what those marks on his love's back looked like—and he certainly wasn't going to forgive them, either—but he didn't have the free time to deal with Morfran himself. Luckily, there were plenty of dark elves willing to chop off body parts for a little extra coin. Valan summoned a globe of acid and destroyed the bloody bag and head, thus fully killing Morfran.

The other bag, largely deflated of its contents, now contained only his old clothing and boots, along with a small jar with a bit of round, shriveled flesh within—all that remained of a red sidhe eye. His twin's obsessiveness had worked in his favor for once, since she'd decided to take his other belongings too and not just his eye. He studied the shriveled eye closely, noticing just how much it had decayed and comparing it to what he knew about how much time it took for flesh to deteriorate. Considering the location of Isla's room in the female-only section, he had to convince another female to steal his stuff back for him. Now there was just Lynet to deal with, but that was a problem for another day. Valan destroyed the jar with acid too, if a bit reluctantly.

The skeleton picked up the old, brittle paper and unfolded it, holding it open for Valan to see. He had to hope that this map of part of the surface world, focused on the area around a lake, was still fairly accurate. If it wasn't, it would lead to a very unhappy Sorn, as they would then have to move on to the next, more local idea of how to sneak him into The Otherworld.

Valan eyed the coins warily, remembering the main reason he had his skeleton be the first to touch everything. The skeleton collected the coins one by one. Some of them immediately reacted to being touched, sometimes blackening the boney fingers with disease, burning holes into the bone with acid or fire, discoloration from poison. Things meant to kill or harm Valan if he tried to pick up the coins on his own. He usually had to deal with a few such attempts, but now the amount far exceeded his expectations. A lot more sidhe were out there with something to gain from his death.

He had the skeleton peel back the metallic exterior of the "coins" to reveal tiny folded messages, holding them up for him to read one by one before summoning fire to destroy the paper. Valan then called forth just enough magic to move the layer of dust and dirt on the ground to form arcane symbols that wrapped around in a circle. Once the last rune joined with the first, the circle flared. Several things on his person and immediate surroundings, like the blank wall, glowed faintly. The map glowed as well, signifying a concentration of magic; he guessed somebody had enspelled those to find out where he went while carrying these things.

Valan studied the map to memorize as much of it as he could, then used acid as well on anything glowing that shouldn't have been imbued with magic. While the spell he used couldn't detect what exact kind of magic had been cast on the items, the overall intent couldn't be good for his continued health. The books, at least, were left alone.

Valan had neither the time nor inclination to memorize multiple books on children's rhymes. His real interest in them had more to do with comparison's sake. The Anartes library having such a large non-magical section always left him puzzled: what use were all those made-up stories? Hardly anyone bothered to read any of it. At best, they were tools to teach children how to read, and Mairead wasn't the maternal sort. Books with lots of hand-drawn, meticulously detailed, pictures. As he studied magic, however, Valan had begun to realize that quite a few of the drawings looked familiar.

He picked up the topmost book and flipped to a poem called *We Three Are Free*, about three divine children who led millions of fey through the stars by spilling droplets of their own blood, along the way promising salvation from a horror they'd left behind. The poem was accompanied by the image of an archway made up of skeletons. The second book contained the same poem with the same words, but the image was of an arch made up of thorny vines that vaguely looked like runes. The third book was badly damaged, with the drawing of *We Three Are Free* torn out long ago, but somebody had written a warning underneath the poem:

LET THE BLOOD OF EMPIRES
KEEP THE WAY CLOSED.

Empires, as in royalty. His blood, that of Anartes, one of the oldest clans of the Unseelie Court, just might count. Valan sliced open his index finger by running it quickly across the bow of his musical instrument. He then used the blood to draw an arch on the stone wall before him, one that happened to be located at the deepest part of the tower. He had to keep cutting his skin to get enough blood before moving on to duplicate the runes that looked most like the drawing, sometimes removing parts when his initial guess didn't match up quite right with the rest.

Once fully drawn, nothing happened. Likely a key of some sort was needed to bring the portal to life. He suspected the missing third drawing might have hinted at the location or design of such a key.

Well, there's all that talk of "empire" blood, so why not flesh?

Valan placed his cut up hand in the middle of the arch, trying to *feel* the magic in the wall for any reaction. Perhaps there was a slight stirring in recognition, but he couldn't rule out that it was probably just him being hopeful in figuring it out so easily.

This arcane magic was hidden in a children's poem, something simple and song-like, so maybe the portal required a verbal component. So, what were the first things he had been taught to say as a child? Valan started by listing off various praises to the Winter Queen, then the general rules males were supposed to live by, to then speaking aloud various ancient sayings about Clan Anartes. Short poems rarely spoken nowadays, if ever taught at all.

The wall reacted to his last spoken poem about the dangers of too much freedom, the stone under the bloody arch developing a glassy sheen, rippling like a gust of wind on the surface of a lake. Valan let out a short laugh, spun around on a heel, and then became dizzy from the unrealized impact of so much blood loss.

"I did it!" Valan hummed a happy tune to himself. "I may not actually be an idiot after all. No, *genius*. I'm a genius. Ahaha!"

Sorn joined him after hearing all the noise, staring at the elf incredulously as if to say, *What insanity are you on about now?*

The lack of positive reaction from the half-sidhe over what had just been accomplished sobered Valan, suddenly embarrassed. He coughed, straightened to his full height, and pretended no twirling ever happened *at all.* Must have been someone else.

"Right. So, if my guess is correct, this should take us to the surface. Hopefully this lake isn't too far away—but if it takes longer than a few days to find, we'll have to return here," Valan warned.

Besides, how big could the surface world possibly be? He then eyed the portal, studying it closely for any errant pulses of energy that suggested it might be unstable. His lack of teleportation knowledge made him wary, worried he would mess everything up because of his inexperience. These particular sorts of pre-set, artificial tears in reality—the opening of a veil—was not something he'd ever seen, nor was he ever trained in since he wasn't female. That this hidden archway even existed had to be the creation of an ancient veiled one who had set the key for his clan's use only.

Valan directed his skeleton to enter the portal first, concentrating inwardly on the connection which told him this undead servant was still attached to him by an invisible rope. The rope did not break apart; the skeleton just felt distant. Too far away to be given commands, but the magic which animated the undead was still very much in place. No unusual reaction by the portal itself, either.

"It seems safe," Valan hedged.

"Follow *immediately* after me," Sorn warned.

"I really should be the one to—oh," the Firstblood replied, then sighed, watching the half-elf walk through the archway first. If the portal really was unstable, Valan had a higher chance of actually doing something about it. He quickly picked up his things and followed soon after, knowing what Sorn really worried about. Walking backwards into the portal, Valan used one last spell, one to stir up the dust and dirt into an even layer on the ground, to hide any trace they were ever there.

CHAPTER 10

TARRANT FOUND IT interesting that the guards did not patrol the deepest section of the torture area. Did Mairead know about this? Something she had ordered to be done, or did the Firstblood pay off the guards? Tarrant needed to find a way to bring it up in conversation with Mairead at some point. If it turned out Valan had resulted to bribery, it'd give Tarrant something to use against the sidhe for his own benefit.

Due to the curving, sloped nature of the path leading down, he couldn't see the bottom of it very well, but dared not get any closer. Especially since, despite how well he thought he'd hidden himself, Tarrant noticed the patrolling guards sometimes glancing in his direction and plugging their noses. He hadn't wandered around in the sewers for long before eventually backtracking, realizing the trick played on him, but apparently he'd been there long enough to ferment the bottom of his shoes. Another thing he needed to pay Valan back for.

Once he heard a noise—laughter?—Tarrant decided to risk going further down to see what was happening. The strange portal was hard to miss. Some of the runes looked thinner than others, more dried out, and he realized the wall was absorbing the blood into the stone. At the rate the blood was disappearing, he doubted the portal would remain open for much longer.

The safe, wise thing to do was to wait for another time to catch Valan alone—even *he* knew about the instability of torn veils. Chances were high that the Firstblood would use the same way to return, but that could take hours, days even, for that to happen, if at all. Valan was just as likely to return using another way. Mairead was even more likely to demand his attention before that came to pass. He could wait around in his room like a properly tame, useless consort until his services were desired, apparently so pathetic of a warrior that the worst of Clan Anartes could defeat him.

Tarrant walked through the portal. His surroundings immediately blurred into nothing, a complete absence of reality, and he struggled to breathe nonexistent air. When he took another step forward, the world rushed back into view to a place he had never seen before. Before he could properly get his bearings, a blade sliced through the skin on the back of his neck, followed by the burning, itching sensation that warned of poison.

Valan was sitting on a fallen stone pillar nearby, holding a small antidote bottle. His animated skeleton carrying books and the coffin case lingered next to him. The violin and bow rested against the pillar on the opposite side.

"I suggest you come up with a very good reason for why I should give this to you."

Tarrant was too in awe of his surroundings to respond immediately. He had already half-expected to be attacked as soon as he used the portal. Beyond where the Firstblood sat stretched a massive, dilapidated temple. Unlike a temple of An Cailleach, there was no frost motif, no bats; instead, the dusty, abandoned art of the temple's exterior featured ravens and hunting hounds of every shape and size imaginable. The bones of a dragon lay across the roof.

"What is a temple of the Erlking doing here?" Tarrant asked.

"The Erlking? This is a temple to Danu's consort?"

You've just doomed your entire clan by coming here, Tarrant thought. *By letting me see this, I can destroy your entire clan, not just you.*

If word ever got out that Clan Anartes had a portal which led directly to a temple of this god, all the Winter Goddess-worshiping clans would unite to obliterate it from existence. No sidhe was allowed to worship a consort of any sort over a goddess, much less have a huge place of worship dedicated to only the Erlking. The very thought left him giddy. All he'd have to do was report his findings to his old Piuthar. The only issue was explaining how he knew what an Erlking temple looked like in the first place, which would lead to his own death. He also doubted his god would appreciate Anartes' destruction if they were actually true believers, or even descendants of ones who could be converted back.

Valan got to live, for now.

Careful not to make any sudden movements, Tarrant slowly pulled out an amulet he wore hidden under his armor. The necklace held the symbol of two ravens with a round blue opal for one eye each. It matched the image above the central doors of the temple. "Give me the antidote and I'll explain everything."

Valan tossed him the bottle. Tarrant easily caught it and drank the contents quickly, also taking the opportunity to glance behind him to discover the identity of his attacker. He didn't see anyone, but the other sidhe did notice his searching.

"Don't even try to figure it out," Valan warned. "The next time won't be just poison. You live as long as you don't get curious. Now, what do you know about the Erlking?"

"Aside from having been Danu's last consort before he disappeared, he used to lead the Wild Hunt and was worshiped by not just sidhe males, but also a human following, too."

"I've never heard anything more about him other than being Danu's dead consort."

"And you know so much about everything? You, who has never stepped outside Fo Erkunia? How often have you even left your clan's tower?" Tarrant retorted. "You are not even a student of Crann Bethadh yet."

Valan scowled. "You can't be much older than me, so where did all this 'worldly wisdom' come from?"

"I grew up at a Clan Osseriates border town near the surface." Tarrant looked at the other sidhe in exasperation, seeing that Valan very clearly still doubted his words. "Just take a look at the Erlking's temple for yourself."

"I might as well, even though this really wasn't what I was hoping to find," Valan muttered, standing up. He started toward the temple. The skeleton remained behind. "And as a reminder: I'm the only one who can open the portal back to the city. It is in your best interest not to kill me."

He gestured to the raven statues, the images of dogs. "What are these meant to symbolize?"

"I thought you didn't trust my words."

"I don't. I plan on comparing what you tell me to what I can find out for myself once I leave here. So, it is *also* in your best interests not to lie to me."

Tarrant's eyes narrowed. He caught Valan's slip in using *I* instead of *we* when it came to leaving. "I know the basics of his faith. I also know of those who are more dedicated to worshiping the Erlking. The ones with artifacts and books. I can introduce you to them once *we* leave here."

Valan said nothing, just gestured at the decorative elements of the temple again as if knowing Tarrant was holding back.

"... The Erlking values knowledge, death, nobility, and the pursuit of power for our people," Tarrant said. "Ravens symbolize the trickery and defeat of others. Hounds are meant to represent the Wild Hunt."

The Firstblood frowned as if he had just thought of something. "What of thorns? Used in an archway."

"I don't know anything about that. Perhaps a more recent symbol of the Erlking."

"Especially not something easily found in a children's book?"

"What?"

"Nothing." Valan tried to open the double doors of the temple to no avail, which apparently had become stuck from not being used for so long. "Help me with this."

Between the two of them, they managed to drag one of the stone doors open by several inches, enough to squeeze through. Valan stepped back for the other sidhe to enter first. Tarrant looked at him in consternation.

"You're a warrior, right? Bravely marching forward into the Great Unknown is more your kind of thing," Valan kindly pointed out.

"And your contribution when things go awry?" Tarrant asked.

"Oh, I usually just stay back and be especially noisy." Valan held up his musical instrument. "Don't worry. I'll cheer you on."

"Wonderful," Tarrant muttered. Like most sidhe, he had a standard ranged weapon and short sword equipped, along with another hidden weapon, and his armor wasn't anything special, just the typical dark elven chainmail. He did not think his chances of survival were high when facing anything that had lived in an ancient temple for who knew how long. Especially if he was the only one actually fighting. The thing that had killed the dragon on the roof might be still around.

"If you are scared—"

"Shut up."

He drew his short sword and entered the temple, his footsteps stirring dust clouds into the air. Excluding current company, everything was quiet, a stillness to his surroundings as if he had intruded into somewhere timeless. The width of the temple *cella*[2] he stood within was several hundred *troighid* wide and *ceithir* times that long, lined on each side with massive pillars. Down the center rested rows upon rows of obsidian coffins that stretched all the way to the back of the room. Against the farthest wall was a giant statue of a robed man holding a spear crossed over his chest, looking down on the resting places of the dead.

"Not a temple, but a tomb," Valan commented as he followed Tarrant.

Most sidhe didn't leave much behind whenever they died. Yet, this new discovery could not be denied. What if the coffins held the bodies of other races that were at some point in history deemed worthy enough to keep? These could all be undead, waiting for a reason to reawaken. Enough corpses here, perhaps, to even kill a dragon. Tarrant didn't move any deeper into the room.

"As much as I want to take a closer look, I like living more," Valan said.

"Turns out I like living, too," Tarrant replied.

"Let's come back once we're better prepared."

Nothing blatantly dangerous prevented them from exploring the exterior of the building. One side of the cavern had collapsed at some point, damaging that side of the temple. Above the rubble, a giant hole in the cavern's ceiling was big enough for a dragon to fly through. Whatever was beyond the hole extended past the limits of their vision. Nothing more of note caught their attention, so they explored the back of the shrine.

---

2 **cella:** The inner chamber of a temple.

Three archways, like the one they had traveled through, formed a rough circle in what could have been the remains of a garden. All the vegetation had long since died, leaving only stone paths and raised beds.

Valan moved past the other sidhe to take a look at the archways first. "There are symbols I don't recognize at the top of each. Rather, they're written in a heavily archaic version of a language I do know, and it'd take me extra time to make sense of the words. I think they are names of places, but I've never heard of them before." He glanced askance at Tarrant, but the other sidhe shook his head, not knowing, either.

"Do you think you can open these portals?" Tarrant asked.

"Possibly, but this is enough exploration for now. I have a lot more research to do, and you have Erlking-related books to find for me," Valan said. He didn't wait for a response as he headed back toward the arch they had come through at the front of the temple.

Tarrant begrudgingly followed. They'd done only a cursory look around so far. There was still plenty that needed to be examined more closely to find anything of worth, but he couldn't deny not wanting to linger. If Lady Mairead called for him and he was not around, he wasn't sure he could come up with an excuse good enough to hide having been here, especially if tortured for answers. Still, Valan's sudden lack of interest seemed too abrupt.

With the Firstblood's back turned, Tarrant took the opportunity to glance around, hoping to spot the *other* who had managed to successfully hit him twice in surprise. He knew his true opponent at the training grounds wasn't Valan, but whoever had cut him with the poisoned knife.

He saw nothing unusual. The footsteps on the dusty floor were only his and Valan's. Some sort of spell? Magical flying weapons weren't unknown to him, but he'd be able to see the user cast the spell before summoning such a thing, or even initially draw the weapon if it was a physical thing already enchanted.

Once they reached the archway, Valan immediately started drawing the proper runes, apparently having forgotten Tarrant even existed. The Firstblood muttered a string of words under his breath and the portal came into being, appearing as a translucent ripple framed by the arch. He moved as if to go through the portal first.

"Hold on," Tarrant finally said. Valan could easily leave him trapped here by going through before him. "I'll go through first."

"Are you certain?" Valan asked. "I don't mind, either way. We've got the start of a great, mutually beneficial relationship going."

"I'm certain," Tarrant replied, glowering. Before the Firstblood could say another word, he strode through the portal. Valan gave him enough time to travel through to the other side, then wiped away one of the runes, the rippling surface disappearing like a popped bubble.

"He is going to be very upset with you," Sorn said in an amused tone. The half-elf came into view several steps behind Valan, having been walking on top of the other's footprints. They both wore the same sized shoes just for this method of subterfuge, with Valan needing to modify the extra space in his own boots with hidden compartments that kept his smaller feet from sliding around.

"I wish I could see the expression on his face once he figures out that only his footprints lead to and from the portal." Valan grinned. "If he has any sense, he won't go to his *dà* Piuthars about what he has seen here."

"I still think it'd be easier to just kill him."

"It may come to that," the Firstblood agreed. "It'll depend on how useful he turns out to be."

Valan eyed the dragon skeleton on the roof of the temple. The damage to the building. He hadn't wanted to say anything when his new "friend" was around, but he found it very interesting that the broken pillars and walls were only on the outside. That the dragon had not made it within the massive building before perishing, where all the undead were. If a battle had been fought between the two, there would have been more signs of a struggle. More corpses strewn about. So if a dragon dying on the temple roof was not enough to disturb any undead within the coffins, and the undead didn't react to him and Tarrant entering, then Valan guessed it should be perfectly safe to explore the interior.

He reentered the temple, this time walking past all the coffins until he stood in front of the giant statue, staring up at its face. He'd really wanted to take a closer look without having to be paranoid about Tarrant attacking him while he was distracted. To see what a representation of a deity of his people looked like who wasn't either Danu, An Cailleach, or the Seelie favored Summer Goddess, Brigid. He also hadn't wanted to explore the room earlier for fear of stirring up dust that would make it incredibly difficult for Sorn to hide from Tarrant.

Up close, he noticed the statue possessed two faintly blue glowing gems for eyes, one of which had cracks running through it, a feature hidden by the statue's downturned face. This sculpture, Valan suspected, was likely some sort of golem and the true protector of the temple. The sheer size of the temple, the number of coffins, and the scale of the Erlking figure towering above it all, suggested that at one point in time, this god was no minor power. Not something hidden away in fear of the Winter Queen.

"What happened to you?" Valan asked as if he expected the statue to actually answer. Nothing replied; even Sorn stood silently beside him.

If Tarrant had been telling the truth, then...how different would things be if dark elves learned earlier that there was more than goddesses to pray to? All his life, he'd been taught of how little the Winter Queen valued males, whose only role was to serve at best, along with valuing the purity and beauty of their race. Both of them would be seen as lacking due to Sorn's half-human side and Valan having grafted monster parts. Combine all of that with their affection toward each other, something An Cailleach most certainly saw as revolting, the subversion of their race's traditional gender roles...what, then, was the value of their two souls to some other dark elven god?

"I like the idea of this deity, but..." Sorn frowned, letting his words trail off. The Firstblood read the self-doubt on his face.

It was one thing for Valan to constantly have questions and doubts, coming up with as many plans as possible to deal with everything—he figured it at least partially helped keep them both alive—but it bothered him to see that Sorn might be having similar uncertainties.

"Hey," Valan said, moving to stand in front of the half-sidhe. "You are worth *everything* to me, you hear me? The rest of the world can burn for failing to recognize just how great you are. I still can't believe how lucky I am to have you in my life, and if all these stupid, supposedly divin—"

"I love you," Sorn said abruptly, shutting the other male up and leaving him flustered. He drew the other sidhe close, covetously wrapping an arm around Valan's waist, his other hand lightly stroking the side of his face. "And I'll crush *anyone* if they dare try to undermine us."

"I love you, too." Valan smiled, leaning against Sorn. He closed his eyes and slid his hand over the one resting against his cheek, keeping it there. "You and I, against them all."

Sorn kissed him, sliding his hands down to either side of Valan's waist. Valan eagerly brought their bodies flush against each other, before deepening their kiss and exploring each other with more than just their hands. There was plenty Valan wanted to accomplish, things he wanted to change, that would be a whole lot easier to do knowing at least one divine force out there might have similar goals and would want to help, but he'd find a way with just the two of them.

And if no deity found them worthy, then so be it; as far as Valan was concerned, the other sidhe must prove their worth to *him*. No one was going to stop him from doing what he wanted to do.

The loud *crack* of breaking stone above them was their only warning. Sorn pulled Valan out of the way of the falling rock just in time, protectively curled over the Firstblood to prevent him from being struck by the rubble. A roiling cloud of dust and debris obscured their vision. Valan used a spell to instantly settle the dirt so they could better see their surroundings.

"Are you alright?" Valan asked.

"I'm fine. You?" Sorn backed away, warily looking up at the statue.

"Same."

It was the upper half of the statue's face that had fallen off.

Well, that's it, then. This isn't the deity for us. I know a murder attempt when I see one, Valan thought. It made sense, he supposed. *If I had to watch people get sappy with each other in my temple, I might be tempted to drop a rock on them, too.*

"Valan, come look at this," Sorn said.

The half-sidhe was in the process of moving aside some of the fallen stone. Two large, oval-shaped sapphires about *dà dheug ordlach* across were partially buried in the rubble. Faint blue light still emanated from the center of the gemstones, same as when they'd been nested in the statue's eye socket. The already cracked sapphire didn't look like it had sustained further damage from the fall.

"Murder *and* a gift?" Valan asked, then he shook his head, seeing Sorn about to pick up one of the gems. "Let me see what kind of gift this is first."

Valan mentally compelled his animated skeleton to leave the books and case next to the portal, then enter the temple and come to him. A good start: no reaction from the gems once the skeleton picked them up. He directed the minion to move to a different spot and drop the sapphires on the ground several *troighid* apart, then followed it by drawing a ritual circle around each with dust, though completing only the runes of one for now. The runes he used were different from the ones from earlier; he wouldn't just sense the magic, but identify it this time.

Placing his hand on the uncracked gem, he whispered the words to activate the spell and tried to feel the magic within the sapphire. The Erlking's Sùil Clé; the magic it possessed was barely there, something distant and locked away. Most of its power had dissipated, but there was still a chance it could be restored for his use. He just had to be strong enough, clever enough, to bring it back.

Valan quickly sifted through the now-depleted abilities this gem had to offer, a smirk forming on his face. "Oh, you're going to be *fun*. All hail the Erlking."

"That good?" Sorn asked.

"Yes! Well, maybe," Valan said. "Right now it can only obscure the thoughts of the wearer."

Which, admittedly, while valuable to a race full of manipulators, it also meant most dark elves with an ounce of self-preservation already had something similar: less elaborate magical devices used to shield one's mind. Or, if no such items were available, to physically make oneself so uninteresting as to not be worth the attempt to mind-read. The second option was Valan and Sorn's preferred method; the more it seemed like something was worth protecting, the more likely other sidhe wanted it. While many often relied on truth-telling abilities to determine if someone was lying to them or not, Valan found an easy workaround by simply having the "truth" he gave them not being one that specifically answered any questions. However, what Sorn had told Valan of his interaction with Rian Cavii made it very clear that this method was no longer good enough.

"There are other abilities," Valan continued, "but it requires…souls?" He frowned. "Sacrifices, maybe."

"So, what, kill a bunch of gnomes? Dwarves?" Sorn shrugged. "That's easy."

"I'm not sure. Not yet." Valan moved to identify the cracked gem next, though he was pretty sure he would just find identical results. Still, it was better to not be surprised later on by any differences during a bad moment. He learned nothing new from The Erlking's Sùil Dheis, but he wondered about its stability because of already being partially broken, so he handed the other gem to Sorn.

"How do we use it?" the half-sidhe asked.

Valan held up his own gem in front of the tattooed half of his face. He hesitated briefly before letting it touch him, wondering if it would be such a good idea when he knew so little about The Erlking, but his magic detected no curses or anything harmful. At this point, denying a gift in a deity's own temple *would* be the thing that lead him to getting cursed. As soon as the gem touched his face, it turned into a sticky molasses that molded itself around his eye and sank into his skin.

In a panic, he dug his fingers into the edges of the mask, into his skin. The mask initially resisted his efforts before very reluctantly rising to the surface of his flesh and letting go of his face, forming back into a gem once removed. This thing possessed a definite life to it, which Valan found deeply unsettling. The only upside was that nothing had seemed different about his vision.

Not my brightest idea, Valan thought, although carrying around a pair of giant gems was certain to bring undue attention. At least he now knew he could take off the mask if it ever became too bothersome to wear. When he put it on again, Sorn mirrored him.

CHAPTER 11

Out of the *trí* arches located at the back of the temple, only *dà* still looked viable. The last, while technically still standing, was riddled with thin cracks, and Valan deemed it too risky to attempt opening. Valan was about to start adding runes along one arch, slicing open his fingers again using the extremely taut string of his violin bow, but Sorn grabbed his wrist to stop him.

"Heal yourself," Sorn demanded.

"What potions we have left need to be for you, for later," Valan replied. "We're on a time limit, remember? And we've already used a lot of it by exploring. A few cuts isn—"

"*Valan*," the half-sidhe practically growled.

The Firstblood's own temper rose. Opening that second portal for Tarrant had not taken as much out of him as the first one did, and as he got better at it, a third portal should be less draining. This wasn't as big of a deal as Sorn was making it out to be. Certainly, he still hadn't spent any time recovering, but it was just a*on* more portal.

He pulled his arm away. "I am fine."

"No, you are not," Sorn said. "Even with you wearing those earrings, I can tell you're barely standing upright."

"I can handle this, Sorn. Are you going to try to stop me every time something seems a little bit difficult for me?" Valan asked. "I *will* become stronger, but that can't happen if you interfere with every attempt I make to become so. Recovering from blood loss is nothing to me. It's like you want me to be pathetic."

Sorn glared at him. "You know that isn't what I meant."

"I already told you, I'm fine. That should be good enough for you." Valan turned away with a sense of finality to make it clear he really was done arguing, focusing back on drawing the runes for the portal, only for Sorn to stand in front of him.

"*I* am not done talking. Drink a damned health potion."

"Move," Valan warned. This time, he did not hide so much of his own anger. "It's bad enough I'm already putting up with these disgusting, useless wings for you because of your fear of me *getting hurt*, despite them being a constant reminder of Sabrene. *You* are the one prolonging any pain."

Sorn cursed at him, used all sorts of expletives describing the other's idiocy, and then faded back into the surrounding darkness. Valan went right back to creating the runes along the archway, his face expressionless even when he finished and the portal opened. Apparently, it didn't need him to say any ancient Anartes words, unlike the other one. Between this revelation and the name above the arch, it was clear to Valan that these portals were meant for more casual use, perhaps by more than just other dark elves.

He sent his skeleton through first, concentrating on the tether between them, and so felt it abruptly *snap*, losing his connection to the undead servant. Either the skeleton moved too far away or something was broken about the other side of the portal. Either way, it was too dangerous for him to travel through. He removed one of the runes to deactivate the portal.

The Firstblood sat down on the edge of a raised stone garden bed, finally allowing himself to pay more attention to his injured hand. It did look pretty awful, with all those cuts and irritated skin from dragging his bleeding digits across the archways. Not to mention the constant stinging pain, but it wasn't anything he hadn't dealt with before. Valan glanced over at the last potentially useful portal, resisting the urge to just go ahead and open it. He *was* tired from all the blood loss—but he'd still done it: *tri* portals without collapsing. He just wouldn't trust himself yet to do another without resting.

Valan pointedly refused to give in to the temptation to look for Sorn. He wasn't feeling guilty. Not at all. He had every right to be angry. Instead, he rummaged through his instrument case, removing the contoured felt bottom to take out some rations and a flat flask of water. He hadn't brought much food with him, thinking this was all going to be a short trip, but eating and drinking was the quickest way to recover from blood loss without using potions. Valan was in the process of spicing up his food with the help of a spell after a few bites proved the flavor to be inadequate when Sorn rejoined him.

The half-elf said nothing, grabbing Valan's old boots out of the bag before sitting down next to him. Sorn took out a knife and pried open the small compartment hidden in one of the heels, revealing *tri* tiny vials. The bottles were nothing more than minor healing potions, not capable of much. Something meant to be used only in emergencies. Sorn rolled all the vials between the fingers of one hand as if trying to decide on something.

Valan looked at his half-eaten ration and suddenly didn't feel like finishing. "I'm sorry I snapped at you. I know you only said what you said because you care. Just…" He held up a hand as if to say *hold on* since it looked like Sorn wanted to interrupt. "To me, it often feels like you end up being the one who does the most dangerous parts of our plans. I'm…just trying to compensate for that in my own way. Very badly," he admitted. "I don't enjoy seeing you hurt, either."

"I'll help you cut off those wings," Sorn finally said.

His words alone felt like a huge weight had been taken off of Valan. He had not been looking forward to the eventual argument about removing them. Worse than useless, the wings were a complete detriment to life in Fo Erkunia. His Fáinne Athrú might help hide his true appearance, but all it would take was one female demanding he remove his clothes, which was bound to happen, leading to a whole host of new problems. He couldn't even practice flying without fear of being seen. Things would be so much easier with them gone.

The cloth texture fell away from Valan's "cloak" to reveal the true bat-like leathery appearance. He stiffly stretched out his wings; holding them so closely to his back, unmoving for hours at a time, was not easy.

Valan noticed that the wings' membranes weren't quite as dark as when they'd been first attached to him, blending in more with the rest of his skin-tone. Becoming more an actual part of him as they healed.

"Why are you really so against me cutting these off?" Valan asked.

"Didn't it ever occur to you that the reason you struggle with walking so much is because you were always meant to fly?"

"… You read too much poetry."

"And whose damn fault is *that*?" Sorn retorted. Then, "That line sounded a lot better in my head."

"You can be very adorable when you want to be," the Firstblood's grin turned more into a self-satisfied smirk.

"Shut up." Sorn handed over one of the potions. "It's *only* one."

Valan begrudgingly took the vial and drank it, if only to call a truce between them. Sometimes things weren't worth continually arguing over, and he figured this was one of those times. It wasn't a bad thing for most of the cuts to heal; Valan tried not to think too hard about what that might mean for him later. He was about to do something that would upset Sorn again, anyway.

The Firstblood drew another ritual circle on the ground and summoned his familiar into existence. A tiny, fluffy, overly cutesy white bat started to fly around the circle, letting out a squeak of acknowledgment to its master. The creature's black button eyes belied a fiendish intent, as if in the process of thinking something truly nefarious. Only Sorn looked happy to see it.

"Squeakers!" Sorn held out his hand, on which the little bad landed to be petted. The half-sidhe obliged by using his thumb to rub Valan's familiar on its forehead. A suspicious glint entered Sorn's eyes. "Wait. Why did you summon Squeakers?"

"Squeakers is going on a little trip," Valan replied.

Sorn covered the little bat's ears. "No."

"Yes!" Master and familiar shot each other a truly malignant look. Squeakers made a point of letting Sorn rub its little round belly, still staring at Valan as if to say, *See? I get pets and you don't.*

"He could die."

"He shou—I mean," Valan corrected himself, "it is just a familiar. A tiny fey. A bit of spirit given temporary form. If that form is ever destroyed, I can always summon it again."

Squeakers chose that moment to fly under Sorn's hood and into his hair, wrapping itself in the blue-dyed strands. Valan couldn't prove it, but he was certain Squeakers just looked down its nose at him as if to say, *Ha ha, I can do this and you can't.*

"It will go through *all the* portals," Valan muttered. Then, something occurred to him. Something truly horrifying. The real reason Sorn had so little issue with his wings. "Sorn, love, you don't…actually have a *fetish* for bats, do you?"

"Don't be ridiculous." Sorn glared at him, the tiny bat still playing with his hair. "I will never understand why you hate Squeakers so much. You *chose* to make him look like this."

"I was *deich* when I first summoned it," Valan said. "And then you gave it that ludicrous name. The one time I changed its form to something more elegant, you cried."

"Now that's a lie," Sorn said. Valan raised an eyebrow at him. "I don't remember that. What I *do* remember is you threatening to set Squeakers on fire. I thought you followed through with that threat."

"It kept vomiting bug parts all over my books because you were overfeeding it."

"By the way, are you going to finish eating the other half of that ration?"

"Sorn…it's just a spirit," Valan said. "It doesn't need to eat."

Squeakers started chewing on some of Sorn's hair as if to deny that claim, those beady little eyes raised in challenge at Valan. *I'm the master. You serve me.*

The things I put up with. Valan grimaced. "Let's make a deal." The tiny fiend perked up a little more. "Every time you go through a portal, Sorn will feed you a treat. If you die while doing this, then the next time I summon you, you get to spend the whole day with Sorn. Everyone agreed?"

"I still don't like it. It's not like Squeakers won't feel anything by dying," Sorn said. Much to his surprise, Squeakers disentangled itself and flew away from him to land on Valan's shoulder. The miniature familiar made a cooing sound at the half-sidhe as if to say, *There, there.*

The bat and Valan shared identical smug expressions. Sorn tilted his head to the side in acknowledgment of his defeat.

"While you see to the portal, I'm going to explore the hole in the ceiling," Sorn said. "Maybe the dragon came from the surface. We might not need these portals after all."

"Alone? But...take Squeakers with you at least. That way it can tell you once I'm done here...or tell me if you get into any trouble."

"I'm not going to leave the cavern without you, Valan. I just want to get closer and see if there is more to explore."

"Well, alright. Do you want to be affected by some gravity altering magic? With all these portals attached to veils nearby, I can command the elements to do that for you."

"Sure." He lifted open part of his cloak to reveal a thin rope and folding grappling hook that was attached to the underside. "I'd originally planned on using these, but being able to walk up the walls and across the ceiling would make things go faster."

Valan moved over and rested a hand on his shoulder, then sent his will out into the world's elements to obey him. To make the gravitational pull of Sorn's surroundings whatever direction the rogue wanted. Defying the natural order of this realm wasn't permanent, but would last long enough for Sorn to make use of it. Valan didn't remove his hand immediately once done, not quite looking up into Sorn's face.

"We're...good now, right?" Valan asked.

"Yeah. I was more upset with myself than with you," Sorn admitted.

Even now, Valan knew if their roles were reversed and he had been the one to decide to check things out on his own, Sorn would have thrown a fit. A pattern was emerging in their relationship that Valan didn't like, one of Sorn constantly pushing what he wanted onto Valan, all but forcing him to just accept it.

Sorn eyed those black wings. "Love, the next time I try to make you do something you don't want, just set me on fire, alright?"

"Really?" Valan asked. "We can start that right now."

Sorn frowned at the disturbing new gleam in the sidhe's red eye. "… Let's stay together and not have one of us wander off alone."

"Excellent suggestion! I approve whole-heartedly. Let's explore wherever that dragon came from together later. We can try this last portal now to see where it goes and then come back if that doesn't work out."

The last of the three portals flared to life.

"You go in, you come back, then you get a treat," Valan said to the fluffy white familiar.

Sorn held up a piece of dried rations—now bug-flavored—as a means of encouragement. Squeakers excitedly dove through the portal. Valan attempted to see through his familiar's eyes, but wherever the spirit had gone, it was too far away. The two males exchanged looks, with Sorn clearly more anxious than Valan, but after a moment, Squeakers returned. The little fiend let out a triumphant squeak and snatched the treat away from Sorn, settling itself comfortably on one of his shoulders to eat.

While Sorn went through the portal after strapping the instrument case across his back, Valan still held onto the violin, deciding to leave the three books behind, before following suit.

His brief trip from one part of reality to the next was made further abrupt by Sorn pushing him out of the way of an incoming arrow. A very rattled Valan found himself squashed between a stalagmite and Sorn as he tried to make sense of his surroundings. The rogue unsheathed two daggers.

The cavern was riddled with stalactites and stalagmites, some forming natural pillars where the mineral-rich water dripping from the ceiling had combined the formations together from dried sediment. Three of the largest stalagmites had been hollowed out to serve as guard towers, each manned by skeleton archers. All three guards aimed their shortbows at Sorn and loosed arrows as he ran out of cover to jump up onto the side of a stalactite within sixty *troighid* of the undead guard towers. Two arrows narrowly missed him, with the third piercing his upper back. From where he now stood, sideways and parallel to the ground on the hanging rock,

Sorn launched both his daggers at an archer, shattering the skeleton into pieces from the sheer force of his throws. He then faded into the deeper darkness of the ceiling.

Valan peered around the stone he hid behind to note the location of the skeleton archer farthest away, before moving out of sight again. He manipulated the surrounding air to condense it into hardened shards, sending them swirling around the stone pillars to hit the distant skeleton, slicing through brittle, undead bones before reverting to its normal density. The broken remains of the skeleton collapsed onto itself. He started to hum a tune.

The remaining skeleton looked around for a visible target, its bones creaking in apparent frustration, and then focused on the sound of footsteps running up the side of its tower. The undead archer aimed his bow over the side and fired down, hitting nothing. Sorn disengaged from the shadows directly behind the archer and severed the skull from the rest of the body, sending splintered bits of bone flying as the unholy light in its eyes faded. Valan stopped humming and the footsteps disappeared.

As Sorn retrieved his thrown daggers, Valan scanned the area for any other threats or anything otherwise unusual. Nothing more seemed in need of killing, at least. Half-hidden in the clusters of stalagmites were more arches with unknown names etched along the tops of them. Four possible portals with more names to places Valan knew nothing about.

The Firstblood fought against his annoyance over discovering more proof that he really wasn't as learned as he thought himself to be. "Let me tend to that arrow in your back. Did you remember to bring bandages?"

"I always have bandages," Sorn said. "And likely still have everything else you wanted me to carry over the past few years."

Valan knew the underside of Sorn's cloak was nothing but layers of pockets full of things he thought he might need at some point. Wearing something like a backpack to carry his things served more as an obvious sign to other sidhe that *There Be Loot Here*; considering Sorn did a lot of his own "acquiring", he wanted to avoid tempting others. From one of these pockets, he handed Valan a flattened roll of gauze.

Sorn's cloak and armor had taken the brunt of the damage the arrow could have inflicted, with the tip of the arrowhead managing little more than deeply scratching his skin. Still, even once the arrow was removed, Valan closely examined the wound for signs of poison and used two small squares of gauze to clean and cover it, then used his will to force the pierced armor and cloak to mend. The pressure from the armor should be enough to keep the bandage in place.

"Poisoned?" Sorn asked.

"Doesn't look like it. No sign poison was ever used to coat it, either."

"Long dead or not, what down here doesn't use poison?"

"That is odd," Valan agreed. "I really wish I knew more about the history of this area."

Sorn eyed the new set of portals. "We don't have the time to explore all of these. Look, let's go back, I don't hav—"

"You are getting what you want," Valan interrupted. "So what if we've gone incredibly off-course and uncovered untold ancient mysteries? One of these must still lead to the surface. We've still got time." He noticed Sorn's frown. "Just a few more portals. A full day hasn't passed yet… probably."

"Fine, and then we'll go back. Try the other choices," Sorn begrudgingly said.

Valan scowled, neither agreeing nor disagreeing, and started working on the runes of the closest archway. Squeakers flew out of Sorn's hood, where it had been hiding this entire time, and went through the portal as soon as it opened. The creature just as quickly came back, covered in spores, its tiny white wings flapping frantically to get the flecks off. Then it suddenly stiffened and crashed to the ground. Sorn jumped to the side of another hanging stalactite to hide in the shadows, and Valan summoned a large sphere of darkness as he backed further away. Six bulbous, vaguely humanoid bipedal creatures wrapped in vines and moss burst through the portal.

Two daggers thrown from the dark above sunk to the hilt into the flesh of two of the plant creatures. A discordant shriek from a violin followed by the beat of other disturbing waves of sound emitted from the center of the magical darkness, rattling the floor directly underneath the portal. Cracks appeared in the ground, the rock lurching under the feet of the monsters. Tremors knocked four of the six intruders to the ground with enough force to break bones. One of the monsters that remained upright expelled a cloud of spores into the surrounding area as the other one ran into the darkness, wildly swinging a clump of vines at the source of discordant music. The sound came to a screeching halt as the plant monster hit its target.

"Valan!" Sorn shouted.

"I'm fine!" Valan yelled back, his voice strained. The half-sidhe obliged by throwing a dagger at the sixth walking plant, hitting it in the head, but the creature remained very much alive. Sorn drew his last two daggers, the first, and tenth anniversary knives, and ran across the ceiling to be directly above the monster. The balance in the blades was so bad that they'd be too ineffective to throw, so he would have to get up close to make use of them.

The four fallen vine-beasts recovered, rushing toward the voice in the magical darkness, while the sixth creature Sorn had just hit ran for the portal. The creatures managed to clear ten *troighid* before another ground tremor—accompanied by Valan's rough instrumental—roiled underneath them, this time smashing them all into the fracturing rock. Only the one nearest the portal survived the impact, but not for long; Sorn dropped from the ceiling to land directly on top of it, using the weight of his own body to smash the creature to the ground and drive both daggers into where its spine should be, killing it. Valan ran out of his globe of darkness and hurriedly removed one of the portal's runes to close it against reinforcements.

"You hurt anywhere?" Sorn asked.

Valan shook his head and bowed, showing off that his musical instrument was now down a string, and dispelled the darkness he had summoned. The missing metal string was wrapped around the neck of the fifth creature, tying it to the stalagmite it had attacked after mistaking it for Valan. Normally a violin had strings made of either animal guts or hair, but some dark elves like himself preferred sturdier materials enchanted to produce traditional sounds, to allow for alternative uses such as garroting. Every time the monster struggled, the string dug deeper into its neck, the wound seeping a greenish ooze. Clouds of spores wafted around it.

"These are fascinating. The books really don't do them justice. It's... an undead and plant, yet somehow alive with its own mind? I wish I had the time to study it further." Valan's eyes were alight with interest, though he made no move to get closer due to the spores.

"We could always leave it here for you to study another time," Sorn suggested.

"I'd rather not give this one a chance to escape," Valan said. "Besides, I suspect there's an entire colony to explore beyond that portal if I'm still curious later." The Firstblood took the time to conjure several globes of acid to finish off the living undead fungus himself. "So, onto the next portal. This is exciting! Finally, a chance to use some of these spells on something."

Sorn eyed Valan warily. "How bad is your headache from using all that magic?"

"Oh, barely any pain."

"Love—"

"I know, I know; I'll be careful," Valan replied distractedly, already wandering over to the next closest archway. "And don't worry! I'll see to Squeakers in a moment."

Sorn sighed and went to collect his knives. By the time he was done, Valan had already brought his familiar in front of another arch, talking to the bat.

"Yes, you ended up as collateral damage, but it wasn't like I tried to specifically kill you—and hey, now you get to spend a full day with Sorn!" Valan said with forced cheerfulness.

Squeakers gave a very miffed squeak in response.

"Squeakers, come here," Sorn called. The bat launched itself into the crook of his arm, snuggling there. He scratched the familiar behind its tiny pointed ears. Valan watched the darkly clad rogue with gray eyes petting something more akin to a fluffy toy, and smiled.

"You're so—" Valan began.

"Don't."

"...mine," Valan finished. His smile widened slightly. *What? Expected me to say something else?*

"Can't argue there," Sorn replied. "After Squeakers and I spend the day together, of course."

Valan contemplated if this was enough of a *set on fire* worthy offense. He suddenly felt more motivated to open the next portal just to send his familiar through it, and so decided to focus on that. Sorn watched Valan's newfound gusto suspiciously, though didn't say anything when the runes were drawn and the portal opened, Squeakers flying through. The bat returned with a triumphant squeak.

CHAPTER 12

THE LIGHT OF the waning gibbous moon shone through the massive hole in the cavern's ceiling. Water poured from one side of the gap to form a small pool of muddy brown, too dense to see more than a couple inches deep. Vegetation that Valan had only seen pictures of grew all along the floor, not quite obscuring the rusted remains of an ancient battle. The broken, ruined pieces of sidhe-like weaponry helped him easily identify the warriors on one side of the ancient skirmish, but he did not recognize the relics of the other faction centered around a destroyed archway: a human family crest on corroded shields.

He wanted to take a closer look, but he was struggling to adjust to the increased amount of light. Dull twinges of pain coming from both the base of his wings and his synesthesia eye confirmed Valan's suspicion that he had not dared to share with Sorn just yet. Part of the reason he had so little interest in exploring the hole in the cavern that a dragon had caused, which the half-sidhe thought might lead to the surface, was because Valan already had a good idea that it probably didn't.

"It is true then," Valan muttered.

He'd hoped the tales of Otherworld-based magic failing on the surface, especially of Unseelie abilities becoming useless under this world's sunlight, were just something made up to scare elves from attempting to escape from their clans. The string Sabrene had used on his monster parts, being partially from the Otherworld, could lead to his wings and eye rotting away from being too far away from a veil. The wings falling off he wasn't too concerned about, but having an acid slime gain its independence so close to his brain all but promised a very painful death.

He made a point of avoiding the moonlight, staying within the deepest shadows near the portal, and noticed that the pain did subside slightly. Just proximity to the surface was enough to make him feel uncomfortable.

Sorn also looked a bit uneasy, though he seemed to have no issue with moving around under the light to look for anything that might attack them. Years of adjusting to reading books by candle and fairy glow turned out to be helpful to them both. Valan guessed Sorn's issue had more to do with it no longer being dark enough to fade into the surrounding shadows practically at will; he'd have to actually put forth an effort to hide here.

"I'm not going to like your next explanation, am I?" Sorn frowned as if noticing the odd role-reversal of him being out in the open while Valan stayed in the dark.

"Yes, well, I'd like to start off by saying I wasn't completely sure what could happen. Like nothing! Nothing was just as likely—and this could still be temporary until my body adjusts completely, I mean…" Valan realized he was starting to babble and so took a deep breath to steady himself. To get it over with. "There's a chance I could slowly waste away and die if I stay on the surface away from a veil, especially under direct sunlight, because of the kind of magic used in converting an acid slime into an eye."

"And you decide to tell me this now, when we're so close to said surface?" Sorn walked over and grabbed Valan by the shoulders, trying very hard not to physically shake some sense into him. "What if the sun was out when we walked through a portal? You could have died, Valan!"

"Oh, that's simple; if the sun were out, I'd have just run back through," Valan said. "See? Easily avoidable problem."

"You…are a complete idiot. No sense of self-preservation *at all*," Sorn growled. "None of this is worth risking so much. If you had told me sooner—"

"You'd force me to stay back? To never leave?" Valan asked. "It's not like I wanted to reach the surface entirely just for *you*. I don't want to only…read about things. I wanted to see the moon for myself. With my own eyes. See what all the fuss is about. A chance to reach the top of the mountain and demand the three-headed beast to grant me my wish."

Sorn abruptly hugged him, and while Valan normally didn't mind a face full of leather-clad muscular chest, he was being held a little tighter than he was entirely comfortable with. Valan didn't tell the half-elf to let him go, even hugged him back, and waited for Sorn to loosen his hold on his own.

"This moonlight isn't going to be a problem…*right*? It is only full sunlight that is an issue?" the half-sidhe grumbled. "You really are going to be the death of me."

"R-right." *If you die, I will follow soon after,* Valan promised. "This'll be *fun*."

Sorn made a noise that could almost be mistaken for a laugh, relaxing his hold even more. "This better be the last thing you haven't told me about."

Valan reluctantly pulled away, making sure there was some space between them. "Do you remember when you stole that cake from Isla, then I asked you to go get some utensils from the kitchen, and by the time you came back all the cake was gone and I told you Lesdorl stole it?"

"I do. Lesdorl was one of my first kills." By the tone of his voice, Sorn almost sounded wistful.

"It was me. I ate the entire cake."

"Oh, I know. I killed him because I hated how he kept looking at you."

"*I* didn't know that. I thought you were that mad because you didn't get to eat chocolate for the first time."

"That wasn't the first cake I ever stole. It was just the first one I wanted to share."

Valan's eyes narrowed. "Hold on. How much have *you* been keeping from *me*?" Sorn tried his best not to look guilty. "We're going to have many long, *thorough* conversations once we're not so busy," he warned, then glanced at the moon, "but for now…" the Firstblood knelt down next to one of the few places on the ground not covered by plants and used a finger to draw a crude copy of the surface map he had destroyed earlier. "We are looking for a place with lots of sand. There should be a river *here* that leads to a lake with a pyramid-shaped building next to it, with some mountains. Along the lake's shore should be what we're looking for."

"Tell me you know more than this."

"It's a location, a town I think, in the southwest named Lez Ghad Beduin. In some place called Orontes," Valan said, stumbling over the names since they weren't in a language he was familiar with, much less entirely understood. Sorn repeated his comment. Valan glared at him. "This is your big chance to wander off and get yourself killed. Enjoy it. With Squeakers."

Sorn raised an eyebrow. "You're staying put?"

"If this place is truly close to our destination, I need to take the time to rest my mind so I can use what magic I can here," the Firstblood said. "Along with staying out of the light as much as possible. I'll look through Squeakers' eyes occasionally."

The rogue went to the cave wall, testing his footing against it to see if he could still walk vertically up its surface. His foot no longer sticking to the stone was a sign that the gravity-altering magic had worn off. Sorn took out his grappling hook and attached a thin rope to it, throwing the hook over the edge of the hole. He had to do this a couple of times before the hook finally snagged on something solid enough to support his weight.

Sorn climbed the rope with ease and pulled himself over the edge, remaining crouched low as he surveyed his surroundings. Squeakers snuggled against the side of his neck. He petted the creature with the tip of his finger, but he did not turn around when he felt a brief gust of wind and heard someone stagger a few steps next to him.

"Thought so," Sorn said.

"I might be really dumb."

"Not arguing that."

"This is an incredibly bad idea."

"Yes."

"And you shouldn't have to face all this alone," Valan added. "This is…a lot of green."

Valan mimicked Sorn in avoiding touching the foreign plants as much as possible. Surely, most were poisonous, if not also being capable of releasing spores or making noises for nearby creatures to kill them easier. Those surface books made it sound like most of the greenery in forests were benign, helpful even, but those could just as easily have been lies. This was, after all, the part of the world that suffered under the horrors of a Seelie-cursed burning sun.

The lack of a true ceiling was incredibly uncomfortable, and if Valan dared pay too much attention to this “sky”, it might feel like he would somehow fall upwards at any moment. The sidhe spared the rogue a worried look. Sorn might think himself incredibly skilled at blending in with the surrounding dark, barely requiring more than a thought and a step to the side, but this place was too bright even at night. He did seem to struggle a lot less to see than Valan, and he thought that had more to do with the human side of Sorn—a side Valan knew the rogue had always viewed as more of a liability. One the society they grew up in would always hold against him, though Valan had tried to make it clear to the half-elf that it never bothered him.

“Light elves are truly disgusting for loving all of this,” Valan said, looking down at the ground. At all the fallen forest debris in different stages of decomposition, all the tiny weird insects, the wiggly things, the sticks that’d be easy to trip over. So many unusual smells and noises. “They *dance* in places like this? Might as well roll in the mud and squeal.”

Sorn grinned, finally standing up. “I don’t think you can navigate without alerting everything, so stay here. I’m going to climb this…tree to see how far the forest extends. Look for any of that sand of yours.”

Valan just nodded, moving to examine a nearby stone of unusual shape, and immediately snapped a stick under his boot. His next step made a squelching noise as his foot sank into some mud and leaves. He made a face.

The rock that had caught his attention was composed of ridges all along one side, which reminded him of a pillar, if buried deep into the ground. In an artistic style that did not match the carved marble’s elegance were rough engravings of human-like figures with pronounced flat, triangle-shaped faces. He looked around and saw other pieces of ruined buildings scattered about the forest, mostly covered in vines and other foliage. A larger piece of a surviving mural was a short distance away, but he figured that wandering off from the relative safety of the cavern's hole wasn't a good idea. Besides, too many things in these woods made noise; he could be attacked by something feral any moment.

Sorn returned from his tree climbing adventure shortly thereafter, if a little paler than usual, from what the Firstblood could see of his face.

"What's wrong?" Valan asked.

"There is too much sky. How is it not bothering you?"

"... I don't know what you are talking about. We're in a big cave with an illusion above." Valan almost sounded like he'd actually convinced himself.

"Right. A big, bright cave."

"Just like when somebody creates too much fire at a party," Valan said, keeping his voice even. "Or when the Archwizard lights all the candles in the library."

Sorn squeezed his eyes shut briefly. "Not anything we can't handle."

The sidhe walked closer, trying not to wince from all the noise he made. Truly, this was a nightmarish land. "If a bunch of dirt-wallowing, plant-hugging weaklings can deal with all of this, then we certainly can as well."

"I *hate* climbing trees."

Valan grinned. "That's the spirit."

The half-sidhe focused on only the Firstblood. They were standing in just another cave, after all. Nothing else worth looking at. "From what I could tell, this forest extends pretty far. I didn't see anything like what you described. There looked to be mountains—giant stalagmites—to one side, on the far end of the cavern."

"So, we go back to trying out portals until we find one in Orontes." Valan glanced at the moon and then very quickly focused back on Sorn. Compared to the rogue, he might have more experience hiding his emotions in front of others, but he couldn't completely obscure how much this was all bothering him, too. "We're not too late yet."

Sorn used his rope and grappling hook to descend back through the opening, while Valan awkwardly flew down and tried to keep from crashing into the cave floor. This time, he kept his hair out of the way. The Firstblood opened the only other portal nearby that wasn't destroyed, sending Squeakers through. The familiar returned to pronounce squeakily that it was indeed not dead, so the two males returned below.

They had soon developed a pattern of behavior for the interconnecting layout of portals: a quick exploration around a cave for enemies and exits to the surface, kill whatever they could, run away from anything they could not, and then take a break after every four portals. Some of the portals led right up to the surface. They emerged upon an abandoned warehouse full of crates with painted symbols they recognized as belonging to an Unseelie merchant, a mountainside of snow and ice, a jungle with brightly colored birds, and this latest one.

"Look, Valan: sand. Water." Sorn did nothing to hide the sarcasm in his voice. A very fat-looking Squeakers rested on his shoulder. He leaned against the side of the cave mouth to steady himself as a wave of ocean water swept over the ankles of his boots before returning further out to sea. The froth left behind by the wave swirled over the pale green rocks and sand around his feet. Beyond the cave was nothing but the unusually colored sand and rock, dotted here and there with the remains of broken towers made of the same stone. Not a single tree nor any other kind of vegetation masked the night sky from view, the moon past its zenith on the way to descending below the horizon.

"I don't understand this. Is this even still the surface world? I..." Valan, standing deeper in the cave to stay more within the shadows next to an archway, scowled at everything in general. "All the maps I could get a hold of made the surface seem small, insignificant. Half of what is mentioned in those books has to be lies, especially since Cernunnos blatantly changed some of the text." Valan changed the tone of his voice to match his father's. "'*In Crociatonum nobody wears pants*' and '*Here be hot dwarf ladies.*'"

"Want to kill them?" Sorn pointed to a group of approaching humans dressed in strange, flowing garb they'd never seen before. When the pair had first exited the portal, they unintentionally scared a human child who had been picking up seashells. The child screeched at the sight of them and ran away to a nearby village made largely of tents. And now half the village's inhabitants had decided to run toward them while fully armed with implements so crude and blunt that the weaponry looked more like something sidhe warriors would only practice with.

"I suppose. No idea what they're shouting about though," Valan said. His understanding of surface languages was shaky at best; whatever language these humans used wasn't familiar at all. One arm's worth of his leather armor was gone, having removed it earlier to expose more skin to cut for blood for portals. His violin, carried in his sliced up hand, was now down to its last two strings. He walked past Sorn to exit the cave, trying not to flinch from the uncomfortable glow of the moonlight.

It's so nice they've grouped up like that, waving a little...flag? Valan wondered, though came to the conclusion that whatever it meant didn't matter all that much. It was many against two; it'd be incredibly foolish to let a potentially dangerous group approach and attack first. He raised his undamaged arm and pointed his index finger at a human in the center of the approaching group, smirked, and said, "Boom."

The area he pointed at exploded in a massive, circular wave of fire that burned the humans and boiled the thin layer of water they walked on, hissing steam rising and scalding their skin further. In contrast, an icy wind carried their screams far across the beach, along with the stench of burned and boiled flesh. As the humans died, charred remains collapsing, the image of Valan faded, being an illusion. The real him stood several feet away and off to the side, with the cuts all along his arm glowing that sickly, necromantic green before healing.

"Looks like you got them all," Sorn said, shielding his eyes from the fire and wrinkling his nose from the smell. His scarf wasn't thick enough to mask the scent of burnt flesh completely. "No...the big one there is trying to stand—never mind, dying spasms. Congratulations."

"Learning more about how magic interacts with killing things this past while has been exceedingly helpful," Valan admitted, rubbing his one normal eye. The light from the fire had bothered him. Living underground with mostly other near-immortals meant he didn't have as many chances to try out magic against more fragile races to see what worked the best. "I've noticed you have a couple of new tricks as well."

"Had to adjust to fewer shadows. And dodging your spells," Sorn replied, eyeing Valan warily.

"In my defense, that was my first time creating a lightning bolt and I wasn't expecting it to bounce off the walls so much… I'll, uh, do better."

Sorn waved that aside. "You want to kill off the rest of the village? They might have stuff worth stealing and we're running low on some basics."

"I doubt it'll be worth the effort. I suspect the ones who are left will be more likely to run away. I'd rather not waste time chasing them down just for a few rations." Valan gestured at the steaming pile of corpses. "They knew enough about sidhe to be scared, but still thought they could kill us with sheer numbers. No magic of their own, half of their weapons made from wood, barely anything that qualified as proper armor, no tactics, and they lived in *tents*. A bunch of weaklings who'd probably have survived longer as slaves than out here on their own."

"Wonder if most surfacers are this easy to kill."

"If they are, then I have some serious questions as to why our race hasn't conquered them all by now."

"Something, something, *An Cleas*. Iron."

"Probably." Valan knelt down to examine the oddly colored sand, grabbing a handful. The strange aura of something alien wasn't from his being unfamiliar with his surroundings, but from a different magic infusing the ground. Judging from all the broken towers made from the grainy substance, he hadn't been the only one who considered the value of this green rock. The bits of stone reminded him of peridot, though he'd need to study it further, consulting a few specific books back home to be certain. "Do you have an extra pouch?"

Sorn begrudgingly removed an empty sack from his cloak and tossed it toward Valan. He shook his head in disbelief. "We're passing up all those supply crates to collect sand instead."

"Crates that'll take months to properly go through, possibly owned by an organization that wouldn't mind murdering us to get it all back," Valan said. "It might serve us better to…exchange it for some 'good will'."

"You really think some other Unseelie would agree to owing us favors?"

"I didn't say it had to be with them. A few independent sidhe come to mind." Valan finished filling the bag and handed it to Sorn. He knew better than to try to carry a sack around openly. Not just because of not wanting to tempt thieves, but for whatever reason, Sorn had gotten it into his head that even though the Firstblood wore enchanted trinkets, carrying anything was still too taxing for him. It wasn't like Valan enjoyed having a lot of gear anyway, so if Sorn wanted to be the walking oddity arsenal, then all the more power to his many pockets. "You know…a lot of those 'romantic' poems dealt with rolling around on a beach. I don't really see the appeal; this sand would get everywhere."

"I wondered why you hadn't tried to throw me down yet. We can still take a stroll, hold hands, breathe in the fresh scent of burning corpses." Sorn grinned. "What is there not to enjoy?"

They looked up at the sky in all its ever-expansive glory, without a single tree obscuring the view, and hurriedly left the exotic beach to try out more portals, eventually coming across another that led to the surface. This latest archway rested in the middle of a much smaller building than the temple to The Erlking, if made from the same material and also long neglected, going by the amount of dust. The interior wasn't more than a thirty *troighid* wide, octagon-shaped room. At one point, it looked like statues of ravens used to rest in each corner, but only broken pieces remained. Even the archway looked like someone had tried—and failed, considering it still worked—to destroy it with a hammer, that someone likely being the heavily armored, desiccated corpse on the ground next to it, welding said weapon.

A badly scorched shield nearby had another human family crest, if different from the one Valan had seen earlier. Each of the eight walls contained a door, with one door being slightly larger than the others and framed by two pillars.

The two of them checked around for traps, discovering nothing unusual, and then stood on either side of the largest door. Since the door looked like it would swing open toward them, as Sorn reached to open it, Valan created the illusion that the door remained closed.

On the other side of the door awaited yet another forest. The trees were a different kind of compact greenery than what they had seen at other locations. Tall vegetation curved out and nearly twisted onto itself, with the leaves looking more like round clusters of spikes. In sharp contrast, rigidly straight plants covered in short needles grew alongside the curvy trees. Tall, dry brush Valan couldn't tell was dead or not made it difficult to see beyond a few *troighid* in the forest. Sorn glanced over at Valan, seeing the disappointment on the other man's face.

"I'll climb up to see if what we're looking for is beyond here," Sorn said. He didn't wait for a response, but got one anyway when Valan grabbed his arm, cautioning him against leaving the building.

"Not yet. There is something wrong here," Valan replied, voice low. "It's too quiet compared to the other forest. Look at all the bones underneath the brush."

Sorn frowned, scanning his surroundings again for any movement, any sign of danger. He merged into the room's interior shadows to then step out of the darkness under the closest trees in the small clearing. This new skill of the half-sidhe's was something Valan found incredibly unnerving; it was something that did not come naturally to either a rogue, human, or a sidhe, and similar short-distance teleporting spells were still above Valan's own abilities to use. Not for the first time did he wonder about Sorn's parentage.

Unlike the other forest, a thick acrid scent pervaded the air, further emphasizing all the remains scattered about on the dry ground. While the bones were of all conceivable sizes and thus certainly belonged to multiple creatures, some were longer than Sorn was tall, and they began to move in protest over such a slight invasion into their territory.

A gigantic skeletal structure assembled itself and lurched upright, towering over the two puny people. Wings of bone stretched and strained against the canopy of trees, breaking branches and showering needles to further expose a sky of changing colors to herald the coming of dawn. The undead dragon's long, whip-like tail thrashed deeper within the forest, knocking down whole rows of trees with such force that the very ground trembled. Sorn stood stock still, incapable of looking away from the horned skull of this creature that loomed above, jaws big enough to swallow him whole. He didn't even notice when Squeakers let out a terrified squeak, followed by a noise that sounded more like a fart. A stream of bat guano dirtied his shoulder and ran down the front of his armor.

Still hiding behind the doorframe and incapable of maintaining the illusion over the doorway due to his own fear, a single thought popped into Valan's head. His voice reminiscent of a noise Squeakers would make, he asked, "Do you know where Lez Ghad Beduin is?"

CHAPTER 13

"Sidhe?! *Here*?!" the undead dragon roared, its breath so overwhelmingly fetid that Valan backed deeper into the room along the wall. He decided he didn't really need directions after all. The growing light spilling through the doorway made it even more difficult for him to see, the unsettling ache in his wings and eye increasing. The most pragmatic solution would be to close the door to block out the sun and then go through the portal in order to escape the dragon, but that meant abandoning Sorn.

Valan reached through his magical link to Squeakers and made the bat smack the half-sidhe across the face with a wing. The abrupt motion startled Sorn enough to at least temporarily break free from the devastatingly intimidating aura of the dragon, allowing him to shift from his current bit of shade back into the shadows within the building. Seeing the Firstblood using his wings to try to block out more of the increasing sunlight finally clued Sorn in to what was going on, so he hurriedly closed the door leading outside, his efforts failing completely when the tip of a giant claw got in the way.

"Puny sidhe! Hiding in there will do you as much good as the last person who tried," the undead dragon chortled mockingly.

Sorn drew his knives and leaned against the door as if he'd somehow be able to keep it closed against the might of an undead dragon. He looked down incredulously at his two daggers as if he couldn't believe what he might have to do, along with how successful he'd turn out to be.

"Valan, go through the portal first, I'll—"

"I didn't smack you just for you to play at heroics," Valan cut in, guessing at what Sorn planned to do as soon as he stepped through the portal. Probably because he was thinking about doing the same thing once he convinced Sorn to go through first. No need to share that, though.

The two glared at each other. Nobody, apparently, was going to be allowed to do anything self-sacrificing at the moment.

"Portal? *You* came from there?" the dragon asked.

A portal that is fading as the bloody runes dry and become absorbed by the archway, Valan noted.

"Aha! That's right, I did! I'm an all-powerful wizard! The most... not-dead magician of my clan!" Valan proclaimed, and then he gestured toward the other doors in hopes that Sorn would get the hint. "Fear me!"

The dragon laughed at him so hard that it shook the door, pushing it open by a few inches. Sorn backed away to check the nearest of the smaller doors, finding it locked, and then got to work on unlocking it using his wires as quickly and quietly as possible.

"What clan are you from, boy?"

It...actually wants to know? Valan questioned. Well, the more they talked, the more time Sorn had to find a safer place for them. "I am from Clan Anartes!" he announced, adding in as much false-bravado as before. He figured since the undead dragon thought he had lied earlier, it would still think he was lying, so wouldn't believe him if he told the truth.

"The full lineage," the dragon commanded, an edge of impatience entering its voice, "not the one which has degenerated into a mockery of itself."

"Right. That one." Valan wondered just how much Mairead would enjoy an unannounced visit from an undead dragon, who would gain the upper hand in that kind of confrontation, and realized he'd very much like to see that bit of chaos play out...and also be far away when that happened. "I'm a descendent of Laruvallhinn de Cailleach."

"Del Anartes'auth..." the dragon added as it removed its claw from the door. Valan heard the rumble and crash of more trees being knocked down as it moved about, a faint tremor passing through the floor underneath him.

Sorn managed to unlock the smaller door, revealing a room that looked very much like a wizard's laboratory. Knickknacks of various magical attunements and piles of books rested on every available surface, with just enough room on the floor to reach a section reserved for rituals. A desk heavily stained with ink and the runoff from ancient alchemical equipment was jammed in one corner. Despite the dangerous situation, Valan couldn't quite hide his look of glee, completely at odds with Sorn's own expression of panic, looking back at him—no, beyond him. The half-sidhe reached out to grab hold of Valan to drag the Firstblood into the room, but he was too slow. Skeletal fingers grabbed onto Valan's shoulder first.

"...o' Nidavellir," the dragon said, standing directly behind the Firstblood and now in the form of an undead elf reduced to nothing but lichen and bones. A cold so deep it felt more like a burning sensation erupted from the hand gripping the Firstblood's shoulder; Valan's skin swelled and split as shards of ice burst forth. He screamed in agony and then found himself transported somewhere *else*.

Tumultuous clouds blanketed the sky, rumbling with thunder and punctuated with streaks of lightning that arched toward the griffins flying through the air. These large eagle-and-lion hybrids were busy attacking dragons that had also taken over the skies, both creatures rending each other's flesh not just with teeth and claws, but also with blasts of ice, fire, or jets of liquid poison. One dragon, a massive green-scaled entity, was biting down onto a griffin's neck when a lightning bolt struck them both, leaving their bodies scorched and wings too tattered to stay airborn. They plummeted to the ground below while still locked together. The dragon twisted itself around just enough to use the griffin's body to soften the impact of hitting the street. The combined weight of their bodies destroyed the immaculately carved white stone path and nearby glass palaces, instantly making a crater out of what moments before had been part of a lavishly decorated district of a Nidavellir city.

"Grandfather!" Laruvallhinn herself cried out and ran toward the fallen dragon. In her hands, she awkwardly brandished a sword bearing her clan's family insignia, holding it more like one would a stick than a martial weapon. Aside from the Anartes'auth symbol engraved into the hilt, the sword possessed no other decoration, though the blade was made from such a highly glossy alloy that looked like it ought to reflect the surrounding toppled buildings yet mirrored nothing.

Despite the dragon's many injuries, he attempted to heave himself upright at the sound of his granddaughter's voice, but managed to lift only his head and long neck off of the ground. As Laruvallhinn reached his side, she could see the unusual curve to his back and his motionless lower body—the result of a broken spine. Using the griffin to soften the fall hadn't been entirely successful, but at least the impact had knocked it out. She tossed the sword aside and threw her arms around his neck in a hug, squeezing her green eyes shut. As severe as his injuries were, she knew that he would heal, but there wasn't enough time for that to happen. There wasn't anything Laruvallhinn could do.

The cloud cover above separated briefly as if by force, rays of bright, pure white light reaching the ground and touching Laruvallhinn's skin, turning what was once fair to a black pitch. The rich green of her hair faded away to white. That light had carried a curse created by the opposition, meant to permanently mark her people, the Dökkálfar, to never be mistaken as any of the Ljósálfar again.

"You need to leave, girl. We cannot hold them off much longer."

The dragon shook his head as if to gently dislodge his grandchild, though his attempt was half-hearted. He made no comment about her appearance; she was far from the first in the war to be changed thus, but she needed to board their remaining black ships kept hidden under the royal palace if she hoped to have any chance of escaping this world. Out of all his descendants, Laruvallhinn had become his favorite, especially once she rose to the position of *Fíada*. Her future was meant to be steeped in fortune and glory—not to see the fall of the Nidavellir Empire—and things could still end well for her as long as she abandoned the city to follow the rest of her family to the safety promised elsewhere.

"I can't," Laruvallhinn replied, finally letting him go and stepping back. She stayed behind not only because her ancestor had not left, but also because she knew that when she had sent her family along with the other evacuees, the elderly, injured, and children would slow down the journey. Extra time was needed to board their ships and rip the veil wide enough to accommodate their passage, with even more time needed to close the tear in reality after them so her people couldn't be followed. Whoever could still fight had to stay behind to give the others more time to escape. The Ljósálfar would slaughter them all if given the chance. They had already done so in other cities.

She picked up the sword and bolted in a circle around the dragon, letting the sharp tip of the blade scrape along the stones. Dragging metal across rock should have caused sparks to fly, but instead the sword easily sunk into the ground, an image appearing on the blade's gleaming surface. Instead of the world around her, the sword reflected another realm made up of impossibly high, twisting towers of books and scrolls that disappeared into the dark distance.

"I'm sorry, Grandfather, but I'm going to need your help. We're all going to need your help once we return," she said.

Once the circle was complete, trapping the dragon within, Laruvallhinn used her free hand to push through the sword's surface to reach into the world it showed, pulling out a book written in a proto-cuneiform script—a book of banned magic capable of ripping apart the world if handled incorrectly, as it most often was. Certainly not something a single elven spellcaster was meant to possess. Such magic had been agreed upon between the elven clans to never be used again, especially since the mere word of such a tome still existing was enough to start wars over obtaining it.

With things so dire, she was past the point of caring about such things; even if she succeeded, this book would kill her and possibly destroy at the very least the rest of the city. To not try at all, however, had crossed her mind as leading to an even worse result.

The book she now held had a ghostly quality to it, as if its very material struggled with being accepted in this world. The pages flickered, translucent, as Laruvallhinn flipped through them, searching. She refused to look at the dragon, scared to see his reaction and the implication of her own. She took his silence as his grudging approval rather than condemnation.

As she spoke the words of the spell, shadows started to bleed from the circular indention Laruvallhinn had drawn with the sword, spilling out as if made of ink, creating magical symbols and other smaller circles across the stones. As the designs became more and more elaborate, so did her own appearance change once more. What was once youthful became wrinkled and frail, her very life being stripped away to power this spell. Inside the smaller circles, creatures crawled out of the ground, their monstrous appearance all but proving that the rumors of the horrific demons humans so feared were involved with the Dökkálfar after all. The humans' accusations were simply wrong about one thing: there was no difference between the two.

Laruvallhinn shouted a single command, her will breaking that of the fey stripped of their humanoid shells and trapped within the smaller circles. While many shrieked curses in protest, as one, they all ripped out their own hearts to add their lifeforce to the spell. The ink on the ground surged and solidified, curving up into thirteen spikes that pierced toward the heavens like some deadly maw of a beast. Several of the flying dragons noticed the enchanted spires, and from their ancient memory perhaps recognized her intentions, one by one willingly impaling themselves on each of the spikes. As soon as the ink touched the dragons, their bodies were reduced to nothing but bones.

"I bind you all to this earth," Laruvallhinn gasped. Ink spilled forth from her mouth with every word. "Until our curse breaks, yours too shall not end."

And all of this was still not enough. There remained one last layer she needed to complete. Her control began to weaken, the ink stretching along the furthest edges of the ground starting to atrophy. For all of Laruvallhinn's own power as a veiled one, she was but one being attempting to defy the limitations imposed on this world. As if to further drive home her own weakness, her preternaturally aged arm, which held up the book, fell off, the limb turning into a pile of salt when it hit the ground.

Laruvallhinn finally looked at her grandfather, saw that he too was starting to deteriorate. He shouted something at her as his scales crumbled, but she could not understand what he was trying to say. Her ears had already rotted away.

Help me, she pleaded inwardly.

Her words were more of a prayer to the god her family worshiped, one who had stopped answering such things years ago. She thought back to her two children, the looks on their faces as they hurried after the cart carrying her wounded, unconscious husband. While the Ljósálfar were the ones invading the city, there were those Dökkálfar who had used the chaos as a cover for their own aspirations for power; one such had tried to kill her husband, a prominent member of Clan Anartes'auth.

Her family's journey to safety, to get away from the light which now cursed them, was far from guaranteed, even if they did make it to another world. Far more of her people were likely to die in search of a new home, with their greatest enemies not so much other creatures but the neighbors who sat next to them. As her eyesight faded, the last things she saw were the remaining living dragons dispersing as the cloud cover broke further.

Her heart knew despair. No allies remained. No hope lingered here.

Please help me keep them safe.

Once the invaders reached the destroyed plaza—the last one that led to the royal palace of the Nidavellir Empire—all that remained was a malformed statue of a shriveled old woman. The first to enter the plaza, a tall elven man with golden hair and bronze skin who led the troop, approached the statue with the self-assurance of one who knew he was in the right and swung his war hammer. The force of the blow was far more than what was needed to break the statue, which was little sturdier than loosely packed salt. A light breeze would have eventually destroyed the figure on its own. The man did not seem to care, gritting his teeth and looking around.

A messenger from Brigid had warned him that the troop needed to stop the vile magics being practiced here as soon as possible, but upon arrival, there was nothing really to see. He'd felt a growing sense of *wrongness* long before reaching the city, and even that feeling had suddenly vanished. Aside from the demolished statue, the only other thing out of the ordinary was the crater, encircled by smaller holes in the earth.

The elven warriors following the commander all cautiously searched the area as well, understanding from past experience that such an open space was perfect for an ambush, especially with so many broken buildings to hide in. They all passed Valan by as if they couldn't see him or the undead elf who kept him anchored within the memory. The Firstblood had long forgotten the pain in his shoulder as he stared at the spot right behind where the statue of his ancestor used to be.

The vision had been brief, nobody noticing, but a robed man had stood there with his upper face hidden in the shadow of his hood. All Valan could see was a pair of glowing blue eyes from the obscured portion, with one eye shining more brightly than the other, and reminding him of the gems on the statue depicting The Erlking. Within the sidhe god's cupped hands was a small mote of light, something that Valan *felt* more than knew through book-learning was all that remained of Laruvallhinn's shattered soul. That little light flared brightly for a moment, as if it too recognized who now held it. The Erlking carefully closed his hands over the glow before fading away, a bitter smile on his face.

Valan tried to take a step forward, overwhelmed with all the questions he wanted to ask, but the undead elf still refused to let him go. He couldn't help but wonder about something else: whose memory was this? Through whose eyes was this all witnessed? And why had no one, not even the undead dragon, noticed what seemed to him was a very obvious robed person wrapped in shadow? Usually one's perception of things was rather sparse in its focus, due to the limitations of sight, hearing, or even recollection itself becoming twisted with the passage of time. No memory should be this complete, unless… Valan's gaze once more turned toward the spot where a deity had once stood.

One of the warriors neared the edge of the crater, unknowingly walking over the original circle of ink that had now disappeared. His foot fell off, no longer made of flesh. He gave a shout of alarm and reeled back, his arms flailing as he struggled to keep balance on a suddenly much shorter leg. The fingers of one hand passed over the invisible spell marker; those too disintegrated into grains of salt on the rock.

Hearing the outcry, one of the group's number, the only female, rushed to the injured warrior's side and immediately started to petition her deity for healing. She finished only half the prayer before she and her hurt compatriot wholly turned into crude salt pillars shaped that vaguely resembled their former shape.

Valan figured that while he couldn't see it either, the edges of the magic circle must have widened after consuming the body parts of the Ljósálfar.

"Back out of the clearing, now!" the commanding Ljósálfar ordered.

Being well-trained, the soldiers listened to the golden-haired elf easily enough, but it was too late. If mere pieces of warriors of light on a crusade against dark elves could cause the spell to expand by a few inches, fully absorbing such elves could only make it expand even faster.

Despite his own orders to run, the commander grabbed the amulet around his neck and spoke the word that activated the power within it. He became quickly enveloped in light so bright that Valan had to turn away and cover his eyes before he went blind. Eventually, the light coalesced into a sexless humanoid being with beautiful white wings. The summoned being, who wore nothing but a golden helm on its head, hugged the commander protectively, and the divine creature's very presence stripped away the illusion that kept Laruvallhinn's spell hidden.

Black runes covered the entire expanse of the plaza, the only place free from the markings being beneath the elven commander's feet. His eyes narrowed, wordlessly noting that some of his warriors had not been fast enough to move out of the area before being reduced to pillars of salt as well. He would have to fight this evil alone.

The winged being raised up its arms beseechingly, and the last of the cloud cover disappeared to bathe the two of them in even more light, this time with the divine power coating the elven commander's war hammer. He took that hammer and smashed it down onto the runes in front of him, splitting open the very earth. Several of the runes evaporated from the force of the blow, and he experienced a moment of elation before the vile markings surged and covered the area once again.

From the distance came screams and shouts of confused terror, the spell having now stretched out into the rest of the city. Unlike him, the other squads of Ljósálfar warriors could not see, much less stop, the danger these black symbols possessed. Once again, he raised his hammer, but this time with the intent to throw it toward the center of the crater. The spell must have originated from that spot; there was a chance that by destroying that epicenter, it'd cause the rest of the magic to fall apart. If his efforts turned out to be in vain, he could always command the winged humanoid to bring his weapon back to him, then try something else. He did not dare recover the weapon himself, as he was trapped by the vile black runes.

His plan might have even worked, if not for a skeletal dragon crawling out of the cracked earth. The undead beast let out a triumphant roar and then lunged toward the elven warrior, jaws wide enough to bite him in half. Before they could, the winged creature summoned a crystalline shield to block the attack and force the beast away. Another undead dragon rose from the earth, and then another, until thirteen surrounded the commander and his protector. The pair fought as best as they could, but there were too many, and so were ripped to pieces.

Valan couldn't find it within himself to feel sympathy despite the gory end. After all, if these Ljósálfar hadn't wanted to die, then they shouldn't have raided—and likely massacred—most of the residents of the city.

Besides, his current interest lay in the construction of the spell itself. This one comprised multiple layers that demanded the sacrifice of a certain amount of souls in order to complete each tier before the next could be powered. Reducing the living beings who came into contact with the spell into grains of salt seemed more of a byproduct, not the main goal, as it used those deaths to power itself further.

Those curved black teeth, so many times taller than Valan, broke through the rock once more, a gaping maw fully emerging as the bisected, worm-like monstrosity freed more of itself into this world. Out of its mouth flew the fourteenth undead dragon, the final one, circling around once before diving down to snatch up the fallen Anartes'auth blade and spellbook, then escaping the area. As more and more citizens died within the city, consumed by the ever-expanding spell, great coils of the worm-beast wrapped around buildings and crushed whomever may have sought safety within. The many-teethed serpent bent its head to stay within the atmosphere, that wide mouth lunging downwards to swallow whole a nearby palace.

"Do you recognize it?" the undead wizard asked.

Finally hearing the undead elf—who still kept a hand clamped down on his shoulder—speak caused Valan to startle. So much was going on that the Firstblood needed a moment to process just what he was being asked.

"It's…The Wyrm at the End of Everything," Valan finally replied.

Any clan that wanted to be taken seriously had a symbol that nobles used to represent them. The older families, like his own, suffered the indignity that their forebears had not been very creative, so they often added jewels or rare materials to help hide that the crude image looked like it was fresh from a cave wall. Families would also go a step further with legends and myths about whatever their Clan Sigil seemed to depict to give even more importance. The Anartes Sigil looked more like a single spiral with the outermost end facing upwards; thus the legend of a mighty worm—or snake, depending on which noble wished to brag—that was so massive it could encircle the entire world, with only a pureblood Anartes having any hope of trying to command it.

"Good. My bloodline has not been reduced to complete buffoonery after all," the skeletal wizard said.

Valan wasn't sure how he felt about the idea of making his undead captor happy, though decided to take advantage of the moment by asking one of the more prominent questions spinning around in his head.

"If we had this kind of power, how did we lose this war? That was just one spell from a book, and one book from an entire otherworldly library. I mean, this alone would—"

"And how many dark elves do you know," the undead elf interrupted, "who would be willing to sacrifice themselves for other sidhe? It wasn't just Laruvallhinn's access to knowledge and power that made her so special, boy."

Valan fell silent. No one from Fo Erkunia came to mind, much less anyone in his family, who cared enough about another person beyond their own pursuit of power. The closest was Sorn, if only because the half-sidhe had no interest in power or prestige unless it was something Valan had expressed an interest in, at which point, his love would have no problem with murdering whoever was necessary just to give it to him. Valan knew of not one single sidhe rumored to be "good" who fit what the old elf seemed to be looking for. Stories of those nice dark elves usually began with "so they ran away to the surface and left everyone else behind" followed by "they wandered around alone and crying until they died." Truly inspiring tales of the ages.

"Well! I certainly hope you find this person," Valan said. "In fact, why don't I help you find them? Let me go and I can introduce you to some people. You should meet the current Piuthar of the Anartes since you care about the clan so much. She doesn't like…sudden visitors, so you'll need me to present you." He continued to babble about all the ways he'd be more useful alive than dead, despite being pretty sure with every word spoken that the undead elf looked increasingly annoyed and regretful for giving that slight praise earlier.

"Enough!" the wizard shouted. It removed its boney hand from Valan's shoulder to make a grab for his neck instead. "You're better off dead than further staining my—"

As soon as it let go, however, Valan disappeared from the memory.

CHAPTER 14

Sorn scooped Valan up and carried him away from the undead elf. What initially had been a laboratory and study full of colorful potions and books suddenly turned gray and rotting, as if everything that could have been mistaken for *life* was stripped from the room. Valan felt that *unlife* starting to feed on him, a tiredness infecting his body and mind that was only made worse with every breath he took.

Sorn carried him to the corrupted twin of the circular chamber, past where the undead elf should have stood in the normal world. His view of things changed once again, and that sense of life returned to his surroundings, this time finding himself in the shadow created by one of the broken statues of the circular portal room. A portal that by now was completely closed. The door leading outside was still slightly open, letting in a narrow band of morning light.

The undead elf, still standing in the doorway leading into the study, whirled around to face the two interlopers and cast a spell. The skeletal hand that once clung to Valan's shoulder had a dagger driven through the wrist. Outside of the memory, Sorn must have tried to cut off that hand, but the enchantments in his blade had turned out to not be strong enough to counteract the magic which held the undead elf's bones together.

"D-don't—" the Firstblood gasped, but his words fell on distracted ears. Once again, the world lost all color as Sorn ran outside, past the clearing, and into the shadows of the surrounding forest. Stepping into the darkness there returned them to the normal world. Valan tried to speak before the negative energy within the shadow world drained him to the point of unconsciousness. "Stop! I can't handle any more!"

"You're going to have to," Sorn practically growled and pulled his cloak over to cover Valan, mistaking the real issue as exposure to too much light. Compared to a full dark elf, being only half-sidhe helped Sorn see farther into the brightly lit surroundings before his eyes started to burn, but a life spent underground meant that they couldn't adjust completely. Aside from providing him safety, jumping from shadow to shadow gave him time to recover his vision before returning to the mortal world again.

"Y-you fool. I can't…"

You're going to kill me. You're going to kill me in your attempt to save me by passing through that other world. I'm going to die, and it'll all be your damned fault!

Valan struggled in Sorn's arms, trying to shove him away, which only caused Sorn to hold him tighter.

Then the Firstblood bit down onto Sorn's ear.

Now Valan had his attention and was promptly dropped onto the forest floor for his trouble.

"What's wrong with you?!" Sorn shouted.

Valan didn't so much as twitch or offer an insulting response in return. Taken aback, Sorn bent down and brushed aside the cloak, finally realizing that the Firstblood's breathing had become shallow, his cheeks sunken, and he overall looked frailer than usual. Valan's eyes were closed, having passed out, with the scarred side twitching on its own. While passing through the shadow world had done quite a bit of damage to him, the sunlight certainly wasn't helping.

Sorn realized that if he had shadow-stepped again, he would have killed the person he loved most. Whenever he entered that dim world of negative energy, Sorn felt better, energized even, and every time he returned, he felt out of place, as if it wasn't the gray and decay that was fundamentally wrong, but all the life outside of it. He assumed that feeling was normal and that Valan wouldn't have any trouble either, yet it turned out to be another reminder that something about him wasn't quite right.

Whenever he compared himself to other thieves, it was apparent just how good he'd become at hiding in the shadows, of being unseen. *Too* good. Sometimes all it took was simply standing still for others to fail to notice him. It was all completely unnatural. Sorn had not dwelled on the differences between him and other fey too much, convincing himself it had more to do with him being a half-elf. That his skill was possibly because of the enchantment woven into his scarf. If Valan had noticed anything odd before, the Firstblood hadn't pointed it out either, making it easier to pretend everything was normal. Pretending those differences didn't exist now was no longer an option if his ignorance led to accidentally harming others.

After wrapping up and carrying Valan once more, Sorn moved through the forest in a more natural way, doing his best to avoid any leaves or branches likely to make noise once stepped on. Plenty of shade from the canopy above provided a measure of relief from the sun, but Sorn still had to pause and find alternate routes in the places where the light filtered down too brightly for him to see through, much less what it would do if it touched Valan. He heard the occasional odd grunts and shuffling noises in the tall brush, usually followed by the smell of rot; he was at too much of a disadvantage and so decided it was best to go out of the way to avoid a fight. He hoped to find a cave that led underground or at least got them far enough away from the undead dragon to make it give up on giving chase.

What Sorn found instead was the edge of the forest. The trees abruptly gave way to a dried, cracked landscape of empty plains. What relief from the sun there was came from the shadows of outstretched wings of the undead dragon flying in lazy circles above. Sorn's grip on Valan tightened, which was enough to snap the Firstblood back into wakefulness.

Before Valan could say a word, Sorn adjusted his hold, placing a hand on top of the cloak covering his mouth as a warning to keep quiet. Any safety found in the woods heavily depended on not alerting the undead searching for them. With unsteady hands, Valan gently pushed against Sorn's chest, and the half-sidhe reluctantly let him stand on his own. Valan still had to lean his shoulder against Sorn's upper arm to keep from swaying on his feet, but at least being upright helped him feel slightly less useless. He didn't dare lift the cloak and risk being directly exposed to sunlight, so Valan tugged on the other man's hands under the fabric as he murmured.

"Tell me what you see."

The half-sidhe reluctantly complied with explaining what he'd been doing and what he had seen beyond the forest. When Valan didn't respond immediately, Sorn added on his suspicions: "I think we were herded here."

It would certainly explain why the undead in the forest had never actually attacked and how the dragon knew what part of the woods they'd most likely try to flee. Their exact location might not have been known, but it was too much of a coincidence to find the dragon waiting for them here. Still, Valan wanted to make sure of something before they acted first, a detail he had noticed when forced to relive that memory from the wizard.

The "memory" could very well have not been a memory at all, but an illusion. As distracting as the pain in his shoulder had been, at no point had Valan felt anyone try to break through the mental barriers he'd created ages ago that protected his mind from such intrusions. An illusion just required tricking the senses and was easily broken by coming into contact with something tangible that didn't match the fabricated scene. Valan was capable of only small illusions that used one sense at a time, like sight or hearing, so it made sense to him that someone like the undead dragon, who'd probably studied magic for hundreds of years, would be capable of fully creating a false reality. When the undead wizard had refused to let him move around in the dream, it might've had more to do with not letting Valan come into contact with his real surroundings than with preventing him from exploring the illusion.

Aside from the limitations of his own skill, nothing prevented the dragon from creating more illusions. Sorn had only heard and smelled the things in the forest, and the image of the undead dragon flying overhead was only sight—smaller illusions easy enough for a master wizard to replicate repeatedly. Valan might have been able to trick the undead dragon into letting him go from the "dream" by being annoying, but he doubted he could get away with that for a second time. The undead wizard would be a lot more cautious now.

The way the dragon was attempting to deal with them interesting as well, since it implied the older elf wanted to capture rather than kill them. At least, rather than killing *both* of them.

Valan ran his thumb over the knuckles of one of Sorn's hands. The half-sidhe had not been shy about his usage of shadow-jumping or how willing he was to rescue someone else. Of course the undead dragon, after revealing what kind of person it was most interested in, wouldn't want to risk damaging such a rare specimen for likely nefarious reasons. If the wizard also managed to capture the *annoying one*, then all the better—someone who could be tortured and used against Sorn.

The silence between them stretched on too long. Sorn twisted his fingers around and gave Valan's hand a squeeze. "What do you want to do?"

"Have a bath and a nice nap," Valan mumbled. He really wanted to tell Sorn to leave, that it'd be so much easier for the rogue to escape on his own without worrying about someone like him, but he knew that Sorn wouldn't go along with it. The Firstblood sighed, then straightened his shoulders, having only just realized that he was starting to slump forward, and tried to clear his mind from the self-doubt plaguing him. "I have a plan."

Sorn smirked behind his scarf. "Of course you do."

The Firstblood explained what he had in mind.

Valan watched as Sorn wasted little time in turning the scheme into a reality. He removed a black string from the instrument case still strapped to his back, then turned to Valan and quickly picked him up. Sorn headed toward the edge of the forest a short distance away from where they had first viewed the dragon, then stepped out onto the empty plains. The not-quite-so-empty plains, since the undead dragon flying overhead dove toward Sorn, and he dodged back into the woods to avoid being attacked. The dragon pulled up at the last moment to keep from crashing into the trees. As it flew higher, a loose, dried bush being blown across the plains by an invisible wind went by unnoticed.

While Valan concentrated on maintaining the illusion of a tumbleweed rolling across the very normal-looking ground above them, Sorn continued to run across the plains with the Firstblood in his arms. It wouldn't fool anyone who caught them running past, but the illusion would have been hard to tell apart from the ground for, say, a wizard using a scrying device to look down upon the land surrounding his lair to help maintain his own illusions. The image of Sorn openly stepping out of the forest earlier was just that—an image which disappeared so Valan could then create the current illusion. With all the shadow-jumping Sorn had done earlier, suddenly disappearing wouldn't have been that odd. Their safety depended on how long it took before the undead dragon noticed that Sorn hadn't reappeared anywhere and figured out what actually happened.

Sorn stopped running when they reached one of the area's very few trees. It provided far too little shade, the half-elf mumbling about "big cave" and "stupid light" while searching for the next closest bit of shadow. Valan looked down at the earth to make sure he was still matching it up with the illusion. He was using his thumbs and index fingers to form the rough shape of a circle, with the black string wound through the center to form a magical rune: what he used to help anchor the magic into place.

Most spells dissipated on their own, the world itself returning a balance to things, but enough will or pure power could be used to extend the time magic remained in place. Usually that came in the form of rune circles drawn on the ground. In theory, any shape with no clear beginning or end could help anchor magic in place, to then be used in a variety of ways. The rune helped form Valan's intent with magic, requiring concentration as he kept his will pitted against that of the world around him, with the circle holding the magic primed. He just had to make sure the circle he formed never broke, in this case from sudden cramps in his fingers, or the spell would fail. Near a veil, like where the Clan Anartes tower or portals were, magic was in such abundance that spells didn't require extra energy to help maintain them. But Valan and Sorn were getting further away from the places where the Otherworld bordered this world.

"There might be…big stalagmites over there, next to a river." The half-sidhe scowled as though his eyes had still not fully adjusted to the amount of light. "I don't know. It looks wavy."

"Good enough," Valan replied.

Instead of running as fast as he was capable, Sorn stuck to a more maintainable jog. The "stalagmites" he'd mentioned turned out to be farther away than expected, and the sun disappeared to finally give way to starlight. Once they reached the boulders and spikey brush growing around the base of the mountains, Sorn set Valan down and then collapsed. The Firstblood didn't join him on the ground, remaining standing to better focus on maintaining and adjusting the illusion, despite how the rocks all looked terribly comfortable.

Both of them were drenched in sweat: Sorn from all the running, Valan from being stuck under a heavy cloth as the sun beat down on them both. His wings especially were not happy about being kept close to his body for so long to make it easier for him to be carried.

"There should be a water flask under the lining on the right side," Valan kindly reminded, seeing Sorn flinch after he had lain down, only to discover a corner of the long-forgotten instrument case digging into his back.

"How is your shoulder? And…" Sorn trailed off, averting his gaze. He busied himself by searching for the aforementioned water.

"I'm fine." When Sorn gave Valan a *look*, the Firstblood quickly amended his response by saying, "I can't really feel it, which probably isn't a good thing, but it isn't something crucial at the moment."

"And?"

Valan scowled. Was he really that easy for Sorn to read? He could barely stand, knowing that if he sat down, he wouldn't be able to get up again. Of course, he still had not recovered from those trips to that dead world, followed by slowly being baked alive by the surface's horrible light, then having to maintain a spell on top of all that, along with the bloodletting and…

Valan decided to stop mentally listing his current woes. Dwelling on it all wouldn't help either of them. His mind felt like it was about to burst out of his skull. Sorn had to do almost all the physical activity and desperately deserved a break, and he didn't need to listen to Valan's list of grievances during the brief moments of rest available. The last thing Valan wanted to do was worry him, but they did have a talk recently about "knowing one's limits".

"And I don't know how much longer I can maintain the illusion," Valan begrudgingly admitted.

"Next time we need to run, I'm going to tie you to my back."

The Firstblood's lips twitched like he wanted to argue, for once choosing silence—at least briefly—on his own. The magical equipment he wore might make him less clumsy and frail than normal, but he was still slower and not as good at obscuring his presence when compared to Sorn. In situations that required speed and silence, things went more smoothly if he just let Sorn carry him, even if it wasn't doing his ego any favors. There was also no denying that with their luck, this would all happen again.

He couldn't resist arguing about one thing, at least. "Next time, at least *try* not to drop me on the ground."

"You bit my ear."

Valan raised an eyebrow. "Normally, you like that."

"There's a difference." Sorn glared. Anyone else might have found the look intimidating, but Valan just smiled in amusement. Teasing the perpetually grumpy-looking half-elf never got old.

Without another word, the rogue stood up stiffly and helped Valan drink some of the water. Sorn made it a point to hold the canister at such an angle that Valan had no choice but to tilt his head back and swallow quickly to avoid gagging. Once the flask was pulled away, it became the Firstblood's turn to scowl furtively. Sorn pretended not to see and put away the remaining water, his every action a little bit energized from his own amusement.

"Terrible," Valan grumbled.

When the half-elf turned around to face the other man, the instrument case had returned to his back, and there was no hiding the all-too-familiar look he gave Valan.

"Yes," Sorn agreed.

"If only there were someone who could do something about that," Valan began, looking down at his hands to help concentrate on keeping his fingers steady. "Now, if you don't mind, I'd much rather we find a place with enough overhead cover so I can rest."

"You think we're far enough away?"

"I don't think any distance will be enough," Valan admitted.

He thought back to how they'd essentially insulted the intelligence of a creature that had lived for who knew how long—not just once, but twice. The undead dragon would never give up on looking for them, stopping only when it captured and then tortured them 'til the end of time for daring to go up against a "superior being". Their best bet was to keep avoiding the beast until they were strong enough to destroy the undead wizard themselves.

As the wizard kept searching for them, it would look further outward as it guessed how far they could travel to Lez Ghad Beduin in a day. There was a chance the dragon would search the more immediate area again to make sure nothing was missed, but then it risked while doing so, Sorn and Valan would even get further away. An arrogant creature would be self-assured they looked thoroughly enough the first time around, anyway. Not that Valan thought the undead dragon would then be stupid enough to leave the portal unguarded, but it'd be wiser to not run away with no idea of where to go.

Valan grinned at his next thought. "It's going to lead us where we want to go."

Sorn looked at him like he'd gone mad. "No."

"Yes!"

"After all this, you want to visit that town." Sorn's tone held more resignation than question. It was apparent that he had assumed that they'd be stuck on the surface. They could try to look for a new path down to Fo Erkunia, but it'd take so long they'd miss the due date for when Valan was supposed to show up for lessons in The Otherworld. Missing *that* meant death at the hands of the Piuthar for daring such a slight. Might as well get used to living aboveground.

As Sorn looked increasingly more despondent, Valan forced himself to appear the opposite with an encouraging smile plastered on his face, as if by sheer will he could convince the half-elf not to give up on their plan to sneak him into Crann Bethadh.

"I'm not sure you heard me, but I might have accidentally blurted out the town's name to the undead dragon earlier," Valan said. "If it can't find us immediately, there's a chance it'll head straight toward that town since it knows that is where we want to go. We'll just follow it at a safe distance and continue to use illusions to hide us."

"We *could* use the portal and go back home once it flies away to that Ghadwhatsis place," Sorn retorted.

"And then still have no way to sneak you into Crann Bethadh." Valan hesitated after hearing his own words, cringing inwardly over how easily he was willing to throw Sorn into dangerous situations. Did he or did he not want to actually protect his love from harm? He already regretted his new plan about essentially running toward instead of away from the undead dragon, directly putting Sorn in harm's way just because of his latest whim. Again. Perhaps it *was* time to stop assuming that somehow he'd always be rescued from whatever mad scheme came to mind.

Valan rallied himself behind the next words to tumble out of his mouth. "But...you are right. It is too dangerous. You don't have to follow me into Crann Bethadh, either. There's... I'll come up with another way."

"No."

Valan slow-blinked. "No? I'm agreeing with you here about this *maybe* not being one of my best ideas."

"Where you go, I go," Sorn replied. The half-elf sighed the long-suffering sigh of someone who knew he was about to go along with something he didn't agree with. "But if this new plan doesn't work, then we stay on the surface."

"I'm sorry. You know I can't do that." Valan struggled with not staring down at the ground, finding it difficult to keep looking at Sorn as a wave of guilt overcame him. He didn't want to make the same bad decisions his father had made with him, though it was starting to feel too much like he just kept creating different problems. "I don't enjoy putting you in danger on my behalf. I'd have left everything behind to be with you ages ago if I didn't feel any responsibility for—"

"Where you go, I go," Sorn repeated, interrupting. He moved closer to Valan to make it harder for the other man to not look at him. "Stop trying to push me away. You are not forcing me to do anything. I want to be the person you depend on the most."

"Even if it kills you? Even if we may never be able to run off and live a 'happily ever after'?" Valan asked, his voice turning soft.

Sorn lightly brushed aside the errant strands of ghostly hair that always seemed to fall in front of Valan's face, especially making sure the scarred side was plainly visible. "Who says I'm not already the happiest person alive just because I get to be with you?"

"My love…" Valan took a deep, shuddering breath. "If you keep going, I'll start kissing you and won't be able to stop."

The half-elf chuckled, obviously very pleased with himself. He wrapped an arm around Valan's waist to hold him steady, and they started searching for a safer place to rest together.

CHAPTER 15

THEY COULDN'T FIND a cave, but they did discover a place that would work just as well. A slab of rock jutted out from the mountainside at such an angle to create a shadow underneath it, with dry bushes of a plant Valan didn't recognize struggling to grow along the ground on one side. Sorn made it a point to clear out the underside of any critters that were taking advantage of the meager protection, kicking out a palm-sized scorpion and over a dozen other small bugs.

Valan eyed those bugs, worried of how likely it was that Sorn might have missed a few, as well as how he'd have to duck down and sit in the dirt to take advantage of the shade. "Maybe the adventuring life isn't for me."

Sorn glanced over at him, taking in Valan's rumpled appearance and all the long, tangled white hair. It had started this trip as a braid that unraveled long since. "Come on, love. It isn't that bad. You need to see to that shoulder and rest."

That's right. Rest. It wasn't just sitting that upset him; Valan needed to lie down in the dirt and bugs if he truly wanted to recover. The noble sidhe begrudgingly ducked under the stone overhang and sat cross-legged on the ground. Sorn kindly didn't point out that the movement caused by sitting made Valan's hair sway back and become caught in the bushes. Valan pulled apart his hands, finally letting go of the spell. Doing so helped abate his building headache, but holding his hands still for so long left them stiff and aching. He started to slowly flex his fingers to get them back to normal. "Remind me once we get home to start looking for spells that make traveling across the surface easier."

Sorn moved to sit next to the other man, removing the instrument case and taking out the supplies they'd need for wound care. "I'm surprised you hadn't already done that."

"I didn't think we'd be gone this long," Valan replied.

The map he'd been given had turned out to be very misleading. He figured there'd be a difference in scale, that what existed on the surface would be more varied than what he'd read about, but to be confronted with how big everything was compared to what was put down on paper really drove home how completely unprepared for the wider world he was. It didn't help that the one person he knew who might be willing to share their knowledge about surviving on the surface was the one he least wanted to talk to.

Seeing the bandages Sorn held, Valan shook his head. "Those are for you. This wound isn't going to kill me, love."

"It still needs to be seen to," Sorn insisted. His eyes narrowed and Valan had a hard time meeting his gaze. Valan wanted to remind Sorn that between the two of them, it wasn't he who was mortal, but the words became lost in the anxiety that tightened his throat. Shouldn't their roles be reversed?

He let Sorn move behind him to better remove his leather armor. From the front, the coverage looked normal, but to get the leather to fit over the wings, he'd had to cut it in half down the back and use leftover strips of leather to tie around the base of the appendages. Sorn made a point of touching the extra appendages as little as possible while undoing the knots, as if he feared the sidhe would shatter into pieces at any moment.

Multiple jagged lines of ripped flesh marked where the ice had burst out of Valan's skin. While the wounds weren't bleeding much, the edges had a rubbery, reflective quality that was slightly darker than his skin tone. The flesh further away from the cuts looked swollen and full of pus. At least the frostbite kept Valan from feeling any pain. Neither said anything as Sorn gently wrapped up the wound and helped Valan put his armor back on.

"Thank you," Valan said, his voice soft. Sorn just squeezed his hand once before letting go.

"I'll take first watch," Sorn said in a very *Don't Argue With Me* kind of tone.

"... Fine," Valan sighed. "Would you mind also keeping an eye out for the dragon? At least for a few hours before we can switch." He'd have preferred to explore now that evening had come, but didn't think it wise to keep pressing forward without giving themselves a chance to recover.

"Did you dismiss Squeakers?" Sorn asked. Usually when they needed another pair of eyes but were both too busy, they'd use the familiar to do so for them, so Valan understood Sorn's meaning.

"Yes," Valan lied. The familiar had died while hiding in Sorn's cloak when the half-elf used shadow step repeatedly. Just a few moments within that dead world nearly killed Valan, so a tiny spirit like Squeakers hadn't stood a chance. Valan thought it too cruel to point that out to Sorn, considering how much he liked the annoying little bat. "Once we ran into that dragon, I called Squeakers back before it could be killed."

"Alright," the half-elf said, not sounding relieved.

Valan gave Sorn a side-hug, resting the side of his face against the other's shoulder, pointedly the side that did not have dried guano on it. "Just give me a few hours and you can spoil it to the point of making me jealous again."

Sorn smiled into his scarf. "Don't worry, love. You'll always be my second favorite."

Valan closed his eyes. "You're lucky I think you make such a useful pillow."

They spoke no more after that, with Sorn paying attention to the location of the moon every so often. At one point, the howls of multiple animals deeper within the mountains echoed in the night, but no wildlife became curious enough to draw near. After a few hours had passed, Sorn lightly shook Valan awake. He didn't give Valan a chance to fully wake up before stretching out and using his lap to rest his head.

"Really?" Valan grumbled, rubbing his eyes to unsuccessfully drive away the need for more sleep, but didn't push Sorn off of him. He had just used the other man for the same purpose, so it was only fair. With his mobility now limited, he had to improvise by drawing a smaller ritual circle into the ground next to him to summon Squeakers. This time when his familiar appeared in the circle's center, instead of looking like a child's flying stuffed animal, it had the appearance of a very ordinary, very unassuming brown bird.

Squeakers squeaked in protest over its new form. How dare its master make it not cute anymore! Sorn turned his head just enough to see what made the familiar so unhappy, then scowled.

"Quit torturing it."

"I'm not." Valan frowned. "You two can bond some more later. Sorn, go to sleep. Squeakers, I'm about to give you a very important mission that will make Sorn very proud of you if you do it well."

At the mention of Sorn, the little bird settled down, though still eyed its master suspiciously. "Very important mission" usually meant "very likely to die".

"I need you to fly around as I look through your eyes." Valan figured if he was right about the dragon flying off to Lez Ghad Beduin, they'd have to follow after on foot in a hurry and couldn't waste time figuring out the best place to walk. Better to scout out the easiest path through the mountains now. Knowing more about their surroundings in general was never a bad thing, either. "You can go back to being a bat later. Right now, you must look like this to better blend in with the local wildlife."

Squeakers hopped over to land on Sorn's stomach, blatantly ignoring Valan. The half-elf rubbed the tiny bird's belly. "Little one, are you okay now?" Sorn asked. The familiar nuzzled his fingers and made a happy chirping sound.

"Sorn. Squeakers. You two can snuggle later," Valan reminded.

Sorn just kept petting the bird. "I know. He's a selfish and horrible sidhe who doesn't like that you are cuter, but if you do this, you'll be helping me out."

The bird perked up over the idea, somehow managing to convey a very smug expression as it decided to acknowledge Valan. *Ha ha, he loves me more than you.*

Valan fought the urge to turn his familiar into a roach and step on it. Squeakers must have sensed the threat, since it decided that now was the time to fly out from under the rock overhang. Thwarted before he had even decided to actually do anything about the familiar, Valan pushed Sorn off of him. The half-elf would have to settle for using the ground as a pillow.

Sorn made a protesting noise. “I wasn’t serious.”

“Enjoy the dirt,” Valan replied.

He closed his eyes and shifted his perception through the bird’s. The arid, inhospitable mountain range Squeakers flew over didn’t look like it was ever visited by civilization, since no blatantly obvious roads cut through all the boulders and smaller rock. Valan directed Squeakers to fly lower to see if any animals might have created their own trails through the mountains, and sure enough, there were. The trails were not perhaps as direct as a human would have made, and it’d take traveling down more than one of these animal-made paths to reach the opposite side of the mountains, but it could be done.

Valan felt a weight against his leg. He snapped his consciousness back to focus on his real body. Sorn had taken advantage of Valan being distracted for the chance to rest his head onto the sidhe’s lap once more. The half-elf’s eyes were closed, at least looking like he was asleep. Valan dug his fingers into Sorn’s scalp as if he was about to pull the rogue off of him by using a handful of messily braided hair, then turned the motion into massaging Sorn’s forehead instead of inflicting pain. Valan didn’t have to see under Sorn’s scarf to know the half-elf was smirking.

As Sorn continued to rest, Valan considered what next needed doing. This time, while still checking his immediate surroundings periodically for anything that might approach their makeshift haven, he returned to looking through Squeakers’ eyes. He directed the familiar back the way they had come, flying along where the mountains met the plains. Sorn had mentioned possibly seeing a river, so. . .just maybe. . .

Valan placed a hand over his mouth and pressed down the corners of his lips to keep from smiling too hard. He’d finally found the place they’d been looking for.

The river seemed more like a ditch with a thin layer of mud on the very bottom, dotted here and there with plants slightly healthier than what Valan saw in the mountains. Squeakers flew along the ditch as it continued westwards, the bottom of it turning from mud to brown water, until it joined with a lake surrounded by sand. Nothing nearby resembled a human settlement. But the scenery matched what the map had shown, so much so that Valan wasn't about to give up looking just yet. This Lez Ghad Beduin had to be around there somewhere.

Something growled.

Valan peered through his real eyes and saw half a dozen skinny, mangy dog-like creatures circling the area around the rocky overhang. The animals looked like drawn images he'd seen of coyotes. Sorn tensed against him, the only sign the rogue was now awake, but neither of them dared to move. Most creatures didn't respond well to sudden movements. He didn't stop massaging Sorn's forehead. The sidhe discretely raised his free hand and made a flicking gesture with his fingers to cause tiny drops of acid to spray outwards at the closest animals. The coyotes hit by the acid yelped in pain, running off. The remaining beasts backed away as well, though not far enough for Valan's liking. Going by how half-starved these animals appeared, they were too hungry to give up so easily.

Valan frowned, looking down at his fingers. He had meant to send out a solid spray of acid to sweep the area, not a few droplets. He knew the farther away he strayed from a veil, the weaker his magic became, but he hadn't expected that lack of power to be so drastic.

A thrown knife embedded itself into the head of one of the coyotes, instantly dropping the creature to the dirt. The other animals backed away even further, then rushed forward to start eating one of their own. There wasn't much meat to share, so they turned on each other in their frenzy for sustenance. Sorn and Valan watched impassively until only three of the coyotes remained. Another thrown dagger and spray of acid finished killing off the survivors.

"Let's go," Sorn said.

He waited long enough for Valan to use the string to create the illusion above their heads before retrieving his thrown knives. He did his best to wipe off the gore covering the blades, taking a moment to stab one of the coyotes that wasn't quite dead yet. Valan followed close enough to ensure they both remained within the influence of the spell, noting how stiffly Sorn moved; their break hadn't been long enough for the rogue to fully recover.

A pile of corpses would inevitably draw other hungry creatures, not to mention become something out of place that would easily be seen by anyone scrying from above. With but a few hours of darkness left, they needed to rest and wait out the day. Valan doubted Sorn had it in him for another long run, much less through mountains while also carrying him again. Neither of them spared much concern over what they had just witnessed; nobody within the Unseelie Court would last long if seeing such sights inspired hysterics. Or worse yet, pity.

"There's an animal trail that can lead us partway through the mountains, which we'll then leave and head toward the river you spotted earlier," Valan said.

"We can probably find another place to rest closer than that," Sorn pointed out. "There's only a few hours left before daylight."

"When I looked through Squeakers, this might be the river we've been looking for!" Valan didn't bother trying to hide his excitement this time. "We might not need to follow the dragon after all."

Sorn gave the other man a flat stare, no doubt thinking there had to be many rivers near sand on the surface and this could just as easily be a coincidence. It wasn't like things had gone smoothly thus far. Valan's good mood began to wilt under the rogue's gaze, which caused Sorn's own to turn troubled. "Alright. Fine. In the meantime, we should have Squeakers look for possible safe places."

"Already done!" Valan exclaimed. He didn't wait for Sorn to follow, just assumed that he would, and headed to where he had seen the animal trail. He didn't even notice the pieces of dried bush stuck in his hair.

Valan sat in a hole.

When they reached the ditch that was once a river, Sorn noticed a small cave had formed near the bottom of one of the banks. If the water level had been higher, the hole would have provided a great place for fish to hide, just barely big enough to accommodate the size of two people. Valan's wings were forced to curl awkwardly along the walls with him partially sitting on them. Trying to fit into the cave left them both smeared with mud, and Valan finally noticed the small sticks tangled in his hair.

"It's not that bad," Sorn tried to console. The half-elf was nearest to the cave exit. Squeakers sat on his bent knee, busy preening. Whenever the little bird thought Sorn wasn't looking, it'd fluff its feathers and look at Valan smugly. *Ha ha, you're dirty and I'm not.*

"I'm going to burn every single one of those books that talks about how fun going on an adventure is," Valan said. He picked up a bit of mud and flicked it at Squeakers. He missed. His familiar squeaked in protest as if it had actually gotten hit, acting so wounded that it calmed down only when Sorn picked it up. Sorn glared at the Firstblood in reproach. Valan just fumed silently.

Outside the cave, the sky continued to lighten and bathe the land with the colors of dawn. Valan called forth darkness, hoping he still had enough innate magic within him to at least prevent any light from reaching the interior of the cave, managing to create only a shadowy film that covered the exit. He made a mental note to study more ritual magic to compensate for how unreliable fey magic was turning out to be.

The use of rituals and objects of power was not something the sidhe solely invented, but involved the ingenuity of human wizards, too. Long ago, one such wizard, who had invented ritual spells to tap into this world's magic, made the mistake of lusting after a sidhe woman. He willingly taught her all that he knew in order to win her favor. She ended up trapping him inside of a tree: a still-celebrated example of a successful *An Cleas,* which became a tradition to decorate random trees with the face of a man and watch the humans get confused over its significance.

This famous sidhe then passed the wizard's knowledge of ritual magic to others, who then further refined it. This type of magic, while useful away from a veil, turned out to be too tedious and time-consuming for many dark elves to put up with. Besides, if an elf found themselves too far from a veil, chances were they'd need to defend themselves against a mortal, which was nothing a sword couldn't fix. Taking the time to draw circles and symbols in the middle of a battle was far more likely to be counterproductive than helpful. But considering his lack of martial prowess, Valan figured using ritual magic was still better than nothing.

He dozed fitfully, unable to get comfortable, until the sun had sunk far enough down for the light to not bother him. His darkness spell had faded at some point. Sorn hadn't moved much, turned to face the exterior of their hiding spot. He had one of his knives out, idly twisting and balancing the blade from one finger to the other. Squeakers rested on his shoulder.

"Were you able to sleep at all?" Valan asked.

"I got enough." Sorn put his dagger away. "No dragon. Did see some birds fly in the direction we want to go. Big ones, with no feathers on their necks and heads. Don't remember what they're called."

"I'll send Squeakers to take a closer look. See if they react like a real bird or an illusion," Valan said. For once, his familiar didn't protest or drag things out unnecessarily, eagerly flying out of the cave. Squeakers chose not to fly as high as it usually would while scouting an area, though once Valan saw the big, ugly birds circling around a corpse near the trench, he understood why, recognizing the animals as vultures from previous drawings he had seen.

The vultures were pecking at the carcass of a four-legged creature resembling a horse—*a dromedary?* Valan wondered. Squeakers didn't go near, afraid of becoming the next meal. The legs and neck of the corpse looked far too long to belong to the horse, with a large lump on its back. It looked fresh, and it certainly hadn't been here the last time Valan used Squeakers to scout this area. What the creature died of, he didn't know, since the birds had already made a mess of the details of the corpse. The birds had also churned up the surrounding sand and left their own prints, but not so thoroughly to hide the footprints of more of the four-legged creatures traveling through the area, along with boot-sized shapes that could belong to humans. Lots of footprints heading toward where Valan knew led to a lake. A whole caravan's worth.

Squeakers hopped across the sand in a panic as a large shadow fell over it. The shape of the shadow's outstretched wings was not of one of the bigger birds, but of a skeletal dragon. The large birds shrieked in protest over their meal being interrupted before abandoning it to fly away. Valan instructed his familiar to keep the dragon within sight and opened his real eyes. He reached over, pulled down the scarf, and kissed Sorn with so much force that the back of the half-elf's head smacked into the wall. Sorn made a sputtering noise in protest over the sudden aggression, but Valan had already let him go to climb over him and exit the cave. In Valan's excitement, his feet slid through the mud a few *ordlach* before righting himself, wings outstretched to help keep his balance. Sorn didn't immediately follow.

"Hurry up!" Valan struggled to fight down the urge to go running off on his own. "We've got a dragon we need to chase."

"Forget something?" Sorn asked. He hurriedly pulled his scarf back up to hide most of his face again.

Valan blinked slowly. "… No?"

Sorn held up the black string the sidhe used to maintain the illusion spell. Valan must have dropped it on him in his haste.

"Oh…that. Never mind that! I know exactly what I'm doing!" This time, Valan really did start to walk off, if only so Sorn couldn't see how embarrassed he was over forgetting to set up the illusion above them. He was supposed to be the smart one who planned out their schemes, after all. "We don't really need an illusion now that the dragon is ahead of us."

The rogue had to help Valan climb over the edge of the trench. Valan tried to fly, couldn't figure out how to land, ended up falling and clinging to the top, and so Sorn pushed him over before climbing up himself. The ease with which Sorn did so made Valan envious, while Sorn was busy trying not to laugh over the new layer of mud now covering the sidhe.

"Careful there," Valan warned. "Or I'll smear some of this on you."

"That isn't the threat you think it is."

Valan tried to wipe off as much of the wet dirt as he could before finally giving up in disgust. He briefly looked through Squeakers' eyes to see how his familiar fared. The tiny bird was following after the caravan, pretending to peck at the sand as if trying to get at the tasty morsels disturbed by all the tracks left behind. The flying dragon was barely more than a dark speck in the sky, though it too seemed to be going wherever the humans on those dromedaries were heading. They seemed to be moving away from where the map had claimed Lez Ghad Beduin was located. Intentionally giving the shores of the lake a wide berth.

"The town should be near a lake, not far from where this 'river' is supposed to meet up, but neither the humans nor dragon are heading there," Valan said.

"How old is the map we used?" Sorn asked.

"No idea."

With the river as dry as it was, it either dried up outside of the rainy season or enough time had passed for the geography to completely change. A human town had even less permanency when faced with the passage of time and ravages of nature. Valan hadn't been too concerned when the sidhe who had traded him the map claimed it was new—"new" to a sidhe meant anything from yesterday to a thousand years ago—he just needed to know where the town was originally located.

He kept walking along the edge of the ditch while speaking to Sorn, who followed off to the side and let Valan take the lead. "The town and its people could have been buried under the sand a millennium ago, but the person we want to meet wouldn't so easily disappear. I think it's worth checking out before following the dragon further."

"Whatever you want." Sorn's already brusque tone sounded even more blunt than usual.

Valan glanced back suspiciously at Sorn. Traveling on the surface was turning out to be a miserable experience for the both of them, but this sudden switch to moroseness seemed odd. A life in the shadows meant Sorn never had to learn how to hide how he truly felt since he rarely bothered conversing with anyone other than Valan. All the sidhe who Valan met had learned to lie not just with their faces, but also with body language and tone of voice, to better manipulate others and hide any perceived weaknesses. Even though Sorn did try to hide his face as much as he could, it wasn't enough of an emotional mask against most sidhe. All the scarf did was make it harder to see any features that leaned more toward human than dark elf.

The winged sidhe mentally kicked himself for not considering that even though Valan saw Sorn as his own unique person, it didn't mean the half-elf saw himself the same way, especially since the Unseelie defined who was worthy of privilege by what was fey and what was not. Sorn had never met a human who wasn't a slave or about to become a fey's next meal. Lez Ghad Beduin could have been the first time Sorn saw how an established group of humans actually lived, but now he might find out the entire town didn't even exist anymore.

"The next time we visit a human settlement, I'll make sure the map is...more modern," Valan offered, and left things at that. He wasn't absolutely certain his guess was even correct.

In the past, Sorn never enjoyed when racial differences were pointed out between the two of them. The day the half-elf had woken up to find stubble on his chin was the day he cried. Most sidhe didn't grow much in the way of body hair, if any at all, until they reached five hundred or so years, serving as yet another reminder to Sorn of the racial differences between them. Valan had told him that the scratchiness wasn't bad at all, but pointing it out had seemed to make Sorn only more upset. Even now, Valan pretended to not see the shadow of a beard on Sorn's face, growing ever since they first traveled to the surface. Normally, Sorn shaved every day whenever he thought the other man wouldn't notice. It worried Valan about how well Sorn would handle more signs of him growing older at a faster rate as time went on.

"But you don't like the surface," Sorn said.

"After we move to The Otherworld, I'll be considered old enough to take part in Samhain," Valan's red eye brightened at the prospect. "Just think of all the free food and drink humans tend to leave out for us."

"And if there isn't free food?"

"Since when do you ask to be given something?" Valan grinned, and he could tell even through the scarf that Sorn smiled faintly back.

It took most of the night to reach the shores of the lake. The sand was smooth and looked like it hadn't been disturbed in a while, nor did anything resemble the ruins of an ancient town or giant pyramid. The area was also very, *very* open, with no place to hide from the sun. The Firstblood wasn't too thrilled about all the obvious footprints they left behind in the sand, either.

"I'm going to start digging a hole for us to sleep in," Sorn said.

"Alright," Valan replied. The sidhe took off his boots to intentionally have his bare feet in direct contact with the ground.

When humans described fey in the books Valan had read, his kind was always associated with nature. Flowers and other niceties of the earth linked to the Seelie Court, with everything that was deemed horrible labeled Unseelie. The Unseelie, though, had just as strong a link to the natural world as the Seelie. That pleasant growth could not exist without the decay and death underneath, nor could death come about without there being life. Nature was neither good nor evil, just not always the prettiest thing to look at.

Neither did it mean everything natural within this realm had a member of the fey linked to it. The fey were not native to this world. He'd once overheard one of his uncles talk about how humans had cut down part of a forest to clear land for cattle, not knowing a veil was nearby, so when a *gruagach* showed up and demanded milk, the humans thought they had disturbed a land spirit they needed to appease to avoid bad luck. The *gruagach* just saw an opportunity for a free drink.

Valan wiggled his toes and tried to feel *through* the sand. The ground refused to budge. Unlike at home near a veil, he couldn't make any nearby rock or dust move by sheer will and intent. This realm did not recognize him, but that didn't mean there was nothing similar between here and the Otherworld. He sought death buried within the earth, of the bones of things the size of humans, and let what he sensed pull him to stand over where the greatest concentration of the ancient dead lay. The earth may not have been willing to move just because he demanded it, but he still sensed a reflection of his own fey nature. Sorn had to grab onto one of the straps across his back as Valan walked right into the lake.

Finding himself suddenly standing knee-deep in water startled Valan badly enough to let Sorn drag him back to the shore without protest. The half-elf was glaring at him. "I can't leave you alone for a single *noimead* without you getting into trouble."

"Hey!" Valan protested. "I'm not that ba—"

The bloated, misshapen hands of a corpse emerged from the water's edge and grabbed onto Valan's ankles, pulling him under.

CHAPTER 16

If he'd been mortal, the unrelieving darkness of the solid stone room Valan found himself in might have been terrifying all on its own. Instead, he felt better being farther away from the sun, the ache in his wings and eye disappearing. Even during the night, the light from the moon and stars had made him uncomfortable.

He crouched down to be eye-level with the only other occupant of the room, letting the majority of his weight rest on the balls of his feet with his arms folded over his knees, his wings partially unfurled to help keep his balance. The Firstblood had thought himself well-informed about what human deities existed from the books he had read, but now he worried how much of that knowledge would still be relevant here. This was the first time he ever had to act on the role *An Cleas* demanded of him when dealing with humans. He made himself smile slightly, as if amused by the entire world, and mentally prepared himself for what he had to pretend to be next.

"I've been searching for you, lovely Tanat," Valan told the shrunken, mummified remains of the corpse sitting across from him. The language he used was not his native tongue, but of *Focal nam Marbh*, a voice that typically only the dead and that which was *other* could hear, much less understand. Mortals who could sense the use of this language were incredibly rare and were usually necromancers. They heard the words as a low, distant echo, an indecipherable noise as if coming from the opposite end of a long tunnel.

Underneath all the layers of semi-transparent cloth, he could tell that the corpse belonged to that of a human woman. A gold and green beetle crawled out of where one of her ears would have been had it not rotted away, and it was from this insect that the voice of an elder spoke.

"A fool you are to seek death and not expect it to find you first," she said.

"I am here to make a deal."

"I do not make deals with your kind, darkling." Under the veil covering the corpse's face crawled another beetle that pushed itself out of the corner of the woman's mouth. "You are allowed here only to be of use to me."

Valan's smile widened, and he tilted his head to the side. His single red eye glowed ever so slightly. The pitch-black of his skin seemed to merge with the dark. He didn't need to turn around to know that dozens of undead hands were reaching through the walls to grab him. "Can you not sense with more than your eyes? I thought you wise, pretty Tanat. If not a deal, then let's call it a trade. A test in usefulness."

The multitude of hands hesitated, then slowly, reluctantly, withdrew back into the stone. The two beetles burrowed into the corpse, and a third bit through the thin skin of the neck to speak in the voice of an old woman again. "I see what kind of shadow follows you and want no part of it."

"Very good, young Tanat." His smile stretched further, past the point of what should be possible in an inhuman expression. When he spoke, his voice took on the tone of every other sidhe noble from the generations before him, as if he were addressing someone much younger than himself. "It is good of you to recognize your betters. Now, tell me what happened to Lez Ghad Beduin."

The beetle hissed. "They now roam elsewhere. They have abandoned me for another."

"A shame." Valan's smile didn't falter. "I remember you fondly. How you danced in your veils over the sacrificial altar… The corpses underfoot cried in envy at your beauty."

"I do not know you."

Valan waved an index finger back and forth in admonishment. "Of course you do not. You may know my name once you prove yourself worthy. For now, we will trade to test that value. I will grant you one hundred years of youth in exchange for one of your skins."

The layers of cloth covering the corpse's torso bulged out in several places. The woman's voice turned suspicious. "You speak as if you are one of their *dajjal.* If you can grant life, then skins should be an easy thing for you to create."

"And so now you understand this test," Valan replied. "Can you trust a hand that offers salvation? You were once the humans' Goddess of Destiny, of Time, and so I offer you a chance to reclaim what you once were, when all others have abandoned you."

Valan held out his hand to the surrounding dark, and a small, ornate vial appeared as if from thin air to fall into his palm. He brought the bottle closer to the corpse's face so the beetles could better see the contents through the crystal. The clear liquid gave off a faint glow, lighting up the wall behind the mummified remains and stretching strange shadows across the room. Hieroglyphics covered every inch of stone. The corpse's eyes were little better than a thin film from insects having hollowed them out. He saw one such insect flinch from the light, cowering behind one of those decayed eyes to crawl back further into the woman's skull.

"This is your last chance to take your fate into your own hands. I will not come again," he said.

A sound halfway between a sigh and a moan escaped the corpse's lips. Whenever a human caught the attention of a sidhe, either because of the human's extraordinary beauty or skill, they'd be brought to live in the Otherworld. This human would eat and drink from the bounty found there, never growing old; if they ever crossed a veil to return to this realm, the missing years would catch up if they ever stopped eating the food of the fey. Outside of the Otherworld, this sustenance only temporarily reversed the effects of aging, though perhaps long enough for the imbiber to find a more permanent means of staying young.

"Which skin do you desire?" a beetle asked.

"The snake," Valan replied.

"And if I wish to trade again in a hundred years?"

"Do not worry, Beautiful One. If such a time comes, I will be the one to seek you."

The beetle within the corpse's skull returned to the hollowed out eye, its many legs caressing the remaining thin membrane of it. "Very well. I agree to this trade."

Valan's smile disappeared, replaced by an empty expression. He set the bottle down next to the corpse and removed one of the veils attached to the body, careful not to touch any of the beetles that swarmed through its flesh. The cloth he pulled free was as yellowed and thin as the rest, though with a weight and pattern like shed snakeskin. A beetle tried to climb over the cloth to reach his hand, but he noticed in enough time to shake out the skin, tossing the insect away. He stepped back further into the darkness of the room where the light from the bottle did not reach.

The corpse did not react. "Stay a moment longer. It has been too long since I've conversed with another."

Valan sighed in exaggerated disappointment, shaking out the cloth to remove another beetle that stubbornly tried to hide there. He made a point of crushing the insect underfoot. "The fair Tanat is not so wise, after all. You will not see me again."

Dozens of beetles shrieked with the dead woman's voice as they swarmed out of the corpse. Valan felt arms wrap around him from behind. He didn't struggle as the world faded to shades of gray, dead, with the very air taking away life instead of providing it. Everything blurred as Sorn quickly half-carried him to another part of this dead realm, stepping into the shadows. The next moment, the two of them stood near the shore of the lake again, in the murky, shallow hole Sorn had started to dig earlier.

Panic won over exhaustion as Valan pushed Sorn away, staggering, throwing the snakeskin aside and frantically removing his clothes. A half-dead beetle fell out of the bandage on his shoulder as he ripped that off, too.

"Give me one of your knives," Valan demanded, holding out a hand. Sorn didn't argue and handed over the tenth anniversary knife. The sidhe started to hack off his long hair. Several more dying beetles fell to the sand along with the severed, tangled white strands. Sorn used another knife to kill the insects and then helped Valan search for any odd lumps on his body, cutting those open to pull out any beetles that had burrowed under his skin. Sorn's turn was next, but apparently Tanat had left the half-elf alone.

Valan couldn't stop checking for anything he might have missed that might have been a bug burrowing into his body. His knee, there, looked slightly different compared to the other one, so he better make sure. He needed to cut himself open to check. To be on the safe side. What if it was another insect? If even a single beetle was overlooked, it could eat him from the inside out, turning him into a toy for Tanat, an immortal puppet that never died. He'd be forced to feel something eat him alive for the rest of eternity.

Sorn gently pried the knife from Valan's hands. "That's enough."

"No!" the sidhe shouted, lunging for the knife. "I have to check! I need to check one more time. Just once more." Valan struggled to hold back the fear threatening to overwhelm him. "Please, I won't be able to handle it if I end up like that. *I can't.* Just let me make sure!"

Sorn forced Valan's arms down to his sides, pinning the other man against him in an attempt to calm him down. "We've already searched for more. We'll recheck every day. I'll help you make sure we get them all."

Valan made a noise like a strangled scream, his hands shaking, but didn't cry. He kept his face pressed against Sorn's upper chest. Sorn adjusted his hold once Valan's trembling eased, his fingers running through Valan's now much shorter hair.

"Do you remember what we used to do as kids when one of us got scared?"

Valan didn't respond; Sorn continued as if he didn't really expect him to.

"We would build a fort out of blankets and your books, then pretend to slay the monsters that'd try to invade our keep."

"We're too big for something like that," Valan mumbled.

"Don't be so certain. You own a lot more books now."

"… I want to build a castle. A real one."

Sorn grinned. "Of course you do."

"A haunted castle so terrifying that no one would dare visit. The ghosts can be our servants."

"Mhm." Sorn's fingers continued to run through his hair. "What else?"

"It'll have a hidden library within a library."

"I'll never see you again," Sorn replied.

Valan leaned back just enough to be able to see the rogue's face. "I suppose I can make time for us between reading all those books."

"Some of those books of yours are thick. That's too long for us to be apart, love."

The sidhe sighed. "Between chapters, then."

"Better," Sorn said and let Valan go. "And we can't stay here."

"I know," Valan replied. He looked around at the ground, assessing what remained of his previously knee-length hair and the soggy, muddy clothing and armor scattered everywhere. He did not look forward to putting any of that back on. There was really only one choice left.

Valan set it all on fire.

At least, he tried to. The size of the flames he produced from his hands was barely enough to light a candle, much less burn away wet clothing. His severed hair started to burn after a couple more stubborn attempts at pyromancy, eventually reducing at least his clothes into a scorched, unrecognizable mess. Only his enchanted equipment and Sorn's cloak were spared.

Sorn shook his head. "We're not around other fey. Any humans who see you like this could become elfstruck. You know that."

"I don't care," Valan practically snarled. Fear had given way to anger. He liked this feeling a lot more. He'd been taught that humans would sometimes become obsessed with any sidhe seen without any covering, usually overwhelmed with desire or hate, which could lead the elfstruck mortal to wither away. Most elves would try to completely cover themselves or rely on illusions to make their appearance more mundane if contact with humans that weren't slaves couldn't be avoided.

After putting on his magical belt and bracers, Valan folded his wings across his shoulders and used his Fáinne Athrú to make them look more like a cloak. He took Sorn's cloak and threw it over himself to protect against light exposure, then reached for his boots. The Firstblood stared down into the shoes, knowing how easy it'd be for a beetle to hide in them and how he'd have to stick his hand in there to check. He removed what he had stored in the boots' hidden compartments and tucked it all into Sorn's cloak pockets. He set the shoes on fire to be on the safe side.

His task done, Valan started walking away from the lake to follow the river that fed into it. There was no possible way he would sleep in yet another hole in the ground. Especially in a hole so close to the lake. He'd rather trek barefoot under the burning sun. Sorn grabbed the snakeskin and stuffed it into the instrument case before following, easily keeping pace with Valan and not pointing out they'd be able to move quicker if he just carried the sidhe again.

Anger gave way to rationality around the time the sun rose and edged closer to midday. Valan stepped more gingerly over the sand as the ground became hotter, resisting the urge to wince every time he stepped on a smaller rock. When they came across the four-legged corpse that the strange birds had been eating earlier, Valan stopped moving. Finally acknowledging that if he continued to push himself, he'd pass out.

Creating undead was a fairly simple process with ritual magic. The less rotted the body, the less power was required to animate a corpse. Undead—like ghosts, wraiths, or anything with a spirit—were harder to control, since those retained enough of the original soul to pit its will against that of the necromancer trying to control it. Bringing a creature like a ghoul, vampire, or death knight under control was several magnitudes harder to do, since not only did those undead have their own will but also quite a bit of personal power to fight off a necromancer's influence. A zombie or skeleton, however, posed no difficulty; being little more than husks, anything resembling a soul was usually long gone, and thus became favorites to use when it came to creating en masse. With the loss of his favored goblin skeleton, Valan decided to make do with what was available.

"I'm going to need some supplies from my case," he said. Sorn dropped the instrument case next to him without a word, uneasily keeping an eye out for anything that might approach. The rogue avoided looking up as much as possible, though did risk glancing briefly skyward once a familiar brown bird flew down to land on his shoulder.

"Half-expected you to keep telling Squeakers to follow the dragon," Sorn commented.

"That is no longer necessary." Valan started to draw a circle around the corpse on the ground, followed by adding the necessary symbols he needed to help focus his intent to bring it to unlife. "There's a chance the dragon might circle back around, but I'm hoping we'll be home by the time it realizes we haven't sought after the current location of Lez Ghad Beduin. What we need now is to move quickly and get through the portal before then."

"I doubt it left the portal unguarded."

"I agree, though we do have one thing in our favor." Valan stood back once he was done with his preparations. He suddenly twitched in surprise, grabbing his arm, then forced himself to relax once he realized that the tickling sensation he had felt wasn't a beetle like he imagined, but sweat running down his arm. The heat and excessive sunlight were beginning to get to him, that's all. He was perfectly fine otherwise, he told himself. "It wants to capture us—well, more like capture you—so any defenses it's set up won't be lethal. Being closer to a veil will also make it easier for me to use my own magic, giving us options."

"Seems more like it is after you more than me," Sorn replied.

Valan shook his head. "For whatever reason, that old sidhe is looking for someone who is not selfish. 'Self-sacrificing'. That's you, not me. No, with me, it is disappointed and wants to kill."

"Then it's going to be even more disappointed because the only thing I care about is you."

Valan opened his mouth as if to say something similar back to Sorn, but ended up biting down on his lower lip instead. When he did speak, he kept his voice low, making the regret plain in his voice. "Even though I—"

"I know," Sorn interrupted. "It's alright. We'll be alright."

Valan lifted the cloak to see Sorn's face, eyes squinting from the light, wanting to say so much more but settling on nothing. He turned away and went back to his spell. The sidhe sent his will against that of the corpse's; finding no resistance, the rune circle flared to life, glowing briefly, the magic each symbol represented now flowing into the dead remains.

Bones and rotting flesh twitched, struggling to stand, with loose bits falling away. Eye sockets long pecked out by scavengers started to emit a red light. The undead animal then stood unnaturally still, waiting to be commanded. Normally, Valan would stitch up the loose-hanging skin or remove all the flesh entirely to make the corpse look a little nicer, but he was past the point of indulging in vanity at the moment.

Sorn tied the instrument case around the undead dromedary's neck and climbed onto its back, then reached down to help pull up Valan to sit behind him. The sidhe couldn't sit in front despite being the one who needed to direct the creature, since his wings would get in Sorn's way. Valan mentally ordered the undead mount to start galloping toward the plains surrounding that small forest containing the undead elf's home.

Neither brought up the possibility of finding a place to rest once they reached the mountain range, so evening came and went by the time the two men arrived at the plains surrounding the small forest of the dragon's abode. Valan ordered the dromedary to stop, staring hard at the dense cluster of trees as he considered their next moves.

"What's going on in that head of yours?" Sorn asked.

"When you first tried to leave the forest, after being herded toward the edge and seeing the dragon, you thought, 'Oh no! I can't cross that!' followed by, 'Wait! If the dragon is here, that means the portal is unguarded and we can go back!' Yes?"

"... Close enough."

"And I bet," Valan said, "if you *had* turned back, we'd have found it waiting for us near the portal. But we figured out it was an illusion—it now knows we're smart enough to not fall for something so simple. Then afterward, from our perspective, it seems like the wizard searched for us, couldn't find us, and so decided to head to the location I said we were looking for. But...but it *knows* that we know that it knows—"

"Pretend for a moment not everyone has a brain as twisted as yours," Sorn interrupted.

"It's possible that our undead friend never left the area. That what Squeakers saw was just another illusion. Granted, if that were the case, it's known where we've been this entire time—so why watch us, try to confuse us with yet another illusion, if the goal is to capture you? More efficient to go ahead and get on with it." Valan continued to mull things over aloud. "No, it makes more sense that the second time we saw the dragon, it wasn't an illusion, and it is at least smart enough to have a way to quickly return to the portal if we trigger any of the traps it has set up for us."

"Do you know what spells it'd use to return?" Sorn asked.

"Nothing instantaneous." Valan frowned. "But there could be. I've never had access to the advanced spells, and most sidhe magicians wouldn't willingly reveal what knowledge they did have."

The Archwizard Ferehar had been put in charge of his education, with the wizard grudgingly teaching the bare minimum so as not to anger the Piuthar-Tri. While Valan understood why Ferehar taught as little as possible, it didn't make him feel any better. Back when he was just the youngest male noble, Valan had been made to understand that he didn't have as many prospects for increased status compared to any other noble of Clan Anartes. Becoming the next Archwizard was one of the few positions he could take, albeit it was more of a lateral move. Still better than ending up as a consort, but no position of power was enough to prevent that. The males who ended up in the royal harem were those deemed the most attractive, but also too weak or with an embarrassingly lacking pedigree to be taken as consort.

Regardless, it was smart of Ferehar to not teach too well the very one who was most likely to try to kill and replace him. Neither did Valan think he could have ever convinced Ferehar that he didn't have any interest in the role of Archwizard. He had other plans.

Valan hugged Sorn from behind. The smart thing to do was to find another way back to Fo Erkunia that hopefully wouldn't take too long. Even Valan had to admit that what they were about to do came too close to being truly suicidal.

"So, I have an idea," Valan began. Sorn didn't react, so he continued. "It's probably the dumbest plan I've ever come up with, but it just might work."

The rogue sighed. He placed one of his hands over Valan's, keeping the sidhe's arm around him. "What do you want me to do?"

Sorn rode alone through the forest. He glanced off into the woods whenever he heard sounds of the more unnatural in nature, just to make sure nothing appeared to accompany that noise, though otherwise headed straight toward the clearing with the small hill surrounded by bones. He dismounted from the dromedary before entering the clearing, retrieved the instrument case still hanging around the undead mount's neck, and used a knife to cut away the outer leather layer to expose the lead lining underneath. Sorn then threw the instrument case at the hill.

Midway across the clearing, the coffin-shaped case stopped midair, hitting an invisible wall that rippled out to surround the hill, then fell to the ground as the magical substance collapsed from contact with the lead. Sorn specifically walked toward and then directly over the instrument case before picking it up and throwing it at the hill again. A few *troighid* before him, a curtain of lightning sprang into being and just as quickly dissipated when the lead box touched it. Behind him, with the case now removed, the magical wall surged once more back into place. He had to repeat his actions a few more times before he could stand directly in front of the hill.

The hill did not contain any visible openings. Even when Sorn approached with the case held out in front of him to touch where he remembered the door should have been, nothing appeared that could be mistaken as an entrance. His frown deepened as he circled the entire earthen mound, and still nothing appeared. Usually, it'd be easy for any of the fey to find and get inside these places, but this hill did not recognize Sorn. The rogue went back to where he had started his search.

"I'm going to try touching it with the amulet," Sorn said toward where the undead dromedary stood.

That shouldn't matter since you are wearing it, Valan thought.

Close proximity to a door belonging to Clan Anartes should have been enough to make it appear and allow passage through. The winged sidhe kept his thoughts to himself over just why a fey mound might not respond to Sorn's presence, deciding to jump down from where he sat on top of the dromedary, an illusion in place to make it look like he wasn't really there. Originally, the plan was for them to move up to the mound together, but Sorn had insisted on going alone after pointedly reminding

Valan of his theory: any spells aimed at capturing the rogue could be set to also kill the other sidhe. Besides, it wasn't as if Sorn didn't have any fey blood.

"Sorn, bring me over so I can check the hill as well," Valan asked. Now that they knew the locations of the spells along the clearing, they could at least shadow step across without finding themselves in the middle of one of the magical protections. "It'll be faster if we search together."

For a moment, the rogue looked like he wanted to argue, those gray eyes narrowing in defiance, then he stepped into the nearest shadows to reappear from the shade of a tree near Valan. He held out his free hand toward the sidhe without a word. Valan grabbed it, and Sorn didn't waste any time shadow-stepping back over to the mound.

Already exhausted from a lack of sleep, going through that decayed world again did not improve things. To hide a wave of weakness, Valan braced himself against the side of the hill, pretending that pressing his hand against the earth had more to do with searching for a door than keeping himself upright. He could feel how near to the veil they now stood, the magic here recognizing him with a close familiarity, unlike the ground further away. Valan sensed that the door leading inside was off to his right, in a different spot from when he had first been there. The entrance moving on its own wasn't odd, since being fey meant linking oneself to the wildness of the Otherworld, so of course anything near a veil was prone to seemingly act at random.

Valan willed the opening to move in front of him; it obeyed, the earth shifting aside to reveal a stone door big enough for him to enter. Sorn stepped forward to press the lead case against the exposed door to check for spells, then entered the hill first. The sidhe decided not to comment on Sorn's continued silence and bad mood; trying to get the rogue to talk would only start another argument that they did not have the time for. When it came to touchy subjects such as the rogue's pedigree, it was best to wait until Sorn brought it up first.

Valan began to hum a tune and followed, rubbing his normal eye closed as if to drive away sleep. The circular chamber looked unchanged, except all the doors were now closed, including the one he knew led to a wizard's laboratory. He shut the door behind him.

"Things are going…well," Sorn commented, sounding surprised, then suspicious. "Have you checked on Squeakers?"

"I'll do that now," Valan replied. He had left his familiar outside on purpose. A quick view through Squeakers' eyes showed that the little bird was flying from one treetop to another, occasionally poking its head above the canopy of needle-like leaves to see if anything was coming toward the forest. "Nothing yet."

That "yet" hung heavy in the air. Triggering all those spells, not to mention successfully entering the faerie mound, should have set off a magical alarm to alert the wizard. It was only a matter of time before it returned, unless… Valan kept his voice low and said, "Check the rooms to make sure they're empty while I activate the portal."

Sorn set down the lead case, retrieved his lock picks, and got to work on the nearest door. Valan opted to use the violin's bowstring to cut into his skin for the blood he needed. He also took off Sorn's cloak to wrap around the case to keep the lead from directly touching the portal once they traveled through it.

Valan then tried to write the runes along the archway as quickly as he dared, switching his vision between his eyes every so often whenever Sorn unlocked a side door, checking if the sounds bounced off of any hidden humanoid shapes. The first door Sorn opened contained a bedchamber as much of a chaotic mess as the wizard's study had been. A second door led to a small kitchen that didn't look like it'd been used for a while. Behind the third door was a small library with a round table and two chairs…

Sitting in one of the chairs was a certain skeletal wizard.

Sorn and the undead wizard gaped at each other for a moment, then the rogue slammed the door right as the wizard began to say something. He dashed toward Valan just as the door behind him exploded into gigantic fragments of ice. Shards of frost pierced one of Sorn's legs. He stumbled, the limb losing all feeling, unable to support his weight. When he tried to take another step, his damaged leg snapped off above the knee, the exposed, broken-off flesh completely blackened from frostbite.

"*No!*" Valan shouted.

He gave up on finishing the portal runes to run to Sorn, summoning a ball of fire in his hand and sending it through the doorway after the quickly retreating ice. He reached down to help Sorn stand. Then the wizard appeared next to him in his periphery. Valan barely had enough time to shield the rogue's body with his own before the wizard slammed the skeletal fingers of one hand through his back to rip out his heart… then used its other hand to crush Valan's head.

The Firstblood dropped to the floor like a rock. Overwhelmed and twitching uncontrollably from the pain, a pool of blood spread out around him along with pieces of his own brain matter. The last thing he could focus on was the dead beetle that had fallen out of his skull.

CHAPTER 17

A DEEP, DESPAIRING wail pervaded the round chamber. Sorn's body collapsed onto itself, enveloped in black smoke and filling the air with the thick smell of sulfur. Malformed faces rose to the surface of that dark cloud, expressions in twisted mimicry of rage, pain, and grief. Half of the faces shrieked again while the other half laughed. A giant, clawed hand with too many joints burst out of the mist and lunged toward the wizard.

The undead elf summoned a shield of ice to block the attack, unsheathing a sword tied to his waist that had been hidden by his robes to then sever another multi-jointed limb that split off from the first. The solid, silvery blade held the reflection of everything in the room along its length except for the writhing black mass. More arms, legs, things made of scales and tentacles formed at random, as if struggling to decide what it should look like. Dueling natures wanting to stay near the fallen Valan or attack the being that had hurt him.

"Tame your pet monster, boy, or I will kill it," the wizard warned.

"D-don't," Valan gasped. It was so hard to focus on anything but the pain, struggling to form anything that could be mistaken for coherent thought. His hands twitched, then pressed against the blood-smeared floor. He needed to move. If he didn't move, didn't get up, bad things would happen. What remained of his brain just couldn't figure out what those bad things were. He pushed himself up onto his knees and nearly collapsed from the wave of vertigo threatening to knock him unconscious. Valan tried to speak again and ended up vomiting blood instead.

Several spider-like legs burst out of the black mass to slam into the surrounding walls, cracking stone. Along the legs, multitudes of gray eyes grew and blinked open, gazing about wildly. Some of the faces began to merge together to form a giant screaming mouth. Valan reached over and grabbed onto one of the faces that hadn't combined with the others yet, one that had on a sapphire half-mask which matched his own. The winged sidhe let himself slump forward against the monster, trying to grab onto whichever constantly shifting parts he could to remain steady.

"S-Sorn…I'm n-not dead," Valan managed to choke out, and then he kissed that grief-stricken, malformed face wearing a mask. He fought against the growing panic threatening to overwhelm him as shadowy limbs wrapped around him with crushing force and dragged him deeper into its body.

"*Mine,*" another face growled, the word then echoed by all the different faces. The limbs tightened until Valan felt several of his ribs bend from the strain. He struggled to breathe, to speak further and to maintain his focus on the face in front of him.

"T-that's right," Valan coughed, spitting out more blood. "And you are…mine." Tears began to fall down his face. He squeezed his eyes shut to keep any more from falling, gritting his teeth. "Come back…t-to me, my love."

"*Valan?*" the grief-stricken face asked, then collapsed along with the rest of its body, coalescing back into the shape of Sorn. Most of the half-elf's left leg and several fingers on his right hand did not reform back into a solid mass, made up instead of pure, semi-transparent shadow. Sorn pulled Valan onto his lap, keeping the other man trapped in a hug, curling his upper body over Valan's slighter frame as if to block out the entire world, forgetting about his surroundings. "I'm sorry. I'm so sorry. I thought you died in front of me and I—then I…what am I? Why did I—"

"W-we'll…figure it out…together," Valan managed to reply. He wanted to pass out so badly, but the still-functioning part of what was left of his brain warned that things were not quite safe, that things wouldn't be until he remembered whatever it was.

Sorn looked up abruptly when he heard the sound of approaching footsteps. He pulled out one of his knives in warning, defiantly glaring at the wizard looming over him.

"I suppose that'll do," the wizard said. "I've worked with worse material. Now get up."

"Fuck off," Sorn replied.

The wizard sheathed his silver sword, then reached into a sleeve of his robes to pull out a large potion bottle, dropping it into Sorn's lap. "Have him drink that, then we're all going to have a nice long conversation with his mother."

"I don't give a shit about what *you* want."

"Do not make me repeat myself again," the wizard warned, "and you two will address me as Lord Bhalorn from now on."

Sorn began to repeat his words, though stopped after feeling Valan squeeze his arm in warning. The half-elf's expression turned surly, studying Valan's pained face and wounds that would have killed the sidhe if Valan had been mortal. After a moment, Sorn bowed his head and begrudgingly did as he was told, if in a roundabout way. He took a sip out of the glass bottle first, making sure he wouldn't experience any ill effects, and only then helped Valan to drink the rest.

Most of the wounds Valan had sustained closed, though the potion didn't fix his exhaustion. Sorn helped him stand and kept a hand pressed against Valan's lower back to steady him, that from Bhalorn's point of view couldn't be easily seen.

"Your attachment to that thing is concerning," the wizard replied.

Valan searched for any expression from the undead wizard that would give him more of a hint to what the wizard's true reaction was, but came up with nothing. It made him recall how openly affectionate he had been with another man ever since traveling to the surface. He hadn't been cautious at all, so caught up in the chance of being able to simply *be* with the person he loved without fear of judgment or death. Even worse in the eyes of his people, Sorn was partly one of those filthy humans, along with something else that certainly wasn't fey. For any sidhe, especially a noble, to take someone like that as a lover would be the height of perversion, and now he'd given someone all the blackmail material that could ever be needed. Years of helping Sorn stay hidden now gone.

The winged sidhe's gaze automatically shifted downwards, toward the floor smeared with blood, brains, and two dead beetles; once he recognized his own ingrained submissiveness, he forced himself to stare defiantly back at Bhalorn. Years of conditioning might have made him try to feel guilty for not being what others expected of him, but it couldn't change what Valan knew deep down: if he had never met and fallen in love with Sorn, he'd have ended up as some twisted, pathetic thing lacking a sense of self. Being with Sorn had always been what made Valan the happiest and made the rest of his life bearable.

"His name is Sorn. He isn't a pet or a monster." Some of the feigned haughtiness faded from Valan's face to turn into a faint smile. He tried not to let it show that the idea of beetles eating away at his flesh bothered him. "And I really can't make him do anything he doesn't want to do."

"Is it even capable of independent thought?"

"Valan, tell the undead trash that I'd rather kill it, not talk to it," Sorn said. He blatantly slid his hand from Valan's lower back to his hip so that the wizard saw.

Valan shot Sorn a warning glance to not go any further. Aggravating a wizard capable of killing them wouldn't be the smartest of ideas. They needed to find a way to kill Bhalorn, just not yet. Not until things were more in their favor. The wizard may not have been actively trying to kill them at the moment, but that could quickly change. Valan was willing to play along with the current power dynamic for now.

"I'll help you talk to the Piuthar-Tri, in recompense for your…" Valan eyed the dead beetles, keeping his voice even-toned. For now, he'd act agreeable and exactly as expected, until he could find a weakness in the wizard to exploit. "…help in ridding me of those parasites."

"Of course you will, boy. Especially since I left one of those bugs in you on purpose," Bhalorn replied, "and will remove it only once we reach *my* clan without issue. Do not even think of teleporting away with your pet monster again, either. Another trip through the shadows will kill you if I don't do so first."

"Great. So, since the threats are out of the way, I should go see to that portal now," Valan said.

He walked away from the other two, ignoring them to pick up the dropped violin bow to cut open his fingers and finish writing the runes along the arch. With the last symbol completed, the portal opened. A brief argument began of who would go through the portal first—not one person, but all three stepped through at the same time—followed by repetition for each subsequent doorway back to Clan Anartes.

By the time they made it back to the large cavern with the temple of The Erlking, Bhalorn made Valan drink another potion to recover from the blood loss, but gave no indication that anyone should take a break. Sorn stayed near the winged sidhe as if he expected Valan to fall over at any moment. As they got closer to the portal leading to the torture chambers, Valan gave Sorn back his cloak.

A nap does sound nice, Valan thought. *Or a bath. Would it be a bad idea to sleep with a pillow in a tub?* He continued to ponder the best combination for maximum comfort as he finished writing the last set of runes he hoped he had to do for a long while.

"You have made a mistake." Bhalorn went to stand next to Valan and pointed at one of the runes. "See? There."

Valan didn't fix the rune immediately. He really didn't understand Bhalorn, of how the wizard would go from helping to harming and back again without a clear motivation as to why. He didn't believe that finding someone "self-sacrificing" was what Bhalorn was really after. It never mattered to any other Unseelie if anyone about to be sacrificed to something was willing or not. With such immense power at the Bhalorn's disposal, he wouldn't have to settle for using someone as low-ranking as Valan, either. Most would murder for the chance of being able to get close enough to steal whatever magical secrets they could from the undead sidhe.

Valan frowned at Bhalorn, making sure his gaze didn't linger to where the mirror-like sword hung half-hidden from the belt around the wizard's waist. "If you're looking for someone like Laruvallhinn, I do have a twin sister that'd be a better fit," he offered. "She'd gladly be used as a sacrifice if given a good enough reason."

Besides, Valan thought, while this wizard was distracted by Isla's lunacy, it'd make Bhalorn less likely to notice his and Sorn's own actions.

"Perhaps," Bhalorn agreed. "Are you truly in such a hurry for me to find you useless? If so, I can dispose of you now."

I just want to be left alone, Valan wanted to say, but doubted he'd be believed. Whoever heard of an Unseelie who didn't thirst for power and prestige? "And how, exactly, are we meant to be useful to you?"

"You were already shown how." Bhalorn didn't try to hide his exasperation. "Now fix the rune, boy."

Valan added the missing line to the symbol and stepped through the portal that formed. The bottom of the torture chamber looked largely undisturbed except for a single set of footprints that had to have belonged to Tarrant. He tried not to smile over that minor victory.

"Since you want to be introduced to the Piuthar-Tri, perhaps it'd be best for us to clean up at the bathhouse first," Valan suggested. He wasn't looking forward to presenting himself to his mother with only a "cloak" and messy, scandalously short hair for a noble. Nudity among the fey may not have been a big deal, but a sidhe seeking a formal audience wouldn't show up naked, especially since that meant fewer places for them to hide weaponry and magical equipment.

"I do not recall asking for your advice," Bhalorn said. He raised a skeletal hand and rammed it through the side of Valan's body with so much force that the bony fingers ripped through flesh. The winged sidhe forgot to breathe from the shock and tried to back away, but Bhalorn merely clenched his fist around a handful of intestines and ripped them out from the hole he made. Only then did Valan scream in pain.

Sorn appeared behind Bhalorn and struck with two of his daggers, aiming for the undead wizard's heart and neck. A thin layer of ice spread out of Bhalorn's back to prevent the knives from sinking into his body, with the frost traveling up the blades to reach the half-elf. Sorn had to let go of his weapons to prevent the ice from touching him, stepping back and blending in with the surrounding dark.

Valan staggered upright from where he had hunched over in agony, his face empty of emotion as he tried to ignore his exposed entrails. One of his own hands was upraised and droplets of acid dripped from his fingertips onto the floor, leaving tiny holes in the dusty stone. His fingers were pointed at his own head. "If you try to kill him again, I'll kill myself, and then you'll never know if I just might be whatever special person you're looking to use. Wouldn't want to ruin your plans, right?"

Bhalorn smiled; at least, Valan thought the undead wizard might be smiling. It was difficult to tell since there wasn't much in the way of flesh left on the skull. The ice melted from his back, and the two knives dropped to the ground. He shook the hand covered in bloody viscera away from him until he held a still very much alive beetle that had been wiggling within. A hollowed out, crystalline shard of ice sprang into being and encased the insect like a cage. "Ah, so now you decide to believe you have value. I think I will keep this for later."

Valan's eyes narrowed, but he said nothing, knowing well the implied threat aimed in his direction. He watched as the wizard placed the crystalized beetle into a hidden pocket of his robes and started up the spiraling path lined by torture cells. He didn't follow immediately, debating on if he should. This was the perfect opportunity to run away. He sighed, clutching his damaged side and began the very annoying, painful task of pushing his exposed guts back within himself. Valan then made it a point to summon more acid to destroy the pieces of entrails that had ended up on the floor.

He followed after Bhalorn, eventually leading the way to the throne room. Since the guards they ran into recognized Valan, he was allowed to move unimpeded, though did get quite a few curious looks over his undead wizard companion—not to mention the horrified double-takes he received over the state of his hair and disheveled appearance, which he tried to ignore. Of course, when it came to his people, the sight of an ugly noble would cause more of a stir than a walking skeleton in robes.

The end of the hallway leading to the throne room had two guards standing in front of the door. Valan didn't recognize them with the helms they wore, but the lack of recognition wasn't mutual since both bowed slightly from the waist.

"I, Lord Valandrius Anartes, the Firstblood Son, seek an audience with the Piuthar-Tri on behalf of Lord Bhalorn," Valan said, trying to project that, yes, despite all appearances, there was still a bit of nobility about him.

"The Piuthar-Tri is entertaining another," a guard warned.

Valan took the hint, especially since he knew what tended to count as entertainment for his mother these days. "Very well, I'd like for word to be sent when she is not as occupied to…hmm…" The winged sidhe turned to Bhalorn. "Visiting…dignitaries usually stay in special housing within the nobility district. I can set up a place for you to rent over there for the next few days. Whatever is keeping her busy should be over with by then."

"I am not to be kept waiting," Bhalorn replied. "You will tell her I am here now, or I will do so myself over your corpses."

The guards reached for their weapons, stopping only once Valan moved between them and the wizard, holding up his hands in a placating gesture. "I know you're doing this only because you think the Piuthar is scarier than dealing with a stranger—especially when she is interrupted—so how about I be the one to go inform her? That way nobody gets punished except for me. You can't be blamed for being ordered aside by a Firstblood claiming there is an emergency. It's not like she specifically told you to let no one pass at all costs."

Valan then strode past the guards to push open the double doors in a hurry before they could decide to stop him. Raising a blade against the Piuthar's heir, even a male one, had its own consequences if caught.

The throne room looked as empty as ever except for the two people occupying the space. Tarrant was the first to react to the suddenly open doors, if only because he was facing them and used Valan's entrance into the room as a reason to hesitate in continuing to use a cat-o'-nine-tails on himself. Further in, and sitting on her throne with a bored expression on her face, was Lady Mairead.

"My apologies, Piuthar-Tri, it is only under these most dire of circumstances that the Lord Bhalorn speaks with you," Valan said, voice apologetic. He walked toward the throne only a few steps closer and knelt, keeping his head down and staying that way.

Bhalorn bowed deeply. "Little Mari, it has been too long."

The Piuthar-Tri continued to look bored, but the sudden stillness to her frame told Valan she'd been caught by surprise. "I did not know your sabbatical to the surface had ended." A faint frown appeared on her face. "I would have sent a proper escort. You may approach, Bhalorn."

"An escort would not have been able to reach me," Bhalorn said. The wizard straightened and walked past Tarrant as if he didn't see the warrior, taking one of Lady Mairead's clawed hands between the two of his with a doting expression. She didn't pull away.

"*That* one managed to find and bring you here?" the Piuthar asked incredulously.

"He used the old ways."

"Get up and approach, Valan." Despite being the one sitting, Mairead gave the impression of looking down at Valan as he neared her throne. "Who helped you?"

Valan decided to lie to her face. It wasn't like she'd ever believe the truth after years of seeing him as the "useless one". Neither did he want to come across as someone holding back information, since all that'd do was make her inclined to have him join Tarrant in hitting himself until he was deemed properly forthcoming.

He looked down at the ground as if to hide the shy embarrassment playing across his features. "I did not want to disappoint you further, Piuthar-Tri, so when I heard that no wizard would accept me as an apprentice, I sent out my own petitions for apprenticeship." Valan struggled to hide his feigned bewilderment. "I did not realize that the list of prominent sidhe magicians was so old as to include Lord Bhalorn's name and location. He reached out to me in return and taught me the quickest way to bring him back here."

"That is ridiculous," the Piuthar-Tri replied. "You barely passed the exam to deem you competent enough to enter Crann Bethadh, much less garner the attention of the most powerful wizard of my clan. It is insulting that you think yourself worthy enough. Doubly so to try to circumvent my own plans for you. I should—"

"I have decided to teach him the higher magics," Bhalorn said. His words were for the Piuthar, sounding amused, with his face turned to look at Valan. "It is partly why I wanted this meeting, so as to be granted your permission."

"… Absolutely any of my other children would be more deserving," Lady Mairead said. "He already has a Mistress, besides. Lady Viviane has agreed to see what she can do with him."

"It pains me to see any weak link within Clan Anartes. If anyone, it is this boy who needs my help the most if he is ever to be useful." Bhalorn shrugged. "Lady Viviane can still have her time with him in the mornings, his general classes during the day, and I will teach him in the evenings. It would be best to keep him as occupied as possible to not cause any trouble—and if he still proves inept, with your permission, I'll kill him myself."

"I suppose it does no harm to indulge this pet project of yours."

"The specifics of my return can be discussed at a more opportune time. Are my rooms on the tenth floor still available?"

"Of course."

Bhalorn finally let go of her hand, bowing deeply again. "I will take my leave, then. Unless there is anything else to be spoken about so openly?"

Tarrant's eyes widened upon realizing he was the one whose presence was being referred to. He looked toward Mairead and saw that her attention was now also on him.

"You may go, Bhalorn, and you will join me for the evening meal later." Mairead's eyes narrowed at her consort, paying no more attention to the wizard as he began to leave. "Who gave you permission to stop? And smile, Tarrant. You are *always* happy to see me."

Tarrant forced his lips to curve into the required expression, looking like he'd rather be grimacing than smiling, and raised the many-pronged weapon to hit himself on the back. Valan took this as his own opportunity to bow and follow after the wizard without a word. He got as far as taking a step back toward the exit before Mairead spoke again.

"Honestly, how did you end up so disappointing?"

Both Tarrant and Valan froze, since the question could have been directed at either of them. The Piuthar didn't seem to notice the lack of response.

"Tarrant, get out of my sight. Valan, stay."

Her consort bowed and immediately left, making a point of not looking at the two other people left in the throne room. Valan said nothing and hoped none of his uneasiness showed over being left alone with his mother.

"You must think yourself very clever," Lady Mairead said.

"I fear any cleverness on my part is purely accidental," Valan replied. This, at least, he felt he could speak honestly about.

"Or it's another sign that you take after your father." The way Mairead spoke made it sound like he had just committed the most vile of offenses. "It must be pure coincidence that Sabrene had been tasked to care for my messenger bats and is now too dead to confirm if you hired any recently."

"I know little about the late Torran." Valan inclined his head. "If my behavior offends, then I apologize, Piuthar-Tri."

"And yet being a pest is exactly what you constantly manage to accomplish." Mairead leaned back on her throne. "Who gave you permission to seek another master after I already assigned you a Mistress?" She idly ran the talons of one hand along the top of her seat's armrest. "Who gave you permission to leave Fo Erkunia? To travel to the surface?" The nail on her index finger started to slowly drill a hole into the stone chair. "To bother Lord Bhalorn? Much less presume yourself important enough to bring him back. You even dared to show yourself as flawed and dirty before me. Not only did you ruin your face, you have now insulted the entire clan by having hair as short as a peasant's! How can you be so stupid? So disgusting!"

Valan knelt, keeping his very empty gaze on the bottom hem of her robes that touched the ground. The edge of the cloth with the screaming faces. "I did not mean to offend, Piuthar-Tri. I wish only to make you proud."

"And now you throw words at me to echo your sister's, as if that will somehow spare you." Her nail dug into the stone a little deeper.

He didn't respond, primarily because he hadn't been asked a direct question and knew if he did, she'd have another excuse to find something disagreeable about him. It had always been this way. There was nothing he could say or do that would make his mother happy with him. He could craft the perfect answers, act exactly as someone of his rank should, and she'd still find fault. It's as if his mere existence bothered her, an insult that could only be fixed once Valan disappeared completely and, for reasons he could only guess at, she deemed him not worth killing over yet.

"Did you know that Sabrene kept notes on everything?" Lady Mairead asked.

"I did not, Piuthar-Tri."

"Too sophisticated a thought for you, I suspect." The Piuthar stopped damaging her throne long enough to gesture to the side of the hall. A guard stepped out of the dark from where she pointed, bowing and moving close enough so that she could whisper something into his ear. He left through the same shadowed entrance to reappear shortly once again, this time with a scorched book in his hands.

"Do you recognize this?" the Piuthar asked, holding aloft the partially burnt tome.

Valan had to work on remaining expressionless once he looked up and saw what she held. "No."

"Really? But these notes have so much to say about you. All these fine details."

"I don't know," Valan insisted.

Inwardly, he wanted to do exactly what his mother wanted and simply disappear. Certainly, not existing would be better than this. He wouldn't have to feel anything anymore. How could he have forgotten about that book? He had even seen Sabrene's assistant write in it before leaving her room. How could he have so little emotional control over himself? And there was no chance that only his mother had seen those notes—Mairead certainly wasn't the type to go poking around in somebody else's room herself; that was a thing to order others to do. What was done to him was likely already known by half of the clan. It'd explain some of the odd looks he had gotten since coming back home—others *knew*. It wasn't the "nothing" he had kept telling himself that never happened under Sabrene's care.

"Perhaps I should read aloud the entries about you. Would you enjoy that?" she asked, a mocking smile curling the corners of her mouth.

"No, Piuthar-Tri."

"What about placing this within the public sections of my library? I'm certain others will enjoy knowing how flexible you are."

"No, Piuthar-Tri."

Valan suddenly felt cold. The smell of something rotting lingered in his nose. He was the one decaying, he realized, like it was coming from the inside out. Covered in a layer of dirt that somehow was more than just on his skin. Filthy. Revolting. He wanted to stop feeling. Just stop. At least for a little while. Just to be away from the ones who *knew*. No, nothing had happened. Sabrene had spent most of her time in a cell toward the end, hadn't she? These could all just be lies spewing out of his mother's mouth. Why would she say these things? What was there to gain?

The thick miasma of emotion threatened to drown him; he could already feel the tightening in his throat, but Valan forced himself to start mentally picking back up the pieces. Despite all the awfulness, he could still be *Valan*. He wasn't just a thing used and discarded by others, reduced to a huddling, quivering mess. No, he was better than that. Stronger. Valan liked books, the ones full of stories too outlandish to be truthful, along with thick texts overflowing with knowledge of things he would have never been exposed to without reading them. Valan enjoyed playing music, since it was the safest way to express what he felt without it getting too personal, and share that feeling with others. He loved the feeling of throwing his arms around Sorn and how this other, wonderful person returned the favor, who knew everything he'd gone through and still loved him back.

Mairead was the weak one to try to use what happened to him for her own entertainment. Not him. Using this to manipulate him emotionally was likely exactly what she wanted. She probably figured out that pure physical torture wasn't quite as effective on him anymore. He then realized that she wasn't quite as intelligent as she thought herself to be, either.

"Then I suggest, from now on, to not flout my authority." The Piuthar-Tri tapped each of her claws to count off each point she began to make. "You will no longer be an embarrassment to my clan—you're Firstblood now, for Goddess' sake. You will do well in Crann Bethadh and will listen to both of your instructors as if I were the one to directly order you. You will no longer be allowed to get away with being such a disappointment, and if you cannot live up to my expectations, I will most certainly share the contents of this journal with others before finally ridding myself of your stupidity. Is that understood?"

"I understand, Piuthar-Tri," Valan replied. More than she knew, he thought.

The threat of that book remained only as long as no others had read it up to this point, which he had a hard time believing her plan was as simple as that. It must have passed through quite a few hands before reaching his mother's, others who would of course read it for themselves before giving her something she found valuable. Even if nobody had read it until she did, probably by killing whoever found and gave it to her, she was allowing him to remain a noble. To knowingly shelter and elevate someone who had the parts of a lesser race grafted on—worse! To also be permanently scarred!—would be enough justification by others to try to kill her as an unfit ruler. Sidhe nobility were supposed to be beautiful, unblemished, of pure blood, and while there were certainly those like his real father and mother who had animal-like limbs, those usually formed after spending hundreds of years in the Otherworld. Of course there'd be physical changes after living directly in the source of wild magic for extended periods of time. It was all part of the inevitable stripping away of *An Cleas.*

"Good. Now leave. Your face sickens me," his mother said. Valan stood up and had nearly reached the double doors before Mairead spoke again. "And if you ever again even *think* of subverting my expectations, I suggest you start reading about the mating habits of bats."

Valan very nearly stumbled over his own feet, resisting the urge to turn around and look at her, and left the throne room without saying anything. He moved past the two guards as if he hadn't seen them, walking down the long hall, which led to the center of the tower with its spiral staircase. He almost managed to successfully ignore Tarrant, who was standing at the opposite end of the hall, but the consort moved directly in Valan's way.

"We need to talk," Tarrant said.

"And we will," Valan agreed. "But not right now."

Tarrant shook his head. "No, it must be now, before I am called on again."

Valan resisted the urge to rub at the corner of his red eye. "Let's call a truce, alright? We're both a little...wrung out. Being the disappointments that we are."

"She doesn't know."

"You're going to need to be a bit more specific." Valan sighed. "Actually, no. I don't really want to know what you're talking about. Certainly *don't* come by my room later."

Maybe if he had been less tired, Valan would have tried to be more clever in his messaging, but he was past the point of caring. The siren's call for the relative safety of his room had become too strong. He went around Tarrant as if the other man had ceased to exist, half-expecting the consort to try to stop him and being pleasantly surprised when that wasn't the case.

He tried to ignore the odd feeling of guilt arising within him, realizing he was treating someone who had just been tortured with the same sort of behavior that he hated being directed at himself. Valan looked back at Tarrant, taking in the other's appearance as if finally seeing the consort for the first time.

Tarrant was one of those rare, tall sidhe with broad shoulders. His yellow eyes were narrowed, the only sign of emotion on an otherwise traditionally handsome face. As a dark elf noble, his skin was as dark as any other, with a bluish bruise-like tinge that gave away his lineage to Clan Osseriates. Light gray hair was tied back in a braid that fell past his knees, bloodstained in spots from brushing against the wounds on his back resulting from the cat-o'-nine-tails earlier. In any clan other than Anartes, Tarrant would have been seen as desirable, but instead he ended up being traded into a clan specializing in wizardry—completely out of place and expected not to survive Lady Mairead's attentions for very long. It was only a matter of time before he became the third consort to commit suicide.

"You still don't know your way around, right?" Valan asked, though continued speaking without waiting for an answer. "You ever want to know where something is located, just ask me." He grinned. "I promise not to lead you to a public privy next time."

"I don't know where your room is," Tarrant grudgingly admitted.

"Oh, well, it's on the fourth floor, the fifth hallway counterclockwise from the staircase, past the fountain full of nightshade and then..." Valan replied, but then he saw the other man frown, "... I'll just show you."

"That would be best," Tarrant said.

Valan led the way for the most part, noting that the longer they walked, the less subdued the warrior came across, as if merely the increased distance away from the Piuthar-Tri helped him remember himself. The winged sidhe decided not to point out that instead of trailing a few steps behind, Tarrant started to walk next to him, like he suddenly remembered that between the two of them, the consort was supposed to be the one of higher rank. When they reached the fountain, Valan put some extra space between them, not particularly enjoying standing next to a trained warrior who easily dwarfed him. Even with Sorn likely lurking nearby, if Tarrant attacked, Valan doubted the rogue could stop the blow in time without relying on magic.

He gestured to the fountain as if pointing it out was the real reason he wanted more distance. The waterworks were made up of three wide tiers decorated with the images of ravens. Along the edges of the two bottommost basins grew what looked like weeds with black berries and withering purple flowers. The hall came to a dead end here.

"Try not to drink or wash your hands with the water," Valan warned. The fountain hadn't always been poisonous—it was something some would-be assassin had done back when Valan used to want a change of scenery and read outside of his room to sit on the fountain edge, putting his feet in the water. Since then, it had become a convenient source of the various poisons Sorn liked to create while Valan resigned himself once again to reading only in more hidden locations.

Tarrant didn't seem too interested in his words, warily glancing around the area. "Did you get lost?"

"No," Valan replied. He walked back down the hall, which ended in an identical fountain, though this time the area had a door directly across and partially hidden by the waterworks. "See?"

The warrior looked back the way he had come, seeing the fountain's twin with no discernable way back to the main tower staircase.

"When you want to go back, all you need to do is turn around again," Valan said. "Now, if you'll excuse me—"

A loud *thump!* came from the other side of the door. Tarrant reached the source of the noise first, already pushing down on the latch to open the door, which caused Valan to raise an eyebrow at such behavior. This led to his room, after all, though he took it as a sign that the warrior thought he was completely useless when it came to investigating or fighting anything despite having won the "duel" a few days ago. The Firstblood wasn't going to dissuade Tarrant of that notion.

The door opened only a few *ordlach* before hitting the dead body of a dwarf lying on the ground. Tarrant tried to push the door open further, but it wouldn't budge.

"Oh, don't worry about that," Valan said. "I'll clean that up once you leave."

"The other one is hiding in your room, isn't it?" Tarrant asked. He didn't back away from the entrance.

"I don't know what you are talking about." Valan folded his arms in front of him and shrugged. "I trap the entranceway against assassins. Probably triggered it once they heard us approaching."

"A trap," Tarrant repeated.

"Yes!" Valan replied cheerfully with a smile. "For some reason, people like to hide above my doorway, so I installed a bunch of spikes that come out whenever they're touched."

Tarrant still didn't look like he believed a word coming out of Valan's mouth. "You still want those books about…what we discovered, right? Well, I want another duel."

"I don't really want to fight you."

"Not you, the other one," Tarrant insisted.

"There is no other one," Valan said. He walked over to his bedroom and squeezed past the warrior to wrap the fingers of one hand around the edges of the door, pushing it open with ease. He stepped inside the room and spun on his heel to face Tarrant again, still smiling. "Besides, you'll just lose again."

He shut the door in the consort's face. Sorn moved away from where he had been standing behind the door to reach over and lock it. The smile on Valan's face disappeared as he heard Tarrant try to open and pound on the entryway, followed by a few choice insults involving "little bastard" and "not over yet". Eventually the noise stopped, though Valan didn't trust the silence and raised an eyebrow at Sorn as if to ask him a question.

The rogue disappeared into the shadows, only to reappear a moment later. He drew Valan deeper into the bedroom, away from the door.

"Still there," Sorn whispered.

"Probably hoping I'll come out so he can force his way in to catch you," Valan replied, also keeping his voice low.

"I don't like him."

Valan genuinely smiled this time. "You don't like anyone."

Sorn tried to glower at him, but the expression faltered a bit over seeing the other man's amusement. "Why are we letting him live again?"

"Because I want those books on The Erlking, which will be easier to obtain by me playing nice."

"It'll be faster for me to beat him again," Sorn suggested. "He might be one of those that gets the wrong idea if you're too nice."

The rogue did have a point. Valan thought back to all the times he had to fend off the advances of other males who had harassed him during the years he'd been made to learn the use of martial weapons. There'd been a few who had thought the nice-seeming, weak-looking pretty boy would make an easy target for unwanted affections, mistaking the times Valan had decided to act pleasant as meaning something more. Those few who had made that error ended up suddenly missing and were never found again. Valan never bothered to ask Sorn what he did with the bodies.

"Tarrant is married. Admittedly unwillingly, but still married. He wouldn't risk the Piuthar-Tri's wrath. I doubt I'm his type anyway," Valan pointed out. "He never once looked anywhere lower than my face." He hugged the half-elf. "So no more duels. Risking exposing you is not worth some books."

Sorn returned the hug, burying his face in the crook of Valan's neck. "Deal with the corpse later. I'm taking you to bed."

Valan was already working on getting the rogue out of his armor.

CHAPTER 18

Valan woke up briefly, his eyes burning and a headache already building behind his temples. He pressed himself tighter against Sorn from where they lay on their bed in the hidden bedroom, not wanting to face the waking world just yet. He drifted off to sleep again, stirring a second time to realize that at some point, Sorn had left the sanctuary of their blankets.. The acrid scent of burning chemicals assaulted the Firstblood's nose. Valan reluctantly sat upright, moving his legs over the edge of the bed.

Scattered on and around their small table were various glass vials, one of which was situated near an alembic with a small, active burner. Sitting at the table, Sorn was busy chopping up different ingredients in what Valan knew to be preparation for more poison and antidote making. Some of the bottles near the rogue's feet were already full.

… Foot. Singular.

The leg closest to Valan didn't really exist anymore. From mid-thigh down, Sorn's limb consisted of a substance that looked like swirling smoke in the shape of a leg, partially transparent. Valan couldn't see them from where he was, but he knew at least three of Sorn's fingers were now like that leg. The consequences of Valan's choices.

"Do you—can you feel anything in your leg?" Valan asked, voice thick.

"No," Sorn said, not looking up from his task. "And don't worry about the table. If I burn another hole, I'll steal a new one."

Normally, Valan would chastise the other man for yet again making poisons on the same surface they ate food off of, but was feeling too wrung out to give in to that urge. Instead, he scratched an itch on his cheek, startled to find moisture there, and hurriedly removed such an obvious sign of how upset he had become. Valan unsteadily stood up and then sat down at the table in the chair opposite Sorn. The rogue finally glanced over at him, his gaze quickly dropping back to his poison-making with a slight frown on his face, obviously not liking whatever it was he saw in Valan's own expression.

"We need to talk about what happened to you," Valan said.

Sorn's frown deepened. "There's nothing to talk about."

"You keep telling me that I need to be more open and honest with you," Valan replied. "That goes both ways, Sorn. If we're going to figure out what is happening to you, then you need to talk to me. Something, anything, you might have noticed during your...transformation that can help us figure things out."

Sorn reached over and turned off the burner, the small flame matching the brief flicker of fear in his gray eyes before disappearing. "I didn't change shape," he began. Valan didn't respond, waiting for Sorn to gather his thoughts before continuing to speak further. "I fell out of this body and spread...everywhere. I couldn't remember what I was supposed to look like until you touched me. Only then did I remember and fall back." He started to put away the rest of his equipment, not looking at Valan. "I think I might be dead. Undead. Even when I came back, this body doesn't feel like it's mine anymore. What you've been attracted to this entire time might have always been just a corpse, love."

"That almost implies I want you only for your body," Valan said, amused.

Sorn's eyes widened. "I—No, I didn't mean it only that way. I meant," he said, scowling, "we both know how I come across."

Valan didn't try to stop the sappy smile from forming on his face. "So socially unskilled that it's downright adorable."

"No." Sorn glared. "And you know what I meant."

Valan hummed briefly in response, still amused, before speaking. "I might be a fledgling necromancer, but I've always been able to sense death. I never got that feeling from you. Besides, if your body is dead, even undead, you would never grow older like you have been doing—that is a thing of life. At worst, we've discovered you are truly mortal, since your limbs didn't physically regenerate. When it comes to your…shadow self—that side of you might be as immortal as me, which is good news. We just need to find out more, and luckily for us, we're about to be sent to a place meant for higher education. While there, you won't even have to worry about aging so long as you eat and drink from the Otherworld."

"And if this body turns out to not be mine?"

"Have you ever felt like there *was* someone trying to speak to you inwardly?"

"No," Sorn said. His complete lack of hesitation didn't go unnoticed by Valan, but the sidhe didn't think it wise to prod too much. Sorn had never lied to him before, so Valan didn't see why the rogue would start doing so now.

"See? It's not as dire as you think." Valan smirked. "And do you really want to tempt me into playing that song about all those fine qualities of yours? It wasn't just a list of physical attributes that I love about you so much. Though, if you'd like, I could start off the song by describing the size of your—"

"I get it," Sorn interrupted. The rogue chose that moment to turn away so Valan couldn't see his face, very busily putting away the last of his poison-making equipment in a hole in the floor, one previously hidden by the flagstone he had lifted up earlier. "And if you ever sing that again, I'll never steal another book for you."

"That's a low blow." Valan pretended to protest. "You leave me no choice but to keep you to myself."

"Do you still want me to cut off your wings?" Sorn asked bluntly, making it blatantly obvious he wanted to change the subject before Valan could spew more embarrassing things.

That was a loaded question. Part of Valan still blamed Sorn for not letting him cut off the wings as soon as possible, before they had fully healed, though his frustration over it had lessened enough for him to consider things further. Now some of that anger was aimed at himself. Valan regretted not being more forceful and clear about what he wanted earlier, why it was so important to not have such a constant, visible reminder of what Sabrene had tried to turn him into. Sorn always hated to see him in pain, but might have been too caught up in the idea that Valan was far gone enough to commit self-harm and needed to be stopped at that time.

The silence between them stretched longer than Valan realized, startled out of his thoughts as Sorn reached over and clasped one of Valan's hands in his. The rogue's brows furrowed, his gray eyes narrowed from grief. "I'm sorry. I thought I knew what was best for you, without—"

"No, no. I should have—"

"But—"

Valan smiled slightly. "We're ridiculous."

Sorn didn't try to argue. Valan squeezed his hand, taking a moment to savor the feeling of not just the familiar callouses on the rogue's fingers—something a full-blooded sidhe couldn't form—but of the fading away of his own resentment, of being able to move forward together.

"Getting rid of them would be for the best," Valan began, "but I think it's too late. They're healed and fully part of the rest of me. If we try to cut them off now, it is highly likely those things will just grow back unless the stumps are also burned, which would just leave scars that would give away I had something attached to my back, anyway."

This time, Sorn closely studied Valan's reaction, as if noticing how the sidhe had phrased things. "I'll help you cut them off as often as we need to."

Valan shook his head. He was well aware of how much Sorn struggled with the idea of anything hurting him, much less being the one who caused any pain. Asking him to do that every day would be too much. "Even if we only cut off the wings, I'd end up with two bleeding stumps on my back. A bandage and a minor illusion could keep it hidden for a few hours, but eventually there'd be too much blood and new growth to hide behind a spell."

"I already have poisons that slow down healing." Sorn's gaze turned thoughtful. Poisons meant to counteract a sidhe's natural ability to heal always served as a base for his more elaborate creations, usually combined with causing the maximum amount of damage as possible to overwhelm his target. "I just wouldn't create the second part. Combine it with what normally would serve as an antidote. Then with a numbing reagent. The problem is that it'll affect all of your ability to heal. You won't be able to recover quickly until it breaks down."

"Hm, then it's worth using in situations where I'm likely to be forced to remove my cloak," Valan said.

Using an illusion to turn his wings into a bulky cloak was little more than a quick, crude solution to hiding them as it was. He couldn't exactly take off the "cloak" if a noblewoman demanded that he sleep with her, leaving him little recourse but to kill her in order to keep the wings hidden. Unlike the disappearance of the males of his species, missing females were something sidhe tended to pay attention to. That was, if he could even successfully kill her in the first place, then be forced to flee the city before others caught on to what had happened. He just wished it didn't have to be Sorn to do the very thing the rogue hated the most.

Sorn finished putting away his poison-creating equipment, placing the stone back over the storage space. "I'll go get what we need."

"And I'll see to the corpse. It has to be stinking up the other room by now," Valan sighed. The body was likely too rotten to feed it to the chest chimera, which left messier methods in getting rid of it.

"No wandering around on your own," Sorn warned.

Valan didn't respond verbally, just shot the other man an exasperated look. It wasn't like he somehow got into trouble *all* the time. Only sometimes. Usually in situations beyond his control. He didn't really appreciate Sorn acting like he couldn't even put on his own boots without tripping over the laces if ever left alone; that happened only *once*, when he had forgotten to put on his bracers first.

As Sorn passed by Valan, he bent down low enough to give a quick side-hug. Valan returned the gesture, but didn't let go. The winged sidhe looked up into the rogue's face, searching for any sign of that familiar fear within those gray eyes.

"I'm…" Valan began, pausing to tamp down on the tears trying to make an appearance on his face again, with this time succeeding in keeping them at bay. "I promise I'll work on becoming better at planning things, so you don't get hurt again. I swear, I'll become stronger, so strong that you'll never be hurt again, okay?"

"Love, it's not your fault. I make my own choices." Sorn kissed the top of Valan's head and pulled away. "And it's me who is going to protect you."

The rogue faded into the shadows behind the repurposed throne in the room. Finding himself suddenly alone, Valan took his time to get dressed, not enjoying how it had been a few days now since he'd last taken a bath. Eating anything was out of the question until the wound in his side fully healed. The most he did with his hair was to brush it free of tangles before giving up on it, focusing on using his will to move the stone in the wall aside for him to step into the staged bedroom. He wrinkled his nose over the smell.

Dwarves being unfriendly to dark elves wasn't unusual. The Svartálfar's long-standing hatred for Unseelie was perhaps well-deserved in Valan's mind. Even in the books written from the Dökkálfar point of view, the dark elves weren't painted in the most positive light. Granted, that also depended on how the Unseelie perceived torture and experimentation on lesser races, and who cared what some weaklings felt? A faction within the Dökkálfar, when primitive humans were first discovered, decided to "help" humans evolve further, which lead to the first Svartálfar: stocky, heavily built bipedal creatures who grew an excessive amount of hair with a crude understanding of magic, which they typically used to reinforce physical objects. They tended to live underground near veils much like their creators did.

What was strange was how one of these dwarves managed to penetrate so deeply within an Unseelie clan's stronghold unnoticed, much less why one would be motivated enough to want to kill Valan specifically.

Valan knelt by the corpse to remove enough of its armor to search for any slave brands, finding one in a similar location as Sorn's. The symbol was even the same. His best guess was that this slave's master promised freedom in exchange for getting rid of the Firstblood. Keeping a dwarven slave was expensive, both in its training and maintenance since it took more time to break their wills. Arguably more useful underground than humans, since dwarves could see in the dark— even if it was not as well as the Unseelie—but were still rare slaves to own. So rare that a noble suddenly missing such a slave would be very easy to track and find its master.

Searching the corpse further revealed nothing unique, leaving Valan contemplating what best to do with the body.

Three human slaves knelt on the slippery floor of the bathhouse. All three women were missing their eyes, replaced by emeralds; matching gems were encrusted on the collars around their necks and sparse clothing. One slave held a golden comb and ran it through what remained of Valan's hair. As the tool went past the cut ends, the hair grew out; she continued to pull the comb away until the hair reached the proper length for someone of his station. The second slave used a pair of scissors to even out the strands, all for the third slave to sweep up and toss into an incense burner. Instead of the smell of burning hair, the room filled with the scent of vanilla.

Valan leaned against the side of the large, heated pool, submerged mid-chest in the shallow end, one arm thrown over the edge. He intentionally kept his back flush against the side so that it was less likely anyone might accidentally touch that area and break the illusion hiding the two wounds that marked where his wings should have been.

"What do you think of this, my lord?" The sidhe male who spoke directed Valan's attention back to the floating mirror held near his face. This other sidhe was dressed in simple robes appropriate for a bathhouse, if made from material not expensive enough to belong to nobility. Neither did this other man have that perfect symmetry to his features that many of the ruling class prided themselves on: lips too narrow, dull blue-gray eyes slightly too far apart. A slight hunch to his shoulders from a lifetime of bowing to others.

The mirror faithfully reflected Valan's appearance, with the only difference being his tattoo. Instead of the dull black ink that made up the mark, the swirling shapes gleamed a bright, sparkly silver. Valan scowled in distaste.

"I'm told that this type of tattoo is very popular with women, though my lord certainly would not struggle to garner their attention even without it," the sidhe pandered.

"Osckar, are you sure this doesn't make me less attractive?" Valan asked. He then cringed inwardly at his own words, since playing the vain, party-happy noble with barely two brain cells to rub together sometimes got on his own nerves—and made him worry that somewhere along the way, this mask had become reflective of his true self. He reminded himself that there was a purpose to this, that calling in a favor to rent out the public bathhouse all day for this specific day was important. It also helped spread rumors that the tattoo on his face was real and needed to be reapplied occasionally. Him enjoying finally being able to remove the remnants of his trip to the surface was pure coincidence. "If this is so popular, then that means I'll look like everyone else. Don't you have anything less…flashy? I *must* not look a fool at Crann Bethadh."

"Of course, my lord."

Osckar waved his hand at the mirror and the image within changed to show the tattoo had turned into a different graphic. This time, the markings looked like an elaborate red webbing that tiny white spiders crawled through. Before Valan could even say something in protest, Osckar had already changed the image again into dripping blood, having caught on that something about the spiders upset him. Valan made the mental note to work on not showing that insects crawling in and out of his flesh truly bothered him, since such an obvious weakness was something others would try to exploit.

"Hm, I didn't like the webbing being red. Go back to that look but turn it blue," Valan said. "And really, dripping blood on my face? I'm not some feral goblin."

"Apologies, my lord," Osckar replied and did as he was told. He barely had enough time to shift the image in the mirror back to the webbing and animated spiders before the doors leading into the bathhouse opened.

Valan pushed the floating mirror to the side and smiled. "Hello, Brother."

Domhnall Anartes, now of Clan Latobici, stood framed in the entrance separating the heated pool and a smaller room scattered with wooden benches and stacks of folded towels. Further into this secondary room were other doors, with the one leading to where Valan knew the foyer to be, usually manned by the owner of the bathhouse, that further separated it from the rest of the city. His brother spared a glance back toward the room full of towels where the standing dwarven skeleton was carrying a large instrument case, with no expression on the older sidhe's harshly handsome face if he recognized the undead servant or not. Domhnall didn't seem to notice the portable table displaying the various inks and needles used in tattooing.

The lack of a greeting in return caused Valan to sigh inwardly. Throughout his life, he never really interacted with his older brother, who always seemed content to pretend he didn't exist. He had hoped for some reaction over finally getting the chance to talk to each other, some acknowledgment that they were kin who both grew up having to survive the Piuthar-Tri's whims. Valan decided to at least try for civility, starting with a bit of honesty.

"I'm glad you came! Did you know I used to admire you? My perfect older brother, who I am supposed to emulate—honestly, I don't know why Piuthar-Tri would bother, since I clearly—"

"Get out," Domhnall ordered.

The mirror instantly turned into water and fell into the pool. Osckar bowed and led his slaves out of the room, looking at no one. The normally pleasant surroundings which mimicked that of a naturally heated spring suddenly became awkward.

"There's no reason for hostility. If you like, I could have some wine delivered," Valan offered. He hadn't moved other than to rub his red eye, closing it briefly as if it had gotten irritated over being hit by the splatter of the once-mirror. "I promise I had nothing to do with Lady Fingula deciding to become too…indisposed to meet you here again, despite her assurances that you are her favorite."

"What do you want?" Domhnall's voice dripped with contempt.

"I want us to get along," Valan said, though despite the hopeful words, he was already getting an inkling that things weren't going to end up how he wanted. The sidhe did not keep to family bonds the same way a lot of human families did in the books he'd read. The significance of blood ties had more to do with how closely a sidhe was related to various gods and goddesses of power. For a race that had never been human, a sidhe relying on the overly-vaunted "humanity" wouldn't get him anywhere.

Though Valan knew of something that did.

"We're all aware that without the other clans stepping in to donate members to Clan Latobici, it would have fallen apart…and you, the celebrated jewel of our mother's eye: instead of gaining a coveted position near An Geata, you were regulated to the role of consort of that jumbled-together mess.

"I'm not enjoying my time as Firstblood—something you were fond of—and I will happily not stand in the way of you reclaiming that title to help get you back into Clan Anartes. I'd be thrilled to take your place in Clan Latobici even, but for the Piuthar to think that a good exchange, I'd need to at the very least graduate from Crann Bethadh. Which is less likely to happen if you and your new apprentice keep trying to kill me."

"Your lack of intelligence is well known, but I did not think you were *this* impaired," Domhnall began. "Might as well shout underneath the waters of Bel that you think you can get the Piuthar-Tri to go along with any 'suggestion' from the likes of you."

The smile fell from Valan's face, pretending to be hurt, his eyes downcast. He idly stirred the water around with a finger, creating minor illusions as if to amuse himself. The image of two ravens with blue eyes formed, the birds flying along the stirred surface before gliding away. Images of black birds were everywhere in the capital city, but it did signify one last way he could reach his brother.

"*I* don't need to convince her of anything. *You* have always been the favorite, not me. She'd jump at any chance to swap the two of us; the problem is her having a good enough excuse when negotiating with the other Piuthar that it'd be an equivalent exchange." He held up a hand as if he could already hear his older brother protest, correcting himself. "A nearly equivalent exchange. All I want is a truce for now. It's not like you can't always kill me later. What do you have to lose? A divorce?"

Domhnall's eyes narrowed slightly, so slightly that it barely registered as a change in expression, then walked out of the bathhouse without saying another word. Valan watched his brother's retreat, thinking of all the things in his life that had come to symbolize everything he was not, and briefly wished he hadn't been exposed to stories about "happy families". He wouldn't have to wonder what it'd be like to have a sibling he didn't have to fear would murder him if he ever made the mistake of appearing too strong, all for the never-ending climb for power.

Too often, Valan had observed that those who constantly dragged down others to reach greater heights would find after all their effort, that they merely stood upon a hill of rotting corpses barely above the muck—not the promised mountain of greatness and glory. Domhnall, who had done everything right according to Unseelie expectations, still hadn't acquired this "greatness" that had been all but assured.

A shallow wave broke across the surface of the pool, the depths hidden by all the mist and herbs mixed within it, and the head of a giant snake emerged from the water. The snake's black-and-gray banded body undulated as it swam toward Valan. A lighter gray hood flared out, framing the sides of its face, starting from the lower jaw and down the neck. Valan didn't struggle as the cobra wrapped itself around him. Instead, he leaned his face against the snake's, feeling his new "familiar" flick out a narrow black tongue to touch his cheek.

"Only a few days left," Valan said quietly. There was still a lot he had to do, threats which needed to be dealt with, before he could leave for The Otherworld in relative safety. For now, this was the best he could manage when it came to his much stronger brother. He would have to content himself with this. Time would tell if he needed to use more violent methods.

Isla admired herself in the mirror. Her long, white hair with a metallic-green sheen matched an outfit made from the gleaming scales of a beast unknown to her, the garment precariously held in place with silver straps. The layers of silver necklaces she wore barely covered the top mounds of her breasts, and she knew when she danced, she would flash even more of her figure.

"Isn't this the perfect outfit for the party?!" Isla asked excitably, unable to keep her glee to herself. She had spent days figuring out what to wear and then even more time making sure everything was custom made and would fit just so.

"It's almost too good," Lynet replied. She was similarly dressed, though in an outfit made from materials not as rare as Isla's dress. "Enough to make Nealie envious, at least. It's so rare for her not to be the center of attention for once."

Isla's smile curved her lips more into a smug look. Her first party and already on her way to being the most stunning one there! Even better, Lynet had told her the band playing for the event would include her brother—in a way, being forced to serve her during her time there—and he had to hide behind the other musicians because of that nasty tattooed face of his. She wondered if there was a way to force him more out in the open at the party, that way even more people would see how awful he looked. *She* was the pretty one now, not him.

Lynet had to clear her throat to pull the other sidhe out of her thoughts. "Do you want me to escort you? If you do, then we'll need to leave now. I'm to help finish setting things up."

"Arriving early? Oh no, that'd be terrible," Isla said. Her nose wrinkled at the very idea. Despite her lack of experience with social events, even she knew that showing up before the party began was not something fashionable, especially for a noble of her rank. "I'll take a carriage."

"Alright, see you there!" Lynet gave a brief wave and a shallow bow before leaving Isla's bedroom. She navigated the maze of paths through the tower to reach the dining hall available to everyone, hurrying through a room that appeared too massive than what the tower should have been able to hold. Every thirty *troighid* along the walls, the stone statue of a monster that didn't match any of the others in the room was framed by floor-to-ceiling curtains. The rest of the room was composed of long tables and benches. Some sidhe sat at these tables in small groups. Lynet walked past the group Valan was with, not glancing his way, to join another group of sidhe further in the dining hall, those dressed more for a social gathering.

Valan had a plate of untouched food in front of him, busy tuning his violin and going over scattered manuscripts of music to assure himself that he had indeed memorized everything correctly. Behind where he sat and off to the right stood the dwarven skeleton diligently holding his oversized instrument case, the exterior freshly covered with leather. One part of the dwarf's skin still had the slave brand of Clan Anartes.

"Are you sure you don't want your slave back?" Valan asked the male sidhe sitting directly across from him.

Niall the Secondblood, newly appointed apprentice to Domhnall, didn't bother to hide his sour expression, sitting stiffly and looking for all the world like he didn't want to be here. Being a couple of years younger didn't prevent him from being taller than Valan, though not as thin, with a softness to his frame like someone more used to sitting at a desk. Long, pale-green hair framed a face that featured unusual pink eyes: Niall would have bordered on pretty if not for the harsh angles to his brow and slightly too-wide chin, as if perpetually unimpressed by everyone. Valan didn't know who Niall's father was, but his mother had been an older sibling of Valan's who had died during the fall of one of their clan's outposts.

"I've already told you, that isn't my slave. Mine wandered off and I haven't seen it since," Niall said.

"My mistake." Valan grinned. "I'm glad to have made such an honest friend."

"Yes, well, my Master has led me to believe it will be to our mutual benefit," Niall muttered.

"I'd ask if you wanted to come to the party, but I suspect that isn't your type of crowd."

"Anything that isn't in the pursuit of knowledge is a waste of time." Niall made the haughty tone of his voice crystal clear. "We're supposed to be studying. The exam is only *tri* days away. I shouldn't even *be* here."

"That almost hurt my feelings," Valan replied. "I think he is trying to hurt my feelings, Tarrant."

"Good," said the third sidhe who made up the group. Tarrant sat on the same side as Niall, though with enough distance between the two of them to make it clear there was no familiarity.

Valan sighed. "With friends like these—"

"We are not friends," Tarrant cut in. "I'm here only to figure out where the other one is hiding."

"What are you talking about?" Niall asked.

Valan answered, "I fear our Piuthar-Tri's consort has been spending too much time with her recently. He's starting to hallucinate."

Niall almost looked like he believed it. "Her husbands usually last a few years before they start to do that."

"I know, it's all very sad."

Tarrant looked about ready to reach over and strangle Valan. "I am not hallucinating!"

The shout drew the attention of nearby sidhe. Valan tilted his head toward Niall as if to say, *See?*

"Of course you're not," Valan placated, using a tone which did anything but. He moved as if to stand, stopping halfway when he saw Tarrant do the same thing. "Are you really going to follow me everywhere? That's a bad look for a consort. I'll be gone in a few more days."

"I'm to be sent back to Crann Bethadh for additional training," Tarrant replied, speaking through gritted teeth. "We're going to be spending a lot of time together."

"Ah, so it's true! You did lose to the worst warrior here," Niall said. He placed his elbows on the tabletop and rested his chin atop clasped hands, making no move to stand up. Preparing to watch a show. "By all means, go ahead and kill each other now."

"Shut up," Tarrant said. "Nobody invited you to sit with us."

A brief flicker of anger flashed across Niall's face, but he remained silent due to being lower-ranked. Not that anyone had any difficulty interpreting the silence as a way to point out that nobody had invited Tarrant either. Valan wondered if the true difficulty of being around these two would be getting them not to kill each other before he could get what he wanted out of them: Tarrant's books and connections about The Erlking, along with convincing Niall—and by proxy, his older brother—to follow through with their deal to switch clans.

"That's not a very nice way to treat your friends," Valan pointed out. He smiled and slowly spun the bow of his violin between the fingers of one hand to spite the dual looks of annoyance now directed at him. "If murder is really going to be on the menu, I hope you two will at least be quieter about it. Maybe not declare your intentions in front of so many people." This time, he did leave the table, putting his things away and not turning around when he heard Tarrant start up again. "Don't follow," Valan warned. "You'll get lost again."

Valan walked over to the sidhe standing with Lynet, his undead dwarf following after him. He resisted the urge to look back to see how Niall and Tarrant were doing and focused on the female sidhe wearing the most flashy outfit. He bowed slightly, remembering only at the last minute to not do so as deeply as when he hadn't been declared Firstblood. Technically, he had the highest rank but was still expected to show some deference to any noblewomen. "I apologize for being late. What did I miss?"

Several members of the group looked up at him while they tuned their own instruments. The heavily decorated sidhe didn't so much as glance at him, busy silently mouthing the words to a song as she read from a scroll held open on the table in front of her.

Lynet replied, "We're about done. Isn't that right, Artia?"

"I guess," Artia said, finally looking up, if only to address the other woman. The males might as well not exist. "Don't forget the center stage is mine, *especially* once I start singing. Nobody better set any of the dancers in front of me this time."

"A mistake that won't happen again," Valan assured.

Artia didn't appear to hear him. "Let's go, Lynet."

The two women took off without another word, dividing the group in two, which led the other male musicians to turn to Valan with an odd sort of deference that left him startled.

That's right, I'm too high of a rank to blend in with the rest of them now, Valan thought.

He didn't say anything as he followed the female musicians through the tower, incredibly uncomfortable with keeping his back turned to the other males as he led that half of the group. He did his best at pretending he'd always taken on a leadership role, confidently moving toward the ground floor, to a side area where black coaches pulled by undead horses were left near the entrance for anyone of Clan Anartes to use. Everyone got into one of the bigger carriages that already had the bulkier musical equipment strapped on top, with Lynet sitting next to Valan, leaning against him.

"What do you think of my new comb?" she asked. Lynet tilted her head so he could get a better look at a ruby-encrusted, strand-pinning decoration in her hair.

Blending in with the other gems was a carefully preserved red eye.

CHAPTER 19

The Undercity of Fo Erkunia held not only tunnels for traveling around in a more covert method but also a few caverns used by merchants to store extra goods that couldn't fit into the stores above. Most of these areas were heavily guarded, but at certain times of the year as the seasonal demand of things changed, some of the caverns lay empty. The biggest of these, with a raised area at the back of the cave, was perfect for one last celebration before the next generation of sidhe youth left for the Otherworld.

Lynet didn't lean against Valan quite so much as they walked across the length of the cave, but she still held onto his arm to keep them close. "You're going to listen to me from now on," she said softly, too low for any of the others in their group to hear. "You are not allowed to hurt me, try to kill me, lie to me, or tell anyone else anything I have and will ever do or say to you."

Tension clenched Valan's jaw and strained the muscles in his neck, his eyebrows raised in surprise. He *felt* that her words weren't some idle declaration, but a magical binding that entrapped his mind into always following her command. Even if his main worry had only been others finding out that he *had* lost an eye, thus becoming too imperfect to retain his status within the nobility, a newer, more pressing worry now took hold. Flesh of immortals had many uses in spells. Spells which allowed the possessor of another sidhe's flesh to compel their target to follow every order, with distance being the only thing that could weaken the level of control. The time to deal with Lynet had come a lot sooner than he originally thought.

"After the party, you are not to leave the area without me," Lynet said. She gave his hand a squeeze. "I know you spent time with Artia recently. Did she tell you about any changes she wanted to the sequence?"

"Yes," Valan said. He then told her what differences Artia planned to take place in the middle of several of the songs they were about to play.

Lynet finally let go of him once he was done talking, stepping back and smiling. A smile which faltered into a look of revulsion as her gaze focused on half of his face. "Once we leave, you're going to get rid of that tattoo immediately. Artia might have lowered her standards, but I will not."

Valan resisted the urge to wipe his hand on his pants to rid himself of imaginary dirt. "I understand."

"Good male," Lynet said. She started walking faster to rejoin the other female sidhe. Artia was beginning to act most upset that the slaves hadn't arrived before her to set up the equipment on stage. Valan didn't increase his own pace, glancing briefly upwards to the roof of the cavern. With no one watching him now, his face emptied of all emotion.

So far, so good.

Isla was not pleased. As it turned out, she had not been the only noble who thought it a good idea to travel through the tunnels in a carriage. Midway to her destination, any progress forward ground to a halt, leaving her no choice but to walk the rest of the way. Also was her moving on foot not much of an original idea; some of the carriages she passed were left empty by others who had thought similarly. With nobody left behind to give the order to move the transports, it all quickly became a problem that only got worse.

When she was finally close enough to see the cavern's entrance, her heart skipped a beat at the flashing lights and the faint sound of music coming from deeper within the cave. Isla's excitement banished any further annoyance as she made her way to the line of sidhe waiting to get inside. The length of the line made her decide that she was much too important to enter with the rest of the rabble, so she bypassed it—smirking once she noticed others reluctantly letting her pass without a word—to move to the front.

Lynet, with two ogre slaves flanking her, blocked the entrance. She didn't seem to notice Isla approaching at first, her attention on somebody else who had tried to move to the front of the line.

"Nobody invited you," Lynet told a much taller male sidhe. "I don't care what you decide to call yourself. You're not getting in."

"Valan invited me," the male insisted.

"I very much doubt that. He already warned us that somebody matching your description might try to sneak in," Lynet said. "So get lost."

"You barely qualify as a noble," the male said. "I outrank you easily—"

Lynet raised an eyebrow. "Save it, sweetie. That sounds dangerously close to threatening a female."

Isla brushed past the male, treating him like the weaker sex she clearly thought him to be, beaming a smile at the other woman. "Lynet! I hope I'm not too fashionably late."

Lynet matched her expression. "You kidding? I'm glad you came at all. Go on in. I'll join you later once I'm done here."

Isla didn't wait for further encouragement, taking a deep breath as the noise suddenly increased dramatically as soon as she stepped inside the cave. The heavy, deep sound of drums reverberated off the walls and pulsed to match streaks of faerie light, keeping in time with shrieking bagpipes. Weaving between the two was the barely audible sound of a violin, upstaged by a woman's singing voice, no doubt amplified by magic, which reached every corner of the party.

As far back as she was, Isla couldn't see the stage clearly over all the other dancing and jumping sidhe, who were far too busy and tightly packed to so much as glance at her. When Isla had imagined this exact moment, it wasn't like this at all. Everyone was supposed to turn in surprise and stare in awe at her appearance, her grand entrance, then move aside as one to let her walk to the front of the stage like the true royalty she was. The singer—Artia, was it?—and the other band members were supposed to bow to her and *only then* continue to play. Valan, cowering in the back, was supposed to see her in a mix of shock and horror as he realized that not even here was he safe from her. That she was invited to these kinds of social gatherings now, too. This was her first appearance at such an event, after all, so of course it was something worthwhile for others to acknowledge.

For a moment, it was almost as if Isla had gotten her wish. The beat of the music suddenly switched, the mellow sound of the violin dipping into a heavier tone as if in warning, and part of the dancing crowd darted out of her way. From the ceiling fell a stalactite to shatter onto the floor, bits of stone shrapnel hitting the nearby dark elves, who only laughed at the cuts before going back to dancing to the song as it increased its pace a little bit faster than before.

An accident? Isla wondered. The others hadn't treated it as an accident, more like something they'd expected, not even meant to hit anyone specifically. Lynet hadn't warned her about this being part of the entertainment. She turned around to confront the other woman, but Lynet was no longer at the cavern entrance, another ogre slave having taken her place. This time, Isla paid attention to her surroundings a little more carefully, spotting several armed males half-hidden by the presence of the ogres, ensuring that nobody uninvited could pass without notice.

The sound of the violin changed to that deeper, warning note again, and another piece of the ceiling fell, this time closer to the stage. Someone who had not been fast enough to move out of the way screamed in pain, the cry blending and barely heard in the music, merely providing a chorus, and the song increased in tempo yet again. While Isla wasn't dancing, she found herself having to dodge and move quickly to avoid being trampled by the others, edging her way toward the stage. She figured there wouldn't be as many falling stones there, if only because the singer getting hit in the head mid-song would ruin the whole party. Besides, just because part of her fantasy hadn't come true didn't mean she couldn't enjoy seeing the terror on her sibling's face.

Artia finished her song, lights flashing behind her to play shadowy figures across the walls, and she immediately launched into singing the next. The crowd surged forward eagerly, more tightly packed than before, and Isla found herself crushed between bodies. A sidhe close to her lost his footing and fell, immediately disappearing underfoot. Nobody seemed to hear or care about the male's agonized cries. The violin gave a third warning noise.

Isla felt more than witnessed the pressure of others lessen behind her as they moved out of the way, so she wasted no time in dodging out of the immediate area as well. She ended up dumping into Lynet, who sneered and pushed her directly under the falling stalactite.

Nobody seemed to care about Isla's screams, either.

Enterprising merchants, having caught word of the party from previously spread rumors, had set up stands selling various food and drink waiting outside of the cavern for the departing sidhe. By this hour, only a few groups of partygoers loitered still in conversation with each other. Several slaves were already cleaning up all the trash left behind. Inside the cave was even more of a mess, the floor smeared with bloody footprints and loose rock, with the odd mangled body scattered here and there.

"Where is Lynet?!" Artia shouted, her voice hoarse from singing for hours. Only when there were no other women to talk to did she decide to pay attention to the males who made up the band, focusing on the highest-ranking one. They were all still on the stage, busy with putting away their instruments. "And you, I told you to change the sequence! How dare you!"

"Oh!" Valan's eyes widened in surprise as if he had just now remembered. "I'm sorry, you were…very distracting at the time." He frowned. "I knew I must have forgotten something but couldn't remember what it was. The last I saw of Lynet, she was by the entrance, still letting people in. Maybe she already left."

"I cannot believe how absolutely useless you turned out to be," Artia said. She looked like she wanted to hit him, but considering he stood on the side of the stage the furthest away from her, she apparently decided the effort wasn't worth it. "It's now your job to clean up all this—and try not to fuck that up, too. See if any of the bodies are Lynet's."

"What? Just me? By myself? But—"

"Shut up, male."

Artia shot him one last look of disgust before jumping down from the stage with the other band members following suit. Valan kept his confused expression long enough to determine none of them were going to turn around and glance back before letting his face relax. He didn't jump down, walking along the edge while still holding onto his violin and bow. After all the non-stop noise earlier, the silence broken up by the occasional muffled groan from those sidhe abandoned on the floor was eerie. His eyes moved from one body to the next until he found the one he was looking for.

With her face smashed in from being repeatedly stepped on by dancers, Valan barely recognized his twin. What remained of the fallen stalactite had nearly bisected her through the belly and broken her spine, with her arms and legs twisted at odd angles. Those limbs twitched occasionally—still alive and trying to heal, but in too much pain to form cognitive thought. Valan's empty visage stayed staring at her broken one as he began to play on his violin. This song started at a slow pace, with no beat that could have been mistaken for joy, each note low and struggling for existence, before turning sharper, angrier, which now matched the too-wide, mocking smile on Valan's face.

The music drew out the magic from the world around him, so close to a veil, and his will helped give it form. All the blood began to evaporate, leaving a dull, brown residue on the floor, and clouds of the same muddy shade formed and swirled between the stalactites. The air grew heavy, thick with the foreboding feeling of oncoming rain, until water fell from those clouds. Acid rain slowly destroyed, droplet by droplet, what remained of Isla forever. The only dry spot in the cavern remained the stage. Valan hadn't stopped playing his violin, his eyes never leaving where his twin's body used to be, now nothing but a darker patch of liquid on the ground. He stopped only once the acid started to riddle the floor with holes, the clouds disappearing along with his final note.

Valan closed his eyes briefly, forcing himself to look away. His odd smile disappeared back into emotionlessness. When he spoke, his voice also sounded empty, distant. His attention focused more on his inner thoughts and memories than on his surroundings. "I wonder what the Piuthar-Tri would think of your dedication in following me around."

Tarrant stopped leaning against one side of the cavern's entrance. He made no move to walk closer to the other sidhe. "It'd be your word against mine over who is following whom, and she'd believe me over you."

Valan sighed. "Fine, then. You want that duel? To prove how mighty a warrior you are, I mean. Well, go ahead and attack me, then you can report to my mother how skilled you are and won't need to go back to Crann Bethadh."

"I want to fight the *other* one," Tarrant emphasized. This time, he did walk over to Valan, searching his face for a reaction. The Firstblood didn't have it in him to twist his features into another fake expression under such scrutiny. "I have to."

"She must have been very convincing," Valan said.

Tarrant hesitated, then nodded. "We're going to be stuck together for a while."

"Until she realizes you are not a very good spy."

"Good thing we're leaving, then."

Valan decided not to point out that no amount of distance could keep the consort out of the Piuthar-Tri's reach. He could flee to one of the smaller, independent courts that remained in the Otherworld, but those were independent for a reason and more likely to hand Tarrant back into Mairead's hands, gift-wrapped. Valan's own brief trip to the surface made it clear that running away to live there would be difficult for a sidhe, though he supposed a warrior might have an easier time than someone who relied on magic.

The Piuthar-Tri's newfound interest in keeping a close watch on Valan didn't really surprise him. Back when Sorn had triggered all those spells surrounding Sabrene's cell, Valan had thought about who would most likely be informed of that happening. Who'd learn that there was someone wandering around Clan Anartes skilled enough to remain mostly unknown and linked to him. Knowing what he knew of the Piuthar-Tri's personality, she wouldn't be able to handle there being someone in the clan she couldn't control in some way.

Valan couldn't help but prod the other man a little bit for a specific reaction. "If not my mother, who are you supposed to attract?"

A deep scowl formed on Tarrant's handsome face. "Not you."

Valan blatantly, with great exaggeration just to irritate Tarrant further, let his eyes rove over Tarrant's muscular form. Too tall. Too broad-shouldered. Didn't have gray eyes. The hair should be the color of dust when it wasn't dyed a deep blue. Not nearly good enough. Valan made his level of disinterest clear in his voice. "Don't worry, you are not pretty enough to be my type, either."

With that, Valan spun a few extra steps away to move around Tarrant on the off chance he was about to be attacked after all. Especially once he saw how offended the warrior now looked. He spoke again before Tarrant could express his outrage. "I'm almost flattered she thought me worth so much effort. Who doesn't normally want a taste of forbidden fruit? Besides me, I mean—"

"You really can just shut up now," Tarrant interrupted.

"Why do people keep telling me that?" Valan wondered aloud.

The warrior didn't bother giving him a response—too busy trying not to be mortified over the direction their conversation had taken, Valan surmised. That, or resisting the urge to punch him in the face. Not many male sidhe reacted well to the idea of another male finding them physically attractive—or if they did, then rejecting any advances. The Firstblood went back to covering up the messes within the cavern, directing the rock underfoot as if it were really made from clay to smooth out the floor and reform the stalactites above. Seeing how much control he had over the earth, so close to the Otherworld, helped remind him that, unlike on the surface, he really wasn't without options when it came to defending himself.

"So," Valan said, once he was done removing all traces of the party, directing his skeleton to jump off the stage and remain near him, "how thorough will you be in following me around? Am I going to find you lurking outside my door every morning until evening?"

"Yes," Tarrant said, not bothering to hide the weight of his misery behind that one word.

"But...I lead a very boring life."

"I would have gone with 'annoying'."

"Oh, of course; very, very annoying. All day long. Every day." Valan grinned. "How about this: I give you a juicy secret to tell my mother so she doesn't find you utterly useless and kill you, then you give me one of those books we talked about…earlier. We can spend most of the day away from each other afterward."

Valan didn't wait for a reply—he didn't want to give Tarrant a chance to immediately disagree—walking out of the cavern with his pet undead following behind. The other man muttered something insulting under his breath, but Tarrant also left. The consort made a point of walking right next to Valan, to at least make it clear to others that he wasn't the type to follow anyone else around. By this point, the slaves had nearly finished cleaning and the last of the partygoers had headed back home. Valan regretted not being able to buy himself anything to drink after playing for so many hours.

Only the two of them walked down the tunnel leading to Clan Anartes. Aside from some trash and an abandoned carriage, there wasn't anything unique to see, much less something for Valan to find an excuse to comment about in order to break the silence. Eventually, the tunnel split into two. Both ways eventually led to the underbelly of the Clan Anartes tower, with one path far more direct than the other.

"Let's take the longer route," Valan said, seeing Tarrant start down the shorter path.

"Why? The other way leads to other clans first."

"Just follow. It'll give you something to share with the Piuthar-Tri."

Valan took the longer path without providing further explanation, his mood slowly souring with every step he took. The tunnel walls became rough and pockmarked with shallow holes, looking like dead coral, branches protruding with glowing polyps that pulsed in time to an unfelt wind. Valan stopped walking once he saw a cloaked figure standing next to a gate, who had a giant crossbow trained on him.

"Greetings," Valan said. He cautiously moved closer after motioning Tarrant to stay back; much to his surprise, the warrior actually listened to him. Valan had expected to meet a slave under the employ of Clan Latobici here, but once he stood in front of the robed figure, he recognized the features of Gwynedd Latobici. She kept most of herself turned away from Tarrant so only Valan could see her clearly.

By all appearances, she looked like she was considering firing at him despite his genial attitude. Eventually Gwynedd lowered her weapon, but she still attacked him with the harshness of her tone. "You're late."

"Apologies—and for the uninvited guest," Valan replied. "My Piuthar's orders."

Gwynedd lightly kicked a large sack on the ground with one of her spiked boots. "Clan Latobici wishes to show its appreciation for *not* changing things."

Valan walked over and picked up the sack, glancing at those boots of hers, his gaze briefly looking upwards and away once he realized Gwynedd was also wearing a very short skirt. Tiny flecks of blood marred her otherwise smooth, toned skin, serving as the only clue she had been at the party earlier. He felt her draw power from across the veil into their world, the air thickening from the sheer density of the magic, which blocked out all sound within a few *troighid* around them. Unlike him, who had to make use of whatever magic and element already spilled across the border between worlds, Gwynedd's training as a veiled one let her pull as much as she could handle from the Otherworld into this one. Valan doubted anyone outside of the noiseless space she created could hear them.

"I'm told we're going to share the same Mistress." Gwynedd didn't sound angry anymore, a hint of amusement in her voice. She had gotten the reaction she wanted out of him.

Valan made sure his gaze didn't wander this time, keeping his eyes trained on her lovely heart-shaped face. Even wearing heels, Gwynedd was just barely his height, although she often gave the impression of being taller. He'd always thought her eyes to be her most unique feature: a molten gold that swirled around narrow pupils, vaguely cat-like, except he'd seen drawings where a shark's eyes would be a closer match.

"You...don't deserve that," he said. He'd been put under the impression that Viviane only took on students who needed "fixing" in some way. To him, nothing was wrong with Gwynedd.

"Really? Now you pretend to care about what I deserve?" Gwynedd practically spat. The shape of her pupils changed, widening, a predator that sensed blood in the water. She still looked angry, but her tone switched to something more neutral. "Val, they're not going to let me be me anymore. This might be the last time I'll be able to—"

"There's never been anything wrong with you," Valan interrupted, "but you shouldn't have wasted any of this on me. We're not—"

"She's pregnant, Val. She thinks…it's mine."

He stared at her, at a loss for words, fully knowing what she implied. Valan started to hold out his arms, but stopped once he realized what he was doing, turning the motion into him folding his arms in front of him instead.

"I'm sorry," he said, and was going to leave his response at that, but also believed she deserved a better response than that from him. Too much of a shared past between them for him to just turn away. "Do you want any help? I…owe you for not revealing how intimate we were."

Gwynedd glanced past Valan to Tarrant. "You already know what I want from you."

"I can't give you that."

"Liar." She smiled bitterly. Gwynedd stepped close enough to invade his personal space, flashing more of her figure underneath her cloak. "To come to me for these books…did you think a few years would be long enough for me to forgive you?"

"No, and I don't want your forgiveness," Valan replied. "I wish—I want you to leave while you still can. I want you to be happy, Gwyn. Far away from here."

"Then make me happy."

"If you want anything I can actually *give*," Valan emphasized, "you know what to do if you change your mind." He swung the bag over his shoulder. This time he did turn away, about to force himself through the sound barrier Gwynedd had created.

"I think…I would have been a great wife," Gwynedd said softly to his retreating back.

"You would have been the best," Valan replied.

His interference with the sound barrier caused it to shatter and dissipate. He had to fight down the urge to walk at anything faster than a casual pace away from her. He didn't turn around. Had to keep moving forward. He didn't know of anything else he could do or say that would make things better.

Valan just barely registered that Tarrant was walking next to him again. The taller sidhe looked like he was trying to—and failing badly at—hide how much he wanted to ask questions.

Only after putting some more distance between them and Gwynedd did Valan decide to speak, not bothering to hide how tired he felt. "Alright, alright...what is it that you want to know?"

"Who was that?" Tarrant asked.

"A slave belonging to the Piuthar-Sia," Valan said.

"Latobici? That's the clan that got nearly wiped out, right? The one that had only one heir, who their previous Piuthar tried to hide wasn't a female."

"... Close enough."

"I heard the original heir isn't allowed outside of the royal harem anymore after the last time he dressed like a girl."

Valan inwardly winced at that description of Gwynedd, but didn't correct Tarrant. He didn't dare disagree with someone who'd only repeat what was said to a Piuthar more than willing to "correct" any behavior deemed unacceptable by Unseelie standards. Instead, he posed a question back at Tarrant. Easier to pretend he knew even less about the inner workings of another clan.

"Hear anything else about the Latobici?"

"Only that after their last Piuthar failed to pass off her only child as a girl, she was killed for her crimes and the old heir sent to the royal harem. A daughter from Clan Cavii took over, and despite having a consort from...our clan, she prefers the harem."

"Kept alive only because Gwyn is the last of the original Latobici bloodline, alive until more heirs are produced..." The normally brilliant red of Valan's eye dimmed slightly. "Back when Gwyn was known only as a girl, she wanted me as her consort. It was all set to be publicly announced, but then someone revealed the…secret the late Piuthar-Sia tried to hide."

"That doesn't explain why you're meeting someone here," Tarrant pointed out.

"Unrelated business transaction. A Latobici paid me more to do something over a competitor," Valan replied. "Nothing personal. Besides, aside from occasionally running into Gwyn at parties in the past, we've never interacted much—especially now since…'he' can only sneak out occasionally."

"I'm surprised he hasn't tried to run away yet."

Valan decided Tarrant didn't need to know that Gwyn had made plans to do just that—how she had come to him and begged to run away together, but he had refused. Valan wasn't going to forget anytime soon how hurt Gwyn had looked back then, when she realized that he didn't care about her enough to leave for just about anywhere else. Ever since that betrayal, Gwyn seemed to have given up on leaving herself. Another person slowly wasting away here.

He let the silence continue to stretch awkwardly between them. More had happened with Gwyn, but nothing Valan was willing to share with his mother's spy. When he had first met Gwyn years ago, it had been around the time he was figuring out his own feelings involving Sorn. Valan had no other explanation back then except that he was under some sort of lust curse that was slowly driving him mad, half-crazed with the desire to always be near Sorn, only to be plagued with a listless, hollow feeling whenever they were apart. It felt like he had been trapped in a strange fever dream he couldn't seem to wake up from, too scared to tell Sorn what he felt because it might drive the rogue away. Did at the time think he'd driven the rogue away when…

Valan's mind skittered past *that* memory, still finding it too painful to dwell on, to focus more on what happened afterward. He remembered practically throwing himself at other people in order to deny his true feelings, not once considering that anyone else might actually want more from him than just some fun. After all, that was all anyone else had ever wanted from him before.

That Valan hadn't been repulsed once he found out Gwyn's secret, she had taken it as a sign that they were meant to be together. That there was more there than lust, even if neither of them understood what else it could be. He had even encouraged the thought of wanting to become her consort, since it meant he'd be out from under the Piuthar-Tri's scrutiny. It would have been a pleasant, possibly even happy future together that appearance-wise kept within acceptable Unseelie standards.

But of course, there had been at least one scheming dark elf out there who had to ruin it. Someone Valan had never been able to find.

CHAPTER 20

Tarrant stopped following him only when Valan was back in his bedroom. Valan made his skeleton go stand in the corner, dropped the bag he held on the ground, and then slid down to the floor, leaning his back against the wall. After a moment, Sorn stepped out of the shadows next to the tall bedroom dresser. The rogue held a withered, emaciated corpse by its neck and tossed it onto the floor. Tangled in the brittle hair of the corpse was a comb embedded with Valan's missing eye.

Valan studied the corpse from where he sat, unwilling to move closer. He could sense the essence of death wafting from the body like an actual smell. No sign of a soul was left. Even if the body did heal, there wouldn't be a mind to control it.

He didn't feel much of anything when looking at Lynet's remains. He'd known she had to be killed the moment she decided to give him somebody else's rotten eye, with Lynet drawing out Isla for him as an added bonus. After all, if Lynet ever wanted to use that comb openly, she had to get rid of the one female who'd recognize it and cause trouble over thinking the eye really belonged to her. The drama that would have ensued once Isla found out her "friend" was the one who stole items out of her room needed to be avoided as well.

"How long did it take for Lynet to die? "

Sorn shrugged. "It wasn't quick, but nice not to have to be concerned about leaving behind any signs of a struggle. Next time, we should consider leaving the bodies in the other world for our kills to be even harder to trace."

"Not until we know more about that dead world," Valan said. "I don't want to risk accidentally triggering or waking up whatever had left it that way by making a mess. Last thing we need is getting chased by otherworldly monsters we know nothing about."

"Fine. The usual spot it is."

Sorn removed the comb, tossing it near the bag, then grabbed the corpse and stepped into the shadows again. It would take the rogue some time, so Valan decided to see to the contents of the sack. If it had been anyone other than Gwyn who had given him the bag, Valan would have gone through his usual routine in making sure nothing was trapped, poisoned, or cursed, but if she had wanted to kill him, she would have done so years ago. She certainly knew enough about his personal life to cause him problems by just spreading rumors if she wanted to. No need to waste any resources in getting rid of him.

The books he pulled out all dealt with the surface world. Several contained the basics of understanding the more widespread of human languages, along with some being about surviving in different climates on the surface. Only one book taught actual spells, though written in a language he wasn't entirely familiar with, but he still hoped it would help make traveling above less of a chore.

Turning to Gwyn of all people to trade for these tomes had been something he had wanted to avoid, considering their past, but she was the only one who likely had access to and would want to get rid of such books. It didn't make him feel any less of a bastard about it.

Opening one book that taught the specific language the book of spells used caused a small, flat clamshell to fall out from between the pages. Valan picked up the thin seashell gently, running his fingers over the orange-streaked exterior. He had a box of similarly colored shells on his shelf of knickknacks, a not-so-subtle reminder that Gwyn wasn't going to let him pretend nothing important had existed between them. He should probably throw them all away—the only person who knew he kept them was Sorn—but for whatever reason, he never seemed to get around to it.

"Did…you ever want something…more?"

"What? Out of life? Then, power of course."

"No, I—well, power is a given, but I meant from…someone. That physical closeness isn't enough, you want to have someone to share everything with and not have to worry about anything personal being used against you. I know none of this is making any sense and sounds weak, but—"

"Like now?"

"What?"

"Like right now. You're trusting me enough to share what you think."

"That's…okay, that's a good point."

"What's your favorite color?"

"That's such a useless question. What could possibly be gained from—"

"No! It's not useless! It's something we can know about each other that's harmless. Mine is purple, so yours is…?"

"It's…"

Valan put the seashell in the bag the books came from, shoving aside the memory along with it. The comb was another thing he knew should probably rid himself of as soon as possible, but images of all those shells kept bringing themselves to the forefront of his thoughts. The way Gwyn had looked at him when her life had fallen apart and he had refused to leave with her. That he thought something *else* was more important than any future they could have together.

What if there came a moment where he once again decided what he wanted to accomplish, his goal here above anything else, and it was Sorn he risked hurting and driving away? The next time he made a choice and Sorn lost more than a leg and several fingers. Valan wasn't sure he could live with making that sort of decision yet again, but knew himself to be stubborn enough to never want to give up despite any consequences.

Valan picked up the comb and stood up, waiting impatiently for the rogue to return. He kept flipping over the hairpiece, giving the impression that his own eye was winking back up at him. Once Sorn did return, Valan practically shoved the comb into the other man's hands, as if that'd be enough to keep himself from changing his mind.

"How do you want me to destroy this?" Sorn asked, perplexed. If Valan couldn't destroy it with either acid or fire, the rogue obviously wasn't sure what he was supposed to do about it.

"I want you to keep it," Valan said. "You're right, earlier… I sometimes go too far, even when I know it'll not just hurt myself, but others around me. If I ever… When that happens again, I want you to use that to stop me."

"I don't need a comb. I'm going to knock you out and drag you away from here if you get too stubborn."

"Well, in that case, I—wait, what?" Valan's eyes widened. "I prefer less violent methods used against me, if you don't mind. Just use the comb."

Sorn smirked and shook his head. "Destroy it, love. I don't want that kind of power over you."

Despite what his frown might imply, Valan took back the comb. He immediately summoned acid to destroy it, examining the preserved red eye that made up the comb's centerpiece as it began to melt and fall into pieces onto the floor. He was unable to look away from the last piece of what had been an ordinary part of himself as it disappeared, a part that had originally been taken away by Sabrene. One less reminder of what had happened to him in the world.

That's right, Isla is gone now too, Valan thought to himself, *but why doesn't it feel that way? Like she can still appear around the corner at any moment?*

The idea that he could now visit the library and not have to read in one of the hiding spots she didn't know about left him feeling better about things. He could even go ahead and do that now despite the late hour—it wasn't like he'd be able to get much rest anyway. With newfound energy, Valan picked up the rest of the books off of the floor, not noticing that the seashell had fallen out of the bag until Sorn grabbed it.

Seeing Sorn holding the shell froze Valan in place, his mind whirling over what he could possibly say in this situation. The rogue said nothing either, just walked over and put the clamshell in the box with all the others on the shelf.

"I should get rid of those," Valan admitted. "I've been telling myself I only keep them to serve as a reminder of my own failures. To not make the same mistakes that I did with Gwyn, but…it isn't fair to you." He set the books on the bed and stepped toward the box. At least, he attempted to; Sorn didn't move aside and Valan came to a faltering step away from the shelf the box rested on.

"I don't like it when you lie to me, either," Sorn said. "It's fine. You can keep them. It's not like this is the first time I've had to share you."

Valan looked down, saw Sorn's boots, and immediately set them on fire.

"When," the sidhe shouted, watching Sorn hurriedly put out the flames, "have I ever chosen anyone other than you? I may not always have a choice, but when I do, I have always chosen you! So don't you dare act like I'm—"

"Then let me kill Gwyn," Sorn practically snarled. While he managed to put out the small flames, the room now smelled like burnt leather. "She knows too much. The smart move is to get rid of her. It wouldn't be the first time I've killed someone who showed too much interest in you. So go ahead, Valan, tell me you don't mind if Gwyn dies."

"Not all our problems can be solved by murdering it, Sorn."

"Why does she get to live but not any of the others, *Val*?" Sorn asked, intentionally saying the other man's foreshortened name the same way Gwyn did.

"Because I hurt her and she didn't deserve that—that's all," Valan said. "The version of me Gwyn knows isn't even the real me. She has only ever known the public side of me. You're the only one I've ever… I… This is a *ridiculous* argument."

"It's because I know you so well that I get she means more to you than what you're willing to admit," Sorn said.

Valan nearly dropped the books he had just picked up off of the bed. "Any sympathy I might have for her is far outweighed by my feelings for you. You're the one I want to spend the rest of eternity with."

"What are you going to do once I die?" Sorn asked, suddenly switching topics. His question rattled Valan further. Usually talks of being together forever were simply endearments repeated to each other, as if eternity together was a given.

"Where you go, I go," the sidhe said.

"No, you won't. We both know you won't. Not if it means abandoning *them*."

"You're jumping to conc—"

"She can give you something that I can't," Sorn replied. The rogue disappeared into the shadows of the room, not letting Valan even have the chance to respond.

The next several days were spent in the Clan Anartes library. Specifically, a narrow space in the ceiling of the library. If someone were to walk into the multi-tiered, square-shaped room lined with bookshelves and happened to look up, all they would see was a finely crafted mural depicting an ancient war fought between goblins and dark elves, broken up into arched sections. Not all the sections lined up neatly with the one next to it, with there being just enough space for an especially skinny elf to squeeze through and find a crawlspace.

Between the books, partially eaten snacks, and half-empty flask of wine, there wasn't much room for Valan to move around in his cramped hiding spot. This had been less of a problem when he was younger, but he barely fit now, fully knowing that if he ever healed enough to grow back his wings, coming here would be an impossibility. As it was, he had to lie on his back with an open book held open directly above him in order to read it. His current mood being what it was made him want to be somewhere more familiar, at least feeling safer, than risking being in the main room of the library. Tarrant not being able to find and bother him was also a bonus.

A giant cobra slithered out from behind a stack of books to coil itself up against Valan. He pretended not to see it and instead turned the page of his current book. The snake wasn't going to give up so easily, so it bit down on the corner of the text to try to pull it away. Valan refused to let it go; when the snake suddenly stopped biting the book, it bounced back and hit the Firstblood in the face.

"Go away," Valan grumbled into the pages.

The skin of the snake split open. Despite the impossibility due to the difference in size, the much wider, bigger body of Sorn pushed out of the snake, the skin deflating into the same size as when Valan had first taken it from Tanat.

"You can't hide here forever," Sorn pointed out in a clipped tone.

Valan lifted the book high enough to glare at the rogue. "Oh, but I can. In fact, this has been a very successful start in the whole 'for forever' process."

"Valan… I don't want us to be angry with each other."

"Why else do you think I am here?" Valan asked sarcastically. This wasn't the first time he felt a short "time out" was needed from one another—or more specifically, that Valan needed in order to make sense of what had inspired the latest argument and try to find some sort of solution. Especially when Valan was pretty sure things going wrong now was his fault, but he didn't want to be at fault, though it wasn't exactly fair to Sorn to lash out because he didn't want to deal with the source of the problem. That Valan decided to come here and thus "not deal" hadn't escaped him, either. Why did he have to have feelings? He *hated* feelings. Feelings never made any *sense.*

"Studying for the exam you take later today?"

"Oh, right, that." The sidhe scowled over that reminder and shifted until he lay on his side, facing Sorn. Now that he was calmer, he might as well attempt to fix things, not particularly enjoying being angry at Sorn, or himself, either. "You're not the one at fault…it's me. I should have considered things more from your perspective. I should have destroyed every single one of those shells as soon as I saw them." Sorn looked like he was about to say something, but the sidhe reached over and pulled down the scarf to see the rogue's face better, leaning over to give a tentative kiss. "I don't just want a life with you for now, but for in the future as well. Nobody can replace you, my love. Not even close. I'm getting rid of the box as soon as I head back."

"Valan, that isn't—I don't doubt you love me." Sorn pushed the usual errant strands of ghostly hair away from Valan's face, using the hand now partially composed of fingers made from shadow. "One of us just needs to start being realistic."

"No. We'll find a way to remain together. It's always going to be us against the world. I swear, I'll find a way to—"

Sorn kissed Valan with near bruising force, pushing the sidhe onto his back before using his lean, far more muscular body to pin him underneath him. Valan made a protesting noise, about to argue once more, but Sorn simply kissed him again.

"We're not discussing this anymore," Sorn warned. "I'm tired of us always arguing."

It took Valan a moment to pull himself out of a daze, realizing at some point he had started to grip onto Sorn's shoulders.

"As soon as I think we solve one issue," Valan admitted, "another pops up and we're back to being annoyed with each other again. I think it's because we're very different people often confined to small spaces, so of course any issues will be exacerbated—I understand that. What I don't understand is how we manage not to run out of things to get dramatic about."

"One of us *is* very dramatic."

"Truly a shame you have such a gigantic personality flaw, Sorn."

"I know," Sorn said sarcastically. "It can't ever stop over-thinking and talking about things." Before Valan could respond to that, Sorn's hands began to idly roam across his body distractingly. "It's…almost cute?" Sorn sounded surprised at his own conclusion.

Valan gave his best glare under his current circumstances. "Can't you choose a less embarrassing word?"

"No. You keep threatening me with a whole damned song's worth of that garbage," Sorn replied. "You're past due experiencing some embarrassment."

Valan joined several of his peers in the mostly empty training hall. Half a dozen sidhe around his own age were spread out in an area that could easily hold hundreds, divided into two groups according to gender. He recognized most of them as distant family relations, though with how far apart everyone stood away from each other, they might as well all be strangers. An intentional distance, Valan knew, especially since the floor was marked by large circles each student was meant to stand beside. The extra space helped prevent any errant spells from interfering with each other, though it wasn't always enough to stop "accidents".

This setup wasn't so different from other tests meant to judge magical affinity that he had taken in his past. A clan's Archwizard and *Fíada*, the most powerful veiled one in a clan, were usually the ones who oversaw any trials, who then passed the results on to the Piuthar. The Piuthar then decided what to do with the tested sidhe for the betterment of the clan. Many of the extended family took these sorts of tests very seriously, since scoring especially well at any specific branch of magic usually meant they were more likely to be favored—and more likely to be rewarded for being useful—by the Piuthar. A better chance to improve one's rank, like how his nephew Niall became Secondblood over other Anartes despite there being similarly distant blood relations.

The front "row" had only two circles, with Niall already standing next to one of them. Valan went to stand by the other front-most circle. The higher one's rank also determined how close a student could stand near the Archwizard. At the moment, Archwizard Ferehar was summoning floating mirrors out of the floor to match the number of circles on the ground, exchanging words occasionally with Bhalorn. Ferehar didn't look too happy to share what was normally his chance to be the center of attention with somebody else. Ferehar's obvious bad mood deepened as time went on, as on the opposite side of the hall where the females were being tested there was still a circle left unclaimed.

The Anartes *Fíada* was not someone Valan ever had much interaction with, so he was taken aback when she walked up to him.

"Valandrius, do you know where Islandria is?" Lady Oifa asked. Despite not shouting, her voice could be heard by the entire hall, using the same sort of sound amplifying skill often used by sidhe musicians.

Valan hid his annoyance over the implication that just because Isla liked to keep tabs on him meant he was doing the same thing to her. Which was true to a certain extent, but his interest in where she was had more to do with what locations to avoid.

"I haven't seen her recently," he replied neutrally. He certainly wasn't going to be the first to inform everyone else that Isla was dead now.

"Just get on with it," Bhalorn told the *Fíada*. "If the girl is too dense to realize the importance of this test, then she is too weak to survive in the Otherworld."

"You are not in charge here," Oifa said. "Keep your suggestions to yourself, male. It was agreed for you to only observe."

An awkward silence filled the hall, as if waiting for the missing Isla to finally show up. The wait was long enough to have Valan become nervous, wondering if he should expect his twin to somehow still be among the living and *he* was the one who just hadn't been informed yet.

Once Oifa finally relented, turning to deal with the female students, Ferehar created a giant sandglass out of the ground. The topmost of the two pear-shaped globes of what could be mistaken for glass—condensed air—filled with sand of the same color as the floor. The gray rock started to slowly fall to the bottom globe at a pace that likely served as a way to measure the length of a full day.

"You may all begin by creating a workstation in the middle of your circle," the Archwizard said. Valan could overhear Oifa giving similar instructions to the female side of the hall. "I expect you to take plenty of notes—of every word."

Valan used a boot to scuff out and break the dirt outline of the circle he stood next to, stepped inside of it, and then willed the dirt to reform back to where it had been earlier. He then focused on the ground in the circle's center, manipulating the stone to rise up and take the shape of a crude desk and chair. Figuring he met the bare minimum required effort, Valan plopped down in his newly created seat and looked over to see how Niall was doing.

Apparently his nephew refused to settle with something simple, manipulating shadow and ice to form a robust desk and an admittedly comfy-looking chair. The speed and skill Niall flaunted was remarkable for his age, enough to make Valan envious, especially since nobody in their right mind would reveal the full extent of one's magical capabilities to a room full of sidhe who were far more likely to become rivals than friends. Either Niall was capable of much more than what he was currently showing, or he was trying to intimidate others into leaving him alone.

A quick glance around the hall showed the other sidhe creating their own desks and chairs out of various elements, with those like Niall using more than one element being on the rarer side. An especially flashy female student created a workstation out of amethyst, obviously pulling the material from across the veil instead of converting what was already in this world. Seeing that caused Valan to spare a thought about Gwyn, who had shown him more than once that despite the body she had been born into, she was proficient in the magic manipulation exclusively used by women. Gwyn wouldn't have been able to convince so many others of her femininity for as long as she had if she had relied only on dressing like other women.

After checking all the mirrors floating in front of him, each one showing images of the students having successfully, to varying degrees, done what they were told, Archwizard Ferehar immediately began a lecture, of all things, about the importance of *An Cleas*. Understanding the albeit one-sided pact the sidhe had made with humans was one of the first things everyone was supposed to learn about—and usually learned from their *buime*, not from the Archwizard or *Fíada* about to send them off to their higher education.

Valan immediately suspected some sort of trick, that maybe this test had to do with finding the hidden meaning behind the lecture, and so stopped paying attention to the other students' actions to focus on Ferehar's words. He reshaped more stone from the floor into thin tablets, then carved into the slabs words that matched what Ferehar was saying. He figured once the Archwizard was done speaking, he'd be able to go over the notes and look for more discernable patterns to find the answer to this test.

Valan had been taught that the sidhe had long been explorers of other worlds, though coming across realms that weren't already dead, dying, or too inhospitable even for a race largely considered immortal was rare. Even harder to find were worlds that already contained signs of intelligent life. When the sidhe had first traveled to this world, the humans were barely smarter than the wild pigs they hunted for food, but the potential was there: another race the sidhe could interact with. Humans just needed more time to develop.

Interacting with an immature race had to be handled delicately, so the elves developed the concept of *An Cleas* as a way to slowly introduce themselves to humans as time went on. The two largest elven tribes, the Dökkálfar and Ljósálfar, could not agree on how to implement *An Cleas*. The Ljósálfar thought the best way to get humans to evolve further and accept other races was to take on the physical appearance of things that humans were likely to find the most pleasing, followed by then going out of their way to help humans whenever it seemed they were in the most trouble. The Dökkálfar considered such gentle methods to be rubbish and would only lead to humans too stupid to accomplish anything on their own, so better to turn to trickery to get them to think for themselves—and if any of them died, well, getting rid of the weaklings was just doing the human race a favor. Better still to take on appearances deemed frightening, so that when humans did run into any fey in their true form, they would be too desensitized to be scared.

The rift caused by the best way to handle *An Cleas* made the elves split further over time, eventually calling themselves the Seelie and Unseelie, with a few independent clans wanting nothing to do with other races. Not that it mattered much in the end, since trying to interact with humans turned out to be a failure. The sidhe noticed fairly early on how little humans liked anything different from themselves, even going so far as killing off their own over any differences. Once the humans discovered and found uses for a material that the sidhe were highly allergic to, his race as a whole agreed the time to decide what to do with the humans had run out.

Despite the mutual acknowledgment of the "human problem", the two largest elven organizations could not agree on what to do once it became clear that trying to interact with humans was not likely to end peacefully. The Seelie wanted to abandon the world and let the humans kill themselves off, to warn away other races from visiting. The Unseelie believed that since humans couldn't be trusted enough to govern themselves, they might as well be turned into slaves. Any humans incapable of listening to their masters could always be turned into food for the fey who didn't mind the taste.

Depending on the book, Valan had learned that the Seelie either left peacefully or were mostly killed off by the Unseelie in one last war, but whatever the truth was, this part of recorded history remained the same: An Geata, the location of a veil that the sidhe had first used to reach the Otherworld from their native realms, was sealed. Very few Seelie remained, and the Unseelie now lived underground to hide from the surface world until An Geata could be restored again. *An Cleas* then became what was done to keep humans and their iron away from dark elven civilization.

Valan inscribed only on his tablets Ferehar's point of view of this history, since he had long learned that this Archwizard didn't care so much over what was actually comprehended but more what could be repeated back. Mentioning alternate points of view seemed to only annoy the old sidhe. He certainly wasn't going to add any details from the "memory" Bhalorn had forced him to see, either.

As Ferehar droned on and on about the history of their race, Valan realized he was beginning to have a problem. The amount of stone tablets needed to record the lecture was turning into veritable stacks that he had to set around him within the circle. Trying to maintain it all with just his will while carving everything into yet more stone was putting an increasing amount of strain on his mind than what he was comfortable with. He glanced around to see how well his peers were doing.

All the sidhe who had started off with manipulating more than one element were struggling the most, with one having switched to using only a single source like he was. Out of the dual-element manipulators, Niall was doing the best, but even with the distance between them, the strain visible in the furrows of his nephew's face was evident. The sole female sidhe he could see from the other group seemed to be struggling for different reasons, with her issue more like not accidentally pulling more than she could handle from the Otherworld, on top of maintaining and manipulating the shape of elements already existing. Valan didn't risk taking the extra effort to pay attention to any other students; he really couldn't allow himself to grow too distracted—and too noticeable—by the others.

"You are not to leave your circle until I give you permission. Your notes will be reviewed once I return," Archwizard Ferehar said once he was done with his lecture. The mirrors followed him as he walked down the center of the rows of circles. Bhalorn moved at a more sedate pace behind Ferehar, going out of his way to scrutinize every student he passed. Lady Oifa had already left.

"Mavie, Dosne, and Corann: you have failed. Leave," Bhalorn told three students near the back of the hall. There was a long, drawn out pause, with Valan trying to not pay too much attention, then—

"Did I give you permission to leave, Dosne?" Ferehar asked.

"But, he said—"

"Now you have truly failed. Get out."

Multiple doors opened and closed along one side of the hall, the failed sidhe and both wizards leaving the rest of the students to themselves. There was an odd feeling of finality to the silence that now permeated the room. Valan was regretting his use of stone as the sandglass marked the passage of each *uair,* since it wasn't exactly the most comfortable material to be sitting on, but it was too late to add a second element into the magic he was attempting to hold in place. He considered himself to be in the very unenviable position of needing to maintain the image of someone who, while worthy of being called Firstblood, couldn't be seen as *too* strong. Certainly couldn't be seen upstaging Niall, who'd report to Domhnall that he was becoming powerful enough to pose a problem that was wiser to eliminate quickly.

He was drawn out of his thoughts—of preventing some of the stone tablets from merging back into the floor—by the sudden flash of bright light that originated from somewhere behind him.

Screams came from one of the students who accidentally set themselves on fire. Valan ignored the cries, not wanting his own concentration broken, sparing only a brief thought for whoever had tried to use ice like Niall. They must have drawn too much chill and moisture out of their immediate surroundings, super-heating their circle to the point of starting a fire, which then made them lose control completely. The smell of burned flesh made his nose itch.

Half the sand was now in the lower globe of the sandglass, the trickling of the tiny stream of stones almost like a tangible, physical weight on his own body as it slowly became more insistent on fulfilling certain functions. He really shouldn't have eaten all those snacks or drank so much earlier. Considering what to do about his current situation caused the stone tablets to start sinking to the floor again, Valan's concentration wavering before once more willing his notes to remain in place. More of his peers eventually gave up, with one followed very quickly by several others as if the first had given them permission to run toward the privies.

None of them came back.

CHAPTER 21

Valan's focus was nearly shattered by the muffled sobs from one of the remaining students. The sound came from one of those who had tried to use more than one element, stone and air, who thought to open a deep hole in the floor to make use of but which turned out to be one task too many, with all that rock snapping back into place with the lower half of the student's body crushed. Despite the obvious need for a rescue, no one reentered the hall to help, subjecting everyone who remained to the ongoing suffering.

He spared a glance behind him and almost immediately wished he hadn't. The female sidhe who had summoned amethyst technically hadn't given up either, but now most of her circle was engulfed by massive shards of purple, including half her face and an arm. She looked like she wanted to scream but couldn't because of the crystal jutting out of her mouth. Valan hurriedly went back to paying attention to his own manipulated stone, noticing that he had lost one of the tablets over his brief inattention.

A headache demanding his notice became the newest problem, with Valan growing increasingly tired despite the lack of physical activity, on top of the other physical needs growing even harder to ignore. He spared a stray thought toward all the tales of fun and adventure he read about, about how none of them ever mentioned the pursuit of a clean bucket and warmed towels along with all that glory. The pursuit of knowledge should always include a feast, Valan decided, or at the very least, alcohol to keep his mouth from drying out.

Valan's mood improved considerably once the sandglass which marked a full day's passing completed its task of having the last of the sand fall into the bottom pear-shaped sphere. He had hoped for Ferehar to return immediately, but as each extra moment blended into the next, that hope slowly died. Just another form of manipulation to test their resolve. It made the weaknesses of his body harder to ignore now that there was no visible way to tell just when this test would end.

He was well on his way to full on delusion, every sense turned inwardly to better ignore physical limitations to keep all those stone tablets in place, by the time Ferehar and Bhalorn returned.

"Hm, less than half," Bhalorn observed aloud. The two wizards strolled toward the sandglass, obviously in no hurry. The *Fíada* was the last to return, busy reviewing the female half of the hall.

"That is to be expected," Ferehar replied. "This latest generation is much weaker compared to previous ones."

The Archwizard turned his attention to his floating mirrors then began to list the names of those who had passed the test, in order of most successful to the least. Niall's name was called out first, with Valan's name more in the middle. This didn't surprise Valan; forming and using plentiful stone in the most basic shapes imaginable wasn't going to impress anyone, despite maintaining enough notes to have passed the test.

"If I called your name, you are now free to leave your circle, and I expect you to return here in an *uair*," Ferehar said. "Everyone else is to go and prepare for remedial lessons tomorrow. I do not want to see you until then."

Despite his every sense screaming at him to hurry, Valan carefully merged all the stone he had manipulated back into the floor before leaving. He did not take the most direct paths to any places meant to see to bodily needs, knowing there were other ways sidhe would try to move up in ranks than doing well in tests. What better time to get rid of someone than when they were guaranteed to be distracted and tired? He hummed a tune, looking through his black eye as the noise bounced off of the walls of the hallways he traveled down. If anything sidhe-shaped was hit by the noise, Valan took an alternate path. He didn't look for Sorn, trusting the rogue was probably a short distance behind him, and while that thought was comforting against the possibility of being attacked by would-be assassins, Valan didn't want to waste the time and energy to kill anyone and dispose of the bodies.

He barely returned in time to the training hall. Not all the students who Ferehar had announced as passing made it back to their circles, though unlike during the earlier lecture, the instructors did not wait longer for everyone to return.

"Manipulation of elements is just as vital as one's ability to maintain concentration," Ferehar began. "You are to begin with the gases, starting with trinium, and end with solids going from lightest to heaviest. Lead, iron, nickel, cobalt, and of course sulfur are to be excluded."

"Try to not be slow," Bhalorn warned.

Valan decided to do just the opposite, even noisily humming several songs that just so happened to rhyme along with all the elements. The truly hard part was being limited to what was within the confines of the circle, though luckily his own body was made up of enough of the rarer materials, such as astatine, for him to borrow from. His tongue piercings were only gold-plated, holding trace elements of things he was least likely to find either around or from within himself. He had to be especially careful of where and how much he willed out of his own body, since he was still under the effects of Sorn's poison and couldn't heal the damage he was doing. Last thing he wanted to do at this stage was pass out.

"Good," Ferehar said, once it was clear that all his students had completed at least this much without making a mistake. He did spare a glare at Valan for reminding them all about the songs that made memorization easier. "You are now to manipulate into being at least a two-part reconstruction of a solid, gas, liquid, and plasma, followed by a combustion of your choice. Valandrius—you are to be tested last."

Valan couldn't help but scowl at that. By now, he had figured out that all this test did was to make sure that any sidhe youth wouldn't vaporize themselves the moment they stepped into The Otherworld. No interesting mystery or puzzle to solve here.

He watched Niall pull clay out of the ground to form into a vase, which was then filled with a pale blue, crystal clear liquid that issued similar-colored smoke. The blue gas quickly became dense enough to react badly with something not visible to the naked eye, causing a brief flash of lightning to arc across the circle and leave behind a scorch mark. He wondered if clapping over Niall's skill would be seen as too sarcastic, so he settled with displaying an expression of wide-eyed awe on his face. His nephew pointedly ignored him.

As each student finished their test, passing or failing, they were allowed to leave immediately, until finally only Valan and the two older wizards remained in the hall. He couldn't help but feel uneasy, wondering if perhaps isolating him like this had been part of a bigger plan other than "keep the useless one from bothering the others". That one of the two senior wizards happened to be Bhalorn only convinced him he probably wasn't going to be killed. Immediately, at least. Subjected to something painful, though, almost certainly.

"Begin," Ferehar encouraged impatiently.

For a solid, Valan simply recreated his stone desk, with liquid manipulating his own sweat into an acid which burned tiny holes into the upraised stone, causing smoke to rise from the holes. Manipulating gas came in the form of thickening the air into a miniature barrier like he normally would use to block projectiles aimed at him—though this time created as he snapped his fingers, the friction causing a static spark that made a bit of fire no bigger than what a single candle could hold to hover above his index finger. Valan held that tiny light in place as he looked expectantly at the two wizards.

Ferehar didn't seem very impressed, with Bhalorn looking even less so. Probably because, Valan surmised, that the last time the old undead wizard saw him use fire, it was a giant ball aimed at his library.

"Better than the last time you tried that," Ferehar admitted. "You *technically* pass. Get your things together to leave first thing in the morning."

"I couldn't have come so far without your teachings," Valan said, actually managing to keep the sarcasm out of his voice. Sounding earnest, even.

"Your test isn't done yet," Bhalorn said.

"It is according to *me*," Ferehar said. "Nobody gets special treatment under my watch, and especially not—"

"*Your* test is done, mine is not," Bhalorn coolly interrupted. "I can do whatever I wish with my apprentice. Now, begone."

Ferehar's jaw clenched, but other than that, he showed no other emotional display. While it hadn't been that long ago since Bhalorn returned to Clan Anartes, the Archwizard must have figured out by now who between them was more favored by the Piuthar-Tri.

"Very well, I shall not get in the way of your master-student bonding moment," Ferehar said, abandoning the two sidhe.

Bhalorn waited to speak once the door the Archwizard exited out of audibly closed behind him. "Create a ball of fire again."

"If I do that here—"

"Don't worry, boy. Everyone will still think you're useless even if I do *somehow* fail to notice a spy."

"Oh, well... When you put it that way...how could I possibly resist showing off," Valan muttered. He raised his hands to about chest-level and brought into being a sphere made of fire, drawing heat, air, and floating dust out of his surroundings to feed and maintain the shape until it was the size of a cantaloupe.

"Don't add anything more," Bhalorn said. "Try to condense it."

Valan's eyebrows rose, really wanting to ask why, but he went along with the given instructions. This really wasn't a good time to risk angering the undead wizard when there were no apparent witnesses. Bhalorn had already proven himself not to be above inflicting physical harm. Slowly, the ball of fire became smaller, the light going from a flickering display of orange and red to a solid yellow. This smaller shape was also a great deal more unstable, with Valan struggling to keep tiny flares from erupting out of the ball.

"Smaller," Bhalorn ordered.

To help shrink the light down further, Valan *willed* it to start spinning to cause the ball to collapse onto itself. He had to glance off to the side to keep from looking directly at what he had created, the yellow color shifting to a brilliant white glow which lit the entire hall despite now being the size of a pea. Even as Valan winced, feeling his control begin to slip, he recognized just where he had seen a similar magic before: the same light that pierced through the clouds in the vision Bhalorn had forced him to see days ago.

The next instant, the ball of light was gone, plunging the area back into a darkness that now felt strangely oppressive. Valan tried to make sense of the odd feeling of loss, coming up with nothing that could provide an explanation.

"That'll do for now," Bhalorn said.

"That wasn't normal light. It looked just like—"

"You are not to do that again without my supervision," Bhalorn interrupted. "Do not dare to even mention this…event around anyone else. Especially other Unseelie. Do you understand?"

"I believe so," Valan replied. "Does this mean I'm not really…"

He couldn't bring himself to say the rest out loud. Saying it out loud would make it more real. Bhalorn was right; if anyone else found out it wasn't only darkness Valan could summon at will, there was no hope in saving him from the Unseelie Court. Just about any sidhe noble could summon a bit of fire, but to turn it into something more, that was something only a certain *other* court was capable of doing.

"No…no way. Everything I've read about them made them sound like a bunch of whiny, self-flagellating freaks with an excessive love for trees. I'm nothing like that! Why did you even want to see if I could create…*that*? And to do so here, no less?!"

"You certainly seem to be fond of wanting me to repeat myself," Bhalorn said. The undead wizard waved a skeletal hand dismissively. "You've passed my test, so go pack your things. Your real lessons with me will start once you reach Crann Bethadh."

"None of this makes any sense!" Valan protested.

"Go, Valan." The undead wizard's voice took on an unmistakable warning tone.

The younger sidhe really wanted to argue further—he had so many questions—but he had enough of a survival instinct to know that pushing the wizard further wouldn't end well for him. Silently fuming, Valan left the training hall and took the most direct path to his room. He hoped somebody would try to attack him this time, even if only to have a distraction with the added bonus of an excuse to kill something.

Midway back to his room, he just barely registered the temperature of the hallway suddenly dropping. Each exhale of his breath turned into a chilly fog. Valan stopped, very carefully using all of his senses to try to perceive anything else that was unusual, or at the very least find anyone about to attack him. The cold grew stronger. He started to hum a tune, using his black eye to see the noise bounce off the walls and not finding anything odd.

"Did you really think you could get rid of me so easily?" Isla whispered behind him.

Valan whirled around and sent out a spray of acid to attack the source of that voice, but all he did was ruin a few paintings on the walls.

Nobody was there.

His breath, while now edged with panic, had otherwise returned to normal. The chill was gone. He did not linger, his overtaxed mind whirling over the possibilities of what he had just experienced could mean, and walked at a faster pace back to his room.

It could have been an illusion, Valan thought. He'd already gotten a first-hand taste of what a truly powerful wizard could do at a distance when it came to creating false sensations and imagery. The problem with this conclusion was that the wizard would also need to be familiar enough with the sound of Isla's voice to mimic it so well, and she hadn't exactly endeared herself to the male half of the clan. The more likely possibility, one which he'd rather not be true, was that his twin's hatred and fixation on him was so strong that her spirit would try to latch onto him even after death.

Ghosts were highly problematic when it came to trying to get rid of them, but…maybe this was all just a onetime event. Her spirit's last attempt to torture him before moving on. Valan nearly convinced himself of that, or that at least it was all just in his head because he was tired and mentally drained. When he reached his front door, his mood dipped further. Of course *now* would be the time that no assassins attempted to bother him. Just when their presence would have been useful!

Valan's bedroom looked the same as when he had left it, with one notable exception in that the box of seashells was gone. Sorn, having decided to get rid of that unprompted, Valan found disconcerting, but he decided he'd rather not confront *that* mix of emotions. The shells were gone, like he's said they should be, so it wasn't like it should matter *how* that ended up coming about. There was another, far more important question on his mind.

"Do I really come across as one of those goody-two-shoe types?" Valan asked.

Do I need to start doing things to make me more like the other Unseelie? he wondered. *What would that even entail? I'm already just like the rest of them... right?*

"I don't think so," Sorn replied, stepping out of the shadow cast on the wall by the bed frame. "Your father even set us up to see how you'd react to Sabrene in a cell and didn't seem too happy about what we decided to do with her—and he's supposed to be one of those independent neutral types."

"With all that's happened recently, it feels like ages ago since I last saw Cernunnos," Valan said. "Good riddance. He can stay in the past."

Neither of them pointed out that Valan was still wearing the ring his father had given him. Ego now assuaged over the near-traumatic conclusion that he just might be in the wrong sidhe court, Valan *willed* apart the rough stone wall to reveal the hidden bedroom. "Did you get those waterproof sacks? Whatever you want to keep that isn't breakable needs to be stored in them now."

"I did. I only want to keep my knives, lock-picking tools, and clothes," Sorn said. The rogue pushed the chest chimera out of the way and went to lift certain flagstones which made up the floor in their real bedroom, pulling out everything hidden in holes for Valan to then go through, including several large empty bags made of a stiff material. Aside from the alchemical equipment too fragile to safely travel with—Valan made a mental note to replace all of that as soon as he could—almost everything else belonged to Valan. Even, Sorn insisted, the half-eaten moldy piece of a cinnamon roll that mysteriously ended up sharing space next to one of those human poetry books.

Sorn shot the other man a *Don't You Dare* look after seeing Valan about to question the hiding away of edibles next to *that* kind of book, which wasn't enough to dissuade the sidhe from leaning over to give him a side-hug. Valan even patted the rogue's back in a *there, there* gesture before letting him get back to packing, struggling not to smile.

One object that had been hidden away was a shallow, wide crystal bowl. Scrying devices came in all shapes and sizes, but the main functional component remained the same: it had to have a reflective surface. In Valan's case, he preferred to try to see across a surface of water added to his multifaceted bowl, light catching on the surface and obscuring all the tiny runes he'd scratched into the quartz to help reinforce and attune this device to him. Magically linking the bowl to only him helped prevent anyone from trying to see back from the opposite side to then spy on him, though admittedly it couldn't prevent someone powerful from brute forcing their way into any detected scrying attempt. He avoided relying on this type of magic as much as possible, having only one exception.

A small, dried streak of his blood still painted the inner portion of the bowl. Valan pulled enough moisture out of his surroundings to fill his scrying device, watching as that blood peeled off of the side and then broke down in the water to stain it all a pale pink. In his mind, he envisioned the capital city and projected it onto the water's surface. The pink in the water began to coalesce back into tiny red droplets, marking the locations in the city of those who were most closely related to his blood. He ignored the red spots where Clan Anartes was generally located, his attention focused on other areas where his blood was thickest.

Four. There were four red dots within other clans. There used to be five.

Valan bowed his head, his concentration on scrying falling apart, and so the overhead view of the city faded and the water ran pink within the bowl. He thought back to when he was little. Too little to stop the beatings. Too little to tell anyone *no*, and how often he had wanted someone, anyone, to make it all stop. To go somewhere far away and not have to feel anything ever again. He had dreamed about how great it would have been to have someone care enough to take him away from here to somewhere safe, but no one ever did. Not then, when he had needed help the most. Now he was older, and Valan wasn't about to let what those little drops of blood represented be abandoned here, too.

"I'm sorry I was too late to save you," Valan told that missing fifth child. Finding them had always been the easy part; rescuing them from their mothers and then trying to keep them safe would be a whole other challenge. He needed to become powerful in a hurry—that much was abundantly clear—and create that safe space himself in the Otherworld. If not that, then find a place on the surface of the human world that could be easily defended from the inevitable hostile incursions. Perhaps if he'd been more like a typical Unseelie sidhe, Valan could have left this nightmare existence behind in order to save himself.

But what kind of life would that be, fully knowing that he'd left behind his own children?

Valan wouldn't repeat the same mistake his own father had.

He'd rather die trying.

EPILOGUE

His cloven hooves made a light tapping noise as Cernunnos walked across the cracked stone floor, sidestepping a wide crevice that revealed what looked like exposed, living musculature. The walls were similarly made out of flesh and rock. The slick red meat marbled with off-white tendons pulsed in time with what sounded like a distant heartbeat. As the size of caverns went, this one was far from the biggest the elder sidhe had ever visited, barely able to accommodate the space of an especially high-backed throne.

This seat was not empty.

A man with dark red hair sat on the stone throne, bound in place by entrails that wrapped around his limbs to make it impossible to move. What wasn't smeared with viscera and blood revealed elaborate, richly decorated clothing and armor that had long since turned brittle and faded with age. His long, unkempt hair and beard framed a face crisscrossed with vicious scars, matching the unnaturally fanatical glow to his gray eyes. The worst of the scarring resided around his mouth, as if at one point in his life his lips had been sewn shut.

"Begone fiend, I make no deals with your ilk," the man rasped.

"You will now," Cernunnos said. "If you value your son's life."

"I already know the value of his life." One of the man's gauntleted hands twitched, pulling on the entrails that kept his wrist bound. "I will not leave again."

"No, your other son." Cernunnos smiled. "He lives, old friend. Made a slave by another sidhe, and I can tell you by whom and where."

"Lies."

"Now, why would I do that to you?"

The scarred man remained silent, refusing to acknowledge the sidhe's presence further. Cernunnos gave an elaborate shrug. "Very well, but do keep in mind that this slave owner *will* get around to killing him eventually," the sidhe said. "Your boy will need to be rescued soon. Reach out to me if you change your mind."

Cloven hooves once more stepped lightly across the floor, this time the sound they made growing increasingly distant as Cernunnos left the cave. The walls bent and flexed like lungs releasing a sigh, followed more distantly by what might have been a wail. The ancient man remained unmoving, his gray eyes narrowed in thought.

TO BE CONTINUED

THREE LIVES.

THREE FATES.

AND THE JOURNEY
TO DESTROY THEM ALL.

THE SHATTERED MIRROR SAGA BOOK 2

COMING 2026

CONTENT WARNINGS

Please note: it should be assumed that basic horror tropes will apply. These include death, gore, and violence. Other warnings include mentions, ideations, or on-page depictions of the following:

body horror

misandry

homophobia

sexual assault

slavery

suicide

torture

transphobia

ACKNOWLEDGMENTS

To protect their privacy I won't be listing specific names--they know who they are. I want to thank the family members who pushed me to not give up on writing the kind of story I wanted the most, the beta readers who put up with my hovering, the editors dealing with someone who'd never taken a formal writing class, and the friends who cheered me on. I also want to thank a certain Enby H, who was the first to give this story a chance.

ABOUT

Skye Crawford is a house-trained, 1,001 year old nonbinary ghoul prone to biting anyone who gets too close, preferring the company of hellhounds, prehistoric beasts, and poisonous plants. If ever caught lurking outside of their California crypt it usually means they got lost trying to smell the roses and should be directed back into the nearest tomb.

Their writing skills come from after years of realizing that grunting noises turn out to be a poor form of communication. What news that escapes their tomb can be found at **skyecrawford.org**

THANK YOU!

Your purchase helped support an indie author and a small press.
We hope you enjoy enough to leave a review!

Want more Dead Fox books? Head on over to our website
, where you can purchase our titles and our partner titles cheaper than
you'll find them anywhere else.

www.deadfoxpub.com